THE WOLFSHADOW TRILOGY | BOOK 3

FOR ALL THE NORMS OUT THERE, WHEREVER YOU ARE.

THE WOLFSHADOW TRILOGY

Saamaanthaa

The Happening

Norm

OTHER WOLFSHADOW BOOKS

Lupinia:

The Selected Poems

of Polly Drinkwater, 2007–2015

OTHER NOVELS

Chosen

Suckage

NOVELLAS

Relict

Summerville

The Day of the Nightfish

NO RM
D T NEAL
N*P
NOSETOUCH PRESS
CHICAGO | PITTSBURGH
THE WOLFSHADOW TRILOGY 3

Norm
© 2021 by D.T. Neal
All Rights Reserved.

ISBN-13: 978-1-944286-51-4

Published by Nosetouch Press
Chicago, Illinois

www.dtneal.com | www.nosetouchpress.com

Publisher's Note:
No part of this publication may be reproduced, distributed, or transmitted in any form or by any means, including photocopying, recording, or other electronic or mechanical methods, without the prior written permission of the publisher, except in the case of brief quotations embodied in critical reviews and certain other noncommercial uses permitted by copyright law.

For more information, contact Nosetouch Press:
info@nosetouchpress.com

This book is a work of fiction. Names, characters, places and incidentsare products of the author's imagination or are used fictitiously. Any resemblance to actual events or locales or persons or werewolves, living or dead, is entirely coincidental.

Cataloging-in-Publication Data
Names: Neal, D.T., author.
Title: Norm
Description: Chicago, IL : Nosetouch Press [2021]
Identifiers: ISBN: 9781944286514 (paperback)
Subjects: LCSH: Horror—Fiction. | Paranormal—Fiction.
GSAFD: Horror fiction. | BISAC: FICTION / Horror.

Cover & interior design by Christine M. Scott
www.clevercrow.com

PROLOGUE

Here is how it happens: she's taken to the police station for questioning. Pretty young woman, maybe a bit too skinny for her own good. She's in a black cocktail dress, burgundy patent leather heels. She has black hair, cut short, but disheveled. She looks distracted.

It's an oddly dissonant note. Big eyes, red lips—first you think she's smeared lipstick all across her face, but then you realize that it's blood. This pretty young woman's got blood across her face.

Two cops question her—big guys. One has short hair, ginger-colored, freckled face. The other guy is the senior partner, brown hair, mustache, bit of a patrolman's paunch.

They have her in the interrogation room because they want to ask her questions. They want to know what happened to her husband. They ask her what her name is, and she tells them, shaky-voiced:

"Polly. Polly Drinkwater."

They know this already, but they just want to hear her say it. They are trying to get a sense of her mental state. The younger cop, Detective Lanslow, he pours her a glass of water. The older cop, Detective Nightingale, just paces. The light in the room is harsh. Others are watching behind the mirror. They want to know.

"Where is your husband, Mrs. Drinkwater?" Nightingale asks. On cue, she takes the water and takes a long drink of it.

"He's dead," Polly says.

"Where's the body?" Lanslow asks. He's seated across from her, big hands folded. The handcuffs are on the table. They reflect the bright light overhead.

"It's gone," Polly says.

"Who took it?" Nightingale asks. This is being recorded.

"Nobody 'took' it," Polly says.

"You called 911, Mrs. Drinkwater," Lanslow says. "You said your husband had been murdered. There were clear signs of a struggle, but no trace of a body. Who took the body?"

She's been wearing makeup because her mascara has run with her tears. It's made black trails down her ivory cheeks. My, what big eyes she has.

"I ate him," she says.

Nightingale and Lanslow exchange looks. They don't believe her. It's not possible. But here's the thing: they're getting weird reports like this all the time, now. Some kind of mass delusions, people are getting violent. They are killing loved ones, killing each other, eating each other.

Something is Happening.

"You'll pardon me for not believing you, Mrs. Drinkwater," Nightingale says. "But your husband was a big man. There's no way you could have eaten him."

"He wasn't *that* big," Polly says, taking another drink of water. "I looked down on him, you know."

Lanslow has her husband's driver's license. "It says he was six feet tall, Mrs. Drinkwater. You're, what, 5'5" at the most? Even in heels, you'd still be too small to do that."

They can't believe she could have killed her husband, let alone eaten him. But the pathologists have already determined that the blood on her face is the same as the blood they found at their nice house in Winnetka.

Lanslow also has a book of her poetry on the table. A woman on the cover with a moon instead of a head, with rays emanating from her. *Lupinia* is the title of it. He pages through it, thick cop hands dwarfing this slender book of poetry. There is blood on the pages. He reads from it:

Marrow

Grisly gristle jiggles
Cracked bones
and broken hearts
Lay bloody bare before me.

On the floor, I want more
I moan,
am on all fours
And I cannot hope to stop.
My beefcake bellyache

Tames me
my appetite
And it completely claims me.

Feast of flesh, evening dress
I know
There's no return
To the what of what I was.

At hearing her words spoken aloud, her eyes lock on Detective Lanslow, her face has taken on another tone, not the grieving murder-widow, but something else.

A feral gaze, darker than the color of her eyes.

"Your words, Mrs. Drinkwater," Lanslow says. "This book is full of them. What do they mean?"

"You want to know what they mean?" Polly asks. "I'm sitting in my husband's blood and you want to know what those words mean to me? You know I changed my clothes after I called. I was naked in all that blood. Our Persian rug drank it up."

"Did you murder your husband, Mrs. Drinkwater?" Nightingale asks.

"I put him out of his misery," Polly says. "Do you want to see how?"

At this point, she looks diabolical in that harsh light. The shadows along the planes of her face, the gaze, a hint of a ghastly grin. She can see herself in the big mirror, and she likes what she sees. She lets out a shriek and throws herself to the ground.

This startles the policemen, who call out for Mrs. Drinkwater to control herself. Nightingale rounds the table, and there she is, curled into a ball, her body heaving, growing.

"What the hell—?" he says. It's what they always said, like when it first started Happening.

She looks up at him, her mouth full of teeth, her eyes aflame, and Detective Nightingale draws his sidearm, a Smith & Wesson .357 magnum revolver. Most everybody else, his partner included, has gone to Glocks or Berettas. They like the comfort of a bunch of bullets, but Nightingale likes the stopping power of a good, old-fashioned magnum.

He draws and he levels the pistol at Mrs. Drinkwater's head, while Lanslow is shouting to him, calling for help. It only takes a second, a diversion of his gaze. When he looks back down at Mrs. Drinkwater, he sees a tearing dress and a mass of black fur sprouting from her body. All across her body. He actually gags at the site of it, the stretching of her limbs, those slender hands lengthening into clawed paws. The claws are long, the nail enamel peeling off in curls as they grow.

Nightingale knows what to do; he is not a fucking rookie. He brings the revolver to the temple of Mrs. Drinkwater and he pulls the trigger. The gun flares, and the blast in the tiny room is unbelievably loud. Even the people behind the glass jump. Ears are ringing.

He'll answer for it later, he's ready for that. The woman-thing flails onto her back, lands in the corner. At this range, the magnum sends her flying, she knocks over her chair.

Nightingale gazes at his partner, who is ghost-pale and shaking, his face greasy with sweat. Nightingale wipes his lip with the back of his hand, the hand that holds the gun.

In the corner, the thing is laying there, still breathing. *Still breathing.*

"You shot her," Lanslow says. "Bobbie, you fucking shot her."

"Do you see this?" Nightingale says. "Are you seeing this?"

The thing in the corner is not a woman anymore: it's a wolf.

A big, bad wolf.

It springs to its feet faster than either man can react. The speed of it is incredible, it's a blur on the closed-circuit camera. It goes from being flat on its back to right up in Nightingale's face, a clawed hand on the officer's arm, effortlessly bending it badly. You can hear the bones snap, can see the man wince. Lanslow might as well be a statue.

"Whoops," the thing says, a trickle of blood at the temple, the bullet, misshapen mushroom, falling free, landing on the ground with a leaden thump. Then the thing raises its other hand, all claws—they are long, like steak knives. "My turn."

It then slashes Detective Bobbie Nightingale across his face. His skin slices, his blood is absolutely everywhere. But she's only getting started. She bites the officer, clamps right down on him with these ghastly teeth, this Lupine muzzle. She takes a bite out of him and Nightingale screams.

Then she's over the table in a single, graceful bound, bloody pawprint on the table, and she's springing for Lanslow, who hasn't even gotten his Glock out of the holster. This is taking place in seconds, this whole thing. He's young, he doesn't know how to react.

She sinks her teeth into his shoulder, tears flesh from bone, throws him aside. He hits the wall, falls like a ragdoll. He's passed out.

Nobody blames him.

Then she's throwing herself against that mirrored glass. It's thick ballistic glass. It's intended to be. It's the kind of thing made to keep some crazed, PCP-addled felon at bay. It actually takes that first charge of hers.

THUMP

You hear the sound as she hurls herself against it, the glass cracking, but not breaking. Not yet.

THUMP

On the other side, there is bedlam as the observers see this horrible thing throwing itself at them, with just some glass in the way. It's not nearly enough. It's like a zoo exhibit from Hell.

THUMP

The glass gives way explosively on the third blow, like a cannon shot and she is free. She tears through the onlookers, who've only had time to get to their feet as she buries her teeth into them.

And when I say she tears through them, I am not exaggerating—she literally tears through them, claws and teeth, she clears a path through the humanity, biting and rending, bounding down the hallway in a confidently practiced loping stride. Anybody in her way, and I mean anybody, gets bitten and clawed. There is method to her madness. She knows what she is doing, here. Or part of her does, on a molecular level.

She's out the door before anybody left standing can react. She goes right through the door, knocking the thing off its hinges. She leaves behind her a wreck of human flesh, blood, and bone. Blood is splattered everywhere, the scent of it intoxicating. People are moaning and screaming. She leaves that behind, leaves her old life behind. It hardly matters, anymore. New world, new rules.

That is how it happens. That's how the world ends. I know, you're complaining, because that's not how you remember it Happening. But what's memory, anyway? It's a lie—the past as prologue. What's the thing they always say?

Life as we know it.

Yeah, that's so over.

Polly sat on her couch, with her laptop, and, after brooding for a moment or two, she pressed DELETE and made all of that go away. Wishful thinking only counted for so much these days. Being quiet was far safer than being noisy, after all, when it came to her affliction.

As much as she hated to admit it, the less attention, the better—there was an undeniable utility in going out with a whimper, versus going out with a bang. It meant she could pretend she was still somehow normal, even if the life as she knew it was long, long gone.

PART ONE

"IF YOU LIVE AMONG WOLVES, YOU HAVE TO ACT LIKE A WOLF."
—NIKITA KHRUSHCHEV

NORM Stockwell brooded from behind the steering wheel of his black jeep. After the Happening, he'd been tapped for the Stinger Program by Director Troy Minton. Four years ago, it was a new thing created by the Hive, the brain trust deep in the labyrinthine heart of the Bureau in faraway DC.

He prowled the city, looking for those who didn't fit in.

Norm caught his reflection in the window of his jeep—strong-jawed, a Gary Cooper kind of face if you squinted, with dark hair cut very short, hints of white at his temples. Black eyes, eyes that had seen a lifetime's worth of trouble in the past eight years. He'd wrapped up several tours in Afghanistan to find some sanity in the BEE, or an enemy he could take down more readily. From one war to another.

The bloodied young man looked naked and afraid. Curbside and furtive. Norm knew this dance. This was the Infective hangover, the morning after a night of rampaging. They're not sure what happened to them, how they found themselves this way. It's harder, now. Nobody hitchhikes anymore.

He watched the young man dart from bush to bush. Curly hair, brown hair. A handsome face, in a conventional sort of way. He's a long way from whatever counts as home.

Before 2011, when he was still a Warden, Norm would simply have shot him down. The last of the Wardens was killed four years after the Happening. That's how quickly it had gone down. This wasn't widely known, but at the Bureau for Extraordinary Events (BEE), it was something that hung heavy in the hearts of all of the surviving staff.

Norm pulled up to where the man was hiding, got out.

"Hey, Guy," Norm said. "You look lost."

The man, hearing himself addressed, said nothing.

"You, in the bushes," Norm said. "I can see you, Sport. If you don't want the cops to pick you up for public exposure, you'd best come with me."

"Are you a cop?" the man said.

"No, I'm not a cop," Norm said. "I'm a driver."

The Happening had been the worst lycanthropic outbreak in American history, and the Bureau worked hard to ensure that nobody would ever know this. To say it was classified was an exercise in understatement. It was a multilevel national gaslighting that would have made even the most corrupt of politicians proud.

Nobody was allowed to say what had really happened. The reasoning was that the truth was simply too bizarre to be believed. So, the Bureau and its backers didn't even try to tell the truth. The truth was too far out there.

"You look like you've got a little Night Fever," Norm said. "Am I right?"

"Night Fever," the man said, still hiding. "Yeah, that's it. I can't remember."

"Nobody ever can," Norm said. "Look, can I drive you somewhere?"

"Are you a serial killer?" the man asked.

It was sort of a hard question for Norm to answer. He was a BEE Stinger. Stingers were deep cover counterinsurgency agents deployed throughout the country. Their entire purpose was to assassinate every Infective lycanthrope they encountered. It was a simple mission statement, covertly communicated. He'd killed scores of Lupines.

"Nah, I'm just a Good Samaritan," Norm said. "You're the one covered in blood, not me, Guy."

"My name's John," the man said. "John Feldman."

"John, the cops will find you soon, if you try to, what, streak your way to wherever you live," Norm said.

Each state had a dozen Stingers in it, the BEE's most elite agents. They were tasked with stopping what remained of the Happening on a case-by-case basis. There was a methodology to it, cooked up by the Hive. The logic was almost ludicrously simple: werewolves were sloppy. The Infectives, that is.

"I live in Wrigleyville," John said. "I don't know how I ended up downtown."

"I do," Norm said. "And, let's be honest, you do, too."

The BEE had categorized Lupines as follows:

- Trueborn: Natural Lupines, born to the condition
- Infectives: Surviving victims of Lupine attack who became werewolves

Nobody knew how many Trueborn there were. The Trueborn historically kept a very low profile. It was the Infectives who were the primary concern of the BEE.

They were the beating heart of the Happening, the ones who'd either been bitten by Zooey Hummel, the late leader of the 2007 insurrection, or, more insidiously, victims who had been infected by the lycanthropic blood that Zooey and her acolytes had so generously donated before the Bureau had figured out what they were doing.

"I don't know what you're talking about," John said. He was still hiding. This wasn't good, from Norm's perspective. Guilty consciences hid.

"I think you do, John," Norm said. He slipped out his Glock 18, quietly screwed on the silencer for it.

"It's Night Fever, like you said," John said.

Those blood donations had spread lycanthropy across the country. This was the Happening that Zooey had sought to create. Her core followers infiltrated blood banks and gave their blood as often as possible.

The retrovirus responsible for lycanthropy hadn't yet been detected. So, anybody using the tainted blood would become an Infective. It spread like wildfire, and nobody knew why.

"Then I should get you to a hospital," Norm said, holding the gun to his side, screened by the shadow of the jeep. They were in Lincoln Park, north of the zoo.

"No, I'm fine, really," John said.

The government hadn't wanted to cause a panic and charged the BEE with keeping this all as clandestine as possible. The agents of the BEE worked around the clock to track down the lycanthropes and dispatch them as quietly as possible. The sheeple weren't to be disturbed by wolves running amok around them.

"You don't sound fine, John," Norm said. "You sound scared."

The Wardens had been the first responders in those first four years of the Happening. They were the crack sniper units who were trying to either capture or kill the Lupines they encountered. It was dangerous work because the Lupines made for deadly prey. The BEE would send out Wardens and Recovery teams under the guise of Animal Control.

Norm glanced at his watch. He was giving this Infective too much of his time. But he was trying to give him the benefit of a doubt.

"I'm not scared," John said. "I'm just confused."

"Right," Norm said.

"I'm not going to get in a jeep with a stranger," John said. "Nobody normal would even do that."

"But you're not normal, John," Norm said. "Are you?"

In theory, it was a simple process:

1. Identify: Infectives would be spotted

2. Neutralize: Wardens would shoot them (bullets or tranquilizers, depending on the administration in charge and the protocols laid out)

3. Recover: Recovery teams would secure the bodies (for either disposal or rendition, again, depending on who was in charge)

But the attrition rate was high among personnel. The Lupines wouldn't give Wardens second chances. They'd attack. And, as there were more of them, packs began to form. When the Lupines formed packs, the Wardens didn't stand a chance. Too many targets, too few Wardens.

"No," John said. The stress was rising in him. Norm could hear it in his voice. Lupines got that way. Infectives did, anyway. The adrenal glands started pumping, the retrovirus flipped limbic switches and the person changed into what they really were. "I'll take my chances. I'll just go home on my own, thank you."

"Alright," Norm said. "If that's how you want to play it."

Minton had found the daily reports intolerable, the attrition rates untenable. Warden after Warden was killed or missing in action. Recovery teams became afraid to venture out in the field. The BEE began to fall behind.

When the Stinger Program came together, Minton was elated. Stingers posed as normal civilians, the kind of people who wouldn't draw another glance from anyone. But they were authorized to hunt Lupines autonomously. Not in the hunter-sniper way of the Wardens, but in something far more stealthy. It was, in many ways, even more dangerous than the work of the Wardens. There was more talking, for one thing.

"What does that even mean?" John asked.

The key to gaining initiative meant moving quickly, before the target had time to react. For Norm, his protocol was pretty clear—find a naked bloody person out at all hours and engage with them. Ascertain their threat level. Deal with them.

It was a carrot and stick type of conversation. The carrot was the tranquilizer dart. The stick was the silver bullet. Which one poor John Feldman got was dependent on how he responded to Norm's questions. Norm was being patient with him.

"You're infected, John," Norm said. "You need help."

"I don't need help," John said. "I need you to leave me alone."

"Right now, I know what you're going through," Norm said. "You're hearing that voice, yes? That voice inside you that's telling you maybe you need to kill me."

"What?"

"Or maybe it's telling you to run away," Norm said.

What made the Stingers so potent was the evolution of customized, proprietary drone technology. The Hive had conjured up a trio of highly effective drones that were deployed in Lupine hunting.

There was a long-term eye in the sky winged Spotter drone. It would fly at night, out of sight, and use night vision and other high-technology optics to spot Lupines from afar. BEE drone pilots would then relay information to the nearest Stinger, who would take care of the problem.

There were smaller-scale Swarm drones. These quadcopter drones were equipped with cameras and tranquilizer guns that were capable of dropping a Lupine. Swarm drones were deployed in situations where the need for timely interdiction superseded a Stinger's ability to respond.

Finally, there were the Stalker drones, which were equipped with a .50 caliber sniper rifle fitted with a suppressor. The Stalker drones had replaced the surviving Wardens in the field, and carrying 50 rounds, were able to maintain an effectiveness against Lupines that had stealthily winnowed down the number of rogue Infectives.

The result of the drone program meant that there were fewer rogue Lupines out and about, and lower rates of attrition among BEE field agents. The other result was that the smart and careful Lupines got very cautious about showing themselves. It's why the Stingers were being increasingly used to sniff out the hiding lycanthropes.

"How do you know all of this?" John asked, still hiding in the bushes.

"Because I know what you are, John," Norm said. "What you *really* are. I'm from the government, John. I'm here to help."

"The hell you are," John said, his voice getting huskier. Norm knew what this meant.

Norm knew the categorization of Infectives went deeper than most acquainted with them thought. He broke them down as follows:

- Smart Infectives
    - Organized Infectives
- Stupid Infectives
    - Disorganized Infectives

Most of them were stupid and disorganized. These were the hapless souls who, when they turned, would just go out and attack and either kill and/or eat whatever they came across. In his jaundiced view, roughly 90 percent of the Lupines were stupid and/or disorganized. They were still dangerous, of course. Nobody who thought otherwise lived long. They were also the ones likeliest to be felled by the drones.

They were easier to catch and kill.

Norm tapped his earphone and dialed up Tiff.

"Driver to Dealer," Norm said, using his secure field radio. Dealer was the codename of Tiff Wilson, who was his partner and handler. She was one of the BEE's best drone pilots and was in his earphone more often than not.

Tiff was a young African-American woman who'd joined the BEE after the Happening. She'd had a background in intelligence and had worked remotely for the Bureau for the past three years. She was short and bright-eyed, with a big smile that was at least as infectious as lycanthropy. She wore her hair short, except at the top, where it was a spray of mahogany curls.

"What is it, Driver?" Tiff said. Her voice was somewhat soothing, despite the crackle of the satellite connection.

It was the smart Infectives and the organized ones that were the real threat. They were maybe 10 percent of the Infective population. They were the ones who were far more circumspect in their predation. They were the ones the Stinger Program was made to catch. And by "catch" of course, it meant "kill"—the BEE had been directed to extradite Infectives to a top-secret facility known as Wolf Island. At considerable expense, Lupines were caught and airlifted to Wolf Island.

"We've got a suspect here at my location," Norm said. "I'd put him at a 3.7 on the Scale."

"Who are you talking to?" John asked.

The Minton Scale was something his boss, Troy Minton, had come up with. A five-point scale of Lupine Threat Assessment. Most fell in the three-to-five range. One was a sleeping Loop. Five was an active rampager. A 3.7 put John at high flight risk.

"John, you need to turn yourself in," Norm said. "I don't know what you did, or who you killed—maybe it's just animal cruelty, not murder. We have people who can determine that. But you need to come with me, or it's going to get very bad for you."

Norm could hear him breathing, like deep breaths.

"You have to be cold," Norm said. "It's a cold night."

"I'm not cold," John said, his voice a growl. This wasn't John's first rodeo. Newbie Lupines screamed and cried out when they turned. Like everything, it got easier with practice. Norm thought John was reasonably well-practiced in his condition.

"Driver," Tiff said. "What's your situation?"

"Mark my position, Dealer," Norm said. "Sitrep is evolving as we speak."

But as the Happening worsened, as the numbers grew, the rendition program was no longer feasible. The BEE had received new directives, including a blanket kill order. It was just safer, cheaper, and easier. The top secret justification was that the Happening was both an epidemic and a domestic insurgency, and had to be stopped.

"Who are you talking to?" John said. His voice was feral, now, monstrous sounding. Norm could see the bushes shaking, trying to accommodate the larger mass bursting from him. He raised his Glock in the direction of the bushes. With Lupines, sometimes you only got one clean shot.

"Nobody you'd know," Norm said.

For four years after the last Warden was torn apart by ravening Infectives, the Stingers had methodically gone to work assassinating Lupines, working closely with the BEE drone pilots. The Stingers would just emerge from the shadows, kill the target, and leave. Their handlers would coordinate recovery efforts. No one would ever see the Stingers. Only the Director knew who they all were.

That was considered a security feature—in the event that a Stinger was compromised, they'd not be able to reveal the identity of the other

Stingers. It was this hyper-secrecy which lent the Stingers added effectiveness in their fieldwork.

The bushes parted and what was John came bursting out at him, a mid-sized monstrosity in brown fur, clawed hands out ahead of him, like the points of a spear as the thing vaulted for Norm, its face a mask of fangs and ferocity, its eyes a bright yellow.

Norm kept his cool and took the shot, catching John the Werewolf between the eyes. The silver bullet stopped John in his tracks and he crashed to the ground, the force of his jump offset by the impact of the bullet, sloppily sliding toward Norm as he fell and died.

"Pickup near Belden," Norm said. "I'll mark him for Recovery."

Norm took out a homing device: a little lozenge with BEE printed on it. It had a little clip on it, and Norm clipped it to John's ear. John was transforming back from his Lupine incarnation to his human disguise, what happened when they were killed. As many times as Norm had seen it, it always was affecting.

"Are you okay, Driver?" Tiff asked.

"I'm fine, Dealer," Norm said. "Target neutralized."

"Recovery is on their way," Tiff said. "ETA is five minutes. Any local difficulties?"

Norm glanced around, but nobody was around. He'd chosen the point of interception well, where there were plentiful shadows and it had been reasonably quiet by city standards. He glanced at John, who was now in his human form again. It was perhaps a cruel joke that only death really cured the infection.

"Nope," Norm said. "All clear. I'm out of here. Driver out."

He got in his jeep and drove away, hanging up on Tiff. Although he was used to it, he'd never really get used to it. Night after night, he'd hunt. There were still way too many to find.

2

"**WHAT** is lycanthropy?" Chad Bastion asked, walking back and forth in front of the audience of Liminalix executives who'd been gathered in the auditorium, cell phones left in another room by order of Bastion himself.

Chad Bastion was tall, tanned, and handsome. Sandy brown hair, grey eyes, a strong jaw with a cleft chin. He was fit. He wore a headset microphone, so he could move around and gesture. Bastion liked to gesture. "Is it a disease? Is it a condition? Is it a curse?"

The Liminalix leaders murmured to themselves, clicking on the interactive remotes they had been given.

"I see you working, there," Bastion said, smiling. His teeth were perfectly polished almost blue-white. "Don't be shy. Tell me what you think it is."

He waited a moment onstage, while they voted.

"Alright, stop voting," Bastion said. "In three, two, one. Now. Tanner, let's see what people said."

The screen behind him, one of three giant screens, flashed the results as a bar graph, which Chad read aloud as they appeared.

"Wow, 45 percent of you said it was a disease," Bastion said. "And 35 percent of you said it was a condition. And 20 percent of you said it was a curse."

Chad affected a frown at the crowd, prompting nervous laughter.

"A curse?" Bastion said. "Bob, I know you're part of the curse contingent, fess up, Buddy. A curse. Hah, that's funny. Very, I don't know, old-time religion, right? Look, I'm not going to pick on Bob Mazurkiewicz in Accounting for saying it's a curse."

Everybody laughed, and Chad laughed with them. It was a rich laugh, because he was a rich man. Wildly rich. Rich beyond belief.

"I know why most of you would say it's a disease," Bastion said. "Something to be cured. It's what we do here at Liminalix, am I right? We cure diseases."

The display screens shifted and showed old illustrations of werewolves, people turning into monsters. The central screen showed their flagship product, Lupitol—a black and white capsule with a crescent moon upon it, and the tagline, "Feel Human Again."

"Everybody here knows how Liminalix has been at the forefront of the treatment of lycanthropy—excuse me, "Night Fever.""

He air-quoted Night Fever as he said it, to the laughter of the executives. Bastion clicked through various spots of the ad campaign, and his executives applauded.

"Lupitol began as a dream for me ten years ago," Bastion said. "What if we could treat lycanthropy? Help people manage their symptoms. Help them live with their affliction? Help them feel human again. What if? Well, we know how that went. We made it happen."

The audience applause grew still more fervent, and Bastion let them work through it a little, walking around onstage, basking in the applause while the display screens did their thing, showing ad stills.

He clicked through stills of YouTube, Twitter, Facebook, and other social media channels, showing people dealing with lycanthropy.

"The government got themselves into a real pickle with all of this," Bastion said. "All of these people out there, claiming to be werewolves. I mean, how insane is that? It's crazy. You know all about the Happening—that's what they call it. The outbreak of '07, when things really went through the roof. All those Infectives out there. I came up with the notion of Night Fever. I got the government contracts to fast track our R&D to get the treatment to market in record time. I can be very persuasive."

More laughter.

"And as we stand in 2015, we're getting Lupitol out there for all of these people suffering from Night Fever," Bastion said. "That's a win in my book."

More applause. The screens showed the tsunami of profit on the release of Lupitol in the pharmaceutical market.

"We know there's no cure for lycanthropy," Bastion said. "We all know this. But Lupitol works, my friends. It's a drug that delivers time-released tranquility that helps Infectives deal with their condition, their disease, their curse."

He winked at Bob Mazurkiewicz in the audience, prompting more chuckles and ribbing from the audience.

"Going back to my poll at the start of this," Bastion said. "What is lycanthropy? I'm going to tell you what it is: it's a lifestyle. It's a way of life."

The screens shifted to show a full moon in the center, a werewolf howling up at it.

"We're helping people live with lycanthropy," Bastion said. "And that means there's a great big Phase II to this whole thing. The marketing and management of lycanthropic lifestyles. Feel Human Again? Sure, that's for the norms, guys. That's for the people who cry in their craft beers as they're trying to pry the safety caps off their Xanax bottles. No, I'm talking about something else, something bigger, grander."

Bastion went to the edge of the stage and looked out at the sea of faces watching him speak.

"The opportunity to guide people in their lycanthropic lives," Bastion said. "To be there for them every step of the way. Whether they're trying desperately to retain some sense memory of their lost humanity, or whether they're openly embracing their lycanthropy. Liminalix will be there for them."

The audience applauded yet again, some of them, then all of them, standing up. Bastion soaked up the applause with his ever-ready, thousand-watt smile.

"Nobody talks about lycanthropy," Bastion said, putting a tanned finger to his lips. "We're not supposed to. We're not *allowed* to. Outside of these doors, it's Night Fever 24/7, friends."

Some boos, but Bastion shook those off.

"I'm okay with that," Bastion said. "If the norms want people to call it that, they don't want the sheeple getting spooked, sure, fine. Night Fever it is. I mean, given that Lupitol is the number one treatment for Night Fever, I'm certainly not going to complain."

Laughter.

"But I'm also talking about those other people," Bastion said. "The ones who find out that they *like* being lycanthropes. What about them?"

The auditorium got quiet, and the screens showed normal, smiling, happy, active people going about their lives in still shots.

"Get your remotes handy," Bastion said. "How many of you are on Lupitol right here, right now?"

There was visible unease among the audience, being put on the spot, even anonymously.

"Oh, don't worry, friends," Bastion said. "What, are you worried that the feds are going to come get you? Not here. They wouldn't dare."

The Bureau for Extraordinary Events logo appeared on the central screen, a big bee in black and yellow, the name circling it.

"No BEEs are going to sting you, my friends," Bastion said. "Answer the poll. I want to know how many of you are on Lupitol. And here's the thing: I already know. I want you all to know just how many. What's the number, Tanner?"

The screen flashed 48 percent.

Bastion laughed.

"How about that?" Bastion said, noting the concern among some of the audience, looking around nervously. "Nearly half of you are on Lupitol. Being treated for Night Fever. You know, lycanthropy."

The BEE screen was replaced by the Wolfman, and there was some nervous laughter.

"Werewolves, my friends," Bastion said. "Right among you. Right in your midst. And look around you, go ahead, take a gander. You can't spot them, can you? You can't tell if Bobbie, or Amy, or Jen, or Gina, or Beth, or Karl are werewolves. You can't tell. Thank you, Lupitol."

The applause came, but it was still fairly wary. Bastion had unnerved the audience with that poll, the realization that so many of them were lycanthropes.

"It's not about blending in," Bastion said. "It's about standing out. Being proud of who and what you are. Now, I'm not judging you. How you managed to get infected. Maybe it was during the Happening. Maybe it was later. Met the wrong person. I don't know, and I don't care. What I do know is that Lupitol is letting you keep on living the way you did before, am I right?"

The executives looked uncertain where Bastion was taking this.

"Only you never can go back to what you were before," Bastion said. "Not truly. And I'm saying that you shouldn't have to. Why pretend? You're different. You're something else. Lupitol keeps you from eating the family dog or killing your neighbor. It keeps you off the streets hunting for prey. But the urges are still there, right? You still want something. You still need something. IT is still inside you. Those cravings. It's like nicotine, only so much worse."

More discomfort in the audience as some squirmed, whether norm or stealth Infective.

"Liminalix is going to be there for you on your journey, friends," Bastion said. "We'll take you where you want to go, where you need to go, where you have to go. Lupitol isn't the end of your journey. It's just the beginning."

The Lupitol logo appeared on the three screens, and the executives applauded it ardently. The central screen showed "Feel Human Again" as the tagline. The left screen showed "For Those Beastly Nights" as the tagline. The right screen showed "You're Something Else" as the tagline.

"Liminalix is there for all phases of lycanthropy," Bastion said. "We're the best friend you never knew you had. I'm asking you to work with me, friends. Help me, help each other, on your journey. Let's get out there and live, dammit!"

There were cheers, although the norms were still nervous. Chad could see it in them. He could practically smell it, the uncertainty and fear.

"For those of you who're Infectives," Bastion said. "And relax, I know who you all are. You don't have to worry about me outing you. You'll find you all have weekend passes to my Free Rein country club and resort in upstate New York. You know the one. We're going to have a weekend retreat there in a month. A chance for you to let your hair down. A chance to get acquainted."

Chad was pleased to see their reaction. Free Rein was elite and very exclusive, one of Bastion's prize properties. The chance to get a weekend there was on the bucket list of every Liminalix executive.

"For those of you norms out there," Bastion said. "Let's just say that there's an open invitation for you at Free Rein if you meet some entry requirements. We can circle back on that, if you'd like. You can talk to Blythe or Lane about it if you need to. In the meantime, let's keep going, folks. Let's make this quarter our best quarter ever!"

The applause shook the auditorium, and the growing sales figures for Lupitol showed on the flanking screens, while the Lupitol logo dominated the central screen, and Chad Bastion accepted the applause and left the stage to a chorus of people talking to one another.

His assistant, Emily Langford, met him backstage. She was a young woman with red hair tied back in ponytail and a perpetually worried expression.

"Your next meeting is all set in Conference Room L, Chad," she said.

"Great," Bastion said. "I don't want to keep Troy waiting."

3

ANOTHER day, another hunt.

"I've lost the target," Norm said, driving parallel to Michigan Avenue. "Do you see them?"

"Yes," Tiff said. "Do you want me to intercede?"

She and Norm had rarely been face-to-face, were most often interacting on the phone, with him in the field and her at Bureau headquarters—the *Argent*—the BEE's state-of-the-art base of operations. She piloted drones from the ship, far from shore.

"Negative," Norm said. "Just let me know where they're at."

The USS *Argent,* an erstwhile hospital ship under BEE administration, operated in Lake Michigan. She had arrived on the lake several years ago. The official story had been that it was there to tend to any sick and injured in the region.

"Heading north on Michigan, just went over the river," Tiff said.

"Copy that," Norm said.

The BEE had originally had a covert facility near Navy Pier, known as the Kennel, but it had been compromised by Zooey Hummel, who had singlehandedly attacked it and infected everyone in the compound. After that disaster, the Bureau had arranged to use the *Argent* as an offshore headquarters.

"I can assist, Driver," Tiff said.

"Negative," Norm said. "I've got it."

To avoid misunderstandings with other naval vessels, she'd been painted white like other hospital ships, but with the hexagonal BEE logo in evidence. She bore the Yellow Jack flag when in port, the yellow and black checkered flag, to indicate that she was under quarantine. That this color happened to match the BEE logo was an added bonus. It also kept other ships and boats away.

"Let me know when you have line of sight," Tiff said.

"Will do," Norm said. "I'm about a block south of their location, yes?"

If that was not persuasive enough, she also had water cannons and a dozen batteries of 20 mm autocannons arranged strategically around her. These were primarily intended for any Lupines that might be inclined to trek out across the water and attack the ship. As prodigious as the Lupine capacity to regenerate was, the military had discovered that 20 mm cannons firing silver-tipped shells proved highly effective in dispatching them.

"Roger, Driver," Tiff said. "They're heading toward a parking garage."

"Copy that, Dealer," Norm said. "I'm turning."

The crew of the *Argent* were BEE Operations personnel, wearing black baseball caps with the BEE logo upon them, as well as black jackets with BEE emblazoned on the back. In the years before the Happening, they had most commonly masqueraded as Animal Control personnel in white vans. Now, they were all sailors. The BEE strictly monitored who was able to board and leave the *Argent*. There were several procedures in place to ensure that no Infectives repeated what Hummel had done to the Kennel.

Norm was stuck at a lingering light.

"I'm backed up here, Dealer," Norm said. "Keep your eyes on them."

"No problem, Driver," Tiff said. "Still have them."

The official story for the *Argent's* ongoing presence offshore from Chicago was it was tied to something the Hive brain trust had called "Night Fever"—Night Fever was the cover story for lycanthropy.

Signs and symptoms of Night Fever included restlessness, nervousness, anxiety, insomnia, delirium, hallucination, memory loss (or lapses), violent and/or unpredictable behavior.

Norm pushed past the light and got onto Michigan, not wanting to speed or otherwise draw attention to himself, but not wanting the targets to get out of reach.

"Heading south on Michigan," Norm said. "Talk to me, Dealer."

"They're out of their vehicle and walking," Tiff said. "Three contacts."

The media was encouraged to share stories of Night Fever, which it dutifully did. Nobody entirely believed in Night Fever, but it at least accounted for why some people might wake up outside naked, bloodied, without a memory of where they'd been and what they'd done.

Night Fever had been branded an epidemic by 2012 by none other than the CDC, which had led to an effort to come up with some treatment for it. Funding research into this, the government had bankrolled a dozen research efforts at treating Night Fever. One had risen to the top of the heap: Liminalix.

Norm strained his vision, could see targets, three blocks away.

"I see them," Norm said. "Thanks for the assist, Dealer."

"Any time," Tiff said. "Be careful, Driver."

"I'm always careful, Dealer," Norm said.

The targets were three Infectives who were part of the pack-gangs who dominated Chicago after the Happening. While the BEE had been phenomenally—almost uncannily, by Norm's estimation—successful in suppressing the Happening nationwide, because it had been the epicenter of the '07 outbreak, the Lupines there had been more deeply entrenched. The Infectives had proliferated more widely, and with the ransacking of the Kennel, the BEE had lost ground it never quite made up in the city.

As a result, the city was under a selective quarantine as an epicenter for Night Fever. What this meant is that anybody going into the city was monitored by the BEE. This was not widely known. For most norms and civilians, it meant a checkpoint here or there. For the Lupines, it was deadly.

What was even less well-known was that anybody who left the City of Chicago was actively monitored using the Archon Program.

"I don't think that's necessarily true, Driver," Tiff said.

"Enough backseat driving, Dealer," Norm said. Tiff had ridden shotgun with him daily. As a drone pilot, she was perfectly situated to assess and evaluate Norm's fieldwork. He was confident she reported on his missions to Minton.

The Archon Program allowed the BEE to hack cell phones and compromise them completely. With Archon, they could eavesdrop, track a person anywhere they went with their phone, access all contacts and communications, any apps they used. Anything and everything a person did with their phone, Archon could track.

For the BEE, it was a very powerful tool they'd brought to bear in force in 2012, after wrestling with the post-Happening breakout of Lupines for several years.

"Only trying to help, Driver," Tiff said.

"I know you are," Norm said. "You're my guardian angel."

"Never forget that," Tiff said.

The BEE had turned to Blackwatch, a private intelligence firm, to supply them with the Archon program, and a handful of hackers to help use it. This was considered less overt than the NSA, offering the BEE more opportunities for covert action, which was thought to be essential in dealing with Infectives.

"Enough chatter," Minton said. He'd clearly been monitoring their banter. Minton sometimes hopped in on communications. Norm didn't like it, but couldn't do anything about it, since the Director was privileged to access any BEE communications.

"Sorry, Big Bad," Tiff said.

"Driver, what's your sitrep?" Minton asked.

"Tracking three confirmed targets," Norm said, wanting to keep it as low-profile as possible.

"Confirmed? Who by, Driver?" Minton asked.

"Me, Big Bad," Norm said. A Stinger had the situational prerogative to identify and intervene on suspected Lupines.

Since then, the BEE had been tracking Infectives by their phones. This had been a move of particular insight from Minton. While Lupines transformed were hard to find, since they were literally off the grid, when they went back to their former lives, in more cases than not, it meant using their phones. For Infectives, often it meant their phones were lost and left behind somewhere when they transformed. The BEE tracked them and used them to hunt down Infectives.

The BEE approach was simple and straightforward—when they had identified a potential Lupine, they'd use Archon to breach their smartphone. Then, they'd track that person, and get the necessary information to ensure that they were, in fact, a positive Infective. When they found a "lost" phone, they'd do the same thing, with more robust surveillance of the target in question.

"Which targets, Driver?" Minton asked. Minton was as direct as he was evasive. He put the "direct" in "Director."

"Still ascertaining, Big Bad," Norm said. He didn't want Minton nosing around on his hunt, and figured Minton was likely asking Tiff on the sly who he was hunting.

Often, the people who were Infectives went through a period of denial and/or exultation—it depended on the individual. That would manifest in communication on their phone—blog entries, tweeting about it, private diaries, texting close friends, and so on. The BEE analysts would then compile that information, the drone pilots would stalk them, and the Stingers would then apprehend or liquidate them. It was far easier taking down an Infective when they were in their human form than when they were in their Lupine form.

That was the brilliance of the Archon approach—where the Wardens had been forced to contend with fully transformed Lupines, the drones and Stingers would zero in on untransformed Infectives and kill them before they even had the chance to change.

Depending on the situation, the BEE would drop them with a timely tranquilizer dart strong enough to take down a horse. This was typically sufficient to take down most Lupines in their human disguises. Once anesthetized, they'd already have some teams on-hand to drive up in a van and secure the Infective, and off they'd go. In the early days of the Happening, it was more haphazard, but since then, the BEE had gotten particularly good at it.

The targets were walking down the street, and Norm was moving into position. With Minton on the line, he should have announced that, but he kept it quiet. Tiff jumped in.

"Driver, do you still have the targets in sight?" Tiff asked.

"Yes, Dealer," Norm said.

"I'm going to share my feed with Big Bad," Tiff said.

"Not necessary, Dealer," Norm said.

"Go ahead, Dealer," Minton said.

With Archon, the field agents were more like delivery people, co-ordinating with the Operations personnel, and could efficiently pack the van with a dozen sleeping or dead Infectives before racing to un-load them, in a waystation bound for the *Argent*. Minton had turned it into a far more efficient enterprise, allowing the BEE to pick and choose the time to take down an Infective.

The three Norm was stalking were part of the Loop Group pack-gang, what Norm and some of the others referred to as "Loopines" in BEE agent parlance. Chad Bastion was said to be the leader of the Loopines, but nobody could ever positively tie him to that pack. He was immaculate.

Bastion was a very rich man, at the head of Liminalix, his pharmaceutical firm, among other things. Loopines had this vision of themselves as being part of an elite lycanthropic social club and kept a tight leash on their members. They epitomized the organized Infective type that Norm considered most dangerous. Bastion had a killer public image. He'd been the one who had trotted out the treatment for Night Fever roughly five years after the Happening in clinical trials. That was Lupitol, which was being widely marketed.

Lupitol was everywhere. The ads were everywhere—on the sides of buses, at bus stops, on billboards, on television, on the radio. Night Fever? Try Lupitol. Feel Human Again.

Whether it worked or not, Norm knew Bastion was making a lot of money from it.

"Negative, Driver," Minton said.

"Please repeat, Big Bad," Norm said. He'd heard Minton perfectly.

"No go on the targets," Minton said. "Driver, please confirm."

"Big Bad, I'm only a half-block away," Norm said.

"Abort, Driver," Minton said.

Norm was tempted to pretend he hadn't heard Minton's communication, but they both knew he'd heard him.

Traffic downtown looked normal. Cars and trucks, coming and going. Pedestrians hurrying wherever they were going. Restaurants and stores open. Everything looked normal. But Norm knew better. None of this was normal. People knew something was off. He could see it in the looks in their faces, the concern.

It was another of the lycanthropic tells—that absence of worry. After the Happening, some of the Infectives decided that their lives were better now that they were Lupines. Sure, many were traumatized by it, but some thought it was a great lifestyle change. The Loopines were among them. They were a bunch of smug bastards.

The targets took a right turn, appeared to be headed to a restaurant, Bizzo's Italian Eatery. They walked in front of it and the hostess scrambled to get to them. The three walked in the place like they owned it and Norm watched them from a safe distance.

"Abort, Driver," Minton said. "Confirm, Driver."

"Driver, please confirm," Tiff said.

Norm bit his lip, hated being leaned on like this. It irked him beyond belief. They were right there.

There was the youngest of the three, a pinstripe-suited young man with brown hair slicked back and the signature Loopie golf and/or tennis tan. He scanned around them with his feral face, making sure everything was okay.

The oldest of the three was Todd Shaw, one of Chad Bastion's lieutenants. The guy was a creep: tall and lean, he shared the feral countenance of the younger Loopie. Long nose, bright eyes, a hint of a sneer on his chiseled face. He wore a navy blue suit and a red tie with a white shirt.

"Driver, confirm," Minton said. His voice was measured relentlessness. Norm could almost imagine getting chewed out by Minton in 24 hours aboard the *Argent*.

"Message received," Norm said, choking it out.

The third member of this Loopie troupe was a woman. She was blond, handsomely pretty, with a strong jaw and a penchant for ivory in her wardrobe. In this case, an ivory blouse and a honey-hued leather skirt. She wore sunglasses and scanned around them a moment before the three of them went into Bizzo's.

He knew that third Loopie very well, because she was Norm's estranged wife, Anne.

4

DR. MINA Milkowski wore her curly black hair in an ever-present ponytail, even before she'd become infected by Zooey Hummel in that savage attack on the Kennel in '07.

After becoming an Infective, Mina's ponytail had become almost symbolic to her, of her desire to retain control. As sharp-nosed and pointy-chinned as she ever was, Mina glared at herself in the laptop screen, her grey eyes unencumbered by glasses anymore.

One of the beneficial side effects of the infection, she assumed—there were no nearsighted werewolves. She saw herself, and she saw Animus, the name she finally gave to her other self. Mina knew it was bad form to name the Lupine alter ego—that doing so made one vulnerable to it. But she did it, anyway. She was resigned to her condition. Just as she was resigned to living as a permanent guest in *Synowie* safehouses.

Even before the Happening, the *Synowie Srebra*, or Sons of Silver, were never a large group. The secret society of Polish werewolf hunters had a centuries-old and bloody history. Such was the way of all werewolf hunters—secrecy and bloodshed. At most, there had been 50,000 members worldwide at the start of the Happening. With another 50,000 loosely affiliated with the secret order. This was something Mina had gleaned in conversations with Patryk Landa, one of the *Synowie* leaders who had originally sheltered her when she'd hidden from the BEE. Landa had been fond of Mina, had been willing to talk to her in the quiet moments they shared.

But after the Happening, the *Synowie* had been very busy coordinating their underground efforts, which meant fighting werewolves from the shadows in a more low-tech manner than the BEE.

However, as with all such efforts, there was attrition. Despite their long experience and skill, *Synowie* members died fighting the Lupines. Mina knew this better than anyone, as she pecked away on her laptop from one of the safehouses that had become her home away from home.

In her time in the *Synowie* safehouse, there only by the grace of the late Patryk Landa, Mina sought to put it all down for posterity. It wasn't a memoir, exactly, more of a blog. But it was something:

> I still call them what they are: werewolves. It's more honest than the gentler and more oblique "Lupines." There is a purity in the word "werewolf" that can't be ignored.
>
> It's an old word. Old English—"wer" for man, and "wulf" for wolf. *Man-wolf.* Old English. A long time ago. I looked it up. Sanskrit: "vira;" Latin "vir;" Norse "verr;" Gothic "wair;" Old High German "wer;" Irish "fear" (that's apt, no?); Lithuanian "vyras;" even Welsh "gŵr."
>
> Norse also used "vargr"—euphemistically for "wolf"—more like "outlaw." I guess a "Vargulf" was a wolf that slaughtered many sheep but ate little of the kill.
>
> Those rogue wolves were the bane of shepherds. The Old English "warg" was used for such a rogue wolf, and was also synonymous with "serial killer," basically. To be called a "vargr" by the Norse was a very bad thing—you were outside of the law, unfit for representation or aid or compensation.
>
> It's what Wikipedia says, so it must be true, right? The point is, they've been around a long time. Old words, for an old problem.
>
> They have a far simpler word for us: prey.

She stopped at the keyboard, thought a moment. Heard howls outside her window. Not close. She paused and waited in the phosphoric glow of her computer, making sure that the danger wasn't near. Then she continued.

> I don't know why I'm writing this stuff. I don't know who out there would even read it. Maybe you werewolves will read it one day for laughs. Maybe that's why I started this journal. Somebody has to say something. I'm in it for the Norms. The folks like I used to be. The ones you're killing and eating, the ones you're infecting.

Maybe I wanted there to be a record, so that when we're extinct, it'll maybe still be out there, so somebody will know that we weren't *always* monsters.

She stopped again, stretched her back, heard the cracks. She'd stopped being a norm the moment Zooey Hummel had bitten her. Eight years an Infective. Landa had helped her manage her infection the only way they knew how—a cage she could occupy when the compulsion to transform had grown too great to bear. Animus was always waiting for a chance to come out.

Mina looked at the chart she'd made, an optimistic forecast for the consequences of the Happening, based on their experiences in Chicago, the rates of infection, if unchecked:

Year 1: 250
Year 2: 2500
Year 3: 25,000
Year 4: 250,000
Year 5: 2,500,000
Year 6: 25,000,000
Year 7: 250,000,000
Year 8: 2,500,000,000

They were ballpark figures, of course, based on high infectivity rates. In actual practice, the lycanthropes killed far more people than they infected, on the order of maybe 10:1 killed to infected. But the optimistic forecast at least helped her get a sense of the stakes of the game, in terms of scaling the problem for the BEE, how to manage and administer it.

Further, there were the countermeasures undertaken by the BEE, which helped reduce numbers of Infectives. Mina wasn't privy to the latest numbers—but she tracked what she could, all the same.

LOCAL

Year 1: 250
Year 2: 2500

REGIONAL

Year 3: 25,000
Year 4: 250,000

NATIONAL

Year 5: 2,500,000
Year 6: 25,000,000

INTERNATIONAL

Year 7: 250,000,000

GLOBAL

Year 8: 2,500,000,000

The Happening had moved from a Chicago problem to a regional problem in only a couple of years, and with outbreaks occurring across the country by means of a tireless blood drive on the part of Zooey's Infective acolytes.

With an estimated 25,000 Infectives in the Chicagoland area, the problem had very quickly moved out of control in '07 and '08.

One Infective would routinely attack approximately anywhere from five to ten victims during a transformation cycle. There was, at least for Infectives, a period of latency—the Infectives were more heavily tied to the lunar cycle, with activity rising over a three-day span coinciding with the cycle of the moon.

Her research had shown her that it was more of a psychological factor than something actually compelling them to transform with the full moon. But, whatever the case, each wave got bigger.

There had been 250 Infectives at the time the Happening first exploded in Chicago. It had begun with Samantha Hain, Patient Zero, who had infected Zooey Hummel, who had then rampaged, infecting approximately 250 people—very much of this was with the benefit of hindsight.

The BEE had been tracking Hain and Hummel but had not successfully apprehended either. The Avalon Incident had claimed many victims, many (but, importantly, not all) of whom had checked into hospitals. While many had been detained or apprehended by the BEE, Zooey had been particularly busy.

In the 24 months since the Happening, she'd been directly responsible for approximately 5000 Infectives, by Mina's measure. The woman had been a fanged fiend. Mina could still remember her attacking her at the Kennel. Mina still carried that guilt with her, how she'd unintentionally helped it happen by mistaking Zooey for a victim and giving her access to the Kennel. It had been a fateful blunder on her part.

Mina clenched her fists and recalculated the numbers, based on what she'd gleaned of the BEE interdiction efforts:

WARDEN PROGRAM

Year 1: 250 (10% clearance, 25 killed and/or caught) = 225 Active Infectives (AIs)

Year 2: 2500 (20% clearance, 500 killed and/or caught) = 2000 AIs

Year 3: 25,000 (35% clearance, 8750 killed and/or caught) = 16,250 AIs

Year 4: 250,000 (44% clearance, 110,000 killed and/or caught) = 140,000 AIs

Up until the time of the cessation of the Warden Program, the BEE had increased their clearance rates. It had amounted to Wardens stealthily killing Infectives, with the Recovery teams occupied 24/7 with taking the bodies. Especially after the rendition program had been replaced with a shoot-to-kill policy. The growing use of BEE drones had taken a bite out of the Lupines, as had the more recent proliferation of Lupitol as a treatment for it.

Mina didn't have access to the Wolf Island stats, but she assumed that there were at least 100,000 Infectives marooned there, including her former boss, Anya Walker, among others she knew, like Zach West, one of the best Wardens. Mina hoped they were still alive.

Wolf Island was more of a slow-motion death sentence, since the Infectives were dropped off onto the island and left to their own devices, with periodic drops of food and water, and a heavily armed BEE observation facility. The intention of the place was to allow for BEE researchers to observe Lupines in a wilderness setting.

The food and water had been a concession after there was concern that there would be human rights implications if word got out about the island, although the government neatly sidestepped it by pointing out that Infectives, by virtue of the retroviral infection, no longer fully qualified as "human"—they were alternately referred to as "transhuman" or "parahuman" in the legal texts. That qualifier gave the BEE considerable (if highly classified) latitude in its prosecution of its mission.

Wolf Island aside, the termination of the Warden Program made no sense to Mina, contrasted with the problem of the Happening—they were overwhelmed by the sheer quantity of Infectives.

How the government had managed to keep a lid on the story of the Happening was almost beyond her comprehension. The stories were out there, people had footage of Lupines. Even Samantha Hain's "Transformation" YouTube video was still out there. It had been the first time anybody had filmed a live lycanthropic transformation on social media. It wasn't the only one. There were so many now that it almost seemed normal.

Although she was not privy to the inner workings of the Hive, Mina thought BEE was waving a surrender flag in the furry face of the Happening. There were simply too many Infectives to be effectively culled by the BEE, at least working alone. Even with drones.

And yet, the country *hadn't* been overwhelmed by Infectives, despite her projections. In fact, while she didn't have the numbers (and hated that she didn't have access to the BEE databases), Mina thought the Happening had been mostly contained on some level. Not eliminated by any means but contained.

She'd tracked the stories online, the references to Night Fever and related coverage. Something—or someone—had quelled the Happening by 2011. The stories persisted, incidents occurred, but Director Minton had managed to prevent the Happening from spiraling out of control in the way that Mina had calculated. She wanted the numbers. She wanted to know why.

There should have been 2.5 billion Infectives out there, but there weren't. So, what happened to the Happening? Where'd they go?

Mina got to her feet, did some stretches, glanced at herself in a mirror she'd put up on the wall.

Patryk Landa had been kind to let her lodge in one of the *Synowie's* safehouses. In the years after the Happening, Mina had been managing her affliction with tranquilizers, but the compulsion to transform had grown too great to sedate. In those moments, she'd sequester herself to her cage and would lock herself in, while members of the *Synowie* would observe her. Those were embarrassing moments for her, raging in that cage as her Animus snarled at them.

I don't belong here, Animus said, in her head.

Animus hated Mina. Animus hated Mina for not letting her take over. Mina wasn't entirely sure how that shook out with most Infectives, but she was fairly confident that no Infective had more forcefully restrained their lycanthropic other half than she had.

But Landa had been sympathetic. He had understood that, in her human moments, she was trying to find a cure for the affliction, or, failing that, a way of managing it. He had been a good man, which was a liability in this new world of werewolves.

Landa and a half-dozen other members of *Synowie* had been killed three years ago by the so-called Wolves of God in a particularly bloody ambush. It had been that attack that had put Sonia Gorski at the head of this branch of the *Synowie*.

Mina clicked a key on her keyboard and posted her blog entry. It wasn't under her own name, of course, and it had been spoofed out so that even if somebody traced it, they'd not track to the ISP of this safe house. Landa had been very careful about that. All of *Synowie* were careful people. They had a saying: *Lepiej być ostrożnym niż martwym.*

Better to be careful than dead, Mina thought. Who could argue with that?

She went over to the sofa and wrapped herself in a blanket, grabbing the remote and turning it on. The news blathered on about curfews and gang activity in the streets. As ever, they didn't really cover the lycanthropic outbreak, not honestly. It was always either gang activity or terrorist activity, coywolf incursions, or outbreaks of Night Fever.

The media was always talking about Night Fever, the counts, the transmissibility. The CDC spokespeople were talking about it, what peopled needed to do, how Lupitol was turning out to be a proven treatment for it.

There came a knock at the door, and Mina jumped back to her feet, alert. Then somebody keyed in, and Mina felt Animus within her twist and turn, wanting to come out and attack the interloper. Any excuse it had to come out, it would take.

But it was Sonia and her brothers, not a threat. They came in, shutting the door behind them, hanging their *Luparas* on hooks on the door.

"How'd it go?" Mina asked. Sonia and her brothers had attended a planning meeting with the BEE, or so she'd told Mina. It had been in a secret location, and had been a teleconference, since Minton refused to leave the *Argent* after what had happened at the Kennel. Mina didn't blame the man but wondered how he could spend that much time aboard that ship without losing his mind. The *Argent* had been offshore in Chicago for years.

"Fine," Sonia said, walking into the living room and taking stock, the way she always did, as if Mina would have left a mangled body on the floor or something. Sonia Gorski was a broad-shouldered, blond-haired woman with the biggest, darkest eyes Mina had ever seen. She had a strong nose and a stronger jaw, but there was a delicacy to her face when she smiled that belied her bloody work for the *Synowie*. All members of the *Synowie* were accomplished killers, following an ancient tradition of hunting and killing werewolves and vampires.

Sonia wore a black-ribbed turtleneck and grey slacks with a stylish, tailored grey leather jacket with matching gloves. Sonia almost always wore gloves, had a seemingly endless variety of them. Mina always assumed she wore them so she wouldn't leave fingerprints at crime scenes.

She snapped her fingers, and one of her brothers, Jan, produced a cardboard box with "Lupitol" marked on it, courtesy of Liminalix. Jan, who looked like a boyish version of his sister, set the box down within reach of Mina. The *Synowie* abided by Landa's edict that Mina was not to be harmed, but it didn't mean they particularly liked or trusted her.

"I can't thank you enough," Mina said, opening the box. It contained dozens of bottles of Lupitol. It would be enough for a year.

Mina could feel Animus writhing.

Don't do it, Milquetoast. Please.

Ignoring Animus, Mina pried out a bottle and opened it, putting a single half-black, half-cream caplet in her palm, with the Lupitol crescent moon symbol printed it like it was a smile. Mina popped the pill and drank it down with some water.

"Caplets this time," Mina said. "Not capsules."

"We take what we take," Sonia said, smiling and shrugging at the same time.

Mina thought about it. After several years of clinical trials beginning in 2011, Lupitol came onto the market at the start of the year as a treatment for Night Fever. Maybe the widespread availability of Lupitol by Liminalix had helped account for the slowdown of the Happening. Lupitol certainly worked to keep her lycanthropic fits at bay, far better than the tranquilizers she'd been using before. Perhaps the ready availability of the drug had kept the Infectives from as widely spreading as they had.

Maybe the treatment let the BEE agents zero in on the problem Infectives, the ones who either rejected the Lupitol treatment regimen or who weren't capable of being pacified by it. There was an insidious logic to it.

Rather convenient that Liminalix had come up with the perfect course of treatment for lycanthropy in the wake of the epidemic. Mina made a mental note to look into that in greater detail when she got a chance. Meantime, she had to manage the sardonic *Synowie*.

"Americans and your pills," Sonia said, shaking her head and half-smiling.

"You're American, too, Sonia," Mina said.

"Barely," Sonia said, even though Mina knew that wasn't true. She'd grown up in Chicago, had lived there for all of her life. But as one of the *Synowie*, there was always that clandestine air they all had about them, the sense of being distinct and different. They were, of course. Anyone who did what they did was different. The work demanded that of them.

By day, Sonia worked at the Landa Library, an independent research library founded in 1888 that held around a million books, totaling around three million manuscript pages, as well as 500,000 maps. The books dated back from the Middle Ages to present. It had a special Occult and Metaphysical Studies collection that was of particular interest. Sonia Gorski, the lethal librarian. It was a thought that made Mina smile, if only to herself.

Mina had taken to working at the Landa Library with Sonia for the past several years, and the work agreed with her. There was something joyous about all of those books, all of that knowledge and history, there for her use. They would carpool there, Sonia working as the head librarian, and Mina as one of the library technicians. The caveat for Mina was she had to not draw attention to herself and hide away if any Bureau people turned up. She was still a fugitive from her former employer.

While she belonged in a research lab, Mina found it satisfying tending to the books at the Landa Library and spent considerable amounts of time in the Occult and Metaphysical Studies collection, trying to learn all she could about her affliction.

Sonia had her stay home that day because of the Bureau teleconference, just to be on the safe side.

"The Bureau has requested the aid of the *Synowie* in attacking the dominant regional packs," Sonia said. "With one key exception: the Loopines under Chad Bastion."

Mina could tell from her tone that Sonia was less than thrilled with this prospect.

"Really?" Mina said. "Given what's happened to the *Synowie* over the past few years? They're compensating you, right?"

Although Mina wasn't privy to the records of the secret order, people still talked, and the attrition suffered by the *Synowie* was significant, particularly in Chicago. Although they were too proud to admit it, Mina thought they might need whatever help they could get.

"Whatever," Sonia said, with a wave of her hand. Her brothers had gone to the kitchen, while Sonia collapsed onto the sofa, tossing her beret to a side table. "You would not believe what they have brought to the table in this latest, I don't know what you'd call it—conspiracy? They threw money our way, yes. We'd be fools not to take it. A society like ours depends on such donations."

Mina took her seat next to Sonia, wrapping herself in her blanket again. She missed working for the BEE and had been tempted to reach out to them again. After so many years, it might not be the death sentence and/or exile that it was under the previous administration. If they were getting enough funding that they were willing to throw some to the Poles, it might bode well for her own prospects of readmittance.

"What is it?" Mina asked. "What did they do?"

"Here is the arrangement: we hunt werewolves," Sonia said. "We are the Sons of Silver. We hunt them. To have the Director trot them out that way, it was like I was being slapped in the face. Two Trueborn abominations looming over us as if they belonged there. The Rupinos. That infernal Gia Rupino and her damnable, innumerable siblings. And another one, Valentina—I think she's a baby sister, or a cousin, who can tell with them? It's impossible to be sure, as they all look the same to me. The same Rupino insolence. They all have it. And Chad Bastion, looking suntanned and splendid, like he was on vacation."

For Mina, Bastion was the very public face of Liminalix, a pioneer in what was called "Farmaceuticals"—using modified agricultural products to produce marketable drugs. Liminalix was very big in the Midwest, and Bastion was always offering up appearances, particularly in recent years with the "Night Fever epidemic" and Lupitol as the only effective treatment of it currently available.

Sonia sat back angrily on the sofa and downed her wine, her mind clearly occupied with what she'd seen.

At the mention of the Rupinos, Mina was even more curious. The mysterious Clan Rupino ran the lycanthropic underground throughout the Midwest. That they were willing to sit down with the BEE either spoke to the precarious position of the BEE or perhaps some ruthless maneuvering by Gia Rupino.

Mina would have loved to talk to other BEE agents about it, but as an Infective fugitive, she would not be welcome there, not like before.

"Weird that Bastion would come out in the open like that," Mina said.

"Minton was very clear: Bastion's people and the Rupinos are off-limits," Sonia said. "We *Synowie* are not to attack them under any circumstances."

"It's not fair," Mina said, drinking her wine. It was very good red wine, this Romanian red.

"You're so right," Sonia said. "It isn't fair."

Her other brother sat down across from them. The two of them, Jan and Abram, glanced at each other. They were a few years younger than their sister and knew better than to cross her when she was in a mood.

"I am to work with someone named Norm Stockwell," Sonia said. "What do you know of him, Dr. Milkowski?"

It amused Mina that there was a degree of formality in her exchanges with Sonia. Patryk Landa had managed to instill an iota of professional respect in the *Synowie* when he'd brought Mina in, despite the protestation of some of the members.

In addition to her efforts to find a cure for lycanthropy, and her work at the library, Mina traded in her knowledge of the Bureau to the *Synowie*. This was clearly another of those moments.

"He was a Warden, years ago," Mina said. "Before the Happening. Cool-headed sort of guy. Dark hair, always cut short. Serious. Like all business, all the time. They used to call him the Walking Death."

"The Walking Death?" Sonia asked, amused.

"He had a very high kill count," Mina said. "He was a war veteran. He knew how to handle himself in the field."

"Okay," Sonia said. "I can work with someone like that. But what do you know about the Stinger Program?"

"I don't know what that is," Mina said. "They are after my time at the BEE. In my day, you had Rangers, you had Stalkers, and you had Wardens. That's the hierarchy of field ops personnel. I don't know who the Stingers are."

Sonia brushed that off with a sip of wine.

"You don't have to," Sonia said. "Minton told me all about them. He said they're elite field operatives, deep cover agents who operate with minimal oversight. This Norm is a Stinger, apparently, operating under the codename, Driver."

"So, he's like a spy?" Mina asked. She wondered why Sonia was asking her questions she already apparently had the answers to. How the *Synowie* operated was itself a sort of mystery, like layers of intrigue. She also wondered why Minton had given that information about Norm so readily, if the Stingers were intended to be covert. She supposed that nobody would ever accuse the *Synowie* of being tied to anything Lupine. Then again, why was he having them abstain from attacking the Rupinos and Bastion?

"An assassin, more like," Sonia said.

"Interesting," Mina said. "Did he reveal Norm's identity at that meeting? Like in front of the Lupines?"

"He did," Sonia said.

"That didn't strike you as odd?" Mina asked. From what she knew of Minton, he was a procedural stickler, a very by-the-books sort of Director.

"Everything about the BEE strikes me as odd," Sonia said. "They are a peculiar bunch."

To Mina, it sounded like they'd abandoned the extradition and rendition program in favor of something both more clandestine and lethal, and perhaps cost-efficient. The rendition program had been expensive and labor-intensive. Moving to highly trained field agents and drones might prove cheaper. Mina wondered how that might play out.

"But you're willing to work with them?"

"What else can we do? I don't want them attacking us," Sonia said, drinking her wine. "Any progress to report on your memoirs?"

Mina shrugged.

"They're not really memoirs. More just an accounting of what we know. I really need a proper lab," she said. "Not that you haven't been great. But I could do so much more in an actual lab."

Sonia shook her head, swirling the wine. Outside, somewhere, someone howled. They listened a moment, but it was nobody close.

"Not possible," Sonia said. "Sorry. We're strictly wetwork here in Chicago for now."

"You can't blame me for trying," Mina said. "I just want to be useful, beyond what I've done at the library. So, no targeting the Rupinos and Bastion."

"Yes," Sonia said. "It offended me."

"I can only imagine," Mina said.

She also wondered about Norm, where he might be in the city. It sounded like the Stingers kept a very low profile.

"So, how are you working with Norm?" Mina asked.

"That remains to be ironed out," Sonia said. "We're supposed to meet up tomorrow. I'm sure I'll have more details then."

Sonia frowned into what was left of her wine, which she drained, setting the empty class on the table with a clank. Her brothers looked on, uneasy.

"You sound like you're not liking that," Mina said.

"*Should* I like that?" Sonia asked. "I want to kill the targets myself. This is our fight, more than it is for the BEE. The *Synowie* have been at it far longer. We know how the Trueborn think. They are taking full advantage of the Happening to increase their power and privilege."

Somewhere, somebody howled, answered by another and another.

"You see?" Sonia said, smacking one hand into the other. "Even *they* agree with me."

WH**E**N Bastion had reached out to Gia Rupino for a dinner meeting at Simmer, Gia had thought perhaps he'd lost his mind. It was a downtown establishment, overlooking Michigan Avenue from a lofty height.

The décor was ultra-modern to the point of being almost dated—antiseptic lines and artfully chosen dark woods to frame the place, with subtropical plants arrayed strategically to offer the hint of exoticism intended to communicate culinary exclusivity and opulence for laypersons. The dark wood tables had white tablecloths and the waiters were immaculately attired in white coats and black bowties and black slacks.

Bastion's invitation had come by way of phone and he'd offered a truce if Gia only showed up with a half-dozen of her own people.

Unsure what his game was, Gia accepted. Her half-dozen were Valentina, one of her younger sisters, as well as Mia, Sia, and Bria, aka, the Furies, as well as her cousins Lorenzo and Antonio. They were all strong and loyal members of the clan, and Gia had no doubt if Bastion had been intending something untoward, they would be able to fight their way out of it.

Bastion included Todd Shaw, Lane Tanner, Blythe Connor, Anne Stockwell, and two other Clan Bastion people upon whom he could depend—Blake and Wade Bastion, his younger brothers, who looked like broader-shouldered versions of Chad.

The back of Simmer had been reserved by Bastion's people, and they had that area to themselves, while other patrons looked on with envy and curiosity.

At Gia's urging, her people had all come well-dressed—Valentina had worn a blood red cocktail dress, while the Furies dressed in black and white dresses, while Lorenzo and Antonio wore black pinstriped suits. Gia had worn a cream-colored silk blouse and a burnt caramel-colored leather pants and low heels.

Valentina turned her big blue eyes on Bastion and his people, who wore various shades of respectable ostentation, a blend of navy blue crested blazers and golf shirts, open collars and ever-present tans.

"Gia," Bastion said, holding out his arms to give her a hug, which she accepted graciously.

"Chad," Gia said, watching everyone else exchange wary greetings. "To what do we owe the honor of this invitation?"

Bastion smiled at her. It was a becoming smile, all-encompassing.

"Who says I have an agenda?" Bastion said. "Maybe I just wanted to see you. Especially after that little teleconference the other day."

They took their seats and Bastion wasted no time ordering red wine for everyone at the great round table at which they sat.

"Is it wise to talk of such things in this way?" Gia asked.

"Meh," Bastion said. "I'm not worried."

Simmer was filling up nicely with evening patrons, who were dismayed at the big group taking the big round table.

"Then let's get down to it," Gia said.

"Of course," Bastion said. "Gia, you've had your special arrangement with the Director for, what, eight years?"

"Yes," Gia said. "Right after the Happening. We came to him and made our deal."

Bastion smiled at this, while the waiters circled the table and gave everyone wine glasses. The head waiter opened the bottle of pinot noir and ran it by Bastion, who approved it and had them pour.

"What kind of man is he?" Bastion asked.

"Reliable to a fault," Gia said, watching the pour proceed.

"Ah," Bastion said. "I can work with someone like that."

"From what I've heard and seen, you already are," Gia said. Bastion smiled, raising the wine glass.

"To good friends, old and new," Bastion said.

"To clear words and clearer heads," Gia said.

They all drank, savoring the wine. Bastion leaned into Gia conspiratorially.

"I know I'm intruding by being here, Gia," Bastion said. "But you know I only bear you the highest respect. I honor the traditions of your clan, and the sanctity of your territory."

Gia turned her gaze on Bastion in a sidelong glance.

"Do you?" Gia asked. "You're making a pretty big splash in Chicago."

"I made sure Liminalix was outside of city limits when I had the headquarters made," Bastion said. "You'd be amazed how crowded it gets out east. So many noses in your business. Out here, I can breathe.

Probably why you like slumming it in Detroit, no? Although I can't imagine why you wouldn't be here in Chicago."

"Detroit is fine for us," Valentina said, looking challengingly at Bastion, who smiled.

"Sure," Bastion said. "Charming Valentina. I've heard so much about you. You're the bright young star among the Black Hand, no?"

"She is," Gia said. "Almost as savage as me, when push comes to shove."

"Ah," Bastion said. "Lovely creature. But enough distractions. Let's talk of more important things."

Valentina scowled at Bastion, who winked at her.

"It seemed pretty clear to me that the Director wanted us to wrap up of the Infective problem," Bastion said, glancing at the Infectives on his team. "No offense."

"None taken," Todd Shaw said, glancing at Anne beside him.

"You know the Infectives I mean, Gia," Bastion said. "The riff-raff. The various gangs—the Brotherhood, the *Volki,* the *Lunares.* All of them."

"Yes," Gia said. "Although I should think the rogues are more of a problem among the *Infettivi.*"

"In English?" Shaw asked.

"Infectives, Stupid," Valentina said. "People like you."

Gia quieted Valentina with a look.

"As I see it, the Wolves of God, the *Volki,* the Daughters of Zooey, the Babas," Gia said. "They're the problem packs."

"The Babas hardly count as a pack," Bastion said. "They're the riffiest of riff-raff. But you exempt the others?"

Gia knew that Bastion had to be aware of her own overtures to the Brotherhood and the *Lunares.* She'd had the Black Hand spare them, as they had worked hard to organize their own neighborhoods and quell the Happening breakouts that had been there.

"I do," Gia said. "Jaden Cole and Octavio Caudillo are good alphas for their packs. They are keeping things calm in their respective territories. Versus the others, who are causing problems."

"Right," Bastion said. "I have something of a carrot and stick approach in mind for those other groups. You Rupinos have always been the stick. You're damned good at it. I wouldn't presume to tell you your work. We do things differently in my clan. I'm more of a carrot frame of mind with the others. The salvageable ones."

The waiters were taking orders, going from person to person, while Gia and Bastion continued.

"What sort of carrot?" Gia asked.

"You'll see," Bastion said. "I just need you to call a Council. It's been too long since we have all been together."

Gia tried to read Bastion, tried to figure out what he was up to, but he was nearly unreadable. He wasn't wrong that Clan Bastion operated far differently from Clan Rupino. Where the Black Hand worked from the shadows and excelled at killing, the Grey Bastions preferred negotiation and diplomacy to win the day. They made deals and alliances.

"I'll call a Council," Gia said. "Although whatever you're offering the *Infettivi,* I want double for Clan Rupino."

Bastion smiled broadly at her, refilling her wine glass by his own hand, raising it.

"To the Trueborn go the spoils," Bastion said, and he and Gia both drank. "You know, I have to hand it to you Rupinos for so quaintly holding onto the traditions of our kind. You're old-school in every sense of the word."

"Are we?" Gia said. "I prefer to think that we are effete sophisticates."

"Oh, abundantly so," Bastion said. "Like the *Synowie,* you're, I don't know, from another time. When I'd found out about the deal you'd struck with the Hive so long ago, I couldn't believe it. Nobody out East could believe it. Not Gia Rupino. It made no sense."

"It made sense at the time," Gia said. "It still does. The BEEs were swarming, and we wanted to make sure their stings were focused on the proper targets."

Bastion smilingly accepted that.

"You are so right," Bastion said. "Still, what I've done with Liminalix has left your approach looking somewhat ham-handed by comparison."

"Drugs can't cure us," Valentina said.

"I'm not talking about us," Bastion said. "I'm talking about them."

He gestured at his people, who squirmed in their seats.

"No, while you Rupinos were butchering 'Infettivi' across the country, I was coming up with Lupitol," Bastion said. "It's a more elegant solution."

"You must be very proud," Gia said.

"He is," Blake said, glaring at Valentina, who glared back.

"I am," Bastion said, tsking his brother. "Better living through chemistry. Anyway, I wanted us to meet to reiterate that I don't have any designs on Chicago. I just want to sell as much Lupitol as possible."

Gia matched Bastion's smile, although on her, it carried an air of predatory menace that spoke of her well-hidden and well-known ferocity.

"Then why have you worked so hard to capture the Chicago Police and Fire Departments?" Gia asked. "My people tell me that you've infected a lot of them."

"Old habits," Bastion said. "Out East, we always try to get them locked down. Makes the rest so much easier."

"Precisely," Gia said. "No more fire or police *Infettivi*, Chad."

Bastion held up a hand.

"Scout's honor," Bastion said.

"I mean it," Gia said. "We're tolerating your presence here, but only just so. Chicago's our city."

Bastion nodded, bringing his other hand up, palms out toward Gia.

"Of course," Bastion said. "See? Nothing up my sleeves."

He did a sleight of hand and produced a red rose, which he held out for Gia, who took it while the Bastion people chuckled and the Rupinos snickered.

"To peace between us," Bastion said, raising his half-full glass again.

"To peace," Gia said, and the others joined in.

Of course, no one there believed a word of it.

NORM and Anne had been happy. She'd known a little about his work at the BEE, and she worked at Liminalix as a sales rep, directly reporting to Todd Shaw and Chad Bastion. They'd done well for themselves, lived in Streeterville in a lovely high-rise condominium.

They'd been married ten years before the Happening. While they'd had no kids, neither had wanted any. It was one of those things.

"The world is crowded enough without us adding to it," Anne said to him one night, on their balcony that let them look out over the city at night. She'd been so beautiful that night, illuminated by the light pollution of the city, shades of lavender and fuchsia by the commercial lighting down below.

How far away the city seemed on those quiet nights together, the two of them. It had been a peaceful time. Anne knew what he did, and she accepted it. She laughed about it.

"The Bureau for Extraordinary Events," Anne said. "I'd tell people you're an event planner, but you don't look like one."

"No?" Norm asked.

She shook her head, leaning forward in her deck chair.

"You look like a soldier. You look like an agent," Anne said. "A middle agent."

"Funny," Norm said.

"I think so," Anne said, smiling at him. Anne's smile was a radiant thing. She could sell anyone anything and spent her time selling people drugs manufactured by Liminalix. She was so good at it that she'd managed to receive stock ownership shares in the company. It made them good money. Like traveling money, seeing things money, doing things money.

They enjoyed trips together, seeing new places. She always wondered what he really did. She'd ask, but he couldn't tell her. Not really. He didn't tell her that he kept an eye on everything Liminalix did because the BEE had been aware of Clan Bastion for decades, and that Chad Bastion was a known lycanthrope, but because he kept everything seemingly above-board, the BEE had never targeted him. But Norm kept an eye on him, anyway.

"It's investigative work, mostly," Norm said.

"Your BEE doesn't exist anywhere," Anne said. "I've looked. It's super-secret, Norm."

"Exactly," Norm said. "Classified."

"Still," Anne said. "It's weird. Why have a logo if you're secret?"

Norm smiled to himself. She'd seen some of his BEE paraphernalia from his Warden days. Patches, badges and such.

"It's more for the benefit of the people we work with," Norm said. "Police and agents from other groups."

"But if it's so clandestine, do they even know?" Anne asked.

"They always know," Norm said. "We keep them informed. We couldn't do what we do without their knowledge of who we are."

"So, law enforcement is complicit," Anne said.

"Complicit makes it sound like we're doing something wrong," Norm said.

"But you are," Anne said. "Killing people is wrong."

"They're not really people anymore," Norm said. "I don't think of a werewolf as a person. Not like you or me. They're monsters."

Anne laughed. Her laughter was always a treasure to Norm, even if it was at his expense.

"Werewolves are people, too, Norm," Anne said. She was always playing devil's advocate.

It had been before the Happening, so his kill missions back then were few and far between. Back then, Wardens would take their time tracking a target, once there was suspicion of lycanthropic activity.

"So are serial killers," Norm said. "That's what a werewolf is. They're supernatural serial killers. I don't think you'd have any compassion for them if you encountered one."

He didn't mention Chad, but she had.

"I know one," Anne said. "Chad freely owned up to being one at a Liminalix meeting this week. He said he was, and nobody believed him. So, he showed us."

Norm couldn't believe she hadn't told him until that moment.

"And you didn't tell me about this why, exactly?" Norm asked.

"I didn't want you finding an excuse to kill him," Anne said. "Chad's a good man."

"We don't just kill any we encounter," Norm said. "We just monitor. With any lycanthrope, there's a risk of them harming or killing people."

"Chad's not like that," Anne said. "He's so smart and charming. He's trying to cure lycanthropy. He told us he's been working on a new drug he's calling a 'game changer' in the field of biomedical research."

Norm couldn't imagine the mindset of a lycanthrope transforming like that in front of a group of norms. It was ballsy in the extreme. But then, as a Trueborn, he likely had more control over his condition than others.

"Why'd he do that?" Norm asked. "Transform that way, I mean?"

"He wanted us to know he had nothing to hide," Anne said. "He said it was what spurred him on to find a cure for lycanthropy."

"There is no cure for the Trueborn," Norm said. "They are what they are."

"Trueborn," Anne said. "What a weird word."

Not half as weird as some of the things he'd seen on the job. The BEE investigated paranormal occurrences, whatever the source. They didn't make a big thing of it, but their agents documented and, if necessary, interceded if there was a public health risk.

When the Happening broke out, the BEE had been thrown into disarray, had been forced to suspend its other surveillance and research activities in favor of the Lupine incidents. Anne had been worried when Norm had been field-deployed.

"It'll be okay," Norm said, not at all sure back then if it would be. He just didn't want her to worry.

"I see the news stories," Anne said. "People being attacked. People going crazy. People getting killed—torn apart."

Norm was torn between telling her and keeping a lid on it. The leadership had been dead serious about keeping it quiet. Norm had been shuttled to BEE offices around the country, giving people crash courses in fieldwork, specifically Warden-related strategy and tactics: surveillance, hunting, stalking, rendition, killing. They were things that had served him well in Afghanistan.

He'd not been in Chicago when the Kennel had been attacked. He'd been in Detroit, training agents, when the distress call had gone out. He'd gone home as quickly as he could, but it had been too late.

"What is going on?" Anne asked, when he'd gotten home.

"Something's happened," Norm said. "Look, you need to get out of the city."

She shook her head.

"I can't do that," Anne said. "I mean, Chad's got a new campaign underway, a new drug we're marketing. I can't just leave."

Norm could see from her expression that she wasn't going to budge, and Norm sought to find a way to persuade her without sounding insane.

"There's an infection breaking loose in the city," Norm said. "People are getting infected."

"All the more reason to keep working," Anne said. "I'm working with Todd Shaw on it."

Todd Shaw. Norm hated Todd Shaw. They'd be at one of the Liminalix office parties and there Shaw would be, inflicting himself on anyone within earshot. He particularly liked Anne. The man was unctuous and smarmy.

Norm's cover during those things was that he was a freelance security consultant.

"Anne could sell ice to Eskimos," Shaw said, patting her shoulder.

"Inuit," Norm said. "They don't call themselves 'Eskimos'."

Shaw snorted.

"I knew that," Shaw said. "Just making a point, Norman. Anne's made for Sales."

"Thanks, Todd," Anne said, rolling her eyes. "He's just jealous because I habitually beat out his numbers quarterly."

"Envious," Shaw said, smirking at Norm. "I'm envious, not jealous."

"Right," Anne said.

That party had been a couple of months before the Happening, when being annoyed by Todd Shaw seemed like a luxury by comparison to what came after.

As a Warden, Norm had been working around the clock trying to hunt down the rogue Lupines. Back then, Zooey Hummel had been an unknown. They'd called her "Princess"—that had been her codename. He and the other Wardens had been busy trying to chase her down.

He hadn't known that she should've been the least of his worries. Anne had disappeared a month after the Happening.

She'd just vanished. It had driven him crazy. There'd been no sign of a struggle, nothing. Even her cell phone had been sitting there on the nightstand, right where she always left it. After all of the stuff Norm had seen from the Happening, all of the messes, the attacks, the carnage, the simplicity of a disappearance was almost unfathomable.

It was difficult to balance trying to find her with the Warden work, which was escalating and taking a toll.

He called Liminalix directly, reached out to Chad Bastion, who actually had taken his call.

"I haven't seen Anne, Norm," Bastion said. "No idea where she's gone. I'll definitely have my people try to find her, though."

Despite what he knew about him, he'd believed Bastion. He'd looked up Todd Shaw, who'd been way too happy to see Norm.

"Norm," Shaw said, shaking his hand forcefully. "How's security consulting going?"

"Anne's missing," Norm said. "Any ideas where she might be?"

Shaw feigned concern.

"Missing?" Shaw asked. "Since when?"

"Since yesterday," Norm said.

"No idea," Shaw said. "She just up and left you?"

Norm fought to restrain himself. He had no idea where she could be.

"I don't know," Norm said.

Shaw broke into a salty grin.

"People are disappearing left and right these days, Norm," Shaw said. "But Anne's tough. She's smart. If I hear anything, you'll be the first person I talk to. Promise."

Norm hadn't known. Not then. He'd been too tired. It had been beyond comprehension. The Happening, the Infectives. The BEE leaning hard on its remaining (surviving) personnel to try to stem the tide.

He'd filed a missing persons report, but one thing Shaw had been right about was people were disappearing all the time. Norm knew what that actually meant. Some of them were being caught and extradited. Others were being killed and eaten.

Norm took out his frustration on the Infectives. He'd taken any excuse he could to hunt them, to be out on the streets, in hopes of finding Anne.

And then, a month after her disappearance, he'd found her. Or she'd found him. She called him while he was out hunting some Lupines.

He picked up on the second ring.

"Anne," Norm said. "Babe, where were you?"

"I'm sorry, Norm," Anne said. "Something's happened."

"What's happened?" Norm asked.

"They came for me," Anne said. "What do you call them? Lupines."

"What?"

"I didn't know," Anne said. "I didn't know. They infected me."

"Who?" Norm asked.

"I can't say," Anne said. "They infected me, and they kept me in some facility. I can't say where."

Norm's head was throbbing. Anne had been targeted. But he knew Lupines. His mind went into business mode.

"What color?" Norm asked.

"What?" Anne said.

"What color were the Lupines that attacked you?" Norm asked. He only directly knew one proper Lupine clan back then. The Rupinos. The Black Hand.

"They were grey," Anne said. "Grey wolves. Werewolves."

"Grey," Norm said. "They all were? Or were other colors represented?"

"No," Anne said. "Only grey. Is that significant?"

Hell, yeah, it was significant. It was a pack of some sort. He hadn't known, not then. Nobody had known back then.

"Where are you now?" Norm asked.

"I can't tell you," Anne said. "They won't let me tell you."

Norm knew something about the chain of infection. Any Infective was bound to the one who had infected them. There was a degree of control, almost subliminal influence. It was one of the ways the Lupines enforced order in their ranks, along with outright violence.

"Who won't let you?" Norm asked. "Tell me, Anne."

"I can't," Anne said. "I'm sorry, Norm. I have to go."

"No, Anne, wait," Norm said.

"Goodbye, Norm," Anne said. "Don't try to find me."

And she hung up. Of course Norm tried to find her. He spent years trying to find her. He tried to find out the identity of those grey Lupines. But there were no known grey Lupine packs in the BEE archives operating in the Midwest. There were, however, ones on the East Coast. Clan Bastion.

The streetside Lupines paid for his consternation. When kill order clearance had come through, Norm happily volunteered for it, taking down Lupines, sparing only any greys he came across. Greys, he would hit with tranquilizer darts, in hopes of finding something out.

But there were many shades of grey, and none of the grey Infectives he'd bagged knew anything about Anne. The years were a blur of blood and bullets for him, of fruitless searching and growing body counts.

When Minton had taken over and the Stinger Program begun, Norm had immediately jumped at the opportunity when it presented itself. He hadn't told anyone at the BEE about the incident with Anne. At the BEE, it never paid to appear vulnerable. People watched and evaluated. Norm had done nothing to indicate that he was anything less than perfection, where Wardens were concerned.

"This is a dangerous gig, Norm," Minton had said. "As a Stinger, you're going solo on a level far beyond what you'd done as a Warden. You're going out into the field as an agent, as an assassin. If you get into a jam, there's nobody to bail you out. The Drone teams can help, but only in the most overt manner. We want to avoid being overt. Our Recovery teams won't be able to get to you in time. So, if you identify a Lupine, if you target them, you have to kill without hesitation. But up close. We're not talking sniper work like you did as a Warden."

The training had taken three months. It was nothing Norm wasn't prepared for. It was tradecraft through a lycanthropic lens. The psychology of lycanthropy. How to spot Infectives and Trueborn. Lupine pack dynamics. Hunting styles of Lupines. Lupine forensics. How to track, surveil, and evade them. How to kill them in close quarters. Lupine countermeasures.

The training had taken place in Michigan, in a secure BEE facility outside of Detroit. All during that time, Norm had been thinking about Anne, wondering where she might have gone.

When he got back home, he'd seen that she'd been there. Her clothes and possessions were gone. She'd left her phone and had left him a note in an ivory envelope with his name on it:

Dear Norm—

I'm so sorry to leave you like this. I can't do anything about it. Like I told you before: they came for me. I suppose it's for the best. If you'd been here when they turned up, they'd have killed you. At least this way, I know you're alive.

You should give up on the work that you do. It's going to get you killed one day. You know that. And you should give up on me, too. Because I'm going to get you killed if you keep after me. There are things in play that are bigger than you could imagine. And there are bigger players out there.

They're letting me write this letter to you, Norm. I've told them who you are, what you do. Do the smart thing and just quit. Retire. Leave Chicago. Go far away and forget all about me.

I can't say anything else. I love you. I miss you. But please, please, for your own sake, don't try to find me. They will kill you.

Love,
Anne

It was handwritten in her lovely script. She had beautiful handwriting. And, of course, her note did nothing to dissuade Norm. If anything, it egged him on.

He thought about it tactically. First, and perhaps foremost, he'd been grateful that the Stinger Program he'd volunteered for had come about after Anne's disappearance, because it meant that whoever had taken her still thought Norm was a Warden. So, he had that to his advantage.

Second, the fact that they'd taken all of Anne's stuff meant that she was still somewhere. Whatever new life they'd made for her, there was enough consideration of Anne that they had let her take her possessions.

They'd left her phone, however, because they knew he'd be able to track her with it. Norm decided to get smart about it and began to investigate Liminalix. Norm had contacted some of the Archon experts at the BEE, had given them several names to check, including:

- Anne Stockwell
- Todd Shaw
- Chad Bastion

They used Archon to track occurrences of those names, and nothing came up. When Norm asked about it, the techs shrugged and said that there were a number of things they could have done to reduce trackability, including adding a SIM card PIN and using an encrypted messaging app. Another possibility floated was that they avoided using cell phones entirely.

It was suspicious, and Norm took advantage of that to spy on Todd Shaw and Chad Bastion. Both of them lived in big houses, with Shaw in Winnetka and Bastion in Lake Forest.

As a Stinger, Norm had considerable latitude in running his operations. He reached out to Tiff. Tiff didn't approve of Norm surveilling Bastion and Shaw.

"Driver, they're high-profile," Tiff said. "You're putting yourself at risk by snooping on them."

"One or both is involved in kidnapping Anne," Norm said.

"Based on what?" Tiff asked.

"A hunch," Norm said. "Her kidnapping wasn't some random thing. She was targeted. The only reason she would've been targeted is because of me. Somebody knew who I was."

Tiff liked that even less.

"You think your cover's blown?" Tiff asked.

"I suppose we'll find out when they come for me," Norm said. He had been staking out Shaw's place. Despite having a big house, Shaw lived a bland sort of life, by Norm's estimation. For a bigshot pharma guy, his house, while nice, wasn't particularly ostentatious. That seemed suspicious, too.

He observed from the shelter of some shrubs across the street from the Shaw residence.

"Somebody knew about me, and they went after Anne because of it," Norm said. "And once they got to her, they probably got her to talk. They don't know I'm a Stinger, but they'd know I was a Warden."

The difference would have only been semantic, in some respects. But if they knew Norm was part of the BEE in any capacity, it put him at risk.

Next door to Shaw's house was the Drinkwater residence. Norm knew this because he'd investigated when he'd seen the young woman there. He turned his binoculars to that place and saw Polly Drinkwater gardening, accompanied by her seven-year-old daughter, who capered around, running in circles.

The little girl was dark-haired like her mother. Mrs. Drinkwater was a poet, apparently, judging from what Norm had looked up about her. She'd gone on television as a friend of Samantha Hain's, had spoken with some knowledge of Zooey Hummel's lycanthropic manifesto, which she attributed to the late Samantha.

Zooey Hummel had been found dead shortly after that broadcast, decapitated in Winnetka. BEE forensic researchers had found that Ansel Rupino was likely involved in the murder, as some genetic traces of him had been gathered there.

The involvement of a Rupino put things in a proper perspective for Norm. As had something else.

Polly Drinkwater had a black dog. Or what looked like one. It looked more like a young wolf. She'd take it out walking. Enough times doing that, and Norm noticed that there'd be Polly with the girl, and then Polly with the dog. But never Polly with the girl *and* the dog. It was either/or. She'd talk to the dog when she walked it. The dog was unruly, would run around, chasing down squirrels. Polly would get annoyed, would call for the dog.

Curious enough to continue watching, Norm donned a portable listening device and spied on her.

"Sloane," Polly said. "Will you stop? Come on, leave it alone. We've been out enough already."

The young dog would ignore her until she nagged it enough. Eventually, they'd get home. Once home, Norm would see Polly and her daughter moving around their big house. Norm knew enough dog owners to understand the regularity of dog owner habits. The walks Polly took were not regular.

And, one night, Norm saw something very particular. Using infrared binoculars, he saw a Lupine come running out of the Drinkwater residence. It was a female, dark-furred and long-limbed, very fast. She'd gone racing out into the night, clearly hunting. It put him on edge, but it was clear the Lupine wasn't hunting him, thankfully.

"Dealer," Norm said. "Polly Drinkwater's an Infective. Next door to Shaw's place."

"Alright, Driver," Tiff said. "You're cleared to proceed."

"I'm claiming that one," Norm said. If a Stinger prioritized a target, no other BEE agents would be able to do so.

"Sure thing, Driver," Tiff said. "It's all yours."

Norm chose not to relay information about the little girl. He didn't know why, but he kept quiet about it.

"I'm actively surveilling," Norm said. "But my primary target remains my main focus."

"You don't even know," Tiff said.

"I suspect," Norm said, turning his binoculars back to Shaw's place. That's when he saw Anne. She was there, plain as day, on the second floor, in the window. She was wearing an ivory nightgown.

He didn't tell Tiff about that, either. The last thing he needed was his handler thinking he was following some personal vendetta. Of course it was personal, but he wasn't such a newbie to let that impair his judgment.

Norm staked them out all night, and nobody left Shaw's place. A night in. He also saw the Drinkwater Lupine return, racing homeward in the shadows. It stopped in front of the Drinkwater residence and sniffed the air a moment, looking around it.

Then it crept to the front door, and Norm saw the thing turn into Polly Drinkwater. He'd seen enough freshly killed Lupines return back to their human form, but he'd rarely seen a Lupine voluntarily return to their human disguise. It was a jarring sight, seeing all of that dark fur and monstrous limbs unmake themselves, returning to the form of a slender, pale-skinned young mother covered in blood that assuredly wasn't her own.

Norm chewed on that a bit. His primary target was the Shaw residence, just took a mental note to revisit Drinkwater at a future date.

In the morning, after an endless night, Norm saw Anne and Shaw come out of his house, dressed impeccably for work—Shaw in a grey suit, Anne in an ivory blouse with a buff-colored leather skirt. They talked for a moment on the front porch, and then a Liminalix company car pulled up curbside. It was a white limousine with the company logo on the side of it. A half-dozen guys in suits came out and escorted them into the limo.

They looked like bodyguards to Norm.

Polly Drinkwater had come out in a red robe, drinking a cup of coffee by the look of it. The picture of suburban ease. She saw Anne and the two of them waved to each other.

"Good Morning, Polly," Anne said.

"Good Morning, Anne," Polly said. "Lovely morning, isn't it?"

"Perfect," Anne said.

"Come on, Babe," Shaw said, ushering Anne to the limo.

"Gotta run," Anne said.

The little girl appeared by Polly's side, looking adorable in her black unicorn flannel pajamas. Her black hair was sleep-tousled. Polly watched the limo pull off, then went back inside.

"Come on, Sloane," she said.

7

THE Chicago Lupine Council had formed about three years after the Happening, in 2010. It wasn't a formal entity, but, rather, was a response to the surge in Infectives that had resulted from it, and to the rise in government agent activity—principally, the BEE and its Wardens. The Council consisted of the dominant Lupine packs operating in the Chicagoland area.

While the first three years after the Happening had been chaotic, the more organized Lupine packs had worked to secure a place for themselves. In this arrangement, the lone wolves were snuffed out by rival packs, and in a short time, order was crafted out of the chaos.

The Council was an underground organization. It operated in absolute secrecy, and while the BEE knew about its existence, they were unable to find out precisely where it took place. BEE agents who got too close to finding out met grisly ends. It was hard to sneak up on werewolves.

The Council met on neutral ground, in a conference room located in the heart of Streeterville, something the norms didn't know about. The space had a lovely view of downtown, with a profusion of glass windows and an L-shaped balcony that afforded sweeping city vistas. Inside were long rows of tables and a well-stocked bar.

It looked like a restaurant, but the only ones being served were the Lupines who came in, arriving in their respective groups.

Bastion's people were first—four sharply-attired men and one woman in blue, grey, brown, and black power suits. Chad Bastion walked a half-step ahead of the rest. His half-smile evident on his face as he surveyed the currently empty room.

The staff at the bar quickly took their orders, as the Loopines took their seats at the grand blondewood table that dominated the far side of the room. As much as he'd wanted to, Bastion did not take the head of the table—he contented himself with the first seat at the right of the head and had his team file down in a row from him: Blake Bastion, Todd Shaw, Lane Tanner, and Blythe Connor. They looked like an executive team, each of them coifed and immaculate. Shaw with his smoothly slicked hair held in place by ample gel. Lane Tanner with his studiously trimmed salt-and-pepper beard and horn-rimmed glasses he no longer needed. Blythe Connor with her shoulder-length honey-blonde hair, red lipstick, and an expensive strand of pearls. Blake wore a crisp white shirt and blue blazer with chinos, and had slicked his blonde hair back, giving him a more feral countenance. They all carried back ledgers that bore the Lupitol logo, the silver crescent moon that looked like a smile.

Next to arrive were the Wolves of God (or Wargs, as the BEE agents called them)—only two of them: Reverend Marcus Nicks, aka, the Saint, and Brother Saul Favineau, also known as the Deacon. The Saint was wearing a white suit and a red necktie, and had a golden cross pinned to his lapel. His face bore a scar along his right cheek, a claw mark from a Lupine battle from years before. He wore his hair almost punishingly short, in a close-shaved blonde burr that only further highlighted his bright blue eyes. Brother Saul had black hair, also cut close, and wore an unassuming pale blue suit and a similarly unassuming expression. He wore a matching gold cross at his lapel and had brought a Bible in with him. Passing the bar without getting anything, the Saint took his place at the foot of the table, as far from the Loopines as he could get, and merely smiled beatifically at them. The Deacon sat beside him, frowningly surveying the others.

Jaden Cole and his Brotherhood arrived next, along with the fully permitted retinue of five Lupines—himself and four of his Lupine brothers-in-arms. His wingmen wore black leather jackets and pants with black turtlenecks, while Jaden wore a black pinstriped suit. The pinstripes were pencil-thick, and Jaden bore a white rose at his lapel. He kept his head shaved bald and had gold earrings at each earlobe. It was a statement, as much as anything else—as a Lupine, those earring holes would heal every day, and he'd have them redone constantly. He raked his big eyes across the conference table, while having his men order their drinks. They took their seats across from the Loopines, to the left of the head of the table.

The lead Daughters of Zooey (known as "Doozies" by the BEE) came in, only the Monroe Sisters in evidence. Tall and broad-built in a rustic sort of way, they wore street clothes, a matched pair in snow-white babydoll dresses and green army jackets, wearing polished black combat boots. They had red star barrettes in their brown hair, keeping it out of their wild eyes. They took their seats beside the Loopines, facing the door. Both Sheridan and Addison Monroe looked over the other Lupines with barely veiled scorn and contempt, and had their looks returned in kind.

The *Lunares* arrived next, with Octavio Caudillo and his men wearing crisp white shirts and tan pants and leather loafers that spoke of ease and comfort. All of his men were fit and formidable, radiating lycanthropic swagger. Caudillo wore his hair in a black ponytail and had a well-groomed black mustache and beard. He and his men sat next to the Brotherhood, acknowledging each other with nods.

Black Sheep came alone, wore a black wool sweater and black jeans, looked for all the world like he had perhaps crawled out of bed shortly before the meeting. He was unshaven and bleary-eyed. He sat by himself at the table.

"Look what the cat dragged in," Shaw said, looking at Black Sheep with disapproval.

Black Sheep didn't respond, simply slouched in his chair. His presence was tolerated only because he led an all-male pack collectively known as the Black Sheep (called the Babas by everyone else, if not to their faces). They were one of the most brutal and ruthless of packs, with a marked fondness for confrontation and carnage. The Monroe Sisters glared at Black Sheep, but he didn't care. He'd been an intimate of Zooey's, one of her first converts, before he'd turned on her.

The Russians arrived next, calling themselves the *Volki*. They arrived in force, much like the *Lunares* had. The *Volki* were led by Sergei Tolkachev, a dark-haired and square-jawed man with a boxer's face and a militant's scowl. His men were strong and silent, every one of them wearing black suits and red shirts. The *Volki* sat next to the Loopines after they'd stopped by the bar.

The Rupinos didn't keep anybody waiting. They came in force—there were a dozen of them, all in black suits. Only they were permitted to exceed the attendance limit, as they were the ruling clan in the Midwest, and had founded the Council here. They looked like the family that they were: dark-haired, blue-eyed, a blend of young men and women. They filled in the empty seats around the table, looked at everybody without emotion on their chiseled faces. The head seat of the table remained open until Gia Rupino entered.

Gia wore a brown leather skirt and a crisp white blouse, as well as some matching brown gloves. She wore her black hair shoulder length, had a white streak that ran the length of her crown to the edge of her hairline. Her eyes flitted over the assembled Council, while her face betrayed nothing.

She took her seat at the head of the table, and regarded the other Lupines present without saying a word.

"She has arrived," the Saint said. "We may begin."

"First order of business," Gia said. "You Wolves of God are abandoning the city, yes?"

The Saint steepled his fingers in front of him on the table.

"That is correct," the Saint said. "We have relocated away from all of this, from all of you."

Bastion's half-smile became a full one.

"You couldn't hack it, eh?" he asked.

The Saint smiled back at him. His pearly white teeth were almost as bleached as Bastion's.

"We go where God Almighty guides us," he said. "He has told us that our future is in the South. So, we've headed there."

"An exodus, is it? Good riddance," said Black Sheep. "We don't need wannabe Nazis here in Chicago, anyway."

The Saint disregarded Black Sheep, while Gia focused on the more worldly concerns.

"What about your church? The First Lupercalian Church of the Apocalyptic Vision?" Gia asked. "And your territory? Are you ceding it?"

"Yes," the Saint said. "We are giving it to you and Mr. Bastion."

Jaden and Octavio looked irked.

"It should be an even split," Jaden said. "Between all of us."

The Saint looked hard at Jaden, his smile withering on his face.

"No," the Saint said. "Not for you or the *Lunares*."

"Racist pig," Jaden said.

Gia raised her hand, quieting them.

"Take your grievances outside the Council," Gia said. "We accept the 50-50 split of Wolves of God territory."

"Don't get me wrong," the Saint said. "Our mission goes on, but as we've watched the Happening wind down, we feel more concern about our future in the city. We go in peace, and leave you in peace, those deserving of it. The rest of you will face our wrath when the Almighty has decided."

"The Almighty told me to tell you to shut up," Black Sheep said.

"Demon," the Deacon said, glaring at Black Sheep, who only grinned.

The Brotherhood and *Lunares* exchanged glances and scowled at the Saint and the Deacon, who stood up to leave, only to be stopped by a look from Gia that kept them in their seats.

"Next order of business," Gia said. "Chad wants to talk to you about the drug his company has put on the market."

Bastion took his cue and leaned forward at the table, while Blythe and Lane worked a remote to show a PowerPoint slide deck. The Lupitol pill was on display on some of the slides, showing happy people.

"After a dozen years of development and testing, Liminalix is pleased to present Lupitol, our answer to the Infective outbreak."

Black Sheep scoffed, folding his arms.

"So, you were developing the drug well before the Happening. Convenient," Black Sheep said. Bastion was unfazed.

"Lycanthropy didn't start with the Happening," Bastion said. "It's been going on for millennia, maybe as long as humanity has existed. Even in this country, it's been there for a couple of centuries. The most important thing about the drug is that it works."

Jaden shook his head.

"A cure?"

"Better. It's a treatment," Bastion said. "Let me be frank, here. Everyone around this table has successfully established themselves a franchise in this whole lycanthropy business. You wouldn't be here if you hadn't. And however you came to the table—whether from the Happening or before—you have a vested interest in your condition."

"What are you talking about?" Jaden said.

One of Bastion's people worked the presentation slides, showing the pace of lycanthropic infections from 2007–15.

"More mouths to feed," Bastion said. "Let's not delude ourselves— the more lycanthropes out there, the more difficult it is for us. You remember how crazy it was those first few years? Before we got things handled? You know what I mean."

He gestured, and Lane Tanner produced a box of Lupitol and handed out bottles to the Lupines around the table.

"This drug will help all of us retain our market share, if you will," Bastion said. "I don't know about you, but the late, great Zooey Hummel aside, I really don't want everybody out there turning into a lycanthrope. With this, we won't have to worry about it. Lupitol is an effective treatment for lycanthropy. You know, Night Fever, just like they say on television."

Bastion finger-quoted "Night Fever" as he said it, with a well-polished smirk. The others looked over the bottles they'd been given, some of them opening them and looking at the pills.

"So, why are you telling us this?" Tolkachev asked. "What do we get out of your drug?"

"First off, my Russian friend, you get fewer competitors," Bastion said. "Let's be honest—every new Lupine, every new Infective, is competition for you. Either they're out there in your territory, making a mess of things, or they're taking prey meant for you. Maybe a bit of both. You get Lupitol out there, and it starts to drop the numbers of active Infectives. People can start suffering in silence, the way they were meant to, versus howling at the moon, killing and eating people, making a mess, drawing BEEs."

Mocking the BEE drew chuckles around the table, but Bastion could see he had to do some more convincing. His team advanced the slides, showing Lupitol ads featuring happy people going about their lives. The Feel Human Again tagline had them snickering.

"'Feel Human Again'—that's funny," Black Sheep said. "So, you're, what, appealing to the norms out there? The people who can't handle being lycanthropes?"

"More or less," Bastion said. "As I said earlier, however you got here, everyone in this room is okay with being what you are. Lupitol is for the folks who *aren't* okay with what they've become. Hey, lycanthropy's not for everybody, am I right? You know the ones who can't hack it. All I've done is monetize their inability to make the psycho-emotive transition from human to werewolf."

"Okay, you're getting your drug out there, people take it. Then what?" Octavio asked.

"Peace and prosperity, my friends," Bastion said. "And because I'm a good guy, I'm willing to give each of you a one percent stake in the profits of Lupitol. Meaning the heads of your factions, obviously. Not every one of you."

"One percent," Tolkachev said.

"Better than nothing," Bastion said. "I mean, a one percent stake in $3 billion in sales would be a nice pile of money for doing nothing."

"You're getting that much in sales?" The Saint asked.

"Not yet, but Lupitol is climbing fast," Bastion said. "Right now, there's a little issue where people are concerned about getting on some federal registry if they're prescribing to the medication. But we have people—sorry, lawyers—who are working on HIPAA and PHI provisions to ensure that anybody taking Lupitol for Night Fever doesn't get on the bad side of our friends at the BEE."

Mention of the BEE again made the Lupines grumble curses. Nobody liked the BEE. Bastion nodded, his smile radiantly predatory.

"I feel you, friends," Bastion said. "I really do."

Sheridan Monroe spoke up, her eyes flame with revolutionary righteousness.

"Don't pretend you're not in bed with the BEE, Mr. Bastion," Sheridan said. "We all know you are."

"Yeah, what's that about?" Jaden asked.

"Gia, do you want to take that?" Bastion said, earning a sigh from Gia.

"No, that's okay, Chad. You have the floor."

Bastion nodded, laughing.

"That's fair," Bastion said. "Sure, the Black Hand and my own clan have partnered with the BEE. Me, most recently, but the Rupinos have been allied with the BEE for years, right, Gia?"

That really bothered the other Lupines.

"We're not allied with them, as you put it, Chad," Gia said. "We're using them. To his point about the *Infettivi* making things difficult for the rest of us, we've been putting them down. The rogues, the wild ones that draw the federal eyes upon all of us. To the BEE, we are all the same—targets to be dealt with sooner or later."

"So, you're selling out lycanthropes to save your own skins," Black Sheep said.

"We are killing lycanthropes who need to be killed," Gia said. "Ones who cannot restrain themselves sufficiently to operate with a degree of discretion."

"Hah," Black Sheep said. "That's rich."

Bastion cleared his throat, seeking to regain control of the conversation.

"You can all be rich if you work with me," Bastion said. "With us."

"You're in with the enemy," Sheridan said. "That's all I know."

"The BEE wants what we want," Bastion said, showing a Venn diagram displaying the BEE as a circle and the Council as another circle, intersecting. "Just not the way we want it. They want lycanthropes gone. We want our competition gone. So, yeah, we're working with them to take out the riffraff. You know about the riffraff. The rogues, the ones who are out of control. What Gia and I have done is promoted dependency from the BEE—they're dependent on us to help them. We're what you'd call 'subject matter experts' on lycanthropy."

Gia spoke up again.

"What the Bureau fears is for the Happening to keep persisting," Gia said. "They fear people really understanding what was going on. They're willing to work with us to tamp down the outbreaks and reduce the lycanthropic population to pre-2007 levels. There is a critical presidential election in 2016, and there is concern that the persistence of the Happening—even if portrayed as Night Fever— will fuel bad elements eager to either capitalize on the bad policy of past years in the form of executions and renditions, or else mismanage it and cause the Happening to wildly spin out of control."

"Still sounds like you're sleeping with the enemy," Black Sheep said. "And, as much as it pains me to agree with a Daughter of Zooey, it sounds like this deal was extended to you Trueborns, leaving us Infectives out in the lurch."

Bastion tackled that one.

"We Trueborns admittedly have a better handle on things," Bastion said. "We have history, and, most importantly, we have organization. You Infectives, you're all still newbies to this. Now, you faction heads, each of you represents the pinnacle of your particular group's reach and ambitions. I can respect that. I think Gia can respect that, not wanting to put words in your mouth, Gia. I mean, I don't think anybody at this table has killed more Lupines than your people."

Gia didn't like the way Bastion framed that.

"Clan Rupino has cornered the market on silver," Gia said. "And we've put it to good use in dealing with outliers and rogues. All of the Trueborn clans have gotten involved in culling *Infettivi* from their territories."

"So, this really is a Trueborn versus Infective issue," Sheridan said. "You Trueborn get a sweetheart deal, and we Infectives get, what, the silver bullet between the eyes? What does it say that the Rupinos are silver merchants? I mean, that's beyond offensive."

"We are diversified," Gia said. "Silver is only one part of a very considerable portfolio."

"It's disgusting," Sheridan said. "Werewolves trading in silver? Werewolves dealing in a treatment for lycanthropy? You both disgust me. You should *embrace* what you are. We should conquer the world of the norms."

Gia and Bastion exchanged looks that spoke to the challenges of dealing with the Daughters of Zooey.

"Where humans are concerned, the harder you push, the stronger the response," Gia said.

"We killed their Wardens," Sheridan said. "We killed their Stalkers."

"They have new weapons," Gia said. "Drone strikes alone are taking a toll on rogue lycanthropes."

"Drones," Black Sheep said. "The BEE is filled with drones."

"Zooey nearly destroyed the BEE," Sheridan said. "All by herself."

"They're on their ship, far from shore," Bastion said. "Untouchable. Unreachable."

"Anybody can be reached," Tolkachev said. "Access is key. What about the Night Fever denialists? The ones who say it doesn't exist."

Bastion laughed.

"Half of them are Infectives already," Bastion said. "They're using it as an excuse to go after the BEE in their own crazy way."

"But it doesn't exist," Black Sheep said. "Not really."

"The lycanthropy exists, whatever they choose to call it," Bastion said. "And it's been noticed by parties hostile to it, whether they cop to it or not."

"Cop to it is right," Black Sheep said. "From the man who is cozy with the police."

Gia spoke up again, and the others reluctantly listened.

"The BEE has a new program," Gia said. "Stinger agents. Deep cover counterinsurgency operatives who work with their drone teams to isolate and kill Lupines."

"Nobody sees the Stingers coming," Bastion said. "They're like ghosts."

"They're not ghosts," Black Sheep said. "They're just people. People can be found."

"I said they were *like* ghosts," Bastion said. "Not that they *were* ghosts. It's a metaphor, smart guy."

"It's a simile," Black Sheep said. "Not a metaphor, Bro."

"We should just sink the ship," Addison said.

"She stays offshore," Gia said. "Sometimes moors at Navy Pier, but only under tightest security, with drones flying about her, buzzing about. Most of the time, she's far from the shore, inaccessible."

"The next time she comes to Navy Pier, we should be ready for her," Sheridan said. "We could swarm her. Zooey was able to single-handedly take out the Kennel."

"We've all heard that story," Black Sheep said, making a "blah blah blah" motion with his hand. "I knew Zooey. She wasn't that great."

The Monroe Sisters' eyes flashed and they glowered at Black Sheep from across the table with renewed vigor. Gia held her gloved hands up and her Rupino kinfolk made moves to restrain the Monroes, who backed off.

"We can't risk surveillance in the field without drawing attention," Gia said.

"I'll put some of my police to work on the case," Bastion said. "The Bureau coordinates with the police."

"Not if they know you've corrupted the force," Black Sheep said.

"Not all of it," Bastion said. "Just a handpicked few. My selection process is rigorous."

"Yeah, they already know you," Jaden said. "Maybe they're targeting you as we speak."

"They *know* all of us, *Contaminati*," Gia said. "Is my guess."

"So, if they know who we are, why haven't they made their move?" Caudillo asked. "If they're as badass as everybody thinks, why are we all still alive?"

"The Stingers aren't like the Wardens," Gia said. "They take their time with their targets. The Wardens were told to just take shots when they had them. The Stingers go about it with far more deliberation and care."

"Why not simply blow us all up with a missile?" Tolkachev asked.

"They want to keep it quiet," Bastion said. "That's the point. They don't want people seeing missiles blow up in their neighborhoods. They don't want bodies in the streets. Everything the BEE is doing is geared toward keeping lycanthropy off the map as much as possible. We're taking advantage of that."

"We might be able to make that work for us," the Saint said. "If the mandate has shifted, then there's an opportunity we might be able to exploit. We might be able to get them to release the identities of the Stingers, through the proper channels."

The Wolves of God hated the current administration and was actively working with hate groups and others to try to combat it. They were aggressively courting groups to organize in 2016 and beyond.

"You're free to explore that option if you like," Gia said.

"What about the ship?" Caudillo asked.

"Yeah, what about that ship?" Jaden asked.

"What about it?" Gia asked.

"Are we gonna do something about it?" Jaden asked.

"Even if Gia and I hadn't negotiated with them, in truth, what can we do?" Bastion asked. "We don't have a navy. I don't think even the Rupinos have a navy. And they never meet with us in person. It's always via teleconference. There's only so far they're willing to go, where we are concerned."

"We all know it's a BEE vessel," Gia said. "It's flying a plague ship banner—I think that's intended as way of keeping everyday people away from it. Further, anyone who gets close to it gets warned off, then firehosed, then shot if they get too near it."

"I'd say your long-lost brother's on the *Argent,*" Black Sheep said. "I mean, that only makes sense. If not there, then Wolf Island. We've all heard about that place."

"The *Argent* has been gathering Lupines for a final trip to Wolf Island," Gia said. "That's what I've been able to determine from my inquiries. They're pulling them from Wisconsin, Illinois, Indiana, and Michigan."

"We should sink it," Addison Monroe said. "Obviously. Liberate our fellow lycanthropes. The ones who haven't sold out to the enemy, I mean."

"Nobody is able to get close to it, like I said," Gia replied. "The BEE learned from their calamity at the Kennel, and with the degree of compromise they experienced. The agents on the *Argent* are all *Normali*. They don't come ashore, so there's no way of reaching them."

"There is one way," Black Sheep said. "Again, obviously, if you put your minds to it."

The other Lupines looked at Black Sheep, who seemed to enjoy the attention he momentarily had. As a University of Chicago graduate, he prided himself on his intellect.

"The Stingers," Black Sheep said. "If the *Argent* is a BEE vessel, which we know it is, and the Stingers are Bureau field agents, then I guarantee the Stingers have to sneak their way aboard her from time to time to debrief and resupply, whatever it is they do. You want a direct path to that ship, you have to catch a Stinger, like I said before."

"How would we even know one if we had one?" Gia asked. "If they're as deep cover as people say, how would we know?"

"You talk out of both sides of your mouth," Black Sheep said. "You work with the BEE and you try to undermine them, as well. So, which is it? Which are you? Friend or foe?"

"We're smart," Valentina said. "Are you?"

"Oh, I'm as smart as they come," Black Sheep said. "Smart enough to know when I'm being jerked around. The Stingers are the way to the *Argent.*"

"Fuck them," Sheridan said. "I'm not scared of ghosts."

"You should be," Gia said. "They're out there."

"Why should we worry?" Sheridan asked.

"It's different from the Wardens," Gia said. "We all remember how the Wardens were. But Stingers are far quieter, sneakier. You never see them coming until you're dead."

"So, they're assassins," Tolkachev said. "And I assume that you and Bastion worked some deal where you're safe from these assassins? Part of your partnership with them?"

Gia sighed, glanced at Bastion and Valentina.

"Enough," Gia said. *"Pecoro Nera* has a point. If we're to find out what's really going on the *Argent,* we need to find and capture a Stinger."

"It won't be easy," Caudillo said. "They'd die before discovery. That's the point of them."

"I'll bring one to you on a silver platter," Black Sheep said. "So to speak."

"We don't know how many Stingers are operating in Chicago," Gia said. "I'd estimate maybe a half-dozen in every major city."

"Based on what?" Black Sheep asked. "What they told you? Did they tell you to tell us?"

"Intel," Gia said. "We know people."

"Of course you do," Tolkachev said. "So, is that the order of business, then? We try to flush out these Stingers?"

"Yes," Gia said. "No killing of them. We want them captured for interrogation. From what we know of the program, they are deep cover operatives. Like spies, basically. They know how to blend in, how to appear innocuous. They target and kill Lupines, so they're trained killers. They know what to look for, and how to avoid detection."

"Who's to say you're not working with them to screw us over?" Jaden asked.

"It's why I'm offering you a percentage of the profits from the sale of Lupitol," Bastion said. "A chance to settle down and make a killing—the only killing that really matters, when you come down to it."

"Sellout," Sheridan said. "You're both sellouts. The BEE probably took your own brother, Gia. And you work with them? Your brother's been missing for years. And you work with them?"

Addison snickered at this. The Monroe Sisters were allowed at the Council table only because it served to keep some semblance of the peace to have them there. They were the most infective of Infectives.

"It matters to me," Gia said. "Nobody kills a Rupino. Especially no *Infettivo*, and no *Normali*."

Black Sheep piped up at this notion, this distinction.

"We're supposed to care what you Trueborn think?" Black Sheep asked. "I don't see why any of this should matter. The BEE could have already killed your brother, dissected him for research, or whatever it is they do on that ship."

"If anything happens to Ansel," Gia said. "Our associations are severed."

"How would you know?" Black Sheep asked. "If you don't even know where he is. He could be dead, for all we know."

"I respect her perspective on this," Octavio said. "Family is everything. Her brother shouldn't be targeted, wherever he has gone."

Gia and Black Sheep glared at one another a moment, before Bastion spoke up.

"I'm being particularly patient, here," Bastion said. "Any takers on my Lupitol offer? It's a good faith offer."

"I'll take it," Octavio said. "The *Lunares* approve. We'll work with you."

Bastion smacked the table with his tanned palm.

"That's what I like to see," Bastion said. "You won't regret it, Octavio."

Jaden didn't want to be left behind, piped up next.

"Me, too," Jaden said. "Fuck it. I want a slice."

"Smart man," Bastion said. "You'll be a rich man in a year. Or richer, anyway. I know you alphas are doing pretty well already. But that's nothing compared to what you'll see with your slice of Lupitol money."

"Do we get an amnesty?" Tolkachev asked. "The BEE leaves us alone if we get on board?"

"You won't have to worry about the BEE any longer," Gia said. "If you partner with us."

"Why didn't the BEE come to us directly with this deal?" Tolkachev asked.

Gia laughed, her voice like honey.

"Can you imagine any BEE agent willingly coming to this Council?" Gia asked.

"They rely on their stoolies," Sheridan said. "I see how it works."

The Rupinos objected to that, piped up with a chorus of protests that Gia had to quell with her outstretched hands.

"I don't think you do," Gia said. "You can't."

"I'm in," Tolkachev said. "Count the *Volki* in on your little Lupitol deal. I can do a lot with one percent if sales are as good as you claim."

"Government contracts," Bastion said. "Lucrative, my friend. Peace can be prosperous."

"You're the one in bed with the police," Black Sheep said. "Selling out and cashing in."

Bastion looked almost pleased with himself.

"I know the value of making friends," Bastion said. "Friends are far better than enemies. Enemies are expensive."

The Reverend Nicks spoke up.

"The Wolves of God would take a one percent share," the Saint said. Bastion laughed.

"Sorry," Bastion said. "This deal only applies to Chicago factions in good standing. You've already cashed out."

Nicks looked displeased at that suggestion, and the Deacon looked apoplectic.

"Are you serious?" Favineau said. "You go through all of that foreplay and just cut us out?"

"You cut yourselves out, *Infettivo*," Gia said. "It was only courtesy had compelled us to keep you in the room at all."

"Yeah," Bastion said. "Have fun in the South, Reverend."

"We don't need your drug money," the Saint said. "We embrace what we are. Our congregations grow weekly."

"Jesus Christ," Black Sheep said, earning a glare from the Deacon he blew off with a hateful grin.

Sheridan looked even more disgusted.

"You're both a disgrace, Trueborn," Sheridan said. "Asking our complicity in your own corruption and duplicity. The Daughters of Zooey will not be part of it."

Bastion and Gia looked at each other a moment.

"Duplicity and lycanthropy are always bedfellows," Gia said.

"We kind of figured you might say that, Ms. Monroe," Bastion said. "But we wanted to at least extend the offer, because we're trying to be good friends to all of you. What about you, Black Sheep?"

"Old news. Not in. What other business do we have?" Black Sheep asked, mindful of the Monroe Sisters still glaring at him from across the table.

"One of my men caught a *Synowie* sniper," the Saint said. "Outside of one of my churches. I believe he was attempting to assassinate me. If I didn't know any better, I'd say someone was having another go at us."

"The *Synowie* are almost spent," Gia said. "Their secret society has borne the brunt of countless werewolf attacks for generations. I wouldn't put their ranks as more than a few thousand across the country, now."

"At most," the Saint said. "But they are still a threat."

"A minor threat," Black Sheep said. "I've killed at least five of them over the past two years. They're easy to spot. They're the ones packing all the silver that you Rupinos haven't hoarded. They have their shiny silver daggers."

Black Sheep pulled out two of the daggers, jabbed them into the conference table. The gaucherie of bringing silver to a Council meeting caused some of the Lupines to gasp.

"I'll take care of the *Synowie* problem for you," Black Sheep said. "For a price."

"We don't need your help," Gia said.

Black Sheep pried the daggers loose and slipped them back into their scabbards, covered them with the folds of his black sweater.

"Suit yourself," Black Sheep said. "Nobody can accuse me of not being a team player."

"So," the Saint said. "Are we cleared to make further war on the *Synowie*, then?"

"Have we ever stopped, *Reverendo*?" Gia asked.

"Last item of business: what about the rogues? Are we free of that problem?"

"Between the Bureau and our own efforts?" Bastion asked. "I can say that my company is free of rogues."

"My territory, too," Jaden said.

"Ours as well," Sheridan said.

"Mine's fine," Caudillo said.

"Our flock has only grown," the Saint said, smiling thinly at the others.

"I don't believe in rogues," Black Sheep said.

"You are a rogue," Bastion said. "Your pack is all rogues."

Black Sheep only shrugged and grinned. "At least we know what we are and aren't pretending to be what we aren't."

Bastion offered a slow clap, dripping with sarcasm. Black Sheep was unfazed, just accepted it with a sneer.

"Rogues aren't the problem," Black Sheep said. "The Nazis are the problem."

The Saint took that in stride, cleared his throat, knitting his long fingers on the tabletop.

"We're not Nazis," he said, which made Jaden scoff. "We are patriotic Americans."

"You were," Black Sheep said. "You're not even human, anymore, Slick. What could being an American werewolf even possibly mean?"

The Saint continued as if Black Sheep hadn't said anything.

"It means we stand for red-blooded American values," the Saint said.

"Red-blooded is right," Black Sheep said.

"We stand for something," the Saint said.

As if to drive the point home, the Saint stood up, with the Deacon standing in his wake. The two of them stood there, looking like they belonged on a poster wheatpasted to a wall.

"I see you standing," Black Sheep said. "But damned if I know what for."

Jaden laughed, while the Monroe Sisters looked on intently. The Rupinos glanced at Gia, seeking guidance, but she gave none, choosing to simply watch the confrontation between two members of the Council. From Gia's perspective, any time *Infettivi* fought, the better off the Rupinos were.

"You clowns don't even see it, do you?" Black Sheep said. "This is bigger than America. It's bigger than you. It's bigger than God. We're above and beyond all of that old stuff. The Saint can go marching out of Chicago, but the BEE will still find him, wherever he goes, God be damned."

"Blasphemer," the Deacon said, baring his teeth. "Take back what you just said."

"Never," Black Sheep said. "Fuck that. Fuck you. Fuck this."

He got up and went to leave.

"You walk out of here," Bastion said. "You can forget about coming back. And if you aren't with us, you're against us."

Black Sheep laughed. "You think I care? This whole Council is a charade. Why pretend to be civilized? We're monsters, you idiots. Get what you need, take what you can."

He went out the door, laughing as he did.

S⚫N⚫A Gorski met up with Norm at their agreed-upon location, in Vanzetti Park. Norm had driven up in his jeep, and Sonia had already been waiting there, looking as nonchalant as possible, strolling amid the leafless trees.

She was wearing a grey wool peacoat and a black beret, as well as black gloves and black lace-up knee boots. She wore black sunglasses, and barely acknowledged when Norm walked beside her.

"You're who you are, aren't you?" Norm asked. It was an agreed-upon code phrase.

"How could I be anyone else?" Sonia replied. It was her own half of the phrase. "Nice to finally meet you. I'm an admirer of your work."

"Likewise," Norm said. "Do you want to meet here, or should we go somewhere?"

"Here's fine," Sonia said.

Norm looked around, wondered where her *Synowie* compatriots were. He doubted she'd traveled alone. If she hadn't, her comrades were very well-concealed. He appreciated the finesse of the *Synowie*. They'd been at werewolf hunting for a long time, and it showed.

"I'm told by your Director we need to work together," Sonia said.

"Okay," Norm said. "Maybe we can compare notes for starters."

"Ladies first," Sonia said. "I suspect the Bureau has vampires working for it."

Norm wasn't prepared for that.

"Huh?"

"You heard me," Sonia said. "Can you confirm or deny that?"

Norm hadn't heard anything about it. While the BEE dealt with vampires in the past, that typically meant staking them, or else hunting and apprehending them for research purposes. Norm had never taken down a vampire before. The handful of BEE agents who had almost never talked about it. It was one of those things that haunted them. Norm never understood that.

"How did you come across this?" Norm asked.

"I can't reveal my sources," Sonia said. "But I'm just looking for you to confirm."

"Wow," Norm said. "Yeah, I don't know. I haven't met any, although I suppose anything's possible. How would someone spot a vampire?"

It was too crazy to believe.

Sonia looked almost hurt at the insinuation.

"We *Synowie* know vampires when we see them, Mr. Stockwell," Sonia said. "So, what's the story?"

"There's no story, as far as I'm concerned," Norm said. "You were on the *Argent?*"

"No," Sonia said. "It was a teleconference with your director, Gia Rupino, and Chad Bastion, among others."

The notion of Director Minton negotiating with the Trueborn bothered Norm. It was one of those things he'd heard about but didn't like to dwell on. The Rupinos had been good partners with the BEE over the past years, despite themselves. Bastion was a more recent thing. The vampire rumor? It was something beyond his imagining and outside of his immediate concern.

"I'll look into the vampire rumor," Norm said. "And get back with you on that."

"Yes, please do," Sonia said, glancing around them with a sigh. Some kids were playing soccer in the park, and one was flying a kite, a bat that was buffeted by the autumn air.

"I honestly don't know anything about it," Norm said. "I've been doing fieldwork for months. I might meet with Minton once every few months. Definitely not part of his inner circle."

He thought of Anne at Shaw's, standing at the window. If Minton knew he'd been tracking her, he likely would have pulled him off of it. Minton wasn't big on vendettas. He wanted his BEE agents to be as dispassionate as the job would allow them to be. It was a requirement for them to be able to do what they did.

Sonia stared at him through her sunglasses, unreadable.

"I believe you," Sonia said. "Your turn."

"You're harboring Dr. Milkowski," Norm said.

"That's not a question," Sonia said, smiling at him.

"No, I suppose it's not," Norm said. "Has she transformed?"

"Of course she has," Sonia said. "We have resources for her to manage...her condition. How did you know we sheltered her?"

Norm smiled. He lived and breathed surveillance, had seen Mina at the Landa Library, when he'd cased that place, once he learned about its association with the *Synowie*. He'd not revealed himself but had seen her shelving books.

"I do my research," Norm said.

"The Library," Sonia said. "Mina so wants to be useful. Patryk kept her under lock and key back in the day, but when she got better at managing her condition, we gave her more latitude. Years in hiding can take a toll on a person. Library work seemed like a good therapeutic tool for her. You haven't told Minton, yes?"

"No, I haven't," Norm said. He could see Sonia cocking her eyebrow behind her sunglasses.

"Why not?"

"Mina's a good woman," Norm said. "And a great researcher. It would be a loss for her to be farmed away to Wolf Island or locked away in some BEE cell."

Sonia regarded Norm a moment or two in approving silence.

"You're kind to consider her," Sonia said.

"You're kind to shelter her," Norm said. "Not part of the *Synowie* playbook, historically."

"True," Sonia said. "But she's proven to be a very resourceful Infective. She has a real handle on her condition and has never actually caused us trouble. Her other self, not so much, but she always knows when a fit is going to overtake her and cages herself. I respect her strength of will."

"I should probably meet with her at some point," Norm said. He knew that Minton would give his eye teeth to get his hands on Mina, but Norm wouldn't let that happen. While they hadn't worked together much, Norm had less than nothing against her.

"That can be arranged," Sonia said. "Perhaps at the Library. A safe location."

They walked slowly through the park, trying to appear casual as they did so.

"Are you harboring Ansel Rupino?" Norm asked.

"No," Sonia said. "I wish we were."

"So, none of your *Synowie* cells has him?" Norm asked.

"Exactly, no," Sonia said. "I've asked, believe me."

"Lupine goes missing. Nobody knows where he is," Norm said.

It was quiet where they were, and Norm glanced around them instinctively, just in case there was something he needed to attend to. But everything seemed typically autumnal to his eyes and ears.

"Not for the last eight years, anyway," Sonia said. "We tracked him in other states, across the country, right after the Happening. Seems like the Rupinos were going to work killing Infectives—we call them *Zakaźny,* in case you ever wondered."

Talking with Sonia, Norm thought about when he'd met with Minton to discuss the *Synowie.* Every BEE agent knew about them and considered them to be allies in the ongoing fight that was the Happening.

"I don't like loose cannons," Minton said. "But you know that, Norm."

"Yessir," Norm said.

"Still, they have the experience and the networking," Minton said. "I would like for us to at least make overtures in their direction."

Norm knew of a few of them, but the Poles mostly kept to themselves.

"They consider us tourists in the realm of werewolf hunting, Sir," Norm said.

Minton nodded gravely.

"That they do," Minton said. "Entirely undeserved, but there it is."

Minton sat at his desk in his nicely appointed stateroom aboard the *Argent,* looking at him down the end of his nose. Minton, a former Marine, was a neat and disciplined man, who had managed to succeed where both of his predecessors—Anya Walker and Phil Sanderson— had failed. His tenure at the BEE had been one triumph after another regarding the Lupine problem.

"Still, I'd like for us to make inroads with them," Minton said. "There's a synergy between us, a common purpose."

"They're pure werewolf hunters," Norm said. "And vampires, I'd suppose. Only makes sense."

At the mention of vampires, Minton shifted in his seat.

"Yeah, well, I'm focused on the werewolf hunting, obviously," Minton said.

"Sure, sure," Norm said. "With all the fur flying, naturally."

"Supernaturally," Minton said, cracking a slice of a smile. "The *Synowie Srebra* have been going at it since the 1500s. I admire that kind of dedication."

Norm had recalled the known history of the Polish order, which wasn't much, since they operated so clandestinely. It was more like glimpses through history, moments, like snapshots.

"We have different problems here in the States," Minton said. "No respect for history, I suppose. I have to give my reports and I know people think we're the crazy ones. They used to laugh about us, you know. The Bureau? We were an inside joke. Who you gonna call? That kind of shit."

Norm knew that most of that went out the window with the Happening. The same smug bureaucratic bastards who were mocking the BEE were the ones frantically calling when they were faced with Lupines tearing the shit out of their officers.

"I don't judge the *Synowie* for their dedication," Minton said. "Or their secrecy. The work we do has to be secret. If the civilians realized what we were doing, they'd go insane, Norm. You know that."

"I do, Sir," Norm said.

"The *Synowie* have endured," Minton said. "We can learn from them. I'd like to bring a few on as consultants, although they're disinclined to take me up on that. They're like deer—you make a move in their direction and they flee off into the woods."

"What are you proposing, Sir?" Norm asked.

"Inroads, Norm," Minton said. "Use your charm. Use whatever you have. Find some *Synowie*, get to know them. Work with them. Help them. Whatever it takes."

"You know, those crazy bastards nearly bagged Big Black in '07," Norm said. "As close as anybody ever got. Before he disappeared a year later. Maybe they got him after all."

"They *didn't* get him," Minton said. His voice was clear and quiet, so matter-of-fact that it put Norm on his guard. "And the Rupinos are off the menu."

"We're *not* targeting Clan Rupino?' Norm asked.

"I can't make it any clearer than that, Norm," Minton said.

"May I ask why?" Norm asked.

"You may ask, but I'm not obliged to answer," Minton said. "We've come to an arrangement with the Rupinos, taking advantage of their considerable expertise in the area concerned, and their ready access to silver. See a pattern here, Norm? I want expertise and experience in our corner in these matters. No more BEE chasing after things. I want us to be thought leaders on all things paranormal."

Norm's mind raced. As a Trueborn lycanthropic clan, Norm knew the Rupinos bore no love for the Infectives. But the idea that the BEE would be working with Lupines to fight other Lupines felt bizarre to him. Then again, counterinsurgency made for strange bedfellows. He could see Minton holding his nose and working with Lupines to take down other Lupines.

"They're helping us against the Infectives?" Norm asked.

"Yes," Minton said. "They've sent three-member consultants to every state, aiding and assisting BEE strike teams. I call it 'Operation Tooth & Claw.'"

"This hasn't been communicated out to the teams," Norm said. "Why?"

Minton folded his hands atop his desk.

"It might be demoralizing for brick agents to know that we're working with lycanthropes," Minton said. "I'm going to ask you to be discreet, Norm. Word can't get out about this."

"Is this why the Warden Program was shut down?" Norm asked.

Minton cleared his throat and shifted in his seat.

"The Warden Program was shut down because the Wardens were getting killed faster than we could replace them," Minton said. "You were one of the only ones to survive. Plus, it reduced the risk of friendly fire where the Rupinos were concerned."

"You shut us down so we wouldn't hunt Rupinos," Norm said.

"I know how you Wardens carried grudges," Minton said. "You still do. I've got no room for grudges in the BEE, Norm."

Norm was going through the possibilities and permutations of Minton's plan. Every Warden had wanted to get a crack at Big Black before he'd vanished. The idea that he was off-limits was almost too much to bear.

"Is there a problem, Norm?"

"No, Sir," Norm said. "It's just a lot to take in."

Minton reached for a remote on his desk which activated some wall screens he had up that showed the status of the Happening. One screen showed a map of the United States, with red dots spattered across it, like blood. Every BEE station was on the map as well, hexagonal icons in every major city and capital.

"The Administration has provided the BEE with the necessary funding to carry out our counterinsurgency operations," Minton said. "On the condition that we do so under utmost secrecy. You yourself know that we're all bound by NDAs and a rigorous classification system. No one can know the full extent of our operations. Gia Rupino came to me, offering the services of her clan in the eradication of the Infectives. I saw an opportunity and I took it. No regrets."

"Wow," Norm said. There was a brutal simplicity to that plan, the idea of using Trueborn Lupines to hunt down Infectives. "Like drug-sniffing dogs."

"Hah," Minton said. "I suppose you could see it that way. They're our own largely-autonomous K-9 unit. They help us sniff out the Infectives, and they help us kill them. Sometimes they do it for us, although we work in tandem with them."

"No more renditions, then?" Norm asked.

"No more renditions," Minton said. "Whatever Lupines we have aboard the *Argent* through 2015 will be the last group to go to Wolf Island, once we put down the insurrection elsewhere. There's a real desired to get this all handled before the next presidential election."

Norm didn't know how many Lupines were still aboard the *Argent* but was sure the research teams were still at it, doing what they did. The *Argent* had the capacity to hold as many as 1,000 Lupines, although he doubted the cells were that full, given the expense of maintaining that many.

"There's something else to consider, Norm," Minton said. "Using the Rupinos in this fashion, it spares our own people from the mental and emotional exhaustion they suffer in carrying out their duties. All of the Ops teams suffered in their deployments. How many Infectives have you personally killed, Norm? Dozens. Scores."

"Confirmed kills?" Norm asked. "As a Warden? Just over a hundred, Director."

"Just over a hundred," Minton said. "And each one of those took something out of you, yes?"

The intimacy of his sniper kills wasn't something Norm ever talked about. As a Warden, he ended the lives of over 100 Americans—either directly or in the case of tranquilizer shots that got them extradited. Yeah, they were Infectives, but it did have an impact on him. Even talking about them made him uncomfortable.

"It's not easy," Norm said.

"Precisely," Minton said. "Gia Rupino comes to me and offers her services in return for a blanket amnesty for the Rupinos. These are creatures who are already killers, through and through. They want to kill, they need to kill, they are happy to kill. Whatever precisely motivates them, they are made for it. Who am I to refuse? The BEE Recovery teams then just clean up the messes. And that takes a toll on them, too, naturally. But we rotate out the Recovery teams and leave most of the wetwork to the Rupinos."

"Okay," Norm said. "I understand all of that. But why bother with the Stingers, then?"

Minton smiled a cool smile, ingratiating and bone-chilling at the same time. His was the face of bureaucratic rigor.

"Government work always involves a certain amount of redundancy," Minton said. "Let's just say that while I value using the Rupinos as our contract gundogs, I also favor having our own capacity to strike at the Lupines where and when we need to. You know as well as I do that it's not the same as when the Happening first broke out. We've been catching the dumb ones, the reckless and sloppy ones. The BEE has become a selection factor in the evolution of lycanthropy. The Lupines who remain are the craftier ones, the smarter ones, the more organized ones. The ones less likely to be vulnerable. That's where the Stingers come into it. They find those sneaky lycanthropes and they kill them. The Rupinos are a machete; the Stingers are a scalpel."

The chilly logic of it made sense to Norm, even though it was mind-boggling. Minton read his face in silence before speaking again, giving a little magnetic floating globe of black and silver on his desk a spin. Norm watched the globe whirl a moment.

"There's another matter," Minton said. "One that is of personal importance to you."

"Yes?" Norm said.

"Chad Bastion is off-limits to you," Minton said. "As are his lieutenants."

"What?" Norm asked.

"We have made an arrangement with him," Minton said. "In return for access to his Lupitol drug, which has proven effective in treating lycanthropy. Bastion has generously reached out to the BEE with this treatment, doing his part to help stem the tide of the Happening. He's as concerned about it as anyone else."

Norm inwardly seethed.

"I don't believe it," Norm said.

"Lupitol has become a best-selling drug," Minton said. "You've seen the ads, haven't you?"

Of course he had. The ads had been everywhere.

Minton pushed a button on the remote, and one of the screens turned into a Lupitol ad, showing a woman tossing and turning in her bed, talking about Night Fever robbing her of sleep and memory, making her hallucinate. But thanks to Lupitol, she's able to get her life back. The ad segued to the woman on the job, looking bright-eyed and engaged with the world around her.

"Thanks to Lupitol, I feel human again," she said. Others joined her, a tapestry of people, a cross-section of Americans, all saying it. "Thanks to Lupitol, I feel human again."

The words appeared, accompanied by the whitish crescent moon, which turned slowly clockwise until it became a smile—*Lupitol: Getting you back to where you belong.*

Minton pushed another button and the screen went to news coverage.

"Liminalix is offering this to us," Minton said. "It's just too useful to pass up, Norm. Between Rupino and Bastion, we're getting this stuff fixed up once and for all. It won't be long before people forget all about Zooey Hummel except as a sort of urban legend or bogeyman. We're ending the Happening on our terms. You served in Afghanistan, Norm. You know how bad it can get when you can't get closure."

"I do, Sir," Norm said.

"So, you understand," Minton said. "We're talking a decisive win for our side in this. I don't know what Hummel had in mind, I don't think anybody ever will. You've read her crazy manifesto. The kid wanted a revolution—some kind of Infective insurrection. But we're stopping that. Rupino's goons kill the Infectives in the field, and Bastion's minions help us distribute the pharmacologic treatment that lets us keep the rest of them at bay until an actual cure is found for it. That's a win-win in my book. We're administering it to the Infectives aboard the *Argent* to test its effects."

"Why Bastion?" Norm asked.

"He came to us," Minton said. "Through intermediaries."

Norm wondered if Anne was part of the group that negotiated that on behalf of Liminalix. He wondered if Anne was using Lupitol. Minton looked searchingly at Norm.

"Off-limits," Minton said. "Do we have an understanding?"

"What about Anne?" Norm asked. He hadn't wanted to come out with it, but he couldn't contain it.

Minton knew all about it. It was known around the BEE that Norm had lost his wife to the infection. It had garnered Norm a degree of sympathy in the ranks, and at least let people understand why he threw himself into his work with such tireless vigor.

"Your wife is part of Bastion's senior team," Minton said. "Again, I don't want anything disrupting our relationship with Liminalix. And I mean anything."

"Bastion's man, Todd Shaw, kidnapped and knowingly infected my wife, Troy," Norm said. "I mean, come on. I'm just supposed to take that?"

Minton affected concern, and Norm believed that he was concerned as far as he was able to be. But he knew Minton well enough to know that he was unlikely to let that sway him, given the progress he'd made.

"Do you have proof of it?" Minton asked. "You saw him infect her?"

"She's with him," Norm said. "She left me for him. He's compelling her. You know how Loop sires can do that, Sir. They can exert a measure of control over their victims. He always wanted Anne."

Minton composed himself a moment, which Norm knew meant bad news was coming in some form. Minton was not one to emotionally overcommit to something, so when he took a moment to compose himself meant he was about to deliver unwanted information.

"Maybe she's with him because she wants to be," Minton said. "People leave their spouses all the time."

"Jesus, Sir," Norm said. "Shaw was always flirting with her."

Minton cleared his throat, clearly uncomfortable with discussing Norm's private life in this manner. He leaned in.

"We'll settle that once we get the Infectives situation dealt with," Minton said. "I promise you that, Norm. In return, you have to promise me that you'll leave Bastion and his people alone until we put an end to the Happening."

It was a painful promise he was asking of him, one that Norm didn't think he could make. Minton could see the conflict in him.

"I put you into the Stinger Program because you had the emotional and mental fortitude for this kind of work," Minton said. "You're the right man for it. You have the ability to not let emotion carry you into hard-to-navigate places. I need my Stingers to be dispassionate and professional. I can't have them in the field carrying out personal vendettas. Promise me, Norm."

"I promise not to let my emotions cloud my judgment," Norm said.

"And promise to leave Bastion and his people alone," Minton said. "I want to hear it from you, Norm."

"I promise to leave Bastion and his people alone," Norm said, choking the words out.

"Mr. Stockwell?" Sonia said, bringing Norm back to Vanzetti Park.

"Sorry, I was thinking about things," Norm said. He didn't normally let his situational awareness wane, but in matters where Anne was concerned, he did sometimes drift. Sonia seemed to understand, accepting it with a polite nod. Norm felt like maybe he'd lost a point or two with the *Synowie* agent.

"Huh," Norm said. "So, when Minton met with you, what was his angle? What'd he want from you?"

"He wants *Synowie's* help taking care of the remaining *Zakaźny*," Sonia said. "And he wanted us to leave Rupino and Bastion alone. He was very clear about that."

Norm wondered what Minton was up to. With *Synowie* being stretched to their limit, what value did they bring, beyond, of course, long history and experience? He was likely just working to cross the *Synowie* off his list.

"What did you tell him?"

"I told him I'd take it to my peers and we'd discuss," Sonia said.

"Well played," Norm said.

"And I'm supposed to work with you," Sonia said. "Not that I need a partner, mind you."

"Me, neither," Norm said. He was laundry-listing a number of questions he'd have for Tiff when he got the chance.

"I won't work with vampires," Sonia said. "Won't. Do. It. My family has…history with them."

"Yeah?" Norm asked.

Sonia nodded solemnly, and, from the look of her, Norm didn't think he'd get that story out of her anytime soon. He opted to be understanding and empathic.

"I don't blame you," Norm said. The kid with the kite was running around, the kite zigzagging on the fitful autumn breezes. "I'll see what I can find out."

"You do that," Sonia said.

"I've got a line on the Loopines," Norm said. "I'm planning to take some of them out."

"Tough targets," Sonia said, nodding coolly. "You're an ambitious man. But the Loopines are part of Bastion's pack, yes? They're *his* people."

"Yeah, well," Norm said. "They have it coming."

"They're hard to reach," Sonia said. "They've got an entire skyscraper to themselves. Wealth and power buys protection."

"I know," Norm said. The Bastion Industrial Architecture building, just south of the river. It might as well have been a 40-floor Fort Knox.

"Bastion seldom leaves it," Sonia said. "I know. We watch him. He never shows. From there to his Lake Forest mansion. Otherwise, the man's a ghost."

"You've been watching him awhile?" Norm asked. Sonia nodded.

"Years," she said. "Waiting for our shot."

Again, Norm admired their dedication. Nobody was more determined than the *Synowie*. They were entirely committed to their mission. Maybe Minton had worked a deal with Bastion, and maybe he'd forced him to promise not to target Bastion or his guys, but as Norm saw it, if he could take out Shaw and recover Anne, it would be easier to ask for forgiveness later than permission before.

The breeze blew, and Norm could feel the hint of winter chill as the trees rustled. The kids kept chasing their soccer ball, and the one kid had gotten their kite stuck in a tree, was tugging on the kite string, futilely trying to free it.

"If the shot came, would you take it?" Norm asked. Sonia side-eyed him through her sunglasses.

"Is this a test, Mr. Stockwell?" Sonia asked.

"Just a question," Norm said. "Look, I'm sympathetic. Nobody wants Bastion and his people more than me. Which reminds me—what does *Synowie* have on him?"

Sonia sighed, affecting studied nonchalance, which made the park bench seem more like an office in that moment.

"You *are* testing me. He's a Trueborn, if that's what you're asking," Sonia said. "But you already knew that."

"Yeah," Norm asked. The BEE files on Bastion didn't have much on Bastion, incredibly enough. "But the Rupinos have the Midwest. What's he doing here?"

"His clan operates out of the East Coast," Sonia said. "Clan Bastion. Grey wolves. But you know this, as well."

Norm had certainly never heard of Clan Bastion going west of Pennsylvania. But then, he didn't operate outside of the Midwest. Sonia seemed to be anticipating his thoughts.

"Bastion keeps a very low profile," Sonia said. "Even more than the Rupinos. Bastion is heavily diversified in construction, chemicals, pharmaceuticals, and industrial manufacturing. Clan Bastion forges close ties with the police, wherever they go. Another difference between the Rupinos and Bastion is that while the Rupinos almost never let in new members to the pack, Bastion actively, if covertly, recruits new blood. They have membership levels."

It made the Loopines make more sense to him, now. Although it also made it seem like Bastion was attempting some sort of power play in the Midwest, if he was actively horning in on what was historically Rupino territory. Or else these Trueborn were colluding with one another and using the Happening as an opportunity to do so.

"How many Trueborn clans are operating in the States?" Norm asked. It embarrassed him to even have to ask, but for the BEE, even admitting that the Trueborn existed had required a cognitive leap that was decades in the making. There were clans they knew about, but he figured it couldn't hurt to hear the *Synowie* take on it.

"There are five Trueborn clans," Sonia said. "The Rupinos in the Midwest. The Bastions in the Northeast. Clan Murtaugh in the South. Clan Esperanza in the Southwest. Clan Mendoza in the West. They represent the Trueborn Pentagram, the lupine underground. Rupinos are black wolves. Bastions are grey. Murtaughs are brown. Esperanzas are gold. Mendozas are red."

"It feels like there should be more Trueborn clans," Norm said.

"There used to be," Sonia said. "In the time of westward expansion, there were more isolated and insular Trueborn clans that had been there for generations. There was a consolidation over time as clans fought on the frontier. The five Trueborn families are the ones who remained standing. There may be others in isolated areas—Alaska, somewhere in the Rockies or the Appalachians to the east. But they're small clans. The Pentagram are the biggest, most powerful clans."

"Right," Norm said. He made a mental note to study up on them more.

Sonia smiled sadly.

"I don't blame the Bureau," Sonia said. "The BEE tracks *all* paranormality. And Lupines are just one part of that spectrum. The Lupine underground, especially the Trueborn, stays that way for a reason. They don't make waves and they don't draw undue attention to themselves. That's how they survive. We track them and hunt them when we can and have done so for centuries. The BEE is modern. The only reason it rose to the level of attention it's getting is because of the Happening. If it hadn't been for that, the BEE would have been buzzing around, attending to whatever else it does. Chasing ghosts, I suppose, or hunting vampires, witches, ghosts, and sea monsters."

Norm laughed bitterly.

"I hadn't expected a *Synowie* to defend the Bureau," Norm said.

"We live in strange times," Sonia replied. "I'm just saying, you had no reason to track the Trueborn, and to be honest, the Trueborn *are* dangerous. Gia Rupino is dangerous. They all are."

"No white wolves among the Trueborn?" Norm asked.

"Not yet," Sonia said. "Although the Wolves of God are trying."

Norm hated the Wolves of God. They were among the most vicious of Infectives, pulling from the very worst sorts of people, wrapping it up in the flag and brandishing a Bible along with their fangs, fur, and claws. They saw their Infective status as a sign of God's favor.

"What do you mean?" Norm asked.

"There's a place called 'The Créche,'" Sonia said. "It's in the South somewhere. You might want to check that out."

"What is it?" Norm asked.

"It's something new," Sonia said. "A place where the Wolves of God are funneling their Infectives. One part cult compound, one part nursery. We haven't found it, yet. But we will."

Norm had been so focused on Bastion and Shaw, he'd perhaps let his focus drift where other Lupines were concerned.

"Why would they be doing that?" Norm asked.

"I'm only speculating, because the Wargs keep it all very hush-hush," Sonia said. "But it appears the Lupercalians are converting people and busing them down to the Créche. White people, white wolves. Lycanthropic Manifest Destiny. That sort of thing. They're aggressively trying to breed their way to Trueborn status."

"What does that mean?" Norm asked, wishing he'd paid more attention to the tutorials about Lupine ecology.

"It means you start with two Infectives, they breed, and they will birth a Trueborn," Sonia said. "Do that enough and you end up with a Trueborn clan within a generation. It's what they're up to in the Créche, I think."

"The South," Norm said. "Out of my jurisdiction."

Sonia shrugged. "Not out of ours. But with how much of a beating we've been taking, we can't do much about it beyond observation at this point. I'm only telling you so you'll know."

Norm made a mental note to add it to his ever-growing list of things to discuss with Minton.

"So, let's go through our action items, then," Sonia said. "You're going to dig in on this whole vampire business with Minton. And I'm going to covertly assist you with the Loopines, despite them being officially off-limits. Is this correct?"

"Yes," Norm said. "If it's not too much trouble."

"Never," Sonia said. "All the same, we should exchange numbers, in case we need to communicate. We should have call names. I'll be Parker."

"Parker?" Norm asked, then glanced around Vanzetti Park, nodded. "Good one. Just call me Ghost."

"Ghost," Sonia said. "Got it."

The two of them quickly, surreptitiously entered their numbers into their respective phones.

"Let's meet again in a few days," Sonia said. "Are you familiar with Tupelo's?"

"No," Norm said.

"Look it up," Sonia said. "You'll find it. Look for me in three days. I'll be there. We can reconnect and see what progress we've made."

"Alright," Norm said. He was already thinking about how he'd connive to get himself aboard the *Argent*, and what he'd bring up with Minton. "I have to ask you, if Minton told you to avoid the Rupinos and Bastion, why are you agreeing to help me?"

"They're *Wilkołaki*," Sonia said. "And I'm *Synowie Srebra*. Fuck them."

Sonia smoothed out her coat, extending her gloved hand.

"A pleasure meeting you, Mr. Stockwell," she said. Norm shook her hand.

"Likewise, Ms. Gorski," Norm said.

Then they parted ways without another word. He watched her go, walking crisply to the parking lot, taking out her phone and talking on it. He couldn't hear what she was saying.

BLACK Sheep ambled through Streeterville like he owned it. Broad daylight, not a care in the world. The Council meeting had left a bad taste in his mouth, and he knew what he needed to cleanse his palate. That was best accomplished with some willful killing.

He fished out his burner phone and dialed up one of the other Babas, a guy who went by Trainwreck.

"Yo, Rex," Black Sheep said. "Get the boys together. We're going on a hunting trip."

"Wheresabout?" Trainwreck asked. Rex was about six years younger than Black Sheep, but was proving himself to be an avid student of the Black Sheep School of Applied Lycanthropy.

Not that Black Sheep went out of his way to gather recruits. But when the packs began to form, he realized that it would suit him more to have more bodies in his corner, so he spent several years infecting guys he handpicked.

"Just get everybody together, and I'll let you know," Black Sheep said.

It became more of a thing after all the crap he had to keep enduring from the Daughters of Zooey, who were still trying to avenge their late leader. One of Zooey's last wishes was for Black Sheep to be killed, and the Doozies kept coming after him, year after year.

The smart thing to do would have been to flee to another state, maybe go up to Alaska or Canada or something, live out there all free and wild. But Black Sheep was still a city boy, had always been one. He couldn't imagine going all rustic.

When Zooey had infected him, she'd upended his life, but she hadn't changed who he was. Well, not completely. He hadn't been a serial rapist and murderer when she'd met him. That had come out with the infection. That part of him blossomed.

It made him almost laugh, and then he actually did laugh. He had long since forgotten his real name. She'd christened him Black Sheep and he'd stuck with it. He had embraced his Lupine self completely, had become it so much that his human form was simply a disguise his werewolf self wore so he could blend in.

From a werewolf to a worewolf, Black Sheep thought.

While he favored Pilsen as his hunting grounds, downtown worked, too. In fact, being able to kill some sheeple downtown right under the noses of the Council suited him just fine. While the Lupitol drug money would have been sweet, Black Sheep wasn't in it for the money. He was in it for the carnage. Carnage killed.

He bounded up the stairs to the El platform just ahead of the rumble of the incoming train and hopped on. Everybody who caught it wrestled with being an Infective, whereas Black Sheep embraced it. That was the secret of his success, why he'd managed to evade (and kill) the Wardens that had hunted him. Why the BEE would never catch him. He was raw, he was elemental. And he was unconflicted. It eased the transition from man to monster. A wolf never worried about what it was. Why would a werewolf?

For all of their posturing, the Doozies were just that—pretenders to Zooey's crazy crown. The Happening, whatever Zooey's thing had ever really been, had already Happened. It had stirred things up, but lycanthropes weren't anywhere close to taking over the world. And they never would.

Case in point: the media bent over backwards trying out different stories. First there was the coywolf stories, coywolves coming in and attacking people and their pets. Then a bizarre story about rogue furries preying on people, like some kind of cult. Then domestic terrorist stories surfaced. The Night Fever story had legs and it became the one the norms fixated on. Night fucking Fever. That was Black Sheep's personal favorite. Hallucinations and memory loss as a way for accounting for lycanthropy, because admitting that lycanthropy existed was just too much for them to take.

It was like the norms never ran out of reassuring stories to tell themselves instead of honestly facing what was coming after them. It was a sick joke.

Nobody credible in the media would go anywhere near saying "werewolves" or even "lupines" or "lycans" or "lycanthropes" on television or radio. They simply wouldn't go near the idea. It was like the full implication of it was simply beyond them.

It was the same reason why they never used words like "fascist" to actually describe real-life fascists. The real words and ideas behind them were just too scary for the corporate norms who ran the media. The Internet was the only place you actually found werewolves called out, and even there, people went from not believing it to maybe believing in it a little too much.

He remembered when Zooey actually went onscreen and attacked a local news team while they were on the air. Even that had been declared to be a publicity stunt. She'd attacked an El train and it had gone much the same. Eyewitnesses saw, and even the ones that believed what they saw wouldn't dare go on the air and talk about it. Nobody wanted to be known as that kind of person.

Only the freaks and conspiracy theorists ran with it. Not because they had any credibility. They didn't. And that's why they ran with it. No one with an iota of reputation to lose would touch the story of the century.

Looking at the passengers on the train, busy with their city faces on, trying not to draw attention to themselves. All types of prey, here. Young, old, pretty, ugly, plain. Scared, impudent, anxious. Cool.

The cool one caught his eye. She was pretty. He'd seen her at the Council session, had already forgotten her name. A Rupino. A young woman in a black leather jacket with shoulder-length black hair cut in a stylish sort of bob. She wore a black and white horizontal striped shirt and blue jeans with polished black boots. Or were they booties? He hardly cared. She had big blue eyes and sensuous lips adorned with red lipstick. She saw him eyeing her and she met his gaze evenly.

Crap, what was her name? He was so bad with names.

Black Sheep could spot his own kind even without giving them a sniff test. Lupines just looked different, carried themselves differently. It was a certain carnal confidence they carried. Black Sheep knew it well because he had that, too. Lycanthropy was like being part of the coolest club in the fucking world. It hardly mattered that it was infectious, that anybody bitten could belong to it. He didn't care. The capacity to infect was its own intoxicant. The ability to survive the trouble one caused was addictive.

He sauntered down the El train, taking a seat across from her.

"Hey," Black Sheep said. "How about that Council session?"

She looked at him a moment, cocking an eyebrow. She had great eyebrows. But a werewolf-babe would, wouldn't she?

"You mean the one you walked out of?" she said.

"Yeah, that's the one," Black Sheep said. "Did I miss anything?"

"You missed out on like $30 million, by my reckoning," she said, seeming to enjoy how much that annoyed him. "We're really not supposed to talk about Council business out here among the norms."

"I'm a rulebreaker, what can I say? What's your name?" Black Sheep asked.

"What's yours?" she said.

"I'm Black Sheep," he said, and she laughed.

"Your real name?"

"Yeah, sure, it is," he said. "Maybe you've heard stories of me, is my guess."

"Maybe," she said, flexing her neck a bit. She was smaller than he was. Not like he was a particularly big guy, but what it meant was that whatever she turned in to, it would be smaller than what he became, and in Lupine terms, as in so much with life, size mattered.

"So, what's your name?" Black Sheep asked.

"Valentina," she said.

"Valentina," Black Sheep said. "Damn, I should have remembered that. That's one heckuva name."

"Better than 'Black Sheep,' anyway," Valentina said, grinning at him. Her grin was something capricious, like a demon's. That's how he saw it, and he'd never seen a demon before, but he assumed that her grin was how a demon would smile upon him. Black Sheep thought demon sex would be hot, if he could only find the right demon.

The El train rattled, rocked, and rolled, and people boarded and people got off. Clueless norms, going through the motions of their inconsequential lives. Black Sheep could have killed everyone on the train in minutes, and none of them could do a thing about it. That thought made him happy. Werewolf live was one of knowing that you were death incarnate masquerading as an everyday person. It was magical that way.

"Where are you headed?" Black Sheep asked.

"I'm going where you're going," Valentina said.

"Oh, are you?" Black Sheep replied. "You like what you see?"

In his human guise, he considered himself good-looking enough. Sometimes that was all it took. The kind of guy who might not quicken a woman's heart, but one who seemed fey and harmless enough to be worthy of some level of consideration. It was enough of a disguise to get him where he needed to go.

"*You're* what I came for," Valentina said, smiling at him. Her smile was a big one. Black Sheep imagined what she could do with that mouth of hers. He was sure she knew how to use it.

"I am?" Black Sheep asked. "You're not secretly one of those Doozies, are you?"

"Hah," Valentina said. "Um, no. Do I look like one of them? Stupid riot grrl wannabes."

"No," Black Sheep said. "No way. You look utterly Rupino. Italian in the best possible way."

"Wow, I'm not sure how to take that," Valentina said.

"Just take it, howsabout?" Black Sheep said. "You know, your whole clan thinks they run everything in the city, but you don't. There's all sorts of dark corners you Trueborn snobs have never seen."

Valentina looked mock-afraid.

"Oh, my," she said. "Are you going to show me your dark corners, Black Sheep?"

She was hot, and Black Sheep dug her. As a self-declared Agent of Chaos, Black Sheep liked to be unpredictable, so, on a whim, he got to his feet, wanted to see how she'd take that. He didn't pay much attention to the Rupinos. They were a navigation hazard best avoided.

"Next stop is my stop," he said. She stood up and joined him. She came up to his shoulder, he noted with satisfaction. Maybe five foot three. A little thing. He liked that even more. Little things could lead to big things.

The train rounded a bend and came to a halt at the Sedgwick stop. Black Sheep gestured for her to precede him.

"Ladies first," Black Sheep said.

"My, such a gentleman," Valentina said, donning a pair of lovely black leather gloves. "You're an endangered species."

"So true," Black Sheep said, watching her get off the train. "Putting on your Black Hands for me? Am I going to get a Black Hand-job?"

Valentina rolled her bright blue eyes as she stepped off, glancing at him over her shoulder.

"Coming?" Valentina asked.

Some part of him, the human part of him that he'd long since locked away, thought about ditching her, staying on the train, and watching her turn and see him leaving, treating her to a shit-eating, Chaos Agent smirk. But looking at her nice ass as she walked on that badly worn wooden platform, something in him told him to give her a follow, and he did, trotting out after her.

"I'm meeting up with some of my bros," Black Sheep said. "We're going hunting. You want to come?"

"Tempting," Valentina said. "But you Babas are such a sausage fest."

"That we are," Black Sheep said. "Problem?"

Valentina shook her head. The El train rolled away, clacking and clattering, leaving them on the platform almost alone, watching the norms shuffle past them, heading for the stairs. Valentina watched them go before replying. She was so sexy, Black Sheep couldn't stand it.

"Not for me," Valentina said.

"So, are you going rogue or what?" Black Sheep asked. "I'm part of the Council, don't forget."

"Ah," Valentina said. "I should be careful, then."

"That you should," Black Sheep said. "It's dangerous out here. Even for you Rupinos."

"Oh, no," Valentina said. "But I'm a *Veronatta*. I've got nothing to worry about."

"Is that so?" he said.

"Decidedly so," Valentina said.

Something about her was triggering him, and Black Sheep became a little nervous. He didn't last as long as he had without having a keen survival instinct. Something was up.

"Veronatta?" Black Sheep asked.

"Trueborn, *Infettivo,*" Valentina said, and then three she-wolves dropped down around him from the roof atop the Sedgwick station. They were three of a kind, long-limbed and fierce-looking, their claws like talons, their fangs bared. He remembered them from the Council, too. The triplets. The Furies. Fuck.

"Whoa, whoa," Black Sheep said, stepping back, only to find that the she-wolves had him surrounded. "You ladies don't want to dance with me, trust me."

"Me, me, me," Valentina said from behind him. "Always me with you, yeah?"

But then something flicked down over his neck, something that burned. It was a loop of silver, and Black Sheep cursed as the loop of silver was pulled tight around his neck. Valentina was on his back, her knee jabbing him, even as the thin line of silver was cutting into his throat.

"You fucking bitches," Black Sheep said, giving free rein to his true self, transforming on the platform. The transformation was always a beautiful and powerful thing, like a rebirth, turning him from his humble human self into his monstrous better half.

For eight glorious years, Black Sheep had ridden the world as a monster among men, fearless and furious, powerful and predatory. He epitomized the lycanthropic *demimonde,* his University of Chicago brain told him. The duality of man and beast. The integration of two competing impulses, the synergy of slaughter and the will to power.

The three black she-wolves backed up, watching him with their incandescent eyes ablaze while Valentina rode his back, strangling him, even as he towered over them. He'd kill all of them and rape their corpses. This wasn't a threat; it was a promise.

Black Sheep was nearly done transforming when he realized something was terribly wrong. The loop of silver that had been throttling him had been sized to his human form. He had thought his transformation would have snapped the thing, but it had not snapped.

The result, as blood began to spray out from his neck, was a kind of self-induced decapitation. As he added mass and size, and the silver loop held fast, retaining its shape and dimensions. His head came right off in a fount of blood even before he fully realized he was dead.

"Smooth move, Bright Boy," Valentina said.

His head dropped to the wooden platform, bouncing once. He saw his great and powerful monster body fall, twitching. And there was Valentina standing there, the bloody loop of silver in her black-gloved hands, covered in his blood, smiling down on him. She picked up his cell phone, tugging it out of his rended black jeans, and slipped it in her pocket.

He saw the three she-wolves leap off the platform onto a rooftop, even as his vision faded to everlasting black.

"Buh-bye, Black Sheep," Valentina said, unspooling the silver loop and pocketing it. She blew him a kiss from her black hands and left him to die on the platform, which he did in three shakes of a lamb's tail.

I don't know why I still try. It's been eight years, and still no Ansel. I ventured to his studio, the way I always do, but he's not there.

He's never there.

I wonder if the BEE agents took him away, something like that. Or maybe he's dead. Either is possible. Missing and presumed dead. It makes sense when you see those ideas together. Missing might as well be dead.

Sorry I'm so grim and dark.

Sloane's getting more demanding as she's growing up. I don't know how I'll be able to manage her as a tween, or as a teen. She's already far more attuned to her condition (I don't know what else to politely call it) than I am. I see the gulf between us, me, the Infective mother, her, the Trueborn daughter.

Just like her missing father.

Maybe he's avoiding me. I thought about that, too. I made a poem, because it's who I am, and what I do:

INFECTIVE

I never liked the word 'disease'
It is a word that doesn't please
The shadow came and stole my heart
And now I don't know where I start

The thing inside me ate my soul
And now I fear I'll lose control

The Beast, the Beast, she lies beneath
She hides, she hides, so deep inside
I feed, I feed, I need, I need

They bleed, they bleed, they bleed, they bleed

Even now, she steals my letters
Not content to mind her betters

And captive to infection, I
With nothing left to do but die.

Polly saved and closed out. She'd given up blogging on the Net years ago when the BEE agents had begun targeting people that way. Her journal entries were her own, now, and Polly hated being in isolation that way. She needed her audience, needed any audience. But since her infection, she'd gotten increasingly socially anxious.

Especially with Sloane in the mix. Sloane's joyful fearlessness and childlike exuberance was like a constant reminder to Polly of how much she had to be afraid of.

Sloane, with infallible instinct, showed up at her door, as if conjured by the Devil himself. She was wearing a black unicorn sweatshirt with black jeans and silver-glittery ballet flats.

"My, aren't you fancy?" Polly said. "Did you pick that out yourself, Scritchers?"

"Of course I did, Mommers," Sloane said. Polly hated when she called her "Mommers" but didn't want to scold her about it. Sloane had brushed her own hair, too, and it reminded Polly that she needed to get her a haircut soon. The girl was blessed with those lustrous Rupino locks.

"You look very fancy," Polly said. "So, what are we going to do today?"

It was a Saturday, thankfully, since Polly didn't think she had it in her to drop Sloane off at school. Motherhood remained an endless cavalcade of indignities she was forced to weather with timely bottles of wine.

"Something fun, I hope," Sloane said. "Something outside."

"Alright," Polly said. "We can do a bit of gardening."

"In November?" Sloane asked.

"There's always work to do with a garden," Polly said.

Sloane looked beyond bored by that, but the prospect of going outside was simply too good to pass up. Polly got her gardening hat and gloves and ventured out with Sloane into the garage.

Polly was wearing a black turtleneck sweater and black leggings and black flats and looked better-dressed for a coffeehouse than for gardening, but she didn't care. She grabbed a rake for herself and a little one for Sloane and went around to the front yard first.

Todd Shaw had pulled into the driveway with his oh-so-special lady friend, Anne. Polly didn't talk to Shaw much, but her late husband Tristan had been on good terms with him. They got out and saw Polly pretending to work in her garden while Sloane ran around the front yard, raking oak leaves and humming happily.

"Howdy, Polly," Shaw said, waving, looking her up and down, like twice. "Doing a little raking, are you?"

Anne looked at Polly and gave her a smile of pure saccharine. The woman wore a coffee-colored wool coat and smiled at Sloane, who either hadn't noticed, or was pretending not to. Her mother's daughter, after all.

"Nothing gets past you, Todd," Polly said. She hated when people asked leading questions like that. "I am, indeed. The leaves get absolutely everywhere."

"Enchanting little girl," Anne said. "Such a lovely little creature."

Sloane could hear every word, of course, but was pretending not to. The girl had amazing hearing and possessed almost inhuman reserve. Polly wondered if that was part of being Trueborn, that sense of being different from everything around you, and whether it allowed you to keep everything in perspective, somehow.

"Thank you," Polly said. "They grow up so fast."

"That they do," Anne said. "Or so I'm told. I don't have any children of my own. I always felt it was irresponsible to bring children into this cruel and callous world."

Polly was certain the woman was shading her. It had been years since she'd had to spar verbally with someone, and part of her nearly welcomed the challenge. It made her think back on her Horrorshow days when they'd debate one another about whatever esoteric effrontery had earned their ire for that particular moment.

"I suppose so," Polly said. "But children symbolize hope, and we all need that from time to time."

Shaw snorted, rolling his eyes.

"Always the Romantic, Polly," Shaw said, giving Polly's figure a third going-over with his hungry eyes. "She's a hopeless Romantic, Anne. Come on, let's go inside, it's freakin' chilly out here."

"Okay, Todd," Anne said, following him, stealing a backward glance at Sloane as she went.

Polly watched them go, while Sloane crept up on her.

"Mommers," Sloane said, conspiratorially. "You know the neighbors are werewolves, right?"

"Yes, Scritchers," Polly said. "I do. We don't use that word, Baby. It's a stupid word."

"I like it," Sloane said. "It's fun to say."

Polly smiled at that, understood at least the impulse to say fun words. "Emulous" was a fun word to say. She was emulous of Sloane's ease in her own supernatural skin, wished she had that for herself.

"It's just one you should use cautiously, then," Polly said. "People get afraid of it."

"If I know they are, then they know we are," Sloane said. Polly had to admit that she was likely right about that. Werewolves knew their own kind. You could just tell. "They're both like you, Mommers."

"Meaning?"

"They got bitten," Sloane said. "Not, you know, born like me."

"How can you tell that?" Polly said. Sloane tapped her nose, like it was the most obvious thing in the world. "You can tell by the smell?"

"Yep," Sloane said. "There's normal-smell, and there's were-smell."

"Were-smell," Polly said, laughing. "With your were-nose?"

"Yep," Sloane said. "I'll grow up to be Were-Woman one day. A superhero."

"Of that I have no doubt," Polly said.

Polly wondered who had made them, and how they were able to function as well as they did. In her periodic Lupine rambles, she never saw either Shaw or Anne transform. How they kept a lid on their own infections was a mystery.

Maybe they were on Lupitol.

Polly had seen the ads for it on television, on the Internet, and had seen the billboard signs for it. She refused to get any, didn't want to out herself as a lycanthrope. She was fairly certain that anybody who took Lupitol got catalogued somewhere. Her younger self would have called that notion paranoid, but Polly knew better now. Paranoia was her baseline after the Happening.

Sloane had made a leaf pile and was throwing herself into it with gusto. The girl was full of boundless energy, and Polly again wondered how that would play out as she matured. What did Trueborn teens do when they started dating?

Before he'd vanished, Ansel had made arrangements with Polly, and she received a monthly stipend, a nice chunk of money that allowed her to live without having to work, for which she was eternally grateful. Wherever he was, whatever had happened to him, there was that.

"Poets should never have jobs," Ansel said, smiling at her. It was his mocking smile, and she loved it and hated it in equal measure.

"Poetry *is* my job," Polly said, petulant.

"Sure," Ansel said. "I mean like *real* jobs. Paying jobs."

"Fuck you," Polly said.

She didn't know how it had come about, or where the money came from, but it had arrived like clockwork every month for years. Anything was better than having to work a day job. That would have made her life even more intolerable than it already was, wasting away in Winnetka.

She knew that Ansel came from real money, and was grateful for it, even as she was frustrated and worried that he'd seemingly disappeared from the face of the Earth. However, people with money could do that without a thought of the consequences.

Polly had thought about looking into the Rupino Urban Frontier Foundation and making some inquiries, but she was also afraid of raising her profile. Ansel had said he was taking care of things and would be back. He hadn't told her what those things were, in his Ansel way. He always kept more inside than outside.

She didn't even know if he knew that she'd been pregnant when he'd left, or that he was a father. She hadn't known until a week or two after he'd vanished. Maybe the prospect of fatherhood had frightened him off. Part of her feared that maybe he was dead. It was easier to think that than thinking that he'd abandoned her.

She'd seen what had happened to him when he'd fought mad Zooey and her minions. The wounds he'd received had been grievous. Polly remembered when she and Ansel had teamed up to take down Zooey, how bloody that had been. Polly had nearly died that night from her injuries. Although her wounds had long since healed, her hands still went to her throat when she thought about them. Even those scars healed, but the memories remained.

Polly had watched the news over the years, had ranged across the Internet, hoping for some sign. The whole Night Fever epidemic story had been picked up by media channels everywhere, tracking the pretend disease.

She knew it was nonsense, that it was just a euphemism for lycanthropy that was being trotted out because the norms couldn't handle knowing that there were actual werewolves out there hunting them, killing them, eating them. Better to frame it as mass hysteria and hallucinations than admitting the obvious.

It had been the kind of performance art that Sam would have loved. Polly still missed her long-dead friends and couldn't believe she'd been the only one to survive. Sam would have marveled at the madness of the Happening and her own role in bringing it about.

"It's like, bigger than the *zeitgeist,*" Sam would have said, with that air of wonder she always carried with her. "It's something more. There needs to be a totally bigger word for it."

Polly teared up a little at their memory. They lived only in her head, now.

She saw Anne cross the yard, coming toward her with a box. Polly immediately shelved her reverie and remembrances and turned her attention to her visitor, blinking away the tears.

"Sorry to bother you again, Polly," Anne said. "I brought something for you. Something I think you might need."

Her eyes flitted over Sloane, who was rolling around in the leaves and giggling to herself, singing some tuneless song of her own invention.

"Ah, to be so carefree," Anne said.

"What is it, Anne?" Polly asked, looking at the box.

"I'm not usually one to play the spoiler in the matter of gifts, but it's a case of Lupitol," Anne said.

"Lupitol?" Polly said. "Why do you think I need it?"

"Night Fever," Anne said. "You have it, don't you?"

"I don't know what you're talking about," Polly said. Anne looked at her evenly, her middle-aged face at once opaque and quite direct.

"I think we both know that I do," Anne said. "You should take it."

"Do you take it?" Polly asked, annoyed enough to put this woman on the defensive.

"Well, no," Anne said. "Todd won't let me take it."

"Todd won't let you," Polly said. Anne glanced over her shoulder and then offered the box again.

"Please take the box," Anne said. "He doesn't know I'm over here."

"Why not?" Polly said. "Why the secrecy?"

"He and I have different views on, well, Night Fever," Anne said. Polly scoffed.

"Call it what it is, and I'll take it," Polly said. "Just say it, Anne."

"Lycanthropy," Anne said. "There, I said it. Now, do your part."

Polly took the box, to Anne's evident relief. "That's a year's supply, Polly. One pill a day—or night—and you can return to normal."

"It's a treatment, not a cure," Polly said. "I've seen the ads."

"It's something," Anne said. "Let's call it a start."

Polly was always suspicious, even on a good day. She masked it with her abundant charm, but these days, she didn't even bother. Charm was so 2007. It had withered on the vine by 2015, as the world warmed and people slowly went insane.

"Do you always have cases of Lupitol handy?" Polly asked. "Why do I get the benefit of this generosity on your part?"

"Because of her," Anne said, glancing at Sloane, who was throwing leaves in the air with gusto. "You need to be there for her. Where's her father?"

"He's away," Polly said, all she was willing to say.

Anne glanced back at Shaw's house.

"I have to go, now," Anne said. "Don't give the Lupitol to the girl, whatever you do. It's only for you."

Then she went back the way she'd come, walking quickly.

"Thanks," Polly said, only half meaning it. Sloane had been so caught up in her yard play that she hadn't noticed Anne showing up. Or she was still pretending she hadn't noticed. "Come on, Sloane, grab your rake. We're going back inside."

Sloane complained but complied, dragging her rake behind her with Sisyphean weariness.

Polly went in and set the box on her kitchen table, opened it up. Inside, as promised, were rows of bottles, sealed in plastic. Polly cut those open and took out a bottle, looking it over. The Lupitol crescent smile was on the bottle, along with the drug name and the particulars of it, in terms of directions for use.

If you care, don't you dare, Pol said inside her. Polly's Lupine self always spoke to her in rhyme, as if to mock her. *That crap is a trap.*

"Go get cleaned up, Sloane," Polly said. "Then we'll have some dinner."

"Squirrel?" Sloane asked.

"No," Polly said. "Not squirrel."

Sloane pouted, then ran upstairs, muttering to herself about squirrels.

Why would the Stockwell woman have brought her this Lupitol at all? Why should she care? And she did it under Todd Shaw's nose. Polly never liked Todd Shaw. The man always lusted after Polly. Polly was used to it. Men enjoyed ogling her, and she didn't fault them for it. But Todd Shaw was one of those particularly icky guys who looked at women like trophies to be had.

Todd won't let me take it.

Polly remembered when Anne had first appeared, several years ago. Shaw had introduced her as his girlfriend, but the vibe had looked anything but friendly when she thought about it.

She'd looked fearfully ingratiating or something. Polly wasn't entirely sure. Polly hadn't thought about it perhaps as much as she should. She'd been so busy laying low and trying to remain inconspicuous, she had perhaps overlooked what was going on right next door.

Polly put the box of Lupitol on a high shelf in her pantry, kept that one bottle close at hand.

Anne was a captive of Shaw's. Polly understood the mechanics of Infective relations. If an Infective Lupine bit someone and didn't kill and/or eat them, the victim could come under the influence of the sire, for lack of a better word. Zooey Hummel had worked that angle aggressively in the duration of her own rampage, using her Infective power to compel her victims to join her on her crazed crusade. It wasn't mind control per se, so much as much as a kind of compulsion. kind of compulsion.

Shaw was clearly a Lupine and had infected Anne. Polly looked Anne up on her laptop and saw she was Director of Sales at Liminalix, and Todd Shaw was VP of Sales. Polly snooped around Anne Stockwell, seeing what there was of her. The woman was a tireless advocate for Lupitol and had been shilling for the product for quite some time, once it had secured FDA approval after clinical trials. There were clips of her at conferences, giving talks on it.

Todd Shaw was all over the Net, giving speeches, pushing Lupitol. Liminalix had gone all in on treating Night Fever. There was a shot of Chad Bastion with the President, with Shaw and Stockwell in the frame, in the background. He probably had no idea they were Lupines.

It was the kind of thing that made Polly miss her friends all the more. Lee would have had a tidy conspiracy theory about it, explaining the depth and breadth of collusion between the government and these corporate lycanthropes.

"Lycanthropy might as well be a metaphor for capitalism," Lee would have said. "It's a dog-eat-dog world, after all. What's a wolf but a big dog?"

"Werewolves are gauche," Clay would have said.

"I think they're sad," Reagan would have said. "No one should have to face their duality so forcefully."

"Duality? I'd be happy if there were *only* two sides of me," Willa would have said. "I'm multivariant."

"I don't believe in werewolves," Sheldon would have said. "They're simply part of the collective unconscious."

"I'm the only *actual* werewolf here," Sam would have said. "And you don't even know it. You're all norms!"

Why would lycanthropes be offering a treatment for lycanthropy? It was weird.

It's all about the money, honey, Pol said, answering her. *Without a cure, it's the treatment du jour.*

Liminalix had already made a fortune off the sale of Lupitol. Made by lycanthropes, for lycanthropes. It was something they'd never say, hiding under the whole Night Fever pretense. It was brilliant.

Still, she looked at the bottle of Lupitol in her hand and wondered what would happen if she took it.

THE Brotherhood and the *Lunares* arrived at the meeting place covertly, and there were two dozen of them present, as had been agreed upon. They met in the back of Disraeli's in the Gold Coast, in one of the special events rooms in the back, cordoned off by mahogany velvet ropes tethered to tarnished brass stands.

Octavio Caudillo was there, as was Jaden Cole. Each brought a pair of lieutenants, while the rest of their numbers were straight-up enforcers. These were big, strong, handpicked Lupines, real legbreakers.

Jaden was wearing a black leather jacket with a black turtleneck and black pants with polished black leather loafers, while Octavio wore a white suit with a grey overcoat. Both men looked around themselves warily, and the patrons present at Disraeli's hung out carefully and cautiously in their dark leather booths.

Waiters quickly descended on the assembled Lupines, taking drink orders. There was some risk in being in the Gold Coast, at least as both Jaden and Octavio calculated it since this was now basically undeclared hostile territory.

But maybe that was the point, when they saw Gia Rupino enter with her own entourage: a dozen Rupino bravos, all of them big and burly with the exception of four young women—the fabled triplets, the so-called Furies, and Valentina Rupino.

Seeing that the others had taken their seats, Gia greeted both Jaden and Octavio with hearty handshakes of her gloved hands. Gia wore a caramel-colored leather overcoat and matching gloves, as well as a white silk blouse and grey wool slacks with honey-hued pumps.

"So glad you could make it, *Infettivi*," Gia said, snapping a finger and having the waiters close the doors to seal off the room. Gia took her seat at the head of the mahogany table, with Jaden to her right and Octavio to her left.

"What's this about, Gia?" Jaden asked. The other Rupinos settled around the table in open seats, with the Furies sitting together, and Valentina smirking from across the table.

"What's it always about?" Gia asked. "It's about us. I thought we should have a meal, a time to talk."

"We're doing this right under Bastion's nose," Octavio said.

"This isn't *his* city," Gia said. "No matter what he pretends. It's my city. Chicago's always belonged to the Rupinos, whether Bastion accepts that or not."

"Yeah, well, you wouldn't know it the way his Loopies are rolling," Jaden said. "Bastion and his people are everywhere. And you Rupinos, I don't know. You seemed real chummy with Bastion at the Council."

Gia nodded, while the waiters reappeared and served up the drinks to the assembled Lupines. Gia waited until they'd left before she spoke.

"We've been very busy the past several years, I'll admit," Gia said. "Quite the mess your fellow *Infettivi* had left us."

"Enough of that *Infettivi* crap," Octavio said. "We're not diseased."

"Ah, but you are," Gia said. "You're all *Infettivi.* You're not like us. But we don't judge. It's why we work with you, instead of killing you."

The breezy way Gia said it rankled some of the *Lunares* and Brotherhood members, who glared at Gia, who, as ever, was impervious to their disapproval.

"Do you understand how it goes?" Gia said. "Yesterday's *Infettivi* are tomorrow's *Veronatti.*"

"What does that mean?" Jaden asked.

"It means that today you're diseased, but tomorrow, you're a dynasty," Gia said. "All you need to do is survive. We Rupinos respect survival. We respect it because *we're* survivors. Bastion and his company men would have you take his drug and, what? Become normal again? Well, almost. You'd still be what you are, but you'd tame the beasts within you. He wants to neuter you."

"Not a chance," Jaden said. "Not going back to what I was."

Gia tapped the table with her index finger.

"Exactly so," Gia said. "There's no going back. Forget going back. Bastion would have you take that Lupitol and become sheep again. Wolves cannot be sheep. We cannot pretend."

"But we'll take his money," Jaden said.

"He offered it," Gia said. "Why *wouldn't* we take that money? Lupitol will only ever go skyward in value. You'd be crazy not to take that deal. Take the money, but don't let it be a payoff."

Octavio drank his scotch and squinted at Gia.

"What are you getting at?" Octavio said.

"I don't know if Bastion has reached out to you or not," Gia said. "But if he has, you should spurn his pills for yourselves. Give them out to people, sell them, whatever. Just don't take them yourselves. You are each one of you a *Mannaro,* now. Take pride in that, little brothers. My little sisters and I, my brothers and cousins, have been crisscrossing the country for the past eight years, now, dealing with *Infettivi.* Not like you, but the rogues. The messy ones. We've been cleaning up their messes."

Wary eyes went to the Furies, who looked bored as they drank their Negronis. The word had gotten out over the years that the Furies were three of the deadliest lycanthropes around, even deadlier than the missing Ansel Rupino.

"Your point?" Jaden asked.

"You're *not* messy," Gia said, taking off her gloves and setting them on the table. "You're organized. And we Rupinos respect organization. We really do. So, we're going to work with you."

Both Jaden and Octavio exchanged glances. Anyone who was anyone in the Midwest wanted to get in good with the Rupinos. While they didn't know much about them, they knew that those who got in their way didn't live long.

Valentina spoke up, her voice sprightly and lighthearted when contrasted with Gia's mellifluous tone.

"Tell them about Black Sheep," Valentina said.

Gia smiled at her youngest sister and looked at the Lupines around the table. She ran a manicured thumb across her throat.

"No shit," Jaden said.

"Wasn't that hard, either," Valentina said. "He went down easy."

Black Sheep had been a thorn in the sides of the Infective packs, mostly because he persistently bucked their efforts at organizing while remaining a reliably savage wildcard, who could be counted on to mess things up when it suited him.

"Why?" Octavio asked.

"Because he was there," Valentina said. "The Doozies are next on our list."

"Man, they're crazy," Jaden said. "Where does this leave us? Why tell us this?"

"I want your help," Gia said. "Against our enemies."

"And who are your enemies?" Jaden asked.

"Everyone," Gia said. "And anyone."

The waiters reappeared with baskets of bread that they set out around the table, along with some antipasto platters which were set at strategic intervals. Gia studied the faces of the others, waiting for the waiters to leave.

"I'm not comfortable talking about this here," Octavio said. "What if it's bugged?"

"It's not," Gia said. "Besides, we own this place."

Jaden laughed, and Octavio shook his head.

"We're quite safe," Gia said. "From Bastion and his police, and from anyone else who might bother us. Can I continue? Please, eat while I talk to you."

The members of the *Lunares* and the Brotherhood had some of the antipasto and the bread, while Gia continued.

"The Wolves of God are a problem for us," Gia said. "They're organized. They're trying to build something up in the South. They have a place somewhere down there, a compound known as the Créche."

"No way am I going to down there," Jaden said. "The Brotherhood is strictly Chicago, Gia."

"Same for the *Lunares*," Octavio said. "It's too far away."

Gia had been prepared for that.

"Don't worry about that," Gia said. "We are going to take care of the Créche. But we want you to help us with the *Lupi di Dio* here in Chicago."

"We want you to send them to God," Valentina said, winking at them. "As soon as possible. Maximum prejudice."

Jaden and Octavio glanced at each other.

"For what? Out of the goodness of our hearts?" Jaden asked. Gia was prepared for them, shook her head.

"For their slice of the city," Gia said. "You help us with them, we'll give you their neighborhoods."

"Didn't the Saint already say you and Bastion could have his territory?" Octavio asked. Gia shrugged, grimaced at the memory.

"He said some things," Gia said. "But he's a talker, that one is."

Jaden liked that idea, but Octavio was more cautious.

"You're asking us to risk ourselves," Octavio said. "The Wargs are pretty tough."

"Yes," Gia said. "It would be hard to fight them. Lots of claws, lots of teeth, lots of blood. You must be clever and careful if you want to cull them."

"Damn right," Octavio said.

The waiters came back in with the next course, steaks all around, all filets, all cooked rare. The scent of the meat was intoxicating to the Lupines, who were eagerly snatching at their plates. Even the Rupinos savored theirs, while Gia looked on, smiling benevolently as the waiters served up the food and quickly left the room to the Lupines.

"You know we Rupinos have lots and lots of silver," Gia said. "More than any other faction. So much more. More than Bastion. More than Reverend Nicks. Far more. Even more than the *Synowie Srebra.*"

At the mention of the Poles, the Lupines grumbled and complained, muttering curses. Gia settled them.

"The Poles are nothing," Gia said. "What I'm prepared to offer you both is silver. The appropriate amount to deal with the Lupercalians."

Jaden laughed again, waving a forkful of filet mignon at Gia.

"You're going to give us silver to deal with the Wargs?" Jaden said.

"It'll make it easier," Gia said.

"And in return, we get their territory," Octavio said.

"Exactly so," Gia said. "You understand perfectly."

"But they're leaving Chicago," Jaden said. "The man said himself they were leaving."

Valentina chimed in.

"Our spies report that the Saint—sorry, Revered Nicks—is staying in Chicago. Whereas Brother Saul, the Deacon, is going to be coordinating things at the Créche. You deal with the Saint here in Chicago, we deal with the Créche. Then the Wolves of God are gone."

Octavio snorted at the thought.

"You make it sound so easy," Octavio said. "They're not an easy target."

"We know," Valentina said. "But you'll be well-equipped."

"We shouldn't even be talking about this," Octavio said. "Not here, not like this."

"I already told you we are safe here," Gia said.

Jaden was interested.

"The Brotherhood's in," Jaden said. "I don't need any persuasion to take down those racist motherfuckers."

Gia accepted that with a nod and a smile, her eyes alighting on Octavio Caudillo, who was more reserved, more reluctant.

"We're all *Infettivi,* like you say," Octavio said. "Who's to say you're not having us take each other out to weaken us, so you can just end us the way you ended the other Infectives around the country?"

Gia looked shocked at the suggestion.

"So suspicious, Octavio," Gia said. "The Black Hand has no problem with you *Lunares,* or with the Brotherhood. You respect territory, you have purged your territories of parasites and predators other than yourselves. We Rupinos respect that, as well. The only thing we'd require from you is that you acknowledge that Chicago is a Rupino city, that we are the first among equals, and not Bastion and his drug-addled East Coast upstarts."

Jaden thought it over.

"We leave you alone, you leave us alone?" Jaden asked.

"Yes," Gia said.

"What about the BEE?" Octavio asked.

"What about them?" Gia asked.

Caudillo shifted in his seat, as if uncomfortable with having to explain this to Gia at all. It should have been very clear.

"They're still hunting us," Octavio said. "Not like before. More sneaky-like, though."

"Let me worry about the BEE," Gia said. "You worry about the Wargs."

"I want your word that you'll not hunt us down," Octavio said. "Not you, not your Furies over there. Nobody."

The Furies paused in their eating to smile across the table at Octavio. The three young women were predatory-pretty, their dark Rupino hair cut in three lengths—one a short bob, one a shoulder-length shag, and one curly and mid-back. Other than that, they were identical.

"I give you my word," Gia said. "You help us, and you're safe from us. Conversely, if you don't help us, then we'll have to worry about you, and that won't go well."

"Alright," Jaden said. "I already told you I'm in, but I'm all the way in. The Brotherhood will work with you."

He held out his hand, which Gia shook. She turned her attention to Octavio, who was thinking about it while his men and everyone else looked on.

"I'm still suspicious," Octavio said. "Bastion offers us money, but you offer us, what, dirty work to do? Why don't you Rupinos just go after Nicks yourselves?"

"We are offering you a piece of the action," Gia said. "Bastion offered you money, sure. But until it's in your hands, it's all just pixie dust. I'm offering you Warg territory by right of conquest. You take the Lupercalians out in the city, you'll not only have that territory; you'll have something far more precious: my favor."

Octavio and Gia looked at one another across the table, studying each other.

"To ask your question more directly," Gia said. "We're leaving the Wargs to you because we're going to take down the Doozies and the *Volki* ourselves. The Wargs are simply your slice of the pie. Once they're all gone, we'll all be stronger, and Bastion will find himself with our three clans allied and him all alone, so far from home. Who knows what can happen then?"

Octavio clearly didn't relish being put on the spot this way. Gia could see his mind working through scenarios.

"What does your favor buy?" Octavio asked.

"The world," Gia said. "Security and the chance for legacy for your clans. Left to your own devices, who knows what could happen? You could found your own Trueborn dynasties."

Octavio glanced at Jaden, then at Gia.

"I don't trust you Trueborn. But okay, fine. We'll help you."

The waiters came back in and refilled everyone's drinks, while Gia rose and gave a toast.

"To new friends, wherever friendship leads us," she said. The others joined in as well, and everyone drank.

TIFF hadn't been helpful in arranging face time with Minton, Norm noted sourly. He'd been driving to his hideout across from Shaw's house, the spot that allowed him the best possible view with the most concealment. The nice thing about Winnetka was the spaciousness of the yards along with the plentiful foliage—there were thick groves of trees absolutely everywhere. In the evening, it was almost criminally easy to hide.

For someone like Norm, it was a cinch to get to a good spot and simply not be seen. Of course, because he was dealing with Lupines, that wasn't necessarily reassuring. They could sniff him out if they got wind of him. Speaking of that, he could hear wolves howling somewhere. He listened for a moment over the fitful breeze, decided they weren't close enough to worry about.

"Why do you want to meet with Big Bad?" Tiff asked.

"I just have some questions for him," Norm said. "Operational type questions."

"You could tell me the questions," Tiff said. "And I could relay them to him."

"No," Norm said. "I'd really rather talk to Big Bad himself."

He knew Tiff wouldn't like that. Minton maintained an increasingly active firewall around himself after the Happening. He could be called up but was reluctant to meet directly with field agents in person. Something about plausible deniability in the face of ongoing operations.

"Not going to happen, Driver," Tiff said. "Big Bad is very busy."

Norm set himself up in his hide across from Shaw's place and took out his trusty M40A5 sniper rifle, to which he'd added a sound suppressor.

"Alright," Norm said. "Well, tell him I met with the contact he wanted me to meet."

"How'd that go?" Tiff asked.

"It went fine," Norm said. "We had a lot to talk about."

"Good," Tiff replied. "Where are you now?"

"Downtown," Norm said. He didn't like lying to Tiff, but the situation required it.

"Where downtown?" Tiff asked.

"Not at liberty to divulge on an open line," Norm said.

"It's an encrypted line," Tiff said. "Where are you, Driver?"

"I'm just south of the river," Norm said. "Gotta go."

He hung up and disabled his phone, hoping Tiff wouldn't be tracking him. He fished out a burner and dialed up Sonia. She picked up on the third ring.

"Who's this?" Sonia asked.

"This is Ghost," Norm said. "No go on meeting with Big Bad."

"Too bad," Sonia said. "We're in position."

"Copy that," Norm said. He turned his attention to the Shaw residence. Shaw and Anne were both there. They were walking around inside his big house, busy doing ordinary-seeming things. Husband and wife stuff.

"Somebody's coming up the street," Sonia said in his ear, on the radio. "Liminalix van."

Norm glanced down the street, saw the van approaching.

"I see it," Norm said. Norm knew that it would have been better, perhaps, to confront Shaw directly, to have it out with him. But the man was an Infective, and Norm knew better than anyone how that typically went. You never crossed Lupines directly, not if you wanted to survive.

The van, a white van with the Liminalix logo on the side of it in black, pulled into Shaw's driveway. Four men got out. They opened the back of the van. They pulled out some trunks, put them on hand trucks. There were four trunks.

"Looks like they're getting their victim deliveries," Norm said. "Curbside service."

"Monsters," Sonia said.

The front door opened, and there was Shaw, wearing a maroon track suit and looking as smug as ever. Norm wouldn't have minded eavesdropping on what was being said, but it would have been too unwieldy.

He saw Anne appear at the door as well, looking on nervously. Shaw moved around a lot, wasn't a sit-still sort of guy. This posed challenges for Norm, trying to get the shot. In moments, Shaw was back inside the house, directing his guys with the trunks.

Norm thought about his promise to Minton, and then he let that go. It wasn't fair for him to ask that of him. Not where Anne was concerned.

In a few minutes, the men came back out, and one of them held a digital clipboard for Shaw to sign. That was Norm's moment. Only Liminalix would have a sign-off for the delivery of victims.

He controlled his breathing and zeroed Shaw in his night vision scope, seeing the man in phosphorescent green, backlit by the open door. His prick face filled Norm's field of vision.

Without hesitation, because, in his line of work, hesitation meant death, Norm squeezed off a shot. The M40A5 gave its suppressive cough and Norm found immense satisfaction in seeing Shaw's head explode from the high-velocity silver bullet that found its mark. Shaw went flying backward, blood spraying the front of the house and the entryway, his body falling on the front porch, flailing as it fell.

The delivery men looked around in shock, while Anne reappeared at the doorway, stunned, mouth open.

"Packaged delivered," Norm said, then noticed that the delivery men were scrambling, zipping off their jumpsuits and transforming on the lawn. All four of them were Lupines. It was almost too easy, Norm thought, watching the men writhe as they turned. He dropped three of them in the amount of time it took for them to transform. The fourth one had managed to fully turn, and had gone bounding across the big lawn, this grey lycanthropic specter, a vision of fur and teeth.

Anne was still shocked, standing backlit in the doorway, clutching her forehead.

Meanwhile, the werewolf had zeroed in on Norm based on the number of shots he'd fired, and the thing was tearing across the lawn at him. It was a terrifying sight, the kind of thing that would have staggered almost anyone without familiarity with this sort of work. The Lupine would be on his position in about thirty seconds. Norm told himself to keep cool but fought to keep calm before the specter of onrushing death.

In this case, the Lupine's aggressive determination would prove his undoing, as he was charging straight at Norm. A better move would have been zigzagging, of course. But this guy wasn't thinking. He was out for blood.

Norm could hear the panting as the Lupine ate up distance between them. Norm knew that if he missed, he would be a dead man. So, he didn't miss. He fired off another shot, the rifle's suppressor nearly gassed out, sounding more like a clap than a cough, but the silver bullet found its mark, right between the eyes, and the Lupine was knocked back by the force of the ballistic impact, thrashing on the lawn before dying.

Norm had put a brass catcher bag on his rifle, the spent casing ringing as they dropped into it. Then he quickly put the rifle into its camouflaged field case and slipped it on his back as he emerged from his hiding place.

Anne saw him approach, while Sonia and her people drove up in their van, pulling into the driveway. All of them wore black ski masks with the *Synowie* cross stitched on their foreheads in silver thread.

Norm walked up to Anne, who looked shocked at the sight of him.

"Norm?" Anne said, although she knew it was him. "Jesus Christ, what have you done?"

"I'm rescuing you," Norm said.

He walked past the bodies of the delivery men, all of them looking human again.

"What makes you think I needed rescuing, Norm?" Anne asked. "What?"

She stared gravely at him.

"This is who I am, now," Anne said. "What I am."

Then she threw herself to the ground and began to transform, her body contorting as she went through the limbic labyrinth of lycanthropy, adding mass, sprouting golden fur, her manicured fingernails lengthening to knife-like claws. Her overly white teeth becoming fangs, her green eyes growing larger and taking on a predatory cast.

She turned quickly, which Norm knew meant that, as an Infective, she'd transformed many times. It always went faster for them when they got used to the stress of the change. A seasoned Infective could turn within a minute. For someone like Norm, however, she might as well have been turning in slow motion. He had all the time in the world.

Norm drew a tranquilizer pistol and fired three darts into her. The gun had heavy duty tranquilizer, the veterinary stuff that they used at zoos to deal with big animals. Three shots, and Anne managed only a half-assed leap for him before collapsing to the ground, deep in dreamland. She turned back to her human disguise, and Norm was quick to grab a blanket from inside Shaw's place to wrap her with. He hoisted her up and walked her to the *Synowie* van, where Sonia looked on, curious.

"We'll take her to the agreed-upon safe house," Sonia said. "You should get out of here."

"Yeah," Norm said. "Don't forget about the trunks they carted in. There might be people in there, instead of bodies."

Sonia nodded, said something quickly in Polish to one of her men, who went in.

Norm set Anne down in the back of the van, which was bisected by a cage. He put Anne in the cage, closing it, locking it.

"Don't hurt her," Norm said.

"Don't worry," Sonia said. "She's in good hands."

Norm could see the *Synowie*—of whom there were four young men, were quickly gathering the bodies of the delivery men and carting them to the back of the Liminalix van, where they set them. They moved with speed and precision. Ordinarily, they would simply leave the dead where they were. But Norm had wanted to be discreet in this case, because of his own involvement in it.

As if on cue, his secure phone chirped. It was Tiff. Norm didn't pick up.

13

SERGEI Tolkachev was not happy. He had planned to have a meeting at Kiosk, one of his favorite restaurants in the Chicagoland area, only to have it interrupted by some talk of attacks on his properties near Buffalo Grove.

Something involving Lupines, by the sound of it. Something bloody.

Tolkachev had been infected in the early days of the Happening, around 2008, when he'd been snapped at by one of his girlfriends. Irina had bitten him during sex, and he'd gotten infected. It hadn't been the worst thing to happen to him that year, which had been a hectic one, in terms of handling his money laundering and sex-slave businesses.

While the lycanthropy Irina had inflicted on him had made his life more complicated, Sergei had found it more than useful after he'd found that he was nearly invulnerable to harm. Without any moral qualms about his condition, he'd transitioned from gangster to were-criminal with almost ludicrous ease. Irina had fled when he'd confronted her about it, but he didn't mind. He'd track her down eventually.

He had put together his *Volki* as a subgroup within the larger Russian criminal underground operating in Chicago. It had taken some planning on his part, some appropriate application of ritual to bring members on board, but once Sergei had made it clear to them what they were gaining, they accepted it. The looks on rivals' faces when they'd transform and tear them apart had been worth it. It was worth it to lose the tattoos they'd earned, when contrasted with the rightful terror they inflicted on their enemies.

Some of the other members of the Russian *Bratva* had put their heads together and realized something was different about the *Volki*. But when Tolkachev got word of others attempting to get infected, he'd have his *Volki* pay them visits and kill them.

The *Volki* were nearly untouchable, except for the required nod to the Rupinos. And even that was something he was prepared to deal with eventually.

He and a dozen of his men pulled up in three white SUVs to see that the police were already there, surveying the slaughter at one of his laundromats.

Tolkachev got out and went to the police officer who appeared to be in charge.

"What's going on?" Tolkachev asked, after introducing himself as the owner of the Jiffy-Wash Laundromat.

"Looks like a multiple homicide, Mr. Tolkachev," the officer said. "We're seeing six dead here. It's pretty brutal."

The police had put up tape around it, but Sergei would see inside. There was blood everywhere. It was run by his three of his men, all three who were presumed to be among the dead. He glanced up the street, saw a black SUV parked. It was enough to catch his eye, but he had a lot on his mind.

"Can I go inside?" Tolkachev. "I can maybe help identify the bodies."

"We actually already have, Mr. Tolkachev," the officer said. "This looks like some kind of animal attack, but we know it couldn't be that. It's a bloodbath. Nothing was stolen from the look of things, and, uh, the wallets and IDs of the victims were lined up on one of the dryers. We're thinking it's some kind of cult thing, honestly. I'd recommend you go home. We'll have detectives get in touch with you if we find anything."

Tolkachev gazed at the blood and the carnage that looked even ghastlier under the fluorescent lighting and nodded. The officer didn't even go there in terms of who Tolkachev might know who would have done this.

There was no way of speaking to this without incriminating himself.

"Thank you, Officer," Tolkachev said. He got back into his SUV and told his man to drive him out of there. Glancing back at where the black SUV was, he saw that it was gone.

Where to start? He'd start at the top and work his way down.

He dialed up Gia Rupino, who picked up.

"Gia," Tolkachev said.

"Sergei," Gia said. "What a nice surprise."

"Someone murdered some of my people near Buffalo Grove," Tolkachev said.

"Someone familiar to us?" Gia asked.

"Yes," he said. "It looks like it. Six people torn apart. I think someone's targeting me."

"Maybe Nicks?" Gia asked. "Where are you now?"

"Don't worry about that," Tolkachev said. "This isn't supposed to happen. I'm in good standing, yes?"

"Who do you think might have done this?" Gia asked.

Tolkachev worked his brain. Who gained most from attacking him? The Poles were the likeliest choice, but it was so clearly a Lupine attack, it couldn't have been them. It could have been rivals within the *Bratva*. He couldn't rule that out.

The Wolves of God were no friends to the *Volki*, of course. Nothing was beneath them. The *Lunares* and Brotherhood were possibilities, but Buffalo Grove was a stretch for them, in terms of reach. The Doozies were strictly city dwellers.

"Maybe the Babas?" Gia asked. Tolkachev and the others had heard about the murder of Black Sheep, found decapitated on a Brown Line El stop the other day. "Maybe they think you murdered their leader?"

"No," Tolkachev said. "Those animals wouldn't have known about my laundromats. Someone knew that was my place. They were sending me a message."

A fist of ice clutched Tolkachev's heart. It wasn't anyone in the *Bratva*. They wouldn't have dared to take him on. It was Gia.

"It was you," he said. "You did this."

"What?" Gia said. "No, not me, Sergei. Maybe Bastion?"

"No," Tolkachev said. "You."

"Why would I even do that?" Gia asked. "We're friends, Sergei."

Sergei muted his phone and ordered his men to drive to their meeting place in Palatine. It was fortified and he'd feel safer there.

"Are we?" Tolkachev asked.

"We've been on the Council together for years," Gia said. "You're a good and faithful partner. Maybe Bastion's having a go at you. Some sort of power play. Maybe he doesn't want to give up those shares after all. We should all worry."

Tolkachev tried to square what he was hearing with what he was thinking, while his men drove him toward Palatine.

"You're saying it wasn't you or your people?" Tolkachev said.

"We aren't animals, Sergei," Gia said. "We're businesspeople. Like yourself."

The light up ahead turned red, and Tolkachev's convoy stopped.

"Business depends on reliable partnerships, people you can trust," Gia said.

A dozen black SUVs approached the *Volki* vehicles, pulling up on either side of them, three on either side, with six behind them.

Tolkachev saw it at once, ordered his men to run the red light, which they did. The fleet of black SUVs pursued his own.

"There are vehicles pursuing me," Tolkachev said.

"Are they BEE vehicles?" Gia asked.

"I don't know," Tolkachev, glancing behind him. The SUVs had fallen back, were merely tailing them. "They're unmarked. Black SUVs."

"You should get somewhere safe, Sergei," Gia said.

There was a flash of something up ahead and, as the tires of the Tolkachev's SUVs burst, he realized someone had set up spike strips. As his three-vehicle convoy careened to a stop in a flurry of torn rubber, Tolkachev cursed.

"They're coming for me, Gia," Tolkachev said, then his call was dropped, and he wasn't able to dial out. They were jamming the phones.

The SUVs that had been pursuing them had held back, and he saw the spike strips were pulled away by black-clad figures.

Tolkachev wasn't going to waste time.

"Get out and kill them," Tolkachev said, but before his men could do so, the black SUVs drove up and pinioned his own, an SUV to either side of them. They couldn't open the doors to get out.

Tolkachev wasn't going to go out this way, trapped like an animal. He started to transform as the bullets began firing. Automatic weapons, suppressed by the soft sound of them, and stinking of silver. Tolkachev took a half-dozen bullets before he even realized they were firing.

His SUV was a spray of bullets and blood and broken glass for ten dreadful seconds, then those vehicles drove off, leaving six more behind them.

Tolkachev managed to crawl out of his SUV, blood pouring from his wounds as he fought to transform, praying that his healing ability would let him recover enough to manage to crawl out into the woods.

The other SUVs pulled up and he could hear people getting out. He heard more shots fired. Double taps to ensure that the dead were truly dead.

Tolkachev growled as his suit split, but the silver bullets remained inside him like burning barbs, white-hot within. He could heal from almost any injury, but silver took such a toll.

A black-gloved hand fished out his cell phone from his shredding pocket, and Tolkachev rolled over to see Valentina Rupino looking down at him, smiling widely, pocketing his phone.

She held a gloved finger to her lips as Sergei sprouted fur and claws and grew large as he bled out on the motorway. It was a tug of war between life and death, his limbs strengthening and lengthening even as the mortal wounds he took bled. He would prevail. This was only a setback. Many had tried to kill him before.

Fearless, she crouched near him, watching him transform. Why she waited this way was perverse to him. Why wait? What could she gain? She glanced over her shoulder, at the beckoning bare trees of the wintering woods, looked back at him meaningfully. She could tell he wanted to go there. There was creature comfort in the woods that every lycanthrope could understand.

"No matter how much you feed a wolf, he will always return to the forest," Valentina said.

Damnable Rupinos, Tolkachev thought, his rage giving him strength. Wounded or not, he would tear them apart. Even as his blood continued to run on the street, the blood of his men poured from their bullet-riddled SUVs, the rage fueled him.

"The wolf changes his coat, but not his disposition," Valentina said. She held a silenced pistol to his forehead, grinning at him. "Sweet dreams."

She fired two shots into his temple, dropped the pistol by his body. She wolf-whistled for the others' attention, who were finishing shooting the others in their heads. They'd left a bloody mess by the roadside, and the sooner they got out of there, the better.

"Pack it up. Turn off the jammer," Valentina said, dialing up Gia once she could. "It's done."

"Good girl," Gia said.

"WHERE THERE
ARE SHEEP,
THE WOLVES ARE
NEVER VERY FAR AWAY."
—PLAUTUS

MINA saw Sonia and her men come to the safe house with an unconscious middle-aged woman who'd been stuck with three tranquilizer darts.

"What's all this?" Mina asked.

"Field trip," Sonia said. "Help us with the doors, Dr. Milkowski."

She did as Sonia asked, opening the doors ahead of them, while the *Synowie* carted the woman to the prison cell in the basement of the safe house. It was Mina's home away from home, where she'd retire when she was about to transform. She'd last been in there a month ago, when Animus had forced herself out of her. It was that transformation that had persuaded Mina to take her chances and try Lupitol.

"Who is that?" Mina asked, while they put her into the cell. Sonia took out the tranquilizer darts and then closed the cage door, checking it to be sure it was locked. She tossed the darts into a trash can and composed herself.

"This is Norm's wife, Anne Stockwell," Sonia said. "She's an Infective, like you."

"What's she doing here?" Mina said, as they went back upstairs.

"Sleeping, for now," Sonia said. "Norm wants to talk to her. Personally, I think it's a waste of time, but he's a surprisingly sentimental fellow, given what he does. Come, join us for a drink."

Around the kitchen table, they'd poured out five shots of Krupnik, which each of them took, holding aloft.

"*Na zdrowie! Do ludzkości,*" they said, drinking down their shots.

To health! To humanity, Mina said to herself, the sweet liquid fire of the liquor hitting her hard.

Sonia set down her glass and guided Mina away from the table, while the other *Synowie* had a few more shots.

"We freed four victims from some Lupines," Sonia said. "They were going to be dinner for some nasty Loopies. But thanks to Norm and us, they're alive. Scared, but alive. One of those rare moments when we weren't simply killing."

"Loopies," Mina said. "What was Norm doing there?"

"Norm was shooting," Sonia said. "He's a very good shot."

"He was a Warden, remember?" Mina said.

"How could I forget?" Sonia said. "Tonight was a good night. Five dead *Wilkołaki*. That makes me happy, Doctor. We disposed of their bodies. No evidence, no worries. *Ogień oczyszcza.*"

Fire cleanses, Mina thought.

"It's going to take more than fire to purify a quintuple homicide," Mina said.

"We'll see," Sonia said. "We're very good at disposal."

Mina found it hard to square the genteel and formal familiarity of the *Synowie* with their conduct in the field, where they were accomplished and experienced killers.

"What about the victims?" Mina asked. "Did they see you?"

"No," Sonia said. "Well, not exactly."

She took out her black *Synowie* ski mask, held it out for Mina, who took it and turned it over in her hands. She could see the silver *Synowie* cross on the forehead, carefully, perfectly stitched.

"We wore our masks, they did not see," Sonia said. "We know what we are doing, Doctor."

Mina was certain that was true but took little solace in it. The *Synowie* were at peace with their mission, but it didn't mean that Mina wouldn't worry. Her own mind was geared toward calculation and analysis, not the mechanics of kidnapping and murder.

"I very much like Norm," Sonia said. "He's very professional. I can respect that. Except in the matter of his wife, of course. Less professional, that. That is rather more personal for him."

"As to be expected," Mina said. "Can't fault him for that."

Sonia took back her mask and ran her hands over the thing.

"It will get him killed, I fear," Sonia said. "You can't help who you love, of course. But there's real danger, there. The woman in our basement, his wife. She's a danger to us. I would have simply put her out of her misery then and there. But Norm wants to talk to her. He's going to be disappointed."

"We're not all bad," Mina said, prompting a sad smile from Sonia.

"You're better than most, Doctor," Sonia said. "I've never seen any Infective suffer through the malady for so many years and retain some semblance of themselves the way you have."

Mina didn't quite know whether to be flattered or insulted by Sonia's frank assessment of her. Was she only a semblance of herself? Sonia hadn't known her before she'd been infected, only knew her when Animus was inside her, gnawing at her soul. It hardly mattered that Animus was forced to take only tiny bits at a time.

I have all the patience in the world, Animus murmured in her head.

"What does Norm expect regarding his wife?" Mina asked.

"I have no idea," Sonia said. "But he was insistent. And we *Synowie* only want to help a fellow hunter of monstrous things."

Sonia guided Mina into the living room, where one of Sonia's brothers had turned on the television, which was covering something about some gangland murders taking place just west of the Loop. A number of members of the First Lupercalian Church of the Apocalyptic Vision had been gunned down by a group of gun-toting gang members.

The Reverend Marcus Nicks was on-camera, wearing a white suit and a hefty gold cross around his neck, and a look of pale-faced indignation. His bright blue eyes seemed to bore into the cameras upon him. His blond hair was slicked back, and his rage was apparent.

"This cold-blooded murder on the doorsteps of our holy church," Nicks said. "It's a testament to the depravity of this city. A dozen good, honest Americans—churchgoing folk—were shot dead in front of our church by cowardly murderers."

Nicks had high cheekbones, and almost effeminate look to him. Sonia made a finger pistol and shot him from where she sat on the sofa.

"The Reverend," Sonia said. "Somebody's having a go at him."

"Looks like it," Mina said. She could see the sheets they'd put on the bodies until they could be removed from the crime scene.

"We will pray for the souls of our lost lambs," Nicks said. "We will pray for them. I'm holding a special service tonight, all are welcome, that we might remember the poor victims murdered by these gangland predators."

Mina wondered who would have done it. From what she'd been able to glean since the pack-gangs took over the city, the Wolves of God were a formidable group, with great numbers and a degree of organized savagery that made them particularly dangerous.

"This is some internecine Lupine conflict," Sonia said. "Turf, I would imagine. Or a message. Perhaps a distraction. Most of the Wolves of God have left the city for the South."

Mina marveled at the matter-of-fact manner of Sonia.

"If you know Reverend Nicks is a Lupine, why wouldn't your people have already killed him?" Mina asked.

"He's almost impossible to reach," Sonia said. "At least for any of us. He has Sniffers in his ranks. It's what we call them. *Wąchacze.* They sniff out silver. Nobody with silver gets near the Saint."

Mina imagined these Lupines ambling around, sniffing the air, like bloodhounds.

"What about a sniper?" Mina asked. "Attacking from a distance?"

"Of course," Sonia said. "But it's not as easy as you might guess. Not in the city. Nicks keeps a busy schedule. To be able to snipe him, we'd have to have someone in position at just the right time, evading detection, and getting the shot. We've certainly tried. He's well-protected. It's why Norm's successful…culling…of his target tonight was so impressive. With someone like that helping the *Synowie,* we'd be able to make a bigger dent than we have in years."

Reverend Nicks excused himself from the reporters and went quickly into the Lupercalian church, where some burly guards in black blocked the doors from any too-ardent observers, while Chicago Police Department was investigating the crime scene and taping it off from onlookers.

"CPD," Sonia said. "Maybe it was Bastion's men who did the killing. Although that seems unlikely. If Bastion were gunning for the Saint, he'd have already sent him to Hell."

If there were security camera shots of the murders, they weren't being publicly shared, yet.

"Before the Happening, we had quite a network," Sonia said. "We had people everywhere. That makes me sad to think back on, relative to today. It makes me sadder that I'm telling this to a *Zakaźny.* Is this what my life has come to?"

Mina again felt put out by the implication and did her best to shelve it for the sake of diplomacy. She feared being kicked out, where who knew what would happen to her.

A breaking news story appeared about a mass shooting up in Buffalo Grove that claimed the life of area businessman Sergei Tolkachev. The cameras showed three bullet-riddled SUVs with dozens of dead men in them, including Tolkachev, who was laid out in the street, victim of an execution-style slaying.

Sonia leaned forward to watch this more closely.

Reporters spoke of a monstrous mass murder in a laundromat near Buffalo Grove, one that had been owned by Tolkachev. In it, six victims had been brutally murdered in what authorities were characterizing as an almost cult-style mass execution.

The area police were speculating that the murders may have been connected, although they were still investigating.

"Ha," Sonia said. "Something *is* going on. First Black Sheep, then the attack on Nicks and his people, and Tolkachev. Somebody's going after the leading factions."

Sonia went to her phone and texted someone. Mina watched the coverage, feeling uneasy. The facility with murder at the heart of lycanthropy stirred Animus within her, and she felt that strongly.

Let me out, you tourist, Animus said. *I don't belong in here with you.*

"I'd like to go to the Landa Library," Mina said. "Might do me some good."

Sonia nodded absently, clicking her way through channels. All of the local channels were covering the shootings in both parts of the city. Sonia was texting like a fiend, her fingers working quickly as she did so.

"Sure," Sonia said. "We'll go tomorrow."

"You know, I'd like to help more," Mina said. "The *Synowie* have been so good to shelter me these years. I'd like to do more than I have been. I want to be useful."

"You have been," Sonia replied. Sonia looked Mina over, that appraising sidelong look she had, giving up nothing, taking in everything.

"About these killings," Mina said. "Not your people, right?"

Sonia shook her head. "If only. Tolkachev was a bastard maneuverer. More an opportunistic criminal than a pure lycanthrope. For him, lycanthropy merely gave him an edge on his rivals."

"Who do you think killed him?" Mina asked.

"Had to be either the Rupinos or Bastion," Sonia said. "The manner of the execution of Tolkachev is curious—feels more Bastion than Rupino in approach. Rupinos like to get their hands dirty. Like that killing of Black Sheep? Pure Rupino. Old school. I don't know about Tolkachev. Maybe the Trueborn in the city are teaming up to take out the Infectives. *Synowie* are increasing surveillance throughout Chicagoland."

Mina felt some comfort and concern about that, almost in equal measure. Comfort in that it might mean more information coming in, but concern in that it would put Sonia and the others at greater risk. Mina became aware of Sonia studying her a moment in silence.

"What?"

"How is the Lupitol working out?" Sonia asked.

"It's effective," Mina said. "Shockingly so."

"Good," Sonia said. "I've been meaning to ask you—while on the drug, can you transform?"

Mina nearly blushed. She hated to think of Animus at all. But thanks to the drug, Animus was bound in opalescent chains inside her. Still able to make her presence felt, but somehow diminished. Quieter, though not tamer.

"I don't think I can," Mina said. "I don't know how it works, but the urge to turn just isn't there. And the incessant head-chatter is nearly gone. It's like it muzzles my other half."

Sonia nodded at this.

"Amazing," she said. "So, even if your life depended on it, you couldn't transform?"

"Uh, I hope not to ever have to test that," Mina said. The clinical way that Sonia asked put Mina on edge. "You're not going to kill me, right?"

Sonia sighed, shaking her head. "Of course not. I promised Patryk that we'd keep you safe, and we *Synowie* honor our commitments far more often than we break them. However, if we were attacked, I'd like to know what you're capable of in your current condition."

"I'm no killer," Mina said. "I'm a scientist."

"Fair enough," Sonia said. "We can go to the library tomorrow."

2

NORM drove through Chicago in his jeep, mindful of not drawing attention. During the day, in the sunlight, it wasn't as easy to tell who was still a person and who was one of them. The killing of Shaw had almost gone too smoothly for his tastes. It made him suspicious.

The murders of the *Volki* in the northwest were curious as well. That degree of gangland bloodshed was willfully visible. Sergei Tolkachev had been one of the more effective Infectives, having put his criminal underground knowledge to work as a lycanthrope. That he'd been targeted by someone meant he'd either crossed the wrong Lupines or else the BEE had been up to something.

He dialed up Tiff.

"Dealer, this is Driver," Norm said. "I saw the news this morning."

"Which news?" Tiff asked.

"Uh, the dirty laundry," Norm said. "Up north?"

"Yes?"

"That wasn't us, was it?" Norm asked.

"No, it was not," Tiff said. "We would have sent Recovery if it had been us."

Norm acknowledged that.

"True, true," Norm said. "So, who was it?"

"Not sure," Tiff said. "There has been an increase in activity—Black Sheep on the El platform, the attack on the Saint's people, and some influential Loopies have gone missing as well. You wouldn't know anything about that, would you, Driver?"

"Not me, Dealer," Norm said, cursing as the call dropped.

The signs of Lupines were everywhere—blood hosed off the sidewalk without comment by the shopkeepers. Graffiti on the walls cursed out the Lupines in furtive corners. Other graffiti praised them with pentagrams—OUT FOR BLOOD. WE SEE YOU. WE ARE COMING, NORMS.

Norm drove and gripped the wheel while Tiff called him again. So she didn't worry, or perhaps worse, contact anyone to check on him, Norm answered.

"Driver here," Norm said. "Sorry about the dropped call, Dealer."

"What's your situation, Driver?" Tiff asked.

"Driving," Norm said.

"Driving where?" Tiff asked. Norm could hear the level of annoyance in her tone. Just a bit, but there, all the same.

"Heading to my place," Norm said. "Is there a problem?"

"We're getting some chatter about a hit on the Saint's people," Tiff said. "But nothing on the *Volki* one."

"Wasn't me," Norm said, although he wished it had been. "Although I've gotten some good information on the Saint. Something Big Bad would like to hear."

Tiff wasn't going to play ball.

"You can leave the information at one of your drops," Tiff said.

"Okay," Norm said.

He was only a few minutes from the Lincoln Park safe house that Sonia had told him they were taking Anne.

Norm watched to be sure he wasn't being tailed. It was possible. While some of the Lupines tried to play werewolf by day, few of the Infectives had the stones to run with their affliction in the daylight. Most who stalked prey by day did so as pretenders, wrapped up tight in their human disguises.

He welcomed the pretenders because they were easier to kill. If he had his choice, he'd take a pretender over a full-furred Lupine any day.

"Pretenders" was his own pet name for them. They were legit lycanthropes. But by the time they realized they shouldn't be chasing Norm in their skin suits, it was too late. Shaw and his goons learned that the hard way. He was still pleased with himself for that one, even though he knew Minton would have a fit once word got out that Shaw "disappeared."

Norm parked his jeep and got out, looking around. He was certain he hadn't been followed but decided to take a leisurely stroll around the block, rather than beelining for the safe house, just in case. Stinger logic required it of him.

He took the scent of the air, like he was one of them. It was chilly, the interminable Chicago autumn that was really only winter wearing a coy mask to disguise itself. For anybody living in Chicago, the good weather was a hopeful promise never fully realized. It was a tease.

Norm caught a glimpse of himself in one of the windows as he walked. Old enough to know better, but young enough to still care. The Lupines had robbed the world of some precious part of itself. the Happening had taken it away. Norm remembered how it had been. Not perfect, but not this.

Strong-jawed, wearing glasses more often than not, short-haired, broad-shouldered. He looked like he'd have been more comfortable as a carved statue, something in a museum. Maybe that's what he was— a museum specimen for a world long lost. It didn't matter, not to him. He was human. That was enough.

He wore a blue baseball cap when he was out in the city. Anything to make it harder for the ever-present cameras to identify him, without standing out too much. He walked on the sidewalk as cars drove by. People made their way, trying not to stand out as targets. They all pretended that everything was normal.

That was the part Norm struggled with the most. The normality of it all. People all around, busy pretending that the abnormal was somehow routine. Even the Lupines went through the motions of their former lives as a kind of atonement for whatever their transformative transgressions were.

If everybody just went through the motions, maybe they could put it past them that they had been eating dogs, or each other, or normal people the night before.

Minton would kill him for transgressing regarding Shaw.

Norm could actually hear Minton chewing him out about it.

But he'd been careful.

He and the *Synowie* had made Shaw and his men simply disappear. Maybe someday the CPD would find the burned-out van and the bodies within it. They'd find the silver bullets and understand that it had been a hit. They might be able to identify the bodies. Bastion would be pissed about it, would seek some sort of reprisals.

But he wouldn't know who was responsible. And, with the attacks on the Lupercalians and Tolkachev and his *Volki*, maybe it would distract Minton. To a certain set of eyes, it would look like the Lupines were killing each other off. Minton was a linear sort of thinker. That would be an acceptable explanation for him.

Norm reached the intersection and waited for the lights to change. He blended in. That was something he was good at, despite being a big man. He looked like he could be anybody. He didn't stand out.

A trio of feral youths joined him at the intersection, full of hubris and youthful fire. They were playing with their smartphones, heads bobbing. They wore bland clothes—army green jackets and ordinary sneakers. One had a Suck Junkies tee shirt that had seen better days. Their hair was unruly, uncolored, unsullied. They wore no earrings, no tattoos. That was a hallmark of Lupines—the healing factor of lycanthropy scoured the body of vanities like that.

One of them, the ringleader of the pack—long-nosed and button-eyed, the kid sniffed the air and glowered at him.

"You smell that, boys?" he asked. The others followed the alpha's lead, sniffing the air.

"Silver," one of them said. He was chubbier than his pack mates, the omega of this trio. He had curly brown hair. As the omega, he had to be smarter than the other two.

"That's right," the alpha said, sneering. "Contraband."

"Whoa, boys," Norm said, holding up my hands. "You've got the wrong idea."

The alpha just held onto his sneer, looked Norm over. He was bigger than these boys, but he knew they could kill him if provoked.

"What have you got on you, old man?" The alpha asked. "Precious keepsakes?"

The light changed, and Norm crossed the street, the pack of boys following on his heels. They had to be Wargs. The alpha was angry at having Norm walk away from him. He clearly wasn't used to that. They were probably 18 or 19, by the look of them. Early college, tops. Local boys.

"Something like that," Norm said. "From my mom."

"Oh, how precious is that?" the alpha asked. He held out his hand. "How about you deposit it here, for safekeeping? You know anything about what happened at the church?"

The three of them circled Norm, clearly spoiling for a fight.

"I don't know anything about it," Norm said.

"Some bangers came to our church," the alpha said. "Shot up a bunch of our people. Silver bullets, yo. You got silver bullets on you, Slick?"

"Yes," Norm said. He hadn't wanted to have a confrontation like this. Not before meeting with Anne.

"So, you heard him, Loser. Cough it up," the beta said. He was ugly, without the lean silhouette of the alpha, or the portly presence of the omega. This was a small pack, low-hanging fruit in the Warg hierarchy. Sniffers, by their own admission. Sniffers were lower-tier Wargs, out to make names for themselves by being useful to the leadership.

Norm looked around them, which the alpha took to be a sign of fear and weakness. In truth, Norm was simply assessing whether

CPD was around or not. He took off running, heading off the main streets, while the Sniffers went after him.

"We were hoping you'd run, Old Man," the alpha yelled, calling after him.

But Norm was in better shape than they expected, as he kept running, dashing down a side street, one with plenty of trees and fewer cameras. He would take them out there.

He drew his Glock 18 and thumbed automatic fire. There wasn't time to screw on a suppressor, so he spun and fired a burst of shots into the chest of the alpha, who was knocked back by it. Norm took out the beta with a burst to the face.

Both of the Sniffers dropped in seconds, leaving the omega standing there, gape-mouthed, stunned. In the span of less than a moment, he'd seen the dynamic shift. He was the alpha, now.

"You…you're HIM," the omega said. "The Walking Death."

Norm fished out his suppressor, screwing it on while the omega looked on, his skin swelling as he gazed down as his dead compatriots, bleeding on the sidewalk. The omega was such a newbie, risking a transform right in front of a well-prepared adversary.

But the instincts were there, and that's where he went. It was a weird moment, Norm screwing on his suppressor for his pistol while the omega split his skin and sprouted fur, claws, and fangs. How this would play out was based on who was faster.

Staying out of arm's reach, Norm leveled his pistol and switched it to standard fire mode, dropping the omega with two shots to the head, putting him out of his misery before his transformation completed.

Norm didn't relish killing these pups. But they were coming for him, and he slipped his pistol into his waistband and called it in quickly while vacating the scene.

"Driver to Dealer," Norm said.

"Go ahead, Driver," Tiff said.

"Cleanup on Webster, one block off the main avenue," Norm said. "Three targets. Can't miss them."

"Alright," Tiff said. "Are you okay?"

Norm thought about that a moment or two. Was he okay? Sure.

"I'm not hurt," Norm said. "Those three were Wargs. Out for blood. Said something about bangers hitting their church."

"It's what I was telling you about," Tiff said. "Somebody hit the Wargs at the First Lupercalian Church. Right out front."

"You want me to find out who?" Norm asked. There was a pause, and then she replied.

"On it already," Tiff said. Of course she was. That was a Dealer thing to do. The Bureau had probably already sent some drones over there to observe.

"Alright," Norm said. "Signing off."

"Driver—" Tiff said, but Norm had already hung up. He could hear some CPD sirens, likely somebody calling because of his shooting, although he'd been very quick, hadn't made too much noise. The proverbial firecrackers going off.

The real issue would be joggers and dogwalkers coming across the crime scene. Not that Norm saw it as a crime scene. For him, it had been simple self-defense.

But since Bastion had assets within the police, Norm had to be careful. He made his way a block from the triple homicide, hearing the police sirens growing louder. Then he ducked into an alley, startled to hear a slow clap.

In the alley was a young woman, dark-haired and big-eyed, wearing a black leather jacket and a black skirt with polished black combat boots. She mockingly slow-clapped some more, so he knew it was her who'd been doing it.

"Nice shooting, *Paisan,*" she said. Norm went to draw his pistol, but she tsked him with a painted, pointing finger, showing three hulking she-wolves standing there, just a few feet away, lurking in the shadows. They were pure Rupino, all rippling muscle and wild blue eyes, black-furred abominations who'd somehow managed to sneak up on him. Norm knew that if they'd wanted to kill him, he'd already have been dead, so he made a point to raise his hand as peacefully as he could.

He had heard about those three Lupines—the Furies, they were called. Some wags called them the Furries, but not to their faces. They were a mini-pack within Clan Rupino, a trio of enforcers.

"I'm Valentina Rupino," the young woman said. "I'm here to talk with you, Mr. Stockwell. We're admirers of your handiwork. You're a real cool under pressure sort of dude, aren't you?"

"What's this about?" Norm asked. He wondered how she knew his name, but wasn't going to ask her that. He'd find out on his own.

Valentina smirked at him.

"You're a Stinger, am I right?" Valentina asked. She wrinkled her nose, imitated a bee flitting around, her index finger a bee trying to find its mark. She mimed looking afraid.

"I'm supposed to be somewhere," Norm said.

"Aren't we all?" Valentina said. A black SUV pulled up beside them. "Want to take a drive with us?"

Norm glanced at the Furies, who were all three watching him with that riveting blue-eyed stare Rupinos always seemed to have.

"Do I have a choice?" Norm asked.

Valentina shook her head, winking at him. Another Rupino, a young man in a black suit, opened the passenger side of the SUV and hopped out, looking dismissively at Norm, before opening the back passenger door.

"Please, Mr. Stockwell," Valentina said. "Before CPD comes rolling on by and things get messier."

He could hear the Furies growling, baring their teeth.

"I don't think we'll all fit," Norm said.

"Oh, don't worry about them," Valentina said. "Just you and me. And, you know, my cousins who're driving and literally riding shotgun. But I want your word you're not going to do anything stupid while you're with us."

"Stupid, like what?" Norm asked.

"Like trying to kill any of us," Valentina said. "You know, Walking Death type stuff."

"Alright," Norm said. "Provided you promise me that you're not taking me to be killed."

Valentina laughed. "Oh, my god. You are so funny. If we wanted to kill you, we'd have done that like forever ago. We're not here to kill you, Mr. Stockwell. I can promise you that."

The CPD sirens were definitely gathering at the scene he'd vacated on Webster. Moreover, Norm assumed the BEE would be sending a Recovery team to the scene. He didn't want to be seen talking to Rupinos, so he hopped into the SUV, joined by Valentina, who slipped in next to him.

"And away we go," Valentina said.

THE Reverend Marcus Nicks looked out at the congregation, a blend of blond-haired, blue-eyed young men and women. They looked like they'd been cut from sugar cookie molds, and that was just fine by him. The Saint had made them all, meticulously assembling his flock. They were God's people, in every sense of the word.

In the wake of the assassination of some of his flock on the very doorstep of his church, Nicks felt the need to address his people, for them to understand the sacred nature of their mission.

He told the story he'd told a thousand times before. It felt as miraculous as it ever did. He remembered it like it was yesterday, when it was almost a decade ago—he had been at the Avalon nightclub, on a field trip, when Skoll and Hati had come—the wolves had come and had attacked everybody in the nightclub, himself included.

It had been bedlam—the wolves snapping, finding flesh, biting people, attacking people. Marcus could not believe what he was seeing. He'd been there with other friends from the Evangelical Institute—Angelica, Joshua, and Ruth—studying the decadence firsthand.

They had been there to watch and better know the ways of sin, that they might combat it more effectively. It had been an amusing night, until Skoll and Hati had come and changed everything.

The others had run screaming in the chaos, but Marcus had stood his ground. It's what a godly man was supposed to do, wasn't it? He had stood his ground, and in so doing, had caught Skoll's eye. The White Wolf had come for him, leaping and savaging him with her dreadful, monstrous fangs.

"I used to be nobody," Nicks said. "Like anybody else. Like everybody else. Then she came to me—the White Wolf who chases the Sun every day: Skoll. She came to me and she spoke to me with her teeth—she bit me. I almost died, Brothers and Sisters. But I didn't die, did I? Or perhaps I died and was born again?"

It had been a blur. His friends had abandoned him in the chaos, and he'd awakened in an ambulance, helped by paramedics, a black man and a Latina, tending to him. He had been too weak to protest, to fight them off. Skoll had left him weak, having bitten him savagely in her Avalon attack.

Marcus had thought he was going to die, had made his peace with God, but he had not died. Angelica came to see him once he'd stabilized. With her golden hair and big blue eyes, the snowy white hairband she always wore. Angelica believed in their mission. She understood.

He didn't yet experience the miracle. Not at first. But in the days after the attack, he'd healed. The grievous wounds Skoll had inflicted on him had healed, as if they had never been. In the chaos of the Avalon attack, Marcus had managed to check himself out of the hospital with a clean bill of health. It had been before the government agents had begun taking people and making them disappear.

"It's a miracle," he told Angelica, who was there. "I'm healed."

He showed her where his wounds were—the spot on his ribs where Skoll had bitten him, and, to her amazement, and to his continued awe, they were gone. The whole thing had been like a dream.

"God saved you from the ravening wolf," Angelica said.

"God has chosen me for a mission," Marcus said. As he'd healed, he'd done research on portentous wolves in mythology, and had come across Skoll and Hati—a pair of wolves who chased the sun and the moon, who signaled the coming of Ragnarok. They were kin of Fenris. It all made sense.

He didn't tell Angelica about Skoll. She would not understand it. Instead, she had told people about the miracle, and how he had been healed. This was not a bad thing, as far as Marcus was concerned. He'd wanted to start a church, to spread the Good News.

And his own miracle of healing had been just the thing to elevate him relative to his peers. He'd been the only one at the Evangelical Institute to be attacked that night. People would ask him about it, and he'd tell them the story. He wouldn't tell them about Skoll back then—or that he knew it had been her. Rather, he just spoke the story about how the wolf had come, and how God had somehow saved him from the wolf.

That was the safer story at the time. It was before the wolf within—the Saint—began to speak to him, to explain it to him. What happened, what it meant. Why it mattered. Why he mattered. Why *they* mattered.

Nicks grinned at the congregation, who watched him with rapturous eyes. At the back of the church was Saul, the Deacon. Tonight's service was Wolves of God only, in reaction to the attack at the church. The Deacon had seen to it. He saw to everything Nicks needed. What Nicks needed was acolytes.

"No," Nicks said. "I didn't. I was reborn. Like Christ Almighty, Skoll did not kill me. She brought me back—I became something stronger. I became the White Wolf. And we all became White Wolves, didn't we? Skoll's gift. From her, to me, to you, Brothers and Sisters."

The Saint grew within him, speaking to him, guiding him, transforming him. And that was the greatest miracle of them all, his transformation. Skoll had struck him down, and he had come back stronger, and able to become a wolf. Marcus had grown into a great, white wolf, just like Skoll had been.

He transformed under the light of the full moon, and had run forth in the darkness, hunting prey. Marcus knew what he was to hunt. He chased them down and he killed them. He ate them, all of the dark meat he could find. And it was good.

Marcus awoke from that first night in the bowels of an old, forgotten church. He was strewn at the head of it, near the altar. The dilapidated church hung in tatters, with beams of light flowing through it, heralding the day. It would become the First Lupercalian Church of the Apocalyptic Vision. It would become his first home.

Angelica had been worried.

"Where'd you go, Marcus?" Angelica asked.

Marcus had no answer for it that she was ready to hear.

"I have been called to do a great thing, Angie," Marcus said. And he did that thing every night, ranging forth and hunting. He felt a tugging in his spirit, the tug of Skoll. She had been making others. Many, many others. She'd told her pack to give blood. That message had been loud and clear—donate blood as often as you can. Give and give and give again.

It had been like a drumbeat, a call that could not be resisted. And Marcus had given his blood eagerly. It was clean blood, holy blood, a sacrament like Christ's. He understood this. What he was giving was a gift to those who needed it most.

Those early days of the end of the world were heady times for him. To be a crusader, to be chosen for a mission as holy as his, was more than he could have even hoped for. But there it was, all the same.

His life had expanded immeasurably, and yet it had followed some routines. Blood donation, transformation, hunting, killing, feasting, converting. That last part, the conversion, was yet another facet of his glorious new existence.

Marcus had found that Skoll's gift was transmissible. If he bit someone, and they did not die from the wounds he inflicted, they would heal as he had, would become born anew as he had, reborn into a marvelous form. And when this happened, Marcus found he attained some influence over that person—he became their leader, their spiritual guide and mentor.

They'd turn up at his door at the Evangelical Institute, and Marcus would recognize them—or the Saint within him would. They would come to him for guidance, and Marcus would guide them. Only he was dismayed—they were blacks, Latinos, and Asians. They were not always whites. It disgusted Marcus to see these other people with the gift bestowed upon them. After killing them, he communed with the Saint for understanding.

"The gift of Skoll belongs rightly with us," Nicks told his congregation. "As Wolves of God, you must understand this as you understand your own breathing. We hunt and kill the nonwhite, for they are not part of our flock. They are our prey, Brothers and Sisters. Our flock are our own people. You know them, you see them. No exceptions to this rule, the rule of the Wolves of God."

He'd turned Angelica. She'd been his first true convert, versus the accidental rabble who showed up at his door. Marcus had given her the gift. She had not known it was him at first. She'd been on the campus at the Evangelical Institute when he had jumped her from the shadows, biting her as the great, white wolf that he was. She'd screamed and fainted, but he'd lifted her up, had taken her to a place of safety, to a rooftop, as the Saint had instructed him.

Do not leave her for the authorities. They will take her away from you, the Saint had instructed him. Instead, it had allowed him to turn back to his disguise. He had prepared for it, had left a backpack with clothes in it, for him, and a first aid kit.

Marcus had dressed himself and dressed her wounds, and Angelica had awakened to find herself in her dorm room, with Marcus attending to her.

"What happened?" Angelica asked. "Where am I?"

"You were attacked," Marcus said. "I was on the campus, I saw it."

Angelica saw her bandages, sat upright, afraid.

"Marcus, I need to get to the hospital," Angelica said. "What if it was a rabid dog?"

"It wasn't a rabid dog," Marcus said. He could not tell her about Skoll. She would think he was insane.

"Still, I need to go to the hospital," Angelica said. "Did you do this?"

She gestured to the bandages.

"You were hurt," Marcus said. "I didn't know how long it would be until an ambulance came. They're very busy dealing with all the wounded in the city. I remember how it was with me—well, not truly. But I'm sure it took too long. You should just rest, Angelica."

She seemed to listen to him, to accept his word. Marcus hadn't wanted to linger in her part of the dorm, lest people be suspicious. Everyone was suspicious at the Institute.

So, he left, and he told her to call him if she needed anything. Angelica had called an ambulance after all, though—because, when he got back to the campus, he found that she'd gone.

When he'd asked some of the other students, they'd said that Angelica had been attacked by some monstrous wolf, the way so many in the city had been, and that she'd gone to the hospital.

Marcus then went to the area hospitals to try to find her. Where the Institute was located, there was only one real choice for her to go, but when he went downtown and inquired, they had told him that there was no Angelica Walters there.

He wasn't sure what that could have meant, so he went to the other hospitals in the city, checked them all, and tried to find Angelica Walters. But Angelica hadn't been at any of them. There were only two possibilities—one was that she'd checked in under an assumed name. That was possible, although it seemed unlike Angelica to do such a thing. She was not duplicitous like that. She was an honest woman, a god-fearing and righteous woman.

The other possibility was that something had happened to her on the way there, and somebody had run off with her. Skoll had warned her flock about the hunters. There were hunters in the city, now— godless persecutors who would kill any wolves of Skoll they saw.

It was possible that someone had become aware of Angelica's af- fliction, and they'd taken her someplace else.

His failure enraged him. But it made him more cautious, less reck- less. He went about gathering his flock more carefully. Seeing the roomful of White Wolves, he could take real pride in his work.

"An assassin tried to kill me the other day, Brothers and Sisters," Nicks said. "He was a man from the Hive—the dreaded agency that has dogged our steps since the dawning of the miracle. Servants of the secular devil. They have hunted us relentlessly. And, where possible, we have hunted them. As it was in the beginning, when Skoll had first come to this place to share her gift. It is a war, Brothers and Sisters.

A black man is in the White House. A black man runs the Hive. These dark men are threatening our lives and our livelihood. They take good, honest people and they spirit them away to prison camps, never to be seen again."

One of the acolytes brought forth their own missing persons board, much like what existed online and elsewhere, in the wake of the Happening. Only this board was the Warg Board—it showed the Wargs who'd gone missing. He had the acolyte place it to his right. Another acolyte came from his left and put another board up.

"And these are our righteous dead," Nicks said. "These are the fallen Wargs, who have martyred themselves for our cause. You know some of them. Every one of you knows someone on these boards. This remains a war, Brothers and Sisters. And you are all soldiers in it. You have all been chosen by Saul and by me. We have enlisted you in the fight for our very lives."

Marcus remembered when Skoll had stopped tugging at his soul— when she'd flown from this world and gone someplace else. It was as if the tether had been cut by silver scissors, and he'd been set free. With her passing, Marcus had become the new, true White Wolf. When Skoll had gone away, the Saint had arisen in her place, and grown his flock.

It was uncanny, that chain of blessing from Skoll on down to him and beyond. Only two other gang-pack-clans maintained the kind of colorful continuity in their bloodline—the Black Hand and their big, black wolves, and the Loopines with their speedy, rawboned grey wolves. White, black, and grey. It was almost cosmic in its divine symmetry.

None of the Infective gang-packs had such continuity of their bloodline. Not the Black Brotherhood, not the Russian *Volki*, not the Latin *Lunares*. Their packs had not been blessed with that—they were mongrels compared with the purebreds of the Wolves of God.

After the Happening, there had been chaos—wolves of every stripe and color. But the grand celestial order had somehow sorted itself out, and there were great packs defined by color. Sure, there were still Lupines of every hue—the free agents, as it were—but the organizing principle of the three great packs was a degree of self-selection. They were defined by it.

"Our rivals would see us destroyed," Nicks said. "Our enemies would drive us from this world, the way those murderous thugs struck upon our very doorstep. But this is our world, Brothers and Sisters. We made it. It falls to us to retain our ownership of it. Skoll's gift to me is a gift to you, as well. Now, I'm going to have to ask something of you. It's important. The White Wolves will win the day when the blood, dust, and ash finally settles."

The congregation was well-trained. They didn't murmur. They didn't squirm in their seats. The Deacon looked happy as could be from his post at the back of the church. This was the moment they had all waited for. Their enemies had struck a blow at them, but it would only be the kindling for the holy war, the one he would start.

The Deacon saluted Nicks and went out through the front doors with a dozen of his men, while the organ player sounded a righteous tune that filled the room and buttressed his holy words.

"I need each of you to find five converts," Nicks said. "Only the best will do—blond, blue-eyed, white. *Our* people. Find them and make them. Don't kill them. Convert them. But you must not be indiscriminate. You must not let the authorities find them. Because if you do, the Hive will buzz in and take them away. No, you must take them somewhere safe. The Deacon and I have acquired a safe place in another state. We call it the Créche. There is a safe compound out in the western suburbs, a place where we have buses to transport you to the Créche. We want you to take your converts there, where the Wargs can oversee them, ensure that they can develop securely. We have white buses available, where the converts can be transported to the Créche. This work must be carried out carefully, and without the Hive or the Poles finding out about it."

The Wolves of God hated the *Synowie Srebra* and killed them on sight. The wiser path would have been to torture them for their Slavic secrets, but the Saint had found that no *Synowie* cell knew anything about the others and could only rat out their immediate associates if compelled to do so.

The Wolves of God were excited by the prospect of a crusade. This particular group was only a quarter of his flock. He'd given a different sermon to another group, had tasked them with hunting down the enemy Lupines and killing them. Any Lupine that was not them was an enemy. Another quarter of his flock was tasked with hunting the Hive and the Poles.

The final quarter of his flock had already worked on the exodus, traveling south in a great pilgrimage. This group, led by Noah Bishop, another of his own most-trusted lieutenants, was quietly setting up the second Lupercalian Church in the Deep South, far away from prying eyes. As much as Marcus wanted to join them on their pilgrimage, he knew that there was simply far too much work to be done up here, at the epicenter of it all.

He had told the Italian Rupinos and the Anglo-French Bastion that he was leaving Chicago, which was true on the face of it. But it was more of a strategic withdrawal, for he was playing a bigger game. Let them have Chicago. He would have the rest of the country. He'd have the rural hinterlands and would strangle the cities when the time came.

Marcus had given strict orders that the Flock—as he specifically dubbed the Bishop's group—to stay off cell phones. They were to stay off the grid as much as possible, and to rely only on burner phones or land lines, if they had to. They were to be as invisible as they could be on their travels. They had crept out of the city for years, as discreetly as possible. In ones, twos, threes, fours. Nothing to catch anybody's eye.

The Bishop was establishing the Lupercalians in the South along the Warg model, and it would be a good and holy thing. The Créche would be the rebirthing place, where the new race of chosen people would spawn and go forth into the world, to kill and to convert.

The Saint had spoken of it to him in midnight whispers, while he'd mourned the loss of Angelica.

You're infected, Brother Nicks. All of your Wargs are. But you don't need to be. There is a way to build a lineage. You must breed. Have your Wargs start families, and you'll have a race of Trueborn—just like the Black Hand. And sooner than you'd think. Be fruitful and multiply.

"Be fruitful and multiply," Nicks said, alone in the dark.

Exactly so, the Saint said. *White Wolves, born true. The second genesis. A new lineage of Trueborn, following your lead. Raised in the proper fashion. Think of it.*

And he did think of it, because Marcus Nicks was a schemer, in addition to being a crusader. It was how he segmented his flock between himself, the Saint, the Deacon, and the Bishop. They were his own Holy Trinity.

"The Deacon will provide you more details about the Créche, and you'll coordinate with the drivers of the buses," Nicks said. "I'm not going to rush you on this, Brothers and Sisters, but you need to quickly find five suitable souls and convert them. Contact your fellow parishioners, do what is necessary to coordinate and get them to the Créche. That is your holy mission I give you tonight, Brothers and Sisters. Go forth, find converts—make converts—get them to the Créche. After you get your five, find five more, my Lupercalians. Five, like the points of a star. Five, five, five, five, five..."

He held out his hand, fingers outstretched, palm outward, facing them, chanting "five" and pleased to see them answer his chant with a chant of their own, escalating.

"Five, five, five, five, five," they said, and the acolytes in the back unfurled a great white banner, upon which had been painted a beautiful red pentagram with a red Cross painted in the center of it. That was to be their holy symbol, the unification of the Cross and the Pentagram. The Bishop already had banners and flags flying at the Créche.

Five was a sacred number to the Saint. It was an angel number, a powerful number, a transformative number. He knew his acolytes would follow his lead and grow their ranks. They would replenish the brethren that they lost in the attack on his church.

"The enemies of God are out there," Nicks said. "The Black Hand, the Grey Wolves of Bastion. The Brotherhood. The *Lunares*. They did this, they sent the assassins. They would destroy us with their diabolical intentions. They offered me a temptation, Brothers and Sisters. They offered drug money to me, that I would join them in their Unholy Trinity. But I refused. I turned them down flat. My mission—our mission—is a holy one. We cannot be bought and sold like Judas. We must make them pay for their greed, for their poverty of spirit."

The moment filled him with holy fire, and the Saint came bursting out of him right there, sprouting fur and fang, and the congregation felt the call, and they transformed as well, until the entire church was filled with Wolves of God, ready to carry out their sacred mission. They howled at the moon as one, a chorus that shook Heaven and Earth that overshadowed the organ player.

The Saint then charged down the main aisle, his transformed pack-flock following him. They would go on their crusade, hundreds of Wolves of God. It would be greater than the Happening. It would be Armageddon.

He would see Gia Rupino's and Chad Bastion's heads on spikes before the night was through, for daring to exclude him from their scheme to profit from the holy affliction.

But as the Saint reached the front doors of the church, he found them to be locked. He slammed against them, heard the rattle of chains as the doors were blockaded against him. Unaware, the rest of his pack surged behind him, and the press of bodies crushed him against the doors of his church. It reminded Nicks of that night in Avalon, the smash of bodies.

Then, moments later, the windows of the church broke, and Molotov cocktails came crashing through all of them at once. Each bottle exploded into a fireball as it landed, dousing and igniting parishioners, who began to run about, howling in terror. Few things could truly kill a Lupine, but fire was one of them.

The Saint snarled and snapped at his followers, trying to get some space, to take control, but the fire was spreading, and more of his Flock were themselves on fire. The fire, like panic, was spreading fast.

True panic was starting to set in as they pressed against him, trying to get out. More fire bottles flew through the open windows, another fusillade, and now the old church was truly ablaze.

"Let me free!" the Saint snarled, but all around him were his pack, howling and biting and trying to get away from the raging inferno that was consuming everything around them.

The Saint threw himself against the front doors again and again, putting his considerable Lupine strength to bear against them, but something was barring the door from the other side, something more than chains, something stronger.

As he shoved against them, he could glimpse a little gap between the doors. He could see that someone had backed a truck against the door after they had chained them.

It was a fire truck.

Cursing, the Saint tore at the wooden front doors with his great claws, even as the smoke continued to rise, and the fire raged. He could hear the cacophonous howls of his burning brethren and could hear the crash of more Molotovs through the broken windows as they exploded. The roar of the fire was deafening as it grew.

The fire was a proper conflagration, now, and he could see his pack bounding and racing for the broken windows, leaping for them. Dozens of Wolves of God were on fire as they tried to make their way to the windows, where gouts of smoke flew up.

Any who made their way to the windows were shot. The Saint could see it from the way they went flying back. He could smell the silver even amid all the smoke and fire. He did not hear gunfire, could only see the results of it.

The fire was roaring louder than the Wolves of God were howling, for the smoke was choking them, robbing them of breath.

The Saint kept tearing at the door, the old wood of the church giving way to his lycanthropic claws. He tore and punched while his congregation burned behind him, while some of them fought to claw their way past him. The fire had spread throughout the church, now, out of control.

The Deacon had been at the back of the church, the Saint thought. He had been responsible for guarding the church. But he was nowhere to be seen. Had he betrayed him?

The Saint tore through the door and climbed through it, gripping the fire truck with his claws and climbing up.

There, on the other side of the ruined doors, were a group of black and brown men and women in hoodies, holding assault rifles with suppressors on them. They didn't waste any time, shooting the Saint full of silver bullets.

In a murderous moment, the Saint became a martyr, falling to the ground in a bloody splash. As he expired on the steps of his own church, hearing the howling of his pack as they burned, he could see the dead Deacon on the ground, riddled with bullets, along with his men. He had been loyal, after all. The assassins had come for him like he was Caesar.

The fire raged, yet there wasn't a siren to be heard above the howls of the burning Wargs. Those few acolytes who managed to dive through the front doors were shot by the assassins. The fire truck pulled away from the doors, and more burning Lupines pushed through them, only to be shot. A couple more Molotovs were lobbed, this time at the front door, and they exploded into blossoms of fire.

A horde of hooded figures surrounded the First Lupercalian Church of the Apocalyptic Vision, all of them armed. Watching, waiting to see who emerged. Any who did, whether burning or not, were gunned down.

Otherwise, they simply observed, waited until the howling was drowned out by the roaring fire that devoured the church. When they couldn't hear howling anymore, only then did they fade into the shadows, as the sound of fire truck sirens broke the night, but too late to stop the blaze that claimed the sundered church.

It took the firefighters five hours to put out the five-alarm fire at the First Lupercalian Church of the Apocalyptic Vision. By the time the fire had been put out, everyone within the church had long since been burned to death—ashes to ashes, dust to dust.

4

POLLY had known something had happened next door. She'd seen some of it through her window, when she'd looked out to see the Lupines running across the yard, only to be shot dead by an unseen assailant.

She'd just tucked Sloane into bed and was going to try to work on some poetry when she had become aware of it.

She turned out the lights and peered through her living room window, watching the ski-masked figures working to remove the bodies of the dead. She saw a masked woman talking to a shadowy man and saw the masked men carting off Anne Stockwell. Whether she was dead or not was anybody's guess.

Polly wondered if it was one of those government hit squads she'd remembered Ansel talking about. Whatever it was, whoever they were, they worked quickly, spiriting away Anne and removing the bodies from the scene. Within an hour, they were gone, and it looked like nothing had even happened there.

But she'd seen it and had been afraid. She went downstairs to her kitchen and pondered that bottle of Lupitol she'd taken out of the case she'd stashed earlier. She'd been on the fence about whether or not to take it since Anne had given it to her.

Maybe it was a reflection of her own bifurcated condition, but while Pol was decidedly anti-Lupitol, was whispering in her ear for her not to take it, Polly also considered taking it to be able to recenter herself somewhat. Part of her argued that if she needed Lupitol to center herself, she was already terribly unbalanced.

Seeing the disturbance next door, however, made her uneasy. Since Pol had come into her life, her primary terror had been getting caught and either killed or sent away by the authorities. She'd murdered—and eaten—her own husband.

At the time, Polly hadn't given much thought as to her future.

Before Sloane had come around, she'd thought that she and Ansel might form their own little Horrorshow, just the two of them. She knew Ansel held her friends in utter contempt, even before they'd been killed. He would consider her desire to form an artistic couple—him the painter, her the poet—beneath him. She thought it would have been great. They were both good-looking, urbane, sophisticated, stylish, elegant. He was rich. It would have been so delicious.

That the two of them were lycanthropes was just another special thing about them. They'd be bestial bohemians. He'd help her find her way to be at peace with her infection.

It was what was *supposed* to happen, but he'd disappeared.

He abandoned you, Pol whispered. It was an open wound that never healed.

He didn't abandon me, Polly said to herself, through clenched teeth.

She thought of the last time they were together. Before she'd known she was pregnant. They were in the master bedroom, having had killer lycanthropic sex, which had become something of a thing between them. The fur flew when they fucked. What could she say? It was spectacular, and she gave as good as she got. He didn't seem to mind.

The limbic lust was just too much and they'd attack one another, him Trueborn, her Infective, and they'd meet in the messy monstrous middle, a couple of fanged and furry fuck machines. It was cathartic. They both took solace in it. Or at least she did. No one could ever truly know what Ansel was thinking about. He kept his own counsel, in his weird, painterly way.

Ansel lounged there beside her, spent, briefly at peace. She snuggled against him, and for a few moments, the horror of the Happening seemed so far away.

"I have to make it right," Ansel said.

"You?" Polly said. "Just you?"

"This whole thing is my fault," Ansel said. "The chain of infection—from me, to Sam, to Zooey, to you, to the Happening."

"I forgave you for it," Polly said. "I'm more special, now. That matters to me. Being special. We're special."

Ansel scoffed, put one of his strong arms behind his head. He was so very strong. Pol stirred inside her, always hungry for more.

"It's not you I'm worried about," Ansel said. "I mean, Christ. If anything's clear, it's that you're a survivor, Polly. Damned if I know how you are, but you are."

Polly smiled at him.

"I'm a ruthless opportunist," Polly said. "The odds favor me."

"Right," Ansel said. "Okay, so, I'm part of a clan. That means there's an obligation. The head of my clan—my oldest sister, Gia—has put it to me to make it right."

"How many siblings do you have?" Polly asked. Ansel almost never talked about his family.

"I've got five sisters and three brothers," Ansel said.

"Wow," Polly said. "Big family."

"Werewolves always have big families," Ansel said. "It's kind of an insurance policy for us. The lifestyle is, uh, taxing."

"You're a middle sib," Polly said. "Right? You seem like it."

"Uh, yeah," Ansel said. "Anyway, Gia wants me to go state-by-state and kill off the Infectives that got turned by Zooey's dipshit blood drive crap. Her Happening."

She could hear the frustration in his voice, wanted to make it better, somehow.

"How would you even do that?" Polly asked.

"It's a hunt," Ansel said. "A massive cull."

"But wouldn't those government agents do that?" Polly asked. "That's their job."

Ansel sighed, a chest-heaving sigh.

"It may be their job, but it's my responsibility," Ansel said. "Only here's the thing—I'm not really a killer. I know that sounds weird, coming from me, but I'm not."

Polly had seen Ansel kill the hell out of any number of Lupines. He was a magnificent monstrosity, she'd seen firsthand. He was poetry in motion, and she loved him for that.

"I get it," Polly said. "You're an artist. You're sensitive. You get wounded."

"Yes," Ansel said. "I guess you could say that. Gia's wanting me to kill all of these Infectives. But I don't have it in me. I know they're Infectives because of me losing control that one night. It's just that those people, it's not *their* fault they became Infectives. And me coming around and murdering them just for being unlucky? For needing blood and getting tainted blood from Zooey's bullshit? It doesn't sit well with me. I'm not that guy. If I was that guy, I'd have been more of a part of the family business. The Rupino family business. But I became a painter. That's who I am. I'm a painter. I'm not a hit man."

Polly could see how it weighed on him and wished she could help him. Ansel was a stoic sort of man. He didn't bare his feelings readily or willingly.

"You could tell Gia you didn't want to do this," Polly said.

"Ha," Ansel said. "Nobody ever tells Gia 'No'—you just can't do it. She's the head of our clan. It's how that goes with us. Lupines, I mean. The head of the clan calls the shots. She's the alpha."

"It all sounds so very mafia-like," Polly said.

Ansel laughed dryly.

"If only it were as easy as that," Ansel said. "Our history lays out a pile of conventions and taboos. The lifestyle demands it. I mean, think about it. We're true predators. We can't just go crazy out there, or else we'll get the norms all stirred up. It's why we've never taken over the world, even though our infectivity would seem to put that in reach. The culling and our rules and rituals are what keep us from getting out of control. Nobody wants a world full of werewolves, least of all, us. If that ever happened, we'd all go extinct."

"Who knew being a werewolf was so complicated," Polly said, trying to make light of it, but Ansel took it seriously.

"It's a Trueborn thing," Ansel said. "Infectives, they're the out-of-control ones. That's the whole problem. But we Trueborn, it's like there's something else. We keep ourselves in line. I mean, we hunt and kill, but it's on our terms, versus just running amok."

"I think I understand," Polly said. Although she knew she never really would. After all, she was an Infective. "Would you kill me if Gia ordered you to?"

"No," Ansel said, a trifle too quickly. "Never."

"But if she did, what would you do?" Polly asked.

"I'd get you out of here," Ansel said. "Take you someplace safe."

Polly imagined that possibility, being a lycanthropic fugitive, running around the country, Clan Rupino were-bravos nipping at her heels.

"Do they even know about me?" Polly asked.

"Hell, no," Ansel said. "I told Gia everything—except you—I left you out of it."

Outside, somewhere, somebody howled. In Winnetka, it wasn't like the city. In many ways, it was worse. Not in terms of the standard of living, which was infinitely better in Winnetka.

Rather, in terms of the Happening. With abundant space, countless trees, groves, and glades, and a less potent police presence, Lupines could carry out their killings with near-impunity. Polly actually pitied the Lupines downtown, having to manage their murderous impulses in such crowded conditions. In Winnetka, a lycanthrope could stretch their legs and hunt in peace.

She knew because she'd taken advantage of it. Not her, but Pol, her other half.

Pol loved hunting prey in the dark.

She relished it, and Polly found she could only control the beast inside her if she killed. She hated it, but it kept Pol quieter if she indulged her. Polly would hunt deer and coyotes.

Pol wanted people-prey, but Polly would steer her toward deer and coyotes. Especially the deer, who seemed always plentiful. She'd kill and eat them in the dead of night, hating herself for it, but unable to resist those beastly binges.

The meat was neat, but the killing was thrilling.

"Okay, so you can stay here," Polly said. "It can be a sanctuary."

"They'll find me," Ansel said. He tapped his nose. "We can find anyone we look for, sooner or later."

"Then let me go with you," Polly said. "We could team up. I could help you."

Ansel leaned over and kissed her forehead.

"Not going to happen," Ansel said. "They'll only see you as a mess I need to clean up."

Polly was irked at being thought of like that.

"I could talk to Gia," Polly said. "I'm very persuasive."

"Oh, no," Ansel said. "You will definitely not be doing that."

Polly had lived her life skirting around the frontiers of No and found Yes far more appealing and satisfying.

"So, how does it go with your people?" Polly asked. "Like does everybody just fuck their cousins or what? How do you get new blood into your clan?"

Ansel shrugged.

"It's complicated," Ansel said. "Anybody a Trueborn gets with will produce Trueborn offspring. And those offspring belong to the clan. It's like a club membership. Once you're in, you're in."

"Don't even tell me that your clan has a say in who you, you know, settle down with," Polly said. She wasn't going to say "marry" in that moment, because it just felt too on the nose. Not like she wanted to marry again, especially how it went with Tristan. But she could easily see herself with Ansel for the rest of her days. They had something powerful together.

"No," Ansel said. "But in terms of relationships, like settling down, all of that. Let's just say that it's hard for outsiders to find a place for themselves in a clan that doesn't want them."

"That sounds ghastly," Polly said. "What, your five sisters and three brothers determining who you can build a life with?"

"My brothers don't care," Ansel said. "It's my sisters, yeah. They're always making sure there's a rightness of fit with any new blood in our ranks. It's part of the reason why I just went off and did my own thing. They tolerated it because I'm a good painter. There's some prestige for the Clan in that."

Polly saw the whole thing more clearly.

"You just need to level with Gia," Polly said. "Tell her you're not cut out to be her button man on this Happening stuff."

Pol was looking Ansel over, his bare chest, the hair on his chest, the packed muscle there. Even the scars. He had a few scars, and she found them all intoxicating.

"I don't know what I'm going to do," Ansel said. "But I'm not going to tell them about you."

"I don't want to be your dirty little secret," Polly said, straddling him.

"Too late," Ansel said, grabbing her hips and holding her to him.

It had been a long and exhausting night. He'd gone the next day. He'd told her he was going to sort it out. But it was the last time she'd seen him. Once Polly had figured out that he'd vanished, she'd gone looking for him. But his gallery was shuttered. He'd fallen off the face of the world.

And she'd searched for him.

She'd hunted for him.

Pol had hunted for him.

The two of them had scoured the city for Ansel, hoping to find a trace of his scent.

The fact that no Rupinos had come knocking on her door had meant that Ansel had made good on his commitment to not tell them about Polly.

Polly put the Lupitol bottle back into her hiding place for it. While she often resented her lycanthropy, she didn't feel comfortable being without it. Who knew whether the drug worked or not, but if it suppressed her lycanthropic urges, that was a good thing.

However, it could also make her vulnerable. While Pol distressed her, not having her there when she might need her distressed her worse. Pol was part of her, and as crazy as it sounded, she trusted her.

Satisfied that things had quieted down next door (although they were very quiet even when they were doing whatever it was they were doing), Polly slipped on a jacket and some ballet flats and donned some black gloves and went outside.

The chilly November air was bracing, and she sniffed that same air as she crept next door. She didn't want to get caught snooping, and the sensible part of her admonished her for even doing so, but she had to see what was going on.

Polly had never been over to Shaw's house, even when Tristan had been around. The man was just too greasily ingratiating for her. He was an artless man of means, which was likely why Tristan got along so well with him, but Polly couldn't stand him.

Her more sensitive nose could pick up the hints of blood that had been otherwise scoured away. One of the side benefits of her condition was her everyday senses were more acute. The house had its lights on, made to seem as if nothing untoward had happened here.

She reached the front porch, where the blood scent was stronger, as was the smell of cleaners that had clearly been used to camouflage what had occurred. And the astringent scent of silver.

Polly reached the front door and checked it, was surprised to find that the door opened. She went inside quickly, not wanting to linger in the doorway.

"Mr. Shaw?" Polly said aloud, only as a formality. "It's Polly from next door. I just wanted to check on you and Anne, to see if you're okay."

Shaw's place was spaciously equivalent to Polly's, only the décor was firmly set to "bro" as she saw it. It was like a modernist man cave, with a massive television screen in a room that was more like an in-home theater, as well as a trophy room full of decorative animal heads.

Of course the man was a hunter. The kitchen was a feast of fine wood, granite, and stainless steel. In his living room were several opened trunks that contained some handcuffs that had been opened.

Polly felt particularly uneasy snooping around in this manner, but she wanted to know what had gone down here.

"Mr. Shaw?" Polly said again when she heard something upstairs. Pol stirred inside her, ears pricked at the possibility of danger.

Someone's here, Dear, Pol said. *Have no fear.*

She went to the foot of the stairs that led up and looked up.

There was a young man at the top of the stairs looking down at her. He was a handsome young man wearing a black turtleneck and black slacks, and was carrying a short, double-barreled shotgun. He was blond and hazel-eyed, with a strong jaw and a sharply defined nose.

"Who are you?" the young man asked.

"Oh, I'm the next-door neighbor," Polly said. She could smell the silver on the young man. "I, uh, heard a commotion, wanted to be sure everything was alright."

The young man went down the stairs, slowly, one step at a time.

"Everything is fine," the young man said. "I'm one of Mr. Shaw's bodyguards. House-sitting, as it were."

The young man wore gloves and had his shotgun still at the ready. Polly knew he was lying. Hell, even he knew it.

"The front door was unlocked," Polly said.

"What are you doing here?" he asked.

"I just wanted to check in," Polly said, backing up as the young man made his descent. "I suppose I should be going."

"No, no," the young man said. "You said you saw something. What did you see?"

He had the faintest hint of an accent, and Polly remembered what Ansel had said about the *Synowie Srebra*. This young man had to be part of that.

"I don't know what I saw," Polly said. "That's why I came over."

She kept backing up, while the young man had reached the foot of the stairs.

"As you can see, there's nothing here to see," the young man said.

Pol wanted to spring at the young man and tear him apart, just as a matter of course, but Polly kept a tight rein on that impulse. Besides, she was confident this young man would cut her down with his shotgun the moment she transformed.

"Yes," Polly said. "I should be going, now."

"What's your name?" the young man asked.

Polly debated whether or not to tell him, whether to simply leave.

"Really, I'm going to go back home," Polly said. "Sorry I disturbed you."

The young man raised the shotgun, pointing it at her directly.

"There's no need to call the police," the young man said. "No need at all, if that's what you're thinking."

"Says the man holding a shotgun to me," Polly said.

"It's called a *Lupara*," the young man said. "Did you know that? It's an Italian word, meaning 'for the wolf.' In Polish, we'd say *'Dla Wilka'*, but *'Lupara'* just has a ring to it. Italians and their musical language."

They were in Shaw's foyer, now, and Polly was unsure if she'd be able to dash off before the young man could shoot her.

"Would you mind terribly not pointing that gun at me?" Polly asked.

"No, I don't think so," the young man said. "What kind of person comes snooping over on her own like that?"

"A good neighbor," Polly said. "A concerned citizen."

The young man smiled to himself, reaching into his pocket. He produced a silver dollar, holding it out.

"Uh, what's that for?" Polly asked.

"Take it," the young man said. "I want you to hold it in your bare hand."

"Why?" Polly asked, and the young man shook his head, smiling to himself.

"Consider it a test," the young man said. "If you can hold that coin in your hand without burning yourself, you can go home safely. If, on the other hand, you can't. Then you and my *Lupara* are going to have a very brief conversation."

He held the coin out, which Polly took. She could smell the silver in the coin.

"Are you insane?" Polly said. "That's insane."

"If you're *Normalna,* then there's no problem," the young man said. "If you're *Zainfekowany,* then there's going to be trouble. Take off your glove and hold the coin in your hand, please."

"I will do no such thing," Polly said. "This is America. I'm not doing it."

The young man brandished the shotgun.

"Only a *Wilkołak* would be afraid to hold a silver coin in her hand," the young man said.

"I don't even know what that is," Polly said. "What's a *Wilkołak?*"

"I think you do," the young man said. "It means 'werewolf.' Take the coin, Ma'am. Hold it in your palm, and we'll see what you are."

Absurdly, in that moment, terrified for her life, Polly took umbrage at being called "ma'am" by the young man. She was older, sure, but was she a ma'am, now? Had her life come to this, at last?

Then, out of nowhere, a little black blur charged at the young man, sinking its teeth into his thigh. The young man let out a startled yell and pivoted with his *Lupara.*

Polly jumped for the young man before he could bring the shotgun down on the Lupine that was biting him. It was Sloane, snarling at him.

The two of them struggled with the gun a moment, while Sloane thrashed at the man with her teeth. The young man was stronger than Polly, so she gave full vent to Pol to even the odds.

"You wanted to know," Polly said. "So, here's your answer."

Her hands grew stronger, her fingers longer, her fingernails lengthening into claws, while her lithe frame stretched and flexed, giving her greater strength than the terrified young man who was saying something in Polish, even as he fought. The transformation came so much more quickly than it had been when she was newly infected.

Polly grew in size as she transformed into her lean lycanthropic incarnation, her face lengthening into a toothy snout, her pale skin giving way to sleek dark chocolate fur, as she maintained her grip on the man's shotgun, forcing him to the ground.

Pol yanked the shotgun out of his grasp and hurled it across the room, while the man struggled to draw a silver dagger from a scabbard at his belt.

Sloane had released the man's thigh at last, snarling at him.

"Bad man," Sloane growled. "Scaring my Mom."

To the credit of the wounded *Synowie*, he had not completely lost his head, swinging with his dagger-wielding hand, a quick uppercut with the dagger that would have found Polly's heart, had she not been so much faster than he was. Instead, she caught his hand and yanked it to one side. She could hear the snap of tendons as the man yelped.

Sloane stood nearby in her black-furred hybrid shape, looking demonic and dark. Still a young pup, but a fearful apparition all the same, standing there, at the ready.

Polly hadn't wanted to kill the man, but as a member of the *Synowie*, he would report what he'd seen if he survived.

It was a brutal calculation to make, but Pol was excellent at that kind of math. She darted at the man and snapped his windpipe with her jaws, feeling his blood splash on her muzzle. Pol turned her head this way and that, until she heard the snap of his neck, and only then released him, tossing him to the ground.

"That family that slays together, stays together," Pol said.

THEY'D taken Norm to an otherwise unremarkable building, the kind of corporate chic sort of place where small conventions might be held for ideation sessions. There was a long wooden table with a score of chairs and a great big window that had a killer view of the lake, although, at night, it was a sea of blackness.

In the room were a dozen Rupinos, Norm figured, by the way they looked, the way they dressed. All black-haired, all in suits, except for young Valentina and the Furies, who lurked nearby, their eyes on him.

The alpha in the room, the handsome-looking older woman with the white-streaked black hair, wearing a cream-colored silk blouse and burgundy leather pants with some golden leather pumps. Norm knew who she must be, although in-person was more formidable than the file photos he'd seen in dossiers from years past.

"Mr. Stockwell," Gia said. "I'm Gia Rupino. I must say, I'm glad to meet you. Please, do take a seat."

They guided Norm to the table, where he sat. Gia sat across from him, while Valentina lurked on the fringes. The other Rupinos, a mix of men and women, simply looked at him. Being in the company of so many Trueborn Lupines was a first for Norm, and he sought to remain composed, although he was pretty sure they could smell the fear on him.

"I don't know why they call you the 'Walking Death' since you seem to do a lot of driving," Gia said.

"It's a nickname," Norm said. "You know how that goes. What do you want?"

Gia smiled at him, a warmly ingratiating thing that was nonetheless predatory in nature. She leaned forward at the table.

"A direct man," Gia said. "I respect that. How many lycanthropes have you killed?"

"I don't keep count," Norm said.

"Ballpark?"

"A lot," Norm said. Gia laughed.

"Our people tell me you killed some of Bastion's men," Gia said.

Norm glanced around the table, seeing all those blue eyes on him.

"Word travels fast," Norm said. "I may have. Was that bad of me?"

Gia sighed and leaned back in her chair.

"Normally, it would be frowned upon," Gia said. "But Bastion has gotten on my bad side with his machinations in the city. I think he has designs on becoming mayor, or something worse, perhaps. He's a very ambitious man. However, we didn't bring you here to talk about him. Rather, I want to talk about you."

Norm shifted in his seat a moment, unsure where this was heading.

"What about?" Norm asked.

"You're, what do they call you, a Stinger?" Gia said. "One of the BEE's busy little drones? Or one who works with drones, at any rate."

"I am," Norm said. "How do you know about me?"

"Do you know my brother, Ansel?" Gia asked.

"I know of him," Norm said. "We call him 'Big Black' at the BEE."

That prompted some amused chuckles among the Rupinos.

"I simply call him *Fratellino,*" Gia said. "At any rate, my brother has been missing for years. And we cannot find him. It has been many years, and he's nowhere to be seen."

"Maybe he's dead," Norm said.

"No," Gia said. "I do not think he is. But I think maybe he might be hiding."

"Hiding?"

It was a peculiar notion. A powerful Trueborn lycanthrope like Ansel wasn't the type to cower. He played it low-key, but he would never hide.

"Yes," Gia said. "I think he's being sheltered somewhere. We ruled out the *Synowie.* Those fanatics would have simply killed him if they'd had the chance. And they would have gloated at that. You know, they shot him years ago, back in '07. Ironically enough, they weren't even trying to kill him. They were going after someone else. He survived it, however. The only other reasonable possibility is that your organization has him."

Norm scoffed at the notion.

"I haven't heard anything," Norm said.

"Nor would you," Gia said. "I think they're keeping it very quiet on board your ship. I think Ansel's on the *Argent.*"

Norm added it to the list of things he needed to discuss with Minton.

"Based on what?"

"Based on our inability to find him anywhere else," Gia said. "We've narrowed it down to either Wolf Island or the *Argent*. That's where you come in. We need you to find out if my suspicions are correct regarding Ansel. Find out where he is."

Norm wondered what this meant for him.

"Why should I do that?" Norm asked. "It's not like we're on the same side, exactly."

"Ah, but we are," Gia said. "I've been helping your BEE get this Happening business settled for good. You're aware of this. We've been traveling the country, killing *Infettivi*, guiding BEE agents to targets. Let's be honest: we want the outbreaks to end as much as you do."

"So, if you're in our good graces, why not just ask Minton yourself?" Norm asked.

"I have," Gia said. "And he tells me he doesn't know. But one thing about being what we are—we can sniff out liars. Minton is lying. He knows where Ansel is, but he won't tell me. It wounds me."

Gia made a mock sad face.

"So, you want me to find out where Ansel is," Norm said. "And then what?"

"I want you to bring him to me," Gia said. "I'm so very worried about my *Fratellino*. He came to me, you know? In Detroit. He asked for my help. And I offered our help. Of course I did. Clan Rupino got right to it, dealing with the *Infettivi*. But when it became time for Ansel to get to work cleaning up his own mess, the mess he'd made, he disappeared."

"Like a ghost departing a séance," Valentina said, making a poofing noise and movement of her hand.

"I still don't see why I should help you with this," Norm asked.

"What can we offer you?" Gia asked.

Before Norm had managed to abscond with Anne, he would have traded anything for that. As it was, he didn't need that.

"How about a lifetime amnesty from the Rupinos?" Norm said. "I don't kill your family, you don't kill or interfere with mine?"

"Your family?" Gia asked. "Who? Your wife, Anne? You have no children."

"Yes, Anne and me," Norm said.

"She's one of the *Infettivi*," Gia said. "You want us to make an exception for her?"

"Yes," Norm said. "She and I are off-limits for your people."

Gia banged the table with a balled fist.

"Done," Gia said. "You find Ansel, let us know where he is, and, if you can, free him—assuming he's even imprisoned. Knowing Ansel as I do, he's probably lounging around, painting portraits of women he's charmed."

The assembled Rupinos snickered at this.

"Sweet Ansel is a lovely painter," Gia said. "I'd hoped he would paint bloody pictures with us, but he lost his inspiration. He forgets himself sometimes. Who he really is, where he belongs."

Norm didn't know or care about that. All he could think about was the challenge of getting aboard the *Argent*.

"It's not easy to get to the *Argent*," Norm said. "Even for me. Minton literally runs a tight ship. Access is strictly limited."

"You'll find a way," Gia said. "I believe in you."

"If I'm to get an excuse to go to the *Argent*," Norm said. "I'll need bait. Something so juicy that Minton will want to debrief me directly."

Norm didn't trust the Rupinos any more than he trusted Minton. Why would Ansel Rupino even be locked up aboard the *Argent*, anyway? He'd seen no indication of any captures, nothing like that. Big Black had been a prime target for the BEE in his Warden days, and he couldn't imagine it not getting out if they'd bagged him.

If it was a big secret, the question was why it was such a secret. Valentina broke his speculations when she spoke up.

"You mean like how you took out one of Bastion's lieutenants?" Valentina asked. "Would that get your director's attention?"

"It might," Norm said. "But I need something more. Like if I could bring in some of the heads of the other factions."

"You mean like literally their heads?" Valentina asked, grinning at him, earning a side eye from Gia, who scolded her quickly in Italian.

"Like Jaden Cole or Octavio Caudillo," Norm said.

"What about the Monroe Sisters?" Gia asked. "Or Sergei Tolkachev?"

"Yeah, that'd help," Norm said. "Something like that. Reverend Marcus Nicks, maybe. But Tolkachev's dead. Shot like a dog in the street."

The Rupinos exchanged glances, and Norm felt like maybe he wasn't in on the joke.

"Nicks is nixed," Valentina said. "Somebody hit the Wargs. Hundreds of them were killed. Burned to death."

Norm hadn't heard about this and wondered why Tiff hadn't radioed him about it.

"When?"

"Earlier this evening," Gia said. "Surprised you hadn't heard."

"I've been busy," Norm said. He would call Tiff as soon as he was done with the Rupinos.

"Who hit the Wargs?" Norm asked. "Was it you?"

Gia shrugged.

"It wasn't us," Gia said. "We were busy tracking you down. You're not an easy man to find. I give you top marks for that."

Norm didn't know if she was making sport of him or not, whether it was sincere or mocking. He thought maybe it was the latter and filed it away for future use.

"Thanks, I think," Norm said. Seeing the Furies lurking, he felt nervous. Their eyes were locked on him.

"Alright, then," Gia said. "Valentina, you take the Furies and fetch the Monroe Sisters."

"You got it, Gia," Valentina said. "Although it's easier for us to kill them, you know."

"Consider it a challenge, *Sorellina,*" Gia said.

He figured he'd tell Minton that the Rupinos offered them up to him in return for him not targeting them. Something like that. No way would Minton believe he'd been able to tag both of them himself.

"There's also the possibility that Minton will simply instruct me to kill them," Norm said. "In which case, no access to the *Argent.*"

Gia pondered that with a nod.

"Why does Minton stay hidden on his ship?" Gia said. "Why is he so shy?"

"Two of his predecessors came to bad ends ashore," Norm said. "I think he's just being extra-careful. On a ship, he's more remote, harder to reach."

"Does he think we can't swim?" Valentina said, scoffing. "We could get to that ship if we wanted to."

Norm wasn't going to let the young Rupino goad him into revealing anything about the defenses. He didn't trust the Trueborn any more than he'd trust an Infective.

"Okay," Gia said. "So, how long will it take for you to fetch the targets, Valentina?"

Valentina did some calculation in the air with her fingertips.

"We should be able to have them both by the end of the week," Valentina said.

"That long?" Gia said, winking at her baby sister.

"The *Volki* were a snap to provoke," Valentina said. "The Monroes, for all of their nuttiness, are cagier. Especially with the whole Warg business, I imagine they're laying low. We'll get them, but you'll have to be patient, *Sorella Maggiore.*"

Gia waved it off.

"Just so long as it's done," Gia said. "Mr. Stockwell, we'll find you a week from now. You have that long to prepare for your visit with Minton, to find out if our dear brother is there."

Norm didn't like being leaned on by the Black Hand but didn't see himself as having much choice in the matter. Plus, he wanted to get to Anne and talk to her. Glancing at his watch, he figured she'd be coming out of her tranquilized state by now.

"Somewhere you have to be?" Gia asked.

"It's been a long night," Norm said. "If that's all, I'd like to go."

Gia smiled at him, her prettily predatory grin.

"By all means," Gia said. "We'll show you out."

CHAD Bastion didn't like finding out about the hits on Tolkachev and the Reverend Nicks via social media. He paced around in his downtown penthouse, handling his tablet and cursing with every breath.

"I really don't like this, Lane," Bastion said into his earphone. "Todd and Anne disappear. The Lupercalians get barbecued. Tolkachev gets gunned down. What the fuck, man?"

Chad's girlfriend and confidante, Dawn Trotter, lurked nearby. He kept her a secret from all but his most inner circle. It was for her own self-protection. That's what he told himself. He had enemies who would love to target him through her. He could not bear that.

She was as ethereally lovely as ever—black hair, long, her bombastic bangs lending an artsy cadence to her pale visage. Black-eyed and darker-hearted, she hovered nearby, a vision in black. Her nose contended with her big eyes, and her lips were cherry red against the snowy-white of her skin.

She watched Chad pace with cool amusement.

"We're looking into it, Chad," Tanner said. "There are a lot of plates in the air."

"Well, you'd best learn how to juggle, my friend," Bastion said. "I need to know what's going on. STAT."

"I'll see what I can unearth," Tanner said, hanging up.

Chad tossed his tablet onto a beige sectional, while Dawn shifted in her seat, like a cat.

"What's the matter, Chad?"

"Nothing," Bastion said. "And everything."

His living room was more a viewing stand, with a stupendous view of the city that glowed at night, the abundant windows lending a spectacular vista that reinforced Chad's sense of power and autonomy in the heart of downtown Chicago. Although he loved his estate in Lake Forest, in the Bastion Industrial Architecture Building, he just felt safer.

"Somebody offed Tolkachev," Bastion said.

"You wanted that, though, right?" Dawn said. "You and Gia, I mean."

"Yeah, but she didn't loop me in," Bastion said. "That makes me uncomfortable."

Dawn got up and walked over to him, almost gliding. She was a tall woman, lean-built and shapely. She'd been wearing a black gown that was nearly transparent.

"I don't like for you to be uncomfortable," Dawn said.

"I wish you could have seen my presentation the other day," Bastion said. "I killed."

"Of course you did," Dawn said, putting her arms around him. She kissed him gently on the lips. "I wish I could have been there."

Chad believed her, kissing her hard. Of all the women he'd known, Dawn understood him most completely.

"We're so close," Bastion said. "Everything, I mean. It's sliding into place. Minton's on board. Gia's, well, she's Gia. I'll deal with her when the moment's right. The *Synowie* are on their last legs. Lupitol's flying off the shelves. Clan Bastion is cleaning up. I can't believe we didn't do it sooner."

Dawn smiled at him. Her teeth were even whiter than her skin. They were as perfect as her complexion. He could lose himself in her smile.

She'd come into his life four years ago, when he'd first pushed hard on his Lupitol solution to the Happening. He'd been working the corporate conference circuit, drumming up interest in what would become Lupitol when he'd noticed her in the audience. First in Cleveland. But he'd seen her in New York. Philadelphia. Boston. San Francisco. Seattle. Hong Kong. On and on, he'd do his speaking engagements, and he'd see her in the crowd, watching him. Listening to him. Not approaching but paying attention. She stood out.

It had been a half-dozen conferences when he'd finally talked to her. She'd been cool and pleasant. Polite and professional to the point of pain, Chad had found her strangely engaging.

Three more conferences and they'd slept together, her agreeing to join him in his penthouse suite, where they'd had sex until sunrise, when she'd left him spent and tangled in the sheets, barely capable of speech.

After that point, Chad considered her part of his entourage. And Dawn had smilingly accepted that, asking nothing of him in return. People thought she was a fashion model in her otherworldly looks and way she carried herself. Dawn knew how to command attention, and her big dark eyes could entrance at a glance.

Chad wasn't the marrying type, and Dawn never put that on him, but if he had been, Dawn would have been that one in a million. She was simply content to be with him. She left him to conduct his business by day, and would join him in the evenings, always sexy and sensuous. She understood him.

"Lupitol is a good thing," Dawn said, whispering in his hear. "It's how you've left your mark on the world. I'm proud of you."

Night after night, she'd be there with him, and he'd wake up bleary and blissed-out, feeling his head swimming as he went about his busy days.

She never talked about work, and Chad was confident she didn't have a job.

"I'm rich," Dawn said. "Richer than you, even. A family fortune."

"Yeah?"

Dawn nodded. "I'm putting some of it to work helping you. Investing in Lupitol and Liminalix. I like what you're doing, Chad."

"Thanks," Bastion said.

She smiled. Her smile was as magical as any he'd ever seen. It was a secretive smile, speaking of arcane imaginings and eroticism that was bound up in bliss and fervent yearning. Chad liked for her to smile. Her smile was a promise she never failed to keep.

"We're going to conquer the world, you know," Dawn said. "I have every faith in you. Your drug is going to solve the problem of those werewolves everywhere."

He'd been with Dawn a year before he realized what she was. That understanding may have come sooner, but he didn't appreciate it back then. Or else she'd looked into his eyes and he'd lost himself in them the way he always did, finding himself awakening in the morning light, sweating and breathless.

Only because he was Trueborn could he have weathered Dawn as successfully as he had. Four years of it. She'd latched onto him and would never let him go.

"I'm here for you, Love," Dawn said. "Whenever, however you need me."

"Yeah," Bastion said. He had known then, but the word wouldn't come to his lips. He'd laugh about it in the gym, working out. It was so easy being a lycanthrope. The strength was there for the taking. He was strong. He was fit. He looked good. Good enough to eat.

And she had found him. How she'd found him was something only she knew. He kept a high profile, so it wasn't like he was some hermit in a cave somewhere. Dawn had found him and she stayed with him.

She was always a good listener. Serene in her willingness to listen to him, offering something insightful at the perfect moment, Dawn was enchanting.

"You should kill the Rupinos," Dawn said. "They're dreadful creatures."

"Are they? Worse than me?"

Dawn smiled at him, treating him to a cool caress.

"Not all Trueborn are created equal," Dawn said. "You are the future. The Rupinos are the past. The past is dead. There's only the now and the future."

"I'm not ready to take out the Rupinos," Bastion said. "Not in the Midwest."

"You need to be," Dawn said. "You need to be ready, Baby."

She kissed him on his chest, along his neck. Each kiss was a blessing. She slow-crawled toward him on their bed, her big eyes on him, holding him fast.

"How will I know?" Bastion asked.

"You'll know," Dawn said. "I'll tell you. I'll make sure you're ready."

She leaned back, smiling at him down the end of her perfect nose. She looked like a painting, like she could have been in a painting adorning a museum wall. Dawn smiled at him and he saw the fangs, as white and pure as his own. Canines, but she was no Lupine.

Dawn bit him on the inside of his thigh, and drank from him, the way she'd done a hundred or a thousand times. He always healed, he recovered, and she helped him forget with her big eyes.

The sensation was blissful to the point of enervation, far above anything else he'd ever experienced. She drank from him and he welcomed it, yearned for it, until she crawled over him, her mouth smeared with his blood, having licked his wound to banish the bite-marks even before his healing could restore him.

Hovering over him, she loomed, her sultry eyes locked on his own, and, as had been so many times before, the memory of the night faded before her soft-spoken words that comforted and calmed him, the ecstasy of abandon.

"Baby, you need to go higher still," Dawn said. "You're so young in your journey. You need me to take you there."

"Yes," Bastion said. Anything she said, he would have agreed to. His blood, her lips. She smiled and made him go far, far away.

7

ANNE Stockwell was enraged when she came to. Sonia had given Mina a *Synowie* ski mask to wear when she went down to check in on her.

"Does this mean I'm part of the team?" Mina asked.

"Let's just say it pays to be discreet," Sonia said, putting on her own mask.

Mina was alternately bemused and horrified to be donning a ski mask to talk to the prisoner in the basement of the safe house.

More so because they heard Anne hollering down there, and heard her transform, her voice going from the generally soft speaking voice she had to a gusty, gravelly growl of her fully realized Lupine form. And the banging on the cell had grown louder.

Sonia and Mina went downstairs, where they saw the tan-colored Lupine that Anne Stockwell had become. She was broad-shouldered and strong, her claws long, her fangs prominent as she gripped the cell bars and strained against them.

"You *Synowie* bastards have stepped in it," she said, speaking quite clearly, despite her condition. Mina was impressed by that. Not all Infectives could speak when they transformed. "Don't you know who I am? Who I represent?"

"We know," Sonia said. "You work at Liminalix for Mr. Bastion."

"I do," Anne said. Mina thought it was funny to think of a werewolf named Anne. Anne the Werewolf. She wondered what her nether-name might be.

"What do you call yourself?" Mina asked. Anne glowered, her monstrous eyes boring into her.

"You mean my real name?" Anne asked. "My wolf-name?"

"Yes," Mina said.

"I go by Ante," she said.

"Ah," Mina said. "Ante. That's a good name."

Ante sniffed the air, her snout pressing against the cage bars.

"You're one of us," Ante said. "You're a Lupine."

"I am," Mina said.

"Never knew the *Synowie* to work with Lupines," Ante said. "Although I'm still relatively new at this."

"It's our internship program," Sonia said, prompting a dry chuckle-cackle from Ante. Mina was intrigued at this opportunity to interview her.

"Your sire is dead," Mina said. "So, you're free."

"Sire," Anne said. "We're not vampires."

Mina accepted that with a nod.

"What would you call it, then? That relationship?" Mina asked.

Anne mulled over it.

"He didn't make me. I mean, I know he's dead. I saw and felt him die," Ante said. "I'm glad for it. You did me a favor."

"Did we?" Sonia asked. "It was your husband, Norm, who did it. We only assisted."

At mention of Norm, Ante went silent.

"Where is he?" Ante asked. She loomed in the cell, which Mina knew was strong enough to hold her. She'd spent many a frenzied night in there over the years.

"He should be here soon," Sonia said. "He's running a bit late."

"They know about him," Ante said. "Bastion and his people. I told them. They asked, and I told them."

Ante backed away from the bars, pacing in her cell.

Sonia grabbed a couple of wooden chairs and pulled them over for Mina and herself. Mina was well-acquainted with the chairs, and they'd talked to her plenty of times when she'd been Animus. Sonia took her seat, and Mina did so as well.

"Let's talk about that," Sonia said. "What's Bastion up to with his Lupitol?"

Ante regarded them both with a lycanthropic sneer.

"What's to say?" Ante asked. "Isn't it obvious?"

"Humor us," Sonia said. "We're only human. Well, I am, anyway."

"Liminalix offers a treatment for lycanthropy," Ante said. "Lupitol keeps the Beast under wraps. With all of the craziness going on after the Happening, Bastion saw an opportunity and he took it. Liminalix has been doing research on it for years. The time was right to bring it to market. And, with everything being as it was, the government was only too happy to speed up FDA approval."

Hearing a Lupine talk about FDA approval had to have been a lycanthropic first, Mina thought to herself.

"That's it?" Mina asked. "Bastion saw a money-making opportunity and he took it?"

"Yes," Ante said. "He's not a complicated man."

"He's not a man at all," Sonia said. "He's Trueborn."

"Yes, I know," Ante said. "Most don't, but I did. Eventually, I found out. We all find out eventually."

"Very generous of him to come up with a treatment like that," Sonia said.

"He's greedy," Ante said. "He knows most people would rather do anything they could to stave off a transformation. Lupitol makes that happen. You're on it, aren't you?"

"I am," Mina said.

"And?"

"It helps," Mina said. "Not completely, but it definitely levels me out."

Ante clapped her hands together.

"And there you have it," Ante said. "Another satisfied customer. Bastion's approach is better than, say, the BEE's. We're not assassinating people, not kidnapping them and sending them to exile on a godforsaken island. We're treating them."

Sonia took out a bottle of Lupitol from a pocket, gave it a shake. The capsules within rattled against the white plastic of the bottle.

"Yet you haven't been taking it," Sonia said. "Why is that?"

"Todd wouldn't let me," Ante said. "He wanted me like this."

"Todd's gone," Sonia said. "So, you have a choice, now. Would you take it if you could?"

"Yes," Ante said. "Do you think I like what I've become? He stole me from my home, from my husband, and turned me into a monster. I've done monstrous things in his service."

With that, Ante began to turn herself back into her human form again, the otherworldly transformation from monster to human disguise again, the surreal inward turning, like a film being run in reverse, undoing what had been done, until, moments later, Ante was gone, replaced with Anne Stockwell.

"A quick transformation," Sonia said. "You've had plenty of practice for an Infective."

"Todd kept me busy. It turned him on to drive me to transform and do horrible things," Anne said, grabbing her clothes, which Mina had noticed she'd placed in a pile when she'd turned. The deliberate nature of her transformation was curious.

Sonia slid the Lupitol bottle within reach. Anne took the bottle and opened it, removing a black-and-white capsule.

"It comes in caplet form, too," Anne said, grabbing the plastic cup of water that had been set on the little table in the cell. She took the Lupitol, sighing with relief.

"It takes some time to take effect," Mina said.

"I know how it works," Anne said. "24 to 72 hours. Time release. Optimal results after a three to ten days of regular daily use."

She set the bottle down on the table, crunched the plastic cup and tossed it through the bars at them.

"Bastion's going to be looking for me," Anne said. "Once word gets out about what happened."

Sonia shook her head, picking up the mangled cup and tossing it into a nearby trash can.

"We cleaned up the site," Sonia said. "It's going to simply look like Shaw disappeared."

Anne laughed to herself, her shoulders shaking as she did.

"It won't matter," Anne said. "He'll still suspect something."

"We'll be ready for him," Sonia said.

Anne looked at her with fear in her eyes.

"I don't think you will be," Anne said. "He's the worst of them all. He's worse than the Rupinos, even."

"Is he?" Sonia asked.

"I think so," Anne said. "He's terribly smart. And he has powerful friends."

"What sort of friends?" Sonia asked.

Anne rolled her eyes. She sat down on the little cot within the cage. Mina knew every bit of that cell.

"I'm not telling you that," Anne said. "Just know that it's true."

"We've dealt with smart Lupines before," Sonia said.

"Not like him," Anne said. "He's diabolical."

"Ah," Sonia said. "We've dealt with the diabolical, too."

Mina glanced at her watch, wondering where the hell Norm was. He was nothing if not punctual, and his absence unnerved her.

"Where does this all go for us?" Anne asked. "I'm not expected to live the rest of my days in this cell, am I?"

Sonia glanced at Mina, who looked back at her.

"No," Sonia said. "It's up to Norm. We are doing him this favor."

"I have something to trade," Anne said. "A couple of things, really."

Ever the businesswoman, Mina thought.

"What do you have?" Sonia asked.

"Not until I see Norm," Anne said. "But they're good things. Valuable things."

Mina tried to get a read on Anne Stockwell, a sense of who she really was. Mina had studied her share of lycanthropes. Infectives fell into various types, depending on the length of infection and what they'd done in the course of it, including:

- THE CLUELESS: No awareness of what they'd done, confusion about finding themselves naked outside. High risk of involuntary transformation.

- THE DENIERS: Some awareness coupled with a strong desire to reject their new reality. High risk of involuntary transformation.

- THE RAGERS: Slight awareness of their condition matched with a fury at their situation. High risk of involuntary transformation.

- THE RUEFUL: An awareness of the atrocities they'd committed while transformed, and deep guilt. Moderate risk of involuntary transformation.

- THE QUIETLY HORRIFIED: High degree of awareness, coupled with a desire to appear as normal as possible. Low risk of involuntary transformation.

- THE PRETENDERS: Full awareness and assimilation with their other self, paired with a willful desire to blend in. Extremely low risk of involuntary transformation.

Mina figured Anne to be either Quietly Horrified or a Pretender. She was fully aware of her condition, but had managed to control it on some level, either through the brute force of repetition, or perhaps strength of character (or lack of character—Mina found that sociopaths were very well suited to lycanthropy).

She put herself at somewhere between Rueful and Quietly Horrified, although eight years into her condition, she didn't put it past herself to be a Pretender, or dangerously close to one. She thought she would never truly sync up with Animus, no matter how much Animus might want that.

They heard someone come in upstairs, and Mina hoped it would be Norm. She was pleased when he came downstairs, glancing at Sonia and Mina with a smirk, while his eyes went to Anne, who jumped to her feet.

"Norm," Anne said. "Babe, you came for me!"

"I did," Norm said. "Despite your warning."

"You never listen to me," Anne said, gripping the bars. "Babe, you've got to get me out of here."

"Not yet," Norm said. "I'm sorry, but not yet."

Anne's relief turned to something else, Mina noticed. Anne was not a woman used to being denied anything she wanted.

"Not yet?" Anne asked. "Are you kidding me? I'm in a goddamned cage, Norm."

Norm glanced at Sonia.

"Did you give her the Lupitol?" Norm asked.

"I'm right here, Norm," Anne said. "Yes, I took it."

"How long until it starts to work?" Norm asked.

"Maybe three days, to be safe," Mina said.

"Three days," Norm said.

"Three days?!" Anne said, yanking on the bars. "Jesus, Norm. It's me, Babe. You're going to keep me locked up? What the hell are you talking about?"

"For your protection and for ours," Norm said.

Tears ran down her cheeks as she regarded him caustically from behind the bars. Norm was like stone, standing there, looking right back at her.

Mina thought the degree of self-control he possessed was impressive. While she'd never been married, she thought it would be difficult to see her spouse like this.

"I can't believe this," Anne said. "After all I've been through, you'd do this to me."

"Consider it detox," Norm said. "You're in detox."

"Hah," Anne said, releasing the bars and stepping away, turning her back to him. "What is it you think I'll do?"

"I don't know," Norm said. "What does a Lupine typically do? Kill people. Eat people."

"I would never kill *you*, Babe," Anne said, turning back to look at him. Her face was pure contrition. "I warned you away from them so you wouldn't get killed."

"But you told them about me," Norm said. "And he told the Rupinos about me. They know all about me."

"Todd made me," Anne said.

Mina exchanged a glance with Sonia, even as Animus writhed inside her. The Lupitol held her in pharmacological chains, but she felt Animus in there. Something about Anne was putting her off.

"What about the information you had to trade?" Mina asked. "You said you wouldn't trade it until Norm was here. Norm's here now."

Anne turned back around, looking hard at Mina and Sonia, her gaze softening when her eyes danced across Norm.

"So I did," Anne said. "First, and most importantly, is I suspect that Todd's next door neighbor is harboring a Rupino child. She's the mother of the child. An Infective named Polly Drinkwater. She was friends with Ansel Rupino. And, I'd say, something more."

Sonia took out her cell phone and dialed someone.

"One of my men is still at the Shaw residence," Sonia said.

"How can you know the child was a Rupino?" Mina asked.

Norm remembered seeing the Drinkwater woman walking her black "dog" and the appearance of her dark-haired daughter.

"I've seen them," Norm said. "When I was staking out Shaw."

Anne smiled at him.

"You've seen her," she said. "So, there you have it. I know a Rupino when I see one."

Sonia paced around, cursing.

"His phone's going to voicemail," Sonia said.

Anne smirked at them all.

"You won't get there in time," she said. "I'd already told Chad about it before you murdered Todd. Chad was *very* interested. We were going to go over there after we'd had a bite to eat. Before you so rudely interrupted us."

Sonia tapped Mina, motioning for her to follow.

"We'll go up there," Sonia said. "You keep her talking."

Anne watched them run up the stairs.

"You'll never make it," Anne said.

POLLY had whisked Sloane out of the Shaw residence after they'd killed the *Synowie* agent, especially when his phone had started ringing. She'd taken the man's wallet and his *Lupara*, and a bandolier of shells he'd had with him, as well as her ripped-up clothes.

Sloane was still in her hybrid form, capering about, man-blood on her muzzle. Sloane was very excited, and Polly didn't know what sort of moral lesson she could impart upon her. The man was going to kill her, and Sloane had defended her.

"That bad man was going to hurt you, Mommers," Sloane said, dogging her steps. Polly hastened her way across the yard, rushing to their own house, where she thought they'd be at least marginally safer. She felt acutely self-conscious and vulnerable, streaking naked in the chilly November night.

"Thank you, Sloane," Polly said. She felt upset that her daughter had helped her kill a man, that she'd tasted human flesh. Was this how it began with the Trueborn? "We have to get home and wash off."

Sloane shot ahead of her, sniffing around, absolutely happy. It was all a big adventure for her.

Polly's head was spinning. The last thing she wanted was more attention coming her way. When she got to her house, she quickly let them in and shut the door as quietly as she could, locking it. She turned on the intruder alarm, something she didn't typically do ever since Pol had become a big part of her life.

Tonight was right, Pol said in her head.

Polly hung the *Lupara* on the coat rack she had by the door, along with the bandolier, and looked over the man's wallet.

His name was Stanislaw Nowack. He'd been 28 years old. Polly felt bad for killing him, but it had been self-defense. That's what she told herself.

Don't be sad, don't feel bad, Pol purred in her head.

She took Sloane upstairs and rinsed the blood off them both, Sloane happily humming while Polly methodically scrubbed them both in the shower. She wrapped Sloane and herself in towels and got some black flannel pajamas for Sloane, ones with silver stars all over them.

"How'd you know where I was?" Polly asked.

"I tracked you, Mommers," Sloane said. "I can track you anywhere. I woke up, you weren't around, and I followed my nose."

"You saved my life, Scritchers," Polly said.

"I love you, Momma," Sloane said. "I'd eat bullets for you."

"Baby, you'll never have to if I have anything to say about it," Polly said.

Polly brushed the tangles from her hair, Sloane smiling at her. Polly hadn't ever imagined being a mom, but she enjoyed her time with Sloane, just the two of them. Motherhood wasn't natural for her, but the intimacy of it was somehow pleasing. To be a mother was something far beyond anything she'd imagined for herself.

The breezy way that Shaw and his men operated was something Polly hadn't a proper frame of reference for. She was used to the frenetic action of Infectives, versus how they behaved. They seemed more like a kind of fraternity than a gang or pack, with an array of exclusive contacts that allowed them to have a reach that went far beyond their own claws and fangs.

That was something she had not expected in the wake of the Happening. Zooey's insurrection had been just that—a fleeting, chaotic uprising that had, in many ways, failed to make the deeper dent that Zooey Hummel had so hungered for. Even within the post-Happening, Lupine-infested world, there was a drive for some kind of order.

Groups like the Lupines next door were avatars for that brutal return to a comprehensible new abnormal. And yet, they'd been killed by those *Synowie* agents, who'd cut them down.

Sloane came in while Polly was drying her hair, brandished some of her drawings. She was fond of drawing and could devote an afternoon to sketching with crayons or colored pencils.

"This is you, Mommers," Sloane said, holding up a drawing that showed a frowning Polly with a great, big wolf shadow hovering behind her, rendered in black crayon with bright red eyes.

"What's that?" Polly asked, pointing to the wolf shadow.

"That's you, Silly," Sloane said. "The *real* you. You keep her hidden, but I can tell she's just under the surface, all the time."

"Why the red eyes?" Polly asked, combing her hair.

"Because she's so angry," Sloane said, as if it was the most obvious thing in the universe.

How can you tell?" Polly asked. Sloane simply tapped her nose. "I smell angry?"

"Very angry," Sloane said. "Anger smells, I don't know, angry. Like hot peppers and hornets' nests."

"Ah," Polly said, feeling uncertain. She didn't feel angry. How could Sloane detect this anger inside her? It made Polly feel vulnerable, exposed. Sloane's sense of smell was uncanny.

"Every feeling has a scent," Sloane said.

"You can smell emotions?" Polly asked.

Sloane nodded. "Can't you?"

"I wouldn't know," Polly said. She had kept her emotions in check most of her life, and after being infected, she'd tried twice as hard to remain level, to not lose control.

"That's sad," Sloane said.

"What does sadness smell like?"

"Cold spaghetti," Sloane said. "A whole plate of it."

Polly laughed at the image. "Cold spaghetti?"

Sloane nodded. "It sure does. You don't want anything to do with it, but there it is, right in front of you."

"When have you ever had cold spaghetti?" Polly asked. "I've never made us cold spaghetti."

"Never," Sloane said. "Why would anybody ever eat that?"

Polly sighed, conceded the point.

"What about happiness?" Polly asked.

"Honey and butterscotch, warmed by the afternoon sun," Sloane said. "It smells rich and wonderful. It never lasts, but it's fabulous, all the same."

"I think you're making me hungry, Sloane," Polly said. "Are you hungry?"

"I'm always hungry," Sloane said. "I know you said I should control my appetites, versus letting my appetites control me."

"We can have some ice cream," Polly said. "Just a cup of it apiece. A snack."

She wanted to get the memory of the man's blood out of them both, took Sloane downstairs and scooped vanilla ice cream into two white ice cream bowls printed with tiny black stars. They ate in the dining room, Sloane humming to herself as she did so. Her primal happiness was bittersweet for Polly. Sloane was happy in a way that Polly had never been, never would be. Sloane was completely at ease with who and what she was.

Polly took to her poems that had communicated something of her state of mind. The ghost of her former self would endure through her poetry, which made her more than a little sad. She knew them all by heart…

Fester

I've waited too long
To sing this sad song
She's coming, I fear
The child that I bear

It's my own fault, yes
Seduced by his kiss
The half of myself
Which had become his

Took hold of my heart
From the very start
In the dark we bred
I did what he said
Not me, no, but her
The fur flew, for sure

And now I sit, fat
She grows inside me
Dark soul bedside, flee!
From lost bliss to that

I wait, O Ingrate!
Reckless endeavor
Now and forever
In fear for my mate.

It was the only reference to her pregnancy in her books of poetry. She'd been so careful to make sure nobody had known about the baby. The blood tests—for Night Fever, hah—hadn't come about until two years after Sloane had been born.

She'd birthed Sloane as Pol, in her Lupine form, beneath the light of a full moon, banking that her strength, vitality, and healing ability as a lycanthrope would make the delivery go easier for her.

And it did, although it was still painful, if perhaps not as painful as her lycanthropic transformations. How she'd howled when she gave birth, baby Sloane in her clawed hands, sweet baby.

Our yes-no-maybe baby, Pol had said, the newly-minted mother, the monstrous midwife in the backyard, beneath the trees, the moon, the starry skies. And Sloane had been so healthy and strong. Her Trueborn daughter.

"Sloane," Pol said aloud, and Polly accepted that name. Sloane was here, and that was that. Polly hadn't been sanguine about motherhood, but had at least wearily resigned herself to it, for lack of anything else.

Whatever her faults as a human being, Polly had a strenuous work ethic, and had produced a massive body of work in the form of her poetry, which she worked on when Sloane slept:

For Sloane

You cannot know the shame
I feel
And feeling,
I feel
I reel
My dear, my dear, my dear
I fear
I fear
I fear for you and me
You and I
Are one.
Alone, alone, alone
I atone
What have I done?

This poem, and the one after it, was a strange one, which was almost contrary to the persona that Polly had conjured and cultivated. She assumed it was Pol, striving to come forth in a more meaningful, less adversarial way:

Dead Meat

I don't like dead meat
Live kills are far better
For I am a hunter

And not a scavenger
I take what I want
and I won't ever ask
You'd know that, my Lamb
When I took off my mask.

Hungry for More

I'm hungry for more
I'll admit only that.
The price of admission:
My lies of omission.

A eulogy for her lost friends occupied another page, something she'd written in 2008, when the pain was still fresh. They were less than ghosts, now:

Horrorshow

BacchUS burned away last year
All of my friends were lost:

Sheldon simply disappeared
Where was his body tossed?

Then Lee, I think, he lost his head
Cops found it most malign

Willa burned on a pyre of books
Ones of her own design

Gabe and Clay both vanished
Their deaths so clandestine

Sam and Reagan died together:
A murder-suicide

Now I'm the only one who's left
And I've no place to hide.

And this one, reflecting her battle with her other self once more. It was the battle that was inherent in the life of an Infective:

Versus

Shattering the syntax
Between the you and me
We're at each others' throats
At war, eternally.

Don't think that you can understand
All of my aches and pain
Those moments pass through open hands
Blood pouring down the drain.
Forgive me, fragrant wallflowers
I know this is not right
But remember: you came here
To this place, tonight.

The memories, the poems, made Polly tear up. Another life, another world. She saw that Sloane had finished her ice cream, was lapping up her empty bowl.

"Let's get you to bed, Scritchers," Polly said. "Brush your teeth, first, though."

Sloane ran upstairs, was always running. Her abundant energy was an inspiration and a blessing. Her little were-child would grow up healthy and strong, fearless and free. Polly was impressed by that.

She tucked Sloane in after she'd brushed her teeth. She kissed her forehead.

"Sleep tight, you little monster," Polly said.

"Nighty-Night, Mommy Monster," Sloane said, giggling. "You're the Momster!"

Polly laughed, turning out the lights in Sloane's room. Her girl would never fear the dark. Whatever fate was in store for her, Polly knew that she loved Sloane like she'd love no one else. She loved Sloane more than she loved herself, which was something her long-dead friends would have found hilarious.

SHERIDAN and Addison Monroe had convened an ad hoc meeting of a handful of the Daughters of Zooey at Finnegan's Plate, an Irish faux-tavern that was dressed up to appear to be a pub of some sort.

Present was Nancy Link, a Chicago schoolteacher with shoulder length red hair and a bunch of freckles and who wore a red track suit. She was also there with Bobbie Wallace, a cross-fit training buff and marathon enthusiast, who wore her hair in a buzz and was in blue jeans and a white tee with running shoes. Across from both of them was Candace Stahl, who had long blond hair she wore in two braids and who wore black leggings and a roll-neck black sweater.

All of them were agitated, as they'd seen the news reports of the killings.

"They're coming after us, aren't they?" Nancy asked.

"We don't know for sure," Sheridan said.

"We know," Bobbie said. "The Wargs, now the *Volki.*"

"Black Sheep is dead, at least," Addison said. Sheridan frowned at her sister. They'd both been furious when they'd found out about it.

"Doesn't count," Sheridan said. "Someone stole our kill. He was ours by rights."

Candace looked very nervous.

"What are we going to do?" she asked. "Are they coming after us? And who?"

Normally, the Monroes had ready answers, but neither of them knew.

"It has to be the Rupinos," Nancy said. "Or Bastion. Has to be one of them."

"Why?" Bobbie asked. "Why does it have to be them?"

The Doozies perused their menus. Finnegan's was sparsely populated, as was so often the case these days. There were maybe a half-dozen other people around, shadowed at other dark wooden booths.

The waitress came up. She was a young woman with dyed red hair. The dye was, as ever, a hallmark of normality—or else a Lupine posing as a norm.

"I'm Rose. Can I get you all something to drink besides water?" she asked.

"Iced tea for me," Nancy said.

"Whiskey, neat," Bobbie said.

"I'll have the same," Sheridan said.

"Water's fine," Addison said.

"Iced tea, please," Candace said.

Rose took their drink orders, her insolent twenty-something meta-sulk on full display.

"Got it," Rose said. "I'll be back with your drinks."

She turned and walked off, leaving Bobbie and Nancy looking on, while Candace and the Monroes stewed.

"They're coming after us," Addison said. She fiddled with her red star barrette in her hair, was clearly agitated.

"But who are they?" Candace asked again.

"We need to leave the city," Addison said.

Nancy sighed and shook her head.

"I can't do that," Nancy said. "I have a life here."

"They're going after the leaders," Candace said. "I mean, right?"

"The followers, too," Sheridan said, grimacing. "Hundreds of Wargs at their creepy church. A dozen *Volki* were shot dead with Tolkachev. And somebody killed a bunch of Babas in Grant Park."

At the mention of their archrivals, the other Doozies went quiet, just in time for Rose to bring their drinks.

"Are you ready to order?" Rose asked.

They gave their lunch orders—Bobbie got beef and Guinness stew, while Nancy opted for cheddar potato soup. Candace got a corned beef sandwich with mashed potatoes. The Twins ordered fried cod and peas.

Rose took their orders and stalked away.

"She'd make a good Doozie," Addison said. "I like her attitude."

Bobbie nursed her whiskey before responding about the attacks on the other pack-factions.

"They're taking out the rival factions," Bobbie said. "It's like how Lupines took out the gangs after the Happening. Simple as that— they kill whoever is at the top of their pyramid, and then cut down everybody else in the gang. The Loops who're left then work for that new boss or they're dead. Maybe they're dead anyway. But if they break the packs, then those who're left are in disarray. Easy pickings."

"Who're they?" Candace asked. "They they they, but who are they?"

"Our enemies," Addison said. "What would Zooey do?"

"She'd attack them," Sheridan said. "Head-on."

"Yeah, she would," Addison said. "But who?"

The Monroes stewed on that a bit, while the other Doozies looked on. It was unfamiliar space for them, being hunted. They were the hunters.

"How many Doozies are there right now?" Candace asked.

"There are around a thousand of us," Sheridan said. "In the tri-state."

"We should have a retreat," Nancy said. "Like at the Forest Preserve. Just get everyone together. They can't pick us off if we're in a massive pack like that."

Bobbie smiled her Mona Lisa Smile, the one that promised secrets without giving any away.

"If we can't figure out who it is, can we at least figure out who it's not?" Bobbie asked. "I don't think it's the Wargs, because they were already hit. The Saint and the Deacon are dead."

"It's not the Babas," Candace said. "Cuz they're already dead, along with Black Sheep."

"It's not the *Volki*," Nancy said. "Same reason."

"And it's not the BEE," Addison said. "Not their style. Disappearances, yeah. But streetside murders? Not their way."

"Totally their way," Sheridan said. "Hello?"

"Jesus, Sis," Addison said. The twins didn't disagree often, but when they did, it could be epic.

The Monroes glared at each other a moment, the others nervously nursing their drinks, unsure where to look.

"That leaves us the Rupinos, Bastion and his corporate people, the *Lunares*, and the Brotherhood," Nancy said.

None of them stood out as likely candidates.

"Maybe the Rupinos?" Addison said. "I mean, Zooey stomped Ansel Rupino in '07. Maybe it's a revenge thing."

"After so many years?" Sheridan said. "Don't be stupid, Sis."

"Jesus, Sher," Addison said, as Rose refilled their drinks.

"The Rupinos are a family you do *not* want to cross," Bobbie said. "Let me just put it to you that way."

Nancy was on her phone in moments, searching.

"They're a crime family," Nancy said, holding out her phone for them to see. There were shadowy surveillance photographs of dark-haired people on a lycanthropic conspiracy website that may have had *Synowie* backing, for all they knew.

"Yes," Bobbie said. "The Rupinos are lycanthropic gangsters, for lack of a better term for it. They jealously guard their ranks and ruthlessly protect their own—their members and their territory."

Nancy read aloud from her phone.

"They call themselves the Black Hand. The original Black Hand were an Italian extortion racket around the turn of the last century," Nancy said. "Terrified people, killed others. They came with immigrants, kept them in check. Anyway, the Rupinos are the Black Hand, reborn. Only, they're not about extortion, so much as out and out racketeering, and enforcing what they consider their kind of order on things."

Nancy said. "Ansel Rupino's paintings are very good. They're lovely."

She turned her phone again so everybody could see the pretty portraits of women of all sorts. The brushwork was impeccable, the renderings were masterly—retaining the essence of the person while not falling into the photo-realistic style that many painters went to in the age of cameras and smartphones. His works were expressionistic framed in a bolder, steady-handed realism.

Addison scoffed.

"Enough, Nancy," she said. "Who were all those women he painted? Victims? Lovers? Both?"

"I don't care about Ansel Rupino's paintings," Sheridan said. "And I don't care about the Rupinos, either. If it's the Rupinos, if they're the ones after us, then fuck them. We'll deal with them."

"Deal with us?" came a voice that made them all turn around to see Valentina Rupino standing there, smiling at them.

"Oh, fuck," Addison said.

"Hiya, Ladies," Valentina said, taking a seat at the table next to them. Rose walked over to say something but Valentina shook her head and she didn't approach. "You talking about us?"

"Valentina," Sheridan said. "Wouldn't have expected you at Finnegan's Plate."

Valentina looked around the place, sniffing.

"Yeah, not really my scene," Valentina said. "You're going to deal with us, Sheridan? Or are you Addison? I can never tell."

"I'm Sheridan," Sheridan said, annoyed. "We were having a private discussion."

"Sure, sure," Valentina said. "A private discussion in a public place. A real Doozy of a discussion, sounds like."

"You killed Black Sheep," Addison said. Valentina smiled, pretending to blush.

"Not to brag or anything," Valentina said. "He had it coming."

Sheridan leaned over and glared at Valentina, who held onto her smile.

"What do you want? Why are you here?" Sheridan asked.

Valentina finger counted the Doozies at the table.

"Are you five, like, the bosses of the Doozies or what?" Valentina said.

"That's right," Sheridan said. "Bobbie's the alpha of the Wisconsin branch. Candace is the alpha of the Indiana branch. Nancy's the downstate Illinois alpha. And Addison and I cover Chicago."

Valentina chuckled.

"Branches," Valentina said. "I don't know why, but that's funny to me. It sounds like libraries or something. The important thing is you all are the heads of the Doozies."

"Are you here to deal or what?" Sheridan asked.

"We're afraid about what's been happening," Candace said. "The killings of the others. Like the Wargs and the *Volki*."

Valentina laughed, shaking her head.

"What, you think you might be next?" Valentina asked.

"Something like that," Addison said, warily. She glanced at her sister. The two of them looked both uncomfortable and ready to strike. The other Doozies looked on. Nancy spoke up.

"It's not unreasonable," Nancy said. "We have reason to be worried."

"Yeah," Candace said. "We don't want to be next."

Sheridan got to her feet, stared hard at Valentina.

"Don't think you can just show up all by yourself and try to intimidate us, Girly," Sheridan said.

Valentina looked up at Sheridan and smiled.

"Girly," she said. "That's funny. I had hoped you'd call me 'Bitch' or something toothier. 'Girly' almost sounds, I don't know, quaint?"

Candace spoke up.

"Let's not escalate this," she said. "Miss Rupino, we don't want any trouble. I mean, you're a woman, we're women. We're on the same side."

Valentina's eyes went to Candace a moment before returning to Sheridan, who was still standing over her, arms akimbo, ready to attack.

"Alright," Valentina said. "You understand about our kind, yeah?"

They all nodded.

"How about a challenge, then?" Valentina said. "For the alpha position of your pack?"

"What?" Sheridan asked.

"You heard me," Valentina said. "I'm challenging you Monroes for the leadership of the Doozies. Unless you're too scared to accept a challenge."

Addison looked at little Valentina Rupino, sizing her up. She and Monroe were both taller than she was.

"Two on one? That wouldn't be fair," Addison said.

"Oh, it wouldn't be me you'd fight," Valentina said. "It would be the Furies."

At the mention of the Furies, the Daughters of Zooey got even more on edge. The reputation of the Furies was considerable.

"That's not fair, either," Addison said. "Three on two?"

"Okay, yeah," Valentina said. "You can pick one of your other Branch Alphas to assist."

"Bobbie," Addison said.

Sheridan raised a hand.

"No," Sheridan said. "This is bullshit. You can't challenge us like that. This has to go through the Council."

"We *are* the Council," Valentina said. "You've said it yourself. You deal with us."

"That wasn't what I was talking about," Sheridan said.

"Girls," Valentina said. "One thing you have to know about lycanthropy is that when you head a pack, there comes a responsibility. Not just for the pack, of course, but for the leader. You have to be able to deal with challenges to your authority. How can you be an alpha if you've never been tested? Now, you Monroes started something to, what, honor Zooey Hummel? I can respect that. But you went and formed your own pack. Ergo, you organized yourselves in a fashion that raised your profile in the region. That organization implies a certain amount of accountability for what you do in the area. And that means being willing and able to weather challenges."

Rose returned with their entrees, eyeing Valentina and the others with concern.

"Do I need to set another place?" Rose asked, giving everybody their meals.

"No need," Sheridan said. "She was just leaving."

Rose looked at them all a moment before hastening to vacate the area.

"Enjoy your meal, Ladies," Valentina said, getting up. "I'll be waiting outside for your answer to the challenge."

Sheridan was fuming.

"Who do you Rupinos think you are, anyway?" she said. "Coming at us like this?"

"We respect Gia," Addison said. "I mean, a woman-led clan like that? We respect her."

Sheridan silenced her sister with a curt air chop of her hand.

"Gia sent this one, Addy," Sheridan said. "Gia's no friend of ours. This little pup wouldn't come here like this without the blessing of Gia. Am I right, Val?"

Valentina looked up at Sheridan, unafraid.

"So, you're the alpha among the alphas," Valentina said. "Duly noted. I mean, what is it? You ladies meet at a restaurant like this, think that it means you'd be safe or something? Didn't you see what happened at that laundromat up north? We're not regular people. We don't play by regular people rules."

The doors to Finnegan's Plate opened and a score of Rupinos came walking in, all of them women, including Bria, Sia, and Mia, who looked at the Monroes with mirthful malice.

"My cousins," Valentina said. "And sisters."

The host of Finnegan's Plate was gamely trying to get the Rupinos seated, while Valentina stared down Sheridan.

"I'm not afraid of you, you little bitch," Sheridan said. "Or your goons."

"Challenge accepted?" Valentina asked. "I wouldn't want all of these nice people to have to pay for your cowardice."

Sheridan looked at her sister, who was looking back at her. They had been at Avalon that night in '07, dancing, having fun, when Zooey had come with Samantha. They had been a staggering vision of snarls and savagery, biting everyone in reach. It had been bedlam, the terror of that moment.

Both Sheridan and Addison had been bitten by Zooey, her beautiful white wolf self as powerful as Death. But neither of the sisters had died that night. They'd been infected, had discovered who they were, and when Zooey had spoken to them in their dreams, had taken command of her pack, the Monroes had eagerly embraced it. The lineage was there, the mission. The Lupine insurrection. It had been beautiful and inspiring, the sense of empowerment they'd possessed.

No longer were they just the quirky, normal Monroe Sisters. They were a couple of fierce predators, fomenting revolution, and when Zooey had been slain, the Monroes honored her name by dubbing their pack the Daughters of Zooey. She would be remembered forever. Every fight they had, every bad man they killed, the Daughters of Zooey honored the memory of their maker.

The Doozies stalked and hunted bad men. They culled them. It was a worthwhile quest. It was one they were happy to undertake. In many respects, they did it more ardently than even Zooey, who was more about stirring the cauldron of chaos than anything else.

"We're fellow sisters of yours," Addison said. "Why would you go after us?"

Valentina glanced at Mia, Bria, and Sia, who were alternately smiling, smirking, and frowning between them.

"I already have sisters," Valentina said. "I don't need any more."

"Enough of this," Bobbie said. "We're not going to let you intimidate us. I don't care who you are."

Bobbie hopped to her feet. She was taller than Valentina, too, but Valentina didn't care.

"This isn't about sisterhood or solidarity," Valentina said. "It's about something more than that. Something deeper."

The Finnegan's Plate host tried to intercede, but some of the Rupino men stopped him, shaking their heads.

Sheridan glared at Valentina, who looked like she was hoping she would try something.

"We accept your challenge," Sheridan said, closing her eyes.

"Great!" Valentina said. "Enjoy your last meal on me."

She took out a couple of hundred-dollar bills and tossed them onto the table, before gesturing to the other Rupinos to leave.

"See you later, Ladies," Valentina said, strolling out, followed by the others. "Trotter Field. Ten tonight. Be there or we'll come looking for you. We know where you sleep."

ANNE looked at Norm closely through the bars. She looked desolately beautiful. Anne didn't belong behind bars. She belonged in happier places. She watched him watching her.

"Alone at last," Anne said. "Babe, you have to get me out of here."

He shook his head. He knew there were at least a couple *Synowie* guys upstairs, likely Sonia's brothers. Norm was grateful they were there, as he looked upon the specter of his wife. She looked good. Healthy, strong, complete. Her disguise was perfect.

"No chance," Norm said. He'd taken one of the wooden chairs and sat on it a comfortable distance from Anne.

She pouted at him. Anne had painful pouts. They were portraits of petulance.

"It's not fair," Anne said. "Judging me the way you do. I'm the victim, here, Norm."

"I know," Norm said. "It's what I told myself over the years. And it's been years, Babe. What did you do with them? Bastion and his guys?"

Anne banished the pout and conjured up a careworn look as she gripped the bars with her well-manicured nails. The varnish was off because of her transformation, but their shape was impeccable.

"I sold Lupitol," Anne said. "Chad had us push that hard. Liminalix has had revenues of over $15 billion this year because of it. And climbing. I get a cut of that. I'm rich, Babe. *We're* rich. We can leave all of this behind us. You can retire, leave the Bureau behind. All the killing. All of that nastiness. We can go anywhere you want. Build a new life, however we like."

Norm brooded over what she was making, what they were all making among Bastion's top people. Liminalix was an up-and-comer among biomedical companies. Bastion had masterfully positioned it. That Liminalix researchers had come up with that treatment for lycanthropy less than ten years after the Happening was almost too good to be true.

"Tell me about the R&D for Lupitol," Norm said.

"What about it?"

"Anything you know," Norm said.

"I'm not saying anything while I'm in this cage, Babe," Anne said. "Let me out, and I'll tell you everything."

"Not gonna happen," Norm said. "You have to look at it from my perspective, Babe. You've been literally sleeping with the enemy for years."

Anne gave the bars a shaking, took her seat on the cot in the cell, buried her face in her hands.

"I was a prisoner," Anne said. "Held against my will. You don't even know how it was. While you were gone, they came for me. Shaw and some of his guys. They turned up at our place, under the pretense of talking business. They came and Shaw turned right there. He transformed while his men held me down. He bit me, infected me. I passed out. When I woke up, I was in some facility, a recovery place. Like a hotel. I didn't know where I was."

"Just like that?" Norm asked. "Shaw didn't say anything?"

"Sure, he did," Anne said. "But I was so scared, I don't really remember it. Only flashes of memory. Shaw talked a lot. He always talked so much."

She cried into her hands.

"So, this recovery place," Norm said.

"I woke up, my wounds were tended," Anne said. "There were people there. Nurses, doctors, lab techs, whatever. Whitecoats. They monitored me. Shaw was there. I was angry with him."

"This is for the best, Anne," Shaw said. "You'll be one of us, now."

"I transformed in three days," Anne said. "They induced it. I don't know how, but they did. They were all in on it. Chad, all of them. The whole board of Liminalix. They're all lycanthropes."

"Are they all Infectives?" Norm asked.

"Everybody but Chad," Anne said. "He infected all of them himself. He let Todd infect me. It was like a gift from him, from Chad to Todd. Babe, they have an entire, I don't know, subculture. Chad has a retreat. A resort back east. Upstate New York. Something like that. He calls it 'Free Rein.' It's like a country club. Super-exclusive. It's on 500 acres, has a lodge. Chad lets his people—his pack—hunt people there. They bring people. They host events."

Because Minton had declared Bastion and his people off-limits, there hadn't been as much intel on his activities as Norm would have liked. While they'd surveilled his downtown location, this country club was another matter. Norm would have to check with the East Coast BEE.

"You see why I warned you away from me?" Anne said. "Chad's dangerous. He's terrifying. I mean, he almost never transforms. And that's what makes him scarier. You see all this stuff swirling around him, and then there's Chad, smiling, above it all, at the center of it all. Always charming, always scary. He's scary *because* he rarely changes. And he's got his creepy girlfriend, Dawn Trotter. She's scary, too."

Norm wondered what that was all about, what level of supreme control did Bastion have. Even Trueborn lycanthropes had to scratch that itch from time to time.

"But you know he's watching all the time," Anne said. "Assessing. Evaluating. Nobody crosses him. Not even Todd. He seems so genial, so genuine."

"Did you participate in those hunts at Free Rein?" Norm asked.

"Of course I did," Anne said. "They were mandatory retreats. All hands on deck, that sort of thing. I think Chad did it to compromise all of us. Like we had to run with his pack, he made us kill—and eat—people. When I was transformed, it was easy to lose myself. You run with them, the other members of his pack, and you just find your place within it. When you're there, anything goes. It's cathartic, I'm ashamed to admit."

She peered at him through steepled fingers.

Norm wondered how much *Synowie* knew about Free Rein. He'd have to check with Sonia.

"Let me out, Norm," Anne said. "Please. I know I've done bad things, but please, without Todd's influence, I'm me again. I'm your Anne. Be my Norm."

Norm didn't know if she understood that her leaning on him that way just validated his conviction to keep her in lockdown. Her attempts to persuade him were persuading him of something else, entirely. He'd dealt with so many Lupines, he knew the tricks they played, particularly the Pretenders.

Anne was a Pretender, and it broke his heart to think of her that way. He continued with his interrogation, wondered if she even knew it was one.

"So, Shaw infected you, and once you were his, you spilled what you knew about me," Norm said. "Did they ask you or did you just give that up?"

"They asked," Anne said. "I didn't know much. I mean, you know how you barely told me anything. I told them you were a Warden for the Bureau. That you'd killed many lycanthropes."

Norm wondered why they'd never come after him. Then again, Norm had made himself scarce when he'd discovered that they'd taken Anne. Maybe they'd tried, and he hadn't known it.

"They were amused by you," Anne said. "They thought you were funny. All of you Wardens. Chad most of all. He said you'd never catch him. That you Wardens were only out shooting lycanthropic losers, making things easier for him. That the real game was far out of your reach."

The real game. It set Norm's teeth on edge. His phone chirped. It was Tiff. He got up, walked across the room, glancing at Anne, who was watching him.

"Yeah?" Norm asked by way of answering his phone.

"Driver, where the hell are you?" Tiff asked.

"I'm safe," Norm said. "What's up?"

"Big Bad said somebody hit Tramp," Tiff said. "Do you know anything about that?"

Norm wondered how Minton could have known that so quickly. They'd been careful.

"Tramp's dead?" Norm asked. They must have found the burned bodies. "Who? How?"

Tiff paused on the line, and Norm imagined her frowning at him in her handler sort of way.

"Never mind how," Tiff said. "Was it you?"

"No way," Norm said. "Big Bad was very clear about that. I'm betting it was the *Synowie*. They've had a hard-on for Bromide's people for a long time."

Norm wondered how they'd found out. Maybe there was a BEE satellite overhead. Maybe they'd been actively surveilling Shaw's place. Maybe Bastion had people observing his place. Given Bastion's propensity for security, it was at least possible.

From the vantage point of a group of surveillance guys, it would have looked like a *Synowie* raid. Except for one thing—Anne.

"Why'd they take Lady, then?" Tiff asked, as if she were reading his mind.

"They took her?" Norm asked, trying to sound surprised.

"They did," Tiff said. "Now, why would *Synowie* do that, Driver? Unless they knew she was important to you. Like maybe you made some kind of arrangement with them."

"I don't know anything about that," Norm said.

"Well, here's something else you don't know anything about," Tiff said. "They put a tracker on Lady."

"Wait, who?" Norm asked.

"Bromide's people," Tiff said. "Subcutaneous. It's like they knew you—or somebody working with or for you—would come for her."

"How do you know this?" Norm asked, glancing at Anne in her cell. She'd fully transformed, which meant she'd have expelled the tracker. His eyes darted around her cell, looking for any sign, but he didn't see it. However, she'd have known about it. She'd have seen it. Moreover, she'd have known they injected her with it.

"They told us," Tiff said. "One of Bromide's people told us."

"What's wrong, Norm?" Anne asked.

"Who's that, Driver?" Tiff asked.

"Nobody," Norm said, putting the mute on the phone. "Where's the tracker, Anne?"

Anne smiled at him from behind the bars. She went over to the little table, next to the bottle of Lupitol, and held up the lozenge-shaped electronic device.

"You mean this?" Anne asked.

"Fuck," Norm said, running upstairs, taking two steps at a time.

"Driver, what's going on?" Tiff asked.

"Gotta go," Norm said, hanging up. Tiff tried calling back, but Norm didn't pick up. He ran to the *Synowie* agents. "Get out of here. Now. This place is blown."

They jumped up, looking at him curiously.

"What are you talking about?" Abram Gorski asked.

"They'd put a tracker on Anne," Norm said. "Get your stuff, get the hell out of here. Now."

The *Synowie* guys sprang into action, moving quickly. They were always ready to go if they had to. It was part of the discipline.

Abram said something in Polish to the other half-dozen *Synowie* guys, and they all hustled, while Norm dialed up Sonia.

"The safe house is blown," Norm said, getting her voicemail. "Anne had a tracker on her. They knew I'd come for her, and Bastion had put a tracker on her. I think they're coming."

He hung up and ran to the window, peered out. Everything looked normal, but that meant absolutely nothing.

"Norm?" Anne asked, her voicing lilting from downstairs. "Something the matter, Babe?"

"Rooftop," Norm said to the *Synowie*. "Don't trust the streets."

Abram shook his head. "Tunnel, Norm. We have a tunnel that connects to the place across the street."

They ran downstairs, while Norm could hear CPD at the doors of the safe house. He was impressed that the *Synowie* had somehow managed a tunnel. Then again, the Poles had been in Chicago since the early 1800s, and who knew how long the safe house had stood, and what sort of arrangements they'd made over the centuries.

"This is the Chicago Police Department," said one of the voices. "Open up or we're breaking down the door. You have one minute."

Norm's mind raced. What to do about Anne? He could see the police at the front and back doors of the safe house, and he knew he'd have to give the *Synowie* guys enough time to make good their escape.

He ran to one door and slid a chair in front of it. And to the other door, he propped a coffee table against it.

Then he turned on the gas on the stove. Anne would have seen the *Synowie* go downstairs. There was another room in the basement. He assumed the tunnel was hidden there.

"Thirty seconds," the policeman said. "Come out of there with your hands up."

Norm wondered if these were legitimate CPD or plants of Bastion's. There wasn't time. He'd have to decide—upstairs or downstairs, fight or flight. Anne or no Anne.

They hammered on the door, and Norm ran upstairs as quickly as he could, looking around for some means of exiting. He saw an attic pull chain and yanked it down, climbing up the fold-out latter, and was pleased to see that there was a means to recall the attic ladder.

Bless these Poles for their Medieval sensibilities, Norm thought, shutting the door by means of rope and pulley.

He also saw that the pull chain could be drawn up and a bolt thrown across the end of the door, which would effectively lock it. That would buy him some time.

"Ten seconds," he heard the policeman yell down below.

In the attic, Norm could see the shadows of what amounted to another bedroom—a couple of futons and chairs, some trunks. It was another place where someone could hide. He heard the cops smash through the door, could hear them running through the house. Norm turned off the ringer for his phone and crept through the attic, his eyes adjusting to the darkness, as the cops worked to clear the safe house.

He hoped the *Synowie* had managed to escape via their tunnel, even as he heard the cops run up the stairs, checking room to room.

Norm knew it wouldn't be long before they'd secured the place, and his best opportunity to escape was now, while things were still in flux.

He went to the end of the attic, where there was a window which he opened. It opened easily, and from here, he could slip onto the roof. Norm did so, hoping there weren't snipers on nearby roofs.

Who knew what Bastion and his people had said to the police. Norm quickly, quietly closed the window and slid down the roof.

In the dark, it was hard to see where he might land. Everything was bathed in shadow, except for the jumpy flashlights of the cops. He hoped he didn't twist an ankle upon landing.

Norm saw a tree in the backyard, one that had branches that hung over the house. He went for those and quickly shinnied his way across it, then slipped down to the ground by means of a tangle of branches.

He could hear the cops in the safe house, could hear Anne talking to them, thanking them for rescuing her. She was pouring on the grateful tears.

Norm jumped to the ground and scanned around him, but the cops in the back had shoved their way inside when they'd breached the house. He moved swiftly through the back lot, past the detached garage, hugging the shadows.

There were two police cruisers in the alley behind the safe house, and Norm scanned them quickly, could see there were two patrolmen in each car. Instead, he cut across the back lots of neighboring houses, climbing fence after fence until he was breathing hard. He was getting too old for this, but the greater distance he put between himself and the safe house, the better he felt.

His jeep was parked a block away, and he'd have to double back for it if he wanted to get it. He weighed his options. The primary focus would be on the safe house, but once they realized he wasn't there, they would widen their search, so it made more sense for him to snag his jeep and try to get out of there, which seemed easier than trekking on foot.

Norm zigzagged his way through back lots and made a quick street crossing once he was a block from the safe house, which was flashing with police lights from the assembled cop cars that were there.

Then he rounded the block and keyed into his jeep, starting it up and slipping out of there as quietly as he could without being conspicuous. He hoped they didn't have surveillance in too wide of a net, even as he heard the sound of a police helicopter, could see its search lights knifing this way and that over the house.

Without wasting another moment, Norm calmly drove out of there. He wondered how long it would take for Anne to spill about him, and how that would shake out, exactly.

He checked his phone as he drove, saw that Tiff had been trying to call. He dialed her up.

"This is Driver," Norm said. "Bromide sent cops after me."

"Why?" Tiff asked. "What did you do?"

"Nothing," Norm said.

Minton broke in on the line, which made Norm wonder if Tiff had patched him in.

"Driver, this is Big Bad," Minton said. "What the hell are you doing?"

"Evading," Norm said. "They're coming after me. Loopies, I think. Lady told them about me."

Minton was quiet on the line.

"Are you compromised?" Minton asked.

"Negative," Norm said. "Nobody knows where my own safe house is. I need to get to the *Argent*. At the very least, she could blow my identity."

Minton was quiet again.

"How many backups do you have?" Minton asked.

"Three remaining," Norm said.

"Use one of them," Minton said. "Get ahead of this before they go on the air."

"Easier for me if I can just get to the *Argent*," Norm said. "I can hunker down there until this blows over. We need to see what Lady's play is."

It hurt Norm to think of Anne plotting against him. He didn't understand what that was about, whether maybe some residual ill effects remained from her time in the service of Shaw.

There was perhaps a worse scenario, one almost too painful to admit—maybe she liked her time in Bastion's service. It was a possibility he didn't want to imagine. But clearly Liminalix was making good money, and Anne was a part of that. It was conceivable.

"Fine," Minton said. "Tomorrow night if you last that long. We'll send a boat for pickup at 2100 hours. Be at the drop-off point. You know the one. Do not be late."

SONIA, Mina, and her brother, Jan, were driving to Winnetka when the calls came through about the raid on the safe house.

"Bastion's making a move against us," Sonia said, riding shotgun with Jan. "And Stanislaw isn't picking up. Something may have happened to him already."

"When we get up there, I'll check out Stanislaw," Jan said. "You and Dr. Milkowski can check on the targets."

Mina watched the cityscape whisk past them as they drove. She was thinking about this child of Ansel Rupino's. She'd never seen a Trueborn child before, thought it would be a good opportunity to study her. Of course, there was the matter of Polly Drinkwater. Polly wouldn't be the type to simply accept them turning up and absconding with her and her child.

"They're not really targets, right?" Mina asked. "You're not going to kill them?"

Sonia sighed, glancing back at Mina.

"A figure of speech," Sonia said. "No, we're not going to kill them."

Jan glanced at his sister.

"We're not?"

Sonia shook her head.

"We don't kill kids, Jan," Sonia said. "Besides, our primary objective is just to secure them from Bastion. Assuming we're not too late."

"Why wouldn't we just let Bastion take them?" Jan asked.

"No," Sonia said. "That doesn't sit well with me."

Jan frowned, while Mina brooded.

"Dr. Milkowski," Sonia said, glancing back at her. "Are you quite alright?"

"I'm fine," Mina said. "Just nervous. What will we do if Bastion already has people there?"

"We'll kill them," Jan said.

"Just the three of us?" Mina asked. "I've never killed anyone."

Sonia smiled reassuringly at her.

"You don't have to kill anybody, Doctor," Sonia said. "Leave that to Jan and me. Your job will be to bring Ms. Drinkwater and her daughter to us."

Mina wondered how that would go, given how late it was. Nothing was worse than having somebody come knocking on your door in the midnight hours.

"She's going to think it's a trap," Mina said. "I don't know what I'm going to say to her."

"Make something up," Sonia said. "Tell her Ansel sent you."

The offhand way she said that made Mina think Sonia was accomplished at such breezy deceptions.

"I'm not a good liar," Mina said.

"You'll learn," Sonia said. "The alternative is letting Bastion get the girl. As I see it, she's leverage against the Rupinos for whoever gets her. That leverage should be with us. Will you be able to handle it in your condition?"

"I'm managing it," Mina said. "Thanks to the Lupitol you got me."

"Yes," Sonia said. "The miracle pill. Americans love their pills, don't they?"

"You're an American, too, Sonia," Mina said.

"Don't remind me," Sonia said, cursing as she looked out the window. Ahead of them, Mina saw a white Liminalix van, and several men in grey jumpsuits getting out at the Shaw residence. "We're too late. They're already here."

Mina tried to remain calm, and the Lupitol helped, perhaps too well. She was unable to feel anything but calm. Sonia and Jan slipped on their ski masks, and Sonia directed Mina to don her own. Mina felt so strange doing so, but she wasn't going to argue the point.

"Six targets," Jan said. "Target-targets."

Sonia fished out a submachine gun and screwed on a suppressor. Mina looked on, incredulous.

"What are you going to do, Sonia?" Mina asked.

"Why, I'm going to kill them, Dr. Milkowski," Sonia said, as Jan whipped the car into the driveway, catching two of the men with the front bumper, sending them flying back into their van.

The moment their own car stopped, Sonia hopped out, bringing the submachine gun to bear on the four men who were standing. The weapon spat silver bullets in short, controlled bursts, as Sonia felled two of them directly.

Jan jumped out of the driver's side and fired shots from his own silenced pistol into two of the men.

Sonia pivoted on the two men who'd been struck by the *Synowie* sedan, who were getting to their feet and transforming, cursing at them. She gunned them down with her weapon.

"Holy hell," Mina said, getting out of the car. She'd never been on a hit before, couldn't believe how quickly it had gone down, or how quietly. They were terrifyingly efficient.

"Secure the area," Sonia said to her brother. She looked around warily, while her brother double-tapped the fallen men in the yard, firing shots into their heads. "Doctor, visit Ms. Drinkwater, be quick about it. There may be more Bastion people on the way."

Mina quickly crossed the yard and headed toward the Drinkwater residence, feeling dizzy and shellshocked. The quick killing had made her weak in the knees. But it had energized Animus.

They're killers, Doc, Animus said. *I could help you, if you'd only let me.*

Mina remembered her ski mask, took it off, tousled her hair, retying her ponytail, and rang the doorbell. She could only imagine how this would go.

She stepped back from the door, looked up at the light coming on, saw Polly Drinkwater at the window, looking down. She opened the window.

"Yes?" Polly said, clearly irritated.

"Ms. Drinkwater," Mina said. "So sorry for the late-night drop-in. I'm Doctor Mina Milkowski. Ansel sent me to help you. You and your daughter are in terrible danger. You need to come with us."

As Sonia had surmised, mentioning Ansel affected Polly.

"Where is Ansel?" Polly asked.

"I can't reveal that right now," Mina said. "But you need to come with us."

"Who's 'us'?" Polly asked, glancing at the Shaw residence. "More vans? Are those government vans?"

"No," Mina said. "They're from Liminalix. They've sent people to kidnap your daughter. We don't have a lot of time."

Polly looked suspicious.

"How do I know this isn't just some ruse?" Polly asked.

"I suppose if I were trying to deceive you, we'd have simply broken into your house and tranquilized you and your daughter and shipped you off without talking to you, first," Mina said. She had little patience for Polly's suspicions.

"It's very late," Polly said.

"I wouldn't be here if it wasn't vitally important," Mina said.

"How do you know Ansel?" Polly asked.

"I'm part of the Bureau," Mina said. Polly's eyes narrowed.

"So, you *are* a government agent," Polly said. "Where is Ansel?"

Mina felt her frustration rising.

"He's at a safe house," Mina said. "I can't say anything more without jeopardizing his safety. All I can tell you is that he's safe, he's terribly worried about you, and that you're in great danger. The longer you remain here, the greater danger you're in. Please get dressed, get your daughter, and let us get you someplace safe. We'll reunite you with Ansel as soon as we can."

Polly grudgingly closed the window and disappeared without a word.

Another Liminalix van appeared, driving into the driveway of the Drinkwater residence. Mina called to Sonia.

Four men in grey Liminalix jumpsuits hopped out. When they saw Mina, their eyes narrowed. One of them went to his phone. They were big men with hard faces.

Sonia appeared from the shadows, her submachine gun pointed at the men. They saw her, and two of them ducked around the far side of the van before Sonia fired, dropping the other two with well-aimed sprays of silver bullets.

"*Synowie* bitch," one of the men called from behind the van. "We're sending more people. More people than you have bullets."

Sonia ran across the yard, motioning for Mina to stay where she was as she jumped around the van, firing two more bursts without a word.

"Jesus," Mina said. She couldn't believe how ruthless Sonia was. "Did you get them?"

"Yes," Sonia said, firing another burst into both of their faces. She reloaded her weapon as she emerged from behind the van.

"Were those men Lupines?" Mina asked.

"Yes," Sonia said. "You can't give them a chance to transform, or you're dead."

"Stanislaw is dead," Jan said, appearing. "Torn apart. Killed by a Lupine."

"Go around the back," Sonia said. "Keep an eye out. There may be more."

Polly opened the front door, wearing a black turtleneck and leggings, carrying her sleepy daughter. When she saw Sonia standing here in her mask, her eyes went big.

"It's okay," Mina said. "They're with me."

"They? And why are 'they' wearing a mask?" Polly asked.

"Have you ever seen how the police and military deal with cartels in South America, Ms. Drinkwater?" Sonia said. "We conceal our identities for our own protection."

Polly reluctantly acknowledged that.

"So, now what?" Polly asked. "Where are you taking us?"

Sonia handed Mina a set of keys to the car they'd driven in on, as well as a set of keys with an address printed on them. Old Town.

"Get to this place," Sonia said. "Another safe house. We'll meet you there."

"How many safe houses do you people have?" Mina asked.

"Never enough," Sonia said.

"What are you going to do?" Mina asked.

"We're going to clean this up," Sonia said. "Two shootings at Shaw's in one night? That's going to get someone's attention, even in Winnetka. Plus, we have to take care of Stanislaw."

Mina nodded, directed Polly to follow her, which she did.

"Who're these people, Momster?" the little girl said.

"They're friends, Sloane," Polly said, giving Mina a scathing look. Mina keyed them into the car, putting Polly and Sloane in the back, while she got out of there as discreetly as she could. Mina's hands were shaking.

"Those were *Synowie,* right?" Polly said. "The werewolf killers?"

"Yeah," Mina said.

"But *we're* werewolves," Polly said, while Mina drove.

"So am I," Mina said, making Polly raise her eyebrows.

"What?"

"I'm an Infective, too," Mina said. "Zooey Hummel bit me."

At mention of Zooey, Polly scoffed.

"That one was all sorts of crazy," Polly said. "But answer me this: why would those werewolf killers be helping us?"

"We'rewolves," Sloane said, giggling. "Get it, Momster?"

"I do, Scritchers," Polly said, patting her head.

Mina sighed, keeping her eyes on the road as she drove. The last thing she wanted was to draw any attention to herself.

"I think the people at Liminalix want your daughter," Mina said. "It's some werewolf politics thing. I think they're kind of doing an enemy of my enemy is my friend-type of deal."

Polly accepted that without a word. She'd laid Sloane down in the back seat, where the girl could sleep, although she looked too excited to sleep.

"I really don't appreciate being rousted out of my home in the dead of night," Polly said.

"We wouldn't have done it if we didn't have to," Mina said. "I don't know what would have happened if they'd gotten to you. They only wanted your daughter."

"Why?"

"She's Ansel's child, right?" Mina asked.

"Yes," Polly said, after a moment or two.

"That's why," Mina said. "It's complicated, but they wanted her as a bargaining chip for dealing with the Rupinos. Not so much for the rest of them, but against Ansel."

"And that's why he sent you," Polly said. "Why didn't he come himself?"

"He couldn't," Mina said. "He's being hunted by enemies."

She was on a limb, but the lies came easier to her.

"Are you on Lupitol?" Mina asked, trying to change the subject.

"No," Polly said. "Although my neighbors—well, Anne Stockwell, anyway—gave me a case of it. I didn't take it, though."

Mina wondered what Anne had been up to. Perhaps the plan had been to get Polly to incapacitate herself and then send in their Liminalix goons to kidnap Sloane. After that, it was anybody's guess what they had in mind.

Polly looked at Mina through the rearview mirror.

"Were you part of that group who came to Shaw's place earlier?" she asked. "I saw what happened."

"No," Mina said. "I wasn't."

"They took Anne away," Polly said. "They shot Shaw and some of his guys."

Mina kept as composed as she was able to be. If Liminalix sent other goons, they were screwed. If the BEE sent agents, they were screwed. If they ran into some random hostile Lupines, they were screwed.

"They were bad guys," Mina said, making Polly scoff again.

"That's what everybody says," Polly said. "Evil's like hipsterism—nobody ever owns up to it."

Mina hadn't heard hipsters invoked in awhile, was amused by it.

"I don't think anybody's a hipster anymore," Mina said. "They're nearly extinct."

Polly accepted that with a sigh.

"I prefer 'young urban creative' anymore," she said. Although she felt anything but young these days, just turning 37 the month before. Her life was practically over, most certainly the life she'd led as a young poet. "What's Lupitol like?"

"It works," Mina said. "Mostly. Maybe not completely, but it keeps the worst of the…compulsions…away."

"You still transform?"

"Sometimes," Mina said. "It's different, now. My triggers are reduced. Maybe absent. I'm not entirely sure. It's better than the tranquilizers I used to take."

Mina glanced in her rearview mirror instinctively, to see if they were being followed. Not that she'd be able to necessarily spot a tail. But she figured it couldn't hurt to keep an eye on those things, just in case. It looked clear, but she wasn't entirely sure.

"But Liminalix is after you," Polly said.

"After us," Mina said.

"How does that work?"

"I don't entirely know," Mina said. "The man at the head of it is a bad guy. I haven't sorted out what he's up to with Lupitol, except that it's making him a lot of money as a treatment for Night Fever."

"Night Fever," Polly said. "They're gaslighting the whole country about it. The stories they tell. Hallucinations, memory loss, anxiety, mood swings. All of it. All just to cover up what's actually going on."

Mina would have loved to have known who was behind that whole campaign. It had been carried out to perfection. There were, of course, people who denied that Night Fever even existed. There were people who denied that werewolves existed, too.

Various politicians from rural and southern areas had come out forcefully against it, and against government interference in their lives. Mina wondered how many of them were themselves lycanthropes, how that worked. She didn't think lycanthropy was well-suited for a political career, but maybe she was wrong. Or maybe they were on Lupitol, managing their affliction the way she did.

"I don't have any part of that," Mina said. "It's big, though. Bigger than we are."

Up ahead, there were police cars gathered, lights flashing. There were at least seven cars and SUVs. Mina slowed down, directed to one side by a police officer.

On the ground were a cluster of dead people, busy being covered by sheets by paramedics. They looked like they'd been torn apart.

The police officer waved Mina past the scene, and she and Polly looked out at it as they passed.

"What the hell was that?" Polly asked.

"Looks like a werewolf attack, judging from all of the blood," Mina said, eagerly putting it behind them.

"It's horrible," Polly said. "So much killing. It's just so ugly."

Mina found herself increasingly immune to shock at such things. She didn't know whether it was a result of her condition, or whether her former line of work had done it to her.

"That it is," Mina said.

"I can't stand ugliness," Polly said.

Mina was sure she meant it, judging from her tone. Polly seemed like the type of person who would wrap herself in beautiful things and wish away the bad. The researcher Mina was couldn't pass that up.

"How often do you transform?" Mina asked.

"Weekly," Polly said. "If I indulge it. Every three days if I don't."

"Indulge?" Mina asked. "Meaning what?"

"If I kill something," Polly said. "If I give her something to kill, I can keep her quiet for about a week."

That seemed roughly in the range Mina had associated with the infection.

"Does it matter what you kill?" Mina asked. "Or who?"

Polly's eyes flashed in Mina's rearview mirror at the insinuation.

"I don't hunt people, if that's what you're asking," Polly said. "Not since I first became this way."

Mina understood that.

"But the temptation is still there," Mina said.

"All the time," Polly said.

"However, you won't take the Lupitol," Mina said.

"I'm not in the habit of taking drugs given to me by the lycan-thropic lovers of creepy pharma industry bro neighbors," Polly said.

"Yeah, that wouldn't be good," Mina said, and they drove in silence for a bit. It was starting to snow a little, just furtive flakes dusting the city. Mina hoped the safe house had enough sleeping accommodations because she wanted to conk out. Sloane was quiet, presumably slumbering after all.

"I'm not a murderer," Polly said. "She is, but I'm not."

"Right," Mina said.

"I hunt deer," Polly said, a trifle defensively. "And coyotes."

Mina wondered how that played out in the local ecosystems. She wasn't going to burden Polly with that possibility. They all had enough on their minds for one night. Mina drove them down a neighborhood side street flanked by low-rise old buildings, managed to find a parking spot after driving around for awhile.

She rechecked the address on the keys. "We're here. I'll help you with Sloane."

Then she saw the Liminalix van behind them, about a block back, and started moving again. Polly looked at her, annoyed.

"What's the problem?"

"Behind us," Mina said. "Liminalix."

She wondered how the hell they'd found them. Maybe it had been another team that had hung back when they'd seen what had happened to their comrades. Polly glanced over her shoulder, could see only the headlights of the approaching van.

Mina texted Sonia.

LIMINALIX ON MY SIX. SEND HELP.

Trying to appear at ease while still intending to evade, Mina began taking turns, seeing if the van was actually tailing them. The van kept after her, turn after turn.

They should have waited until you stopped, Animus said through her Lupitol muzzle. *They jumped the gun.*

"What do we do?" Polly asked, checking on Sloane, who was sleeping the way only a child could.

"I'm trying to evade while I think up options," Mina said, glancing at her phone. She texted Sonia again.

VAN ON MY TAIL. NOT SURE WHERE TO GO.

She did another neighborhood circuit, not wanting to get too far from the safe house address, but also not wanting to get too close to it. The van was maintaining distance, likely radioing for help.

"They're just staying on our tail," Mina said. "Maybe calling for assistance."

Polly scowled at her from the back seat.

"Some rescue," she said. "I would've been better at my house. More comfortable."

"No, I don't think so," Mina said. "Liminalix is after you—and they won't stop until they catch you."

"Okay, I have an idea," Polly said. "Next turn where you get out of direct sight, let me hop out. Then you keep driving. I'll take care of them."

"You?" Mina said. "Doesn't seem your style."

"Not mine," Polly said, tapping her forehead. "Hers. Believe me, I'm no hero. But Pol—my other half—she lives for this kind of business."

"Pol," Mina said.

"Yep," Polly said, taking off her clothes in the back seat, methodically setting them down on the seat next to sleeping Sloane. "Believe me, I don't want to do this. But she does. And I know better than to argue with her."

Sonia's text came.

WE'RE ON OUR WAY, TRY TO KEEP MOVING.

Mina made another turn and Polly hopped out as Mina momentarily stopped before she got rolling again. As before, the van turned and followed, maintaining distance.

She wondered how that would go with Polly. Mina only had to wait a block to find out, when she saw the van swerve behind them, crashing into some of the parked cars. Mina resisted the urge to stop and watch, deciding instead to take another turn and try to get to the safe house. Her first priority was to keep Sloane safe, and out of the clutches of Liminalix.

12

NORM was casing the rendezvous point at Navy Pier an hour before the appointed time. It wasn't that he didn't trust Minton to send people there. It was that Norm didn't trust anyone, anymore. Not after what Anne had pulled. He'd parked his jeep in a parking deck near the Pier and walked carefully to a spot where he could keep an eye on things without drawing attention to himself.

He was still processing all of that. Anne had gone on the local news, tearfully recounting herself being kidnapped by her husband, who was in league with a group of European terrorists known as the *Synowie Srebra.*

This group was being blamed for a variety of terrorist acts in the city, including the apparent firebombing of the First Lupercalian Church of the Apocalyptic Vision, where several hundred people had been killed in what was called the worst act of domestic terrorism since the Oklahoma City bombing of 1995.

The *Synowie* were said to be dangerous fanatics, identifiable by their cryptic symbol, which the news station helpfully showed, along with a photograph of Norm that Anne had helpfully given them. The group had been implicated in a number of shootings throughout the city and were considered armed and extremely dangerous. Anyone with information was encouraged to call the hotline they flashed on the screen.

Norm wondered what kind of strings Bastion had pulled to get this to happen, pinged Tiff for some details.

"What is this crap about the Lupercalians?" Norm asked. "That wasn't *Synowie.*"

"We know," Tiff said.

"But it's being blamed on them," Norm said. "So, who's feeding that to the media?"

"We're still looking into that," Tiff said.

From where Norm was, he had a good view of Navy Pier and the pickup spot.

"Are you?" Norm asked. "I feel like you're all pulling my chain."

"You'll be safe soon enough, Driver," Tiff said. "Just be patient and don't get caught by any locals."

Sonia texted him.

PACKAGE RECOVERED INTACT. BUT MONA PEOPLE ARE TAILING DOC.

He replied quickly.

YOU'D BETTER LIE LOW. DOES SHE NEED HELP?

Sonia texted back directly.

WORKING ON IT.

Norm listened, thought maybe he heard a howl or two, although with the ever-present whir of traffic on Lake Shore Drive, it was hard to be sure.

"Wasn't planning on it," Norm said. He planned on combing the *Argent* while he was there. He'd find Ansel.

He saw some CPD cruisers driver around Navy Pier, half-wondering if they were there for him. They weren't moving too quickly, were just tooling around. They parked between him and the rendezvous point.

"Of course," Norm said.

"What is it, Driver?" Tiff asked.

"Locals," Norm said. "Right at the dropoff."

"You're early," Tiff said. "Maybe they'll be gone by the time your ride shows up."

"Or maybe they won't be," Norm said. "Did somebody tip them off?"

"I don't think so, Driver," Tiff said. "I'm sure it's fine."

Norm took out a little night vision spyglass and looked at the cops. Four officers, parked side-by-side so they could shoot the shit. They didn't look to be unusually alert or staking anything out. Sometimes, coincidences were just coincidences. But in his line of work, you never knew. Failing to be paranoid could get you killed, or worse.

"Have you seen the news?" Norm asked.

"Of course," Tiff said. "We're monitoring all broadcasts."

"I don't understand it," Norm said. "She's still with them."

"We can debrief when you're here, Driver," Tiff said. She was not the sort to communicate too openly anywhere but in-person. "See you soon. Don't get caught."

Then she hung up. Norm didn't like that, either. Everything was making him edgy. He chalked it up to lack of sleep and him shooting several Lupines that night.

"Hey, there," said a voice near him, making Norm jump. It was Valentina, who'd managed to creep up on him. She smiled at him, wearing her black leather jacket and some black leggings. She had on a black stocking cap, too.

"What the hell are you doing here?" Norm asked. "How'd you find me?"

Her smile remained.

"We've been tracking you for awhile," Valentina said. "In case you got into trouble you couldn't handle. Not that you couldn't, mind you. No disrespect."

Her smile remained, and Norm looked around.

"Are *they* here?" Norm asked.

"The Furies?" Valentina said. "No, they're busy. We have big plans later tonight. Gia just thought I should check up on you after that whole thing with your wife. Bad break, Bro."

Her cocksure manner rankled him.

"Why are you here?" Norm asked. "For real."

Valentina looked wounded.

"Maybe I just enjoy your company," Valentina said. "Have you thought of that? You're a killer like me."

"I doubt that," Norm said.

Valentina gave him a playful rap on the shoulder.

"Nice escape from that safe house, by the way," she said. "You're pretty limber for an old guy."

"You saw that?" Norm said. He felt even worse knowing that the Rupinos were apparently monitoring his every step.

"Yep," Valentina said. "Those *Synowie*, they have quite a little network. I can respect that. Although, judging from the news, they're going to have a tough go of it. Domestic terrorism, that's a tough stain to wash out, if you know what I mean."

Norm could see her amusement at it all. This young Trueborn was having the time of her lycanthropic life.

"Yeah, about that," Norm said. "Was that your people?"

"Norm," Valentina said, shocked. "We wouldn't do that. We tear people apart and garrote them. We don't firebomb churches. What do you think we are?"

Norm tried to get a read on her, found her unreadable.

"So, you're saying you didn't do that?" Norm asked.

"Nope," Valentina said. "Although the Wolves of God had it coming to them, to be honest. I mean, really—neo-Nazi werewolves? How on the nose is that?"

"Who did it?" Norm asked.

"Act of God?" Valentina said, throwing her hands in the air. "Just kidding. If I had to wager, I'd say it was a Bastion hit. Seems on-brand for him."

Norm decided to push forward on that a bit more. Valentina liked to talk, and he'd indulge her.

"Are you Rupinos working with Bastion?" Norm asked.

"Hell, no," she said. "Dude, we're rivals. We hate Bastion."

He believed she was telling him the truth. Hate was hard to hide. She watched him watching her, the two of them in the shadows.

"What's Bastion's play?" Norm asked.

"He wants to run the world, I suppose," Valentina said. "He probably wants to be president or something."

It seemed absurd, imagining Chad Bastion as a politician. Somehow, that felt beneath him, condescending to running for office.

"I don't think so," Norm said. "He'd have to give up too much for that. Maybe he'll infect the Mayor and run things from the shadows."

Valentina smiled at that. Her smile was full of mirth and menace. Though she was young, she carried herself with considerable power, far more than mere youthful moxie. She was serenely sociopathic.

"I like the way you think, Norm," Valentina said. "You'd make a good Rupino."

"Right," Norm said. He glanced out at the rendezvous point, but the boat hadn't shown up, yet. And the police hadn't left.

"You've got to get me aboard the *Argent,*" Valentina said.

"Hah," Norm said. "I don't think you'd want that. The whole ship is full of people whose entire mission in life is stopping people just like you."

Valentina pursed her lips and blew her bangs out of her eyes.

"Aww, you called me people. I'm not worried," Valentina said. "I mean, crazy Zooey Hummel ransacked the Kennel all by herself. I would have loved to have killed her. I was still a kid, though. Crazy how time flies, right?"

"Yeah," Norm said. "'Crazy' being the operative word, there. She only succeeded because nobody had ever done something like that before. The folks on the *Argent* are much better prepared against that sort of stuff these days."

Valentina gazed out across the dark waters of the lake and squinted.

"I like a challenge," Valentina said.

"That's more like suicide," Norm said, making her laugh. Her laugh was a nasty little thing, short and sharp, like little barks.

"I'm a lot tougher than I look," Valentina said. "Small but mighty."

"I'm sure you are," Norm said. "But having you along for the ride would be awkward."

Norm wondered why the young Rupino woman was here at all. There was some game being played, and he was unsure what it was.

Two more police cruisers drove up to Navy Pier, joined their buddies.

"Damn, it's like a police convention," Norm said.

"Don't you worry," Valentina said. "We'll take care of it. When's your boat arriving?"

Norm checked his phone.

"Fifteen minutes," Norm said.

"Alright," Valentina said. She took out her own phone and called somebody. "Fifteen minutes."

"What are you up to?" Norm asked.

"Helping you out, Bro," Valentina said. "You're welcome."

"Why?"

"Because you're going to find Ansel and get him the hell off of that ship," Valentina said. "That's why."

"Assuming he's there," Norm said. He wanted to make sure to properly set her expectations.

"Oh, he's there," Valentina said. "I'm sure of it. If I could go with you, I could track him, if he's there. I'd find him and free him."

Norm shook his head.

"The pickup's for me," Norm said. "They won't take you."

"What if you pretended to capture me?" Valentina said. "And I, like, escaped?"

"Maybe, but I don't want to have to deal with that," Norm said. "They'd put the ship on lockdown, and I wouldn't be able to travel freely aboard her."

"You're no fun at all, Norm," Valentina said. "Fine, but you'd better not come ashore empty-handed, is all I'm saying."

She went to her phone and dialed up whoever was on the other line.

"Alright, start it up," Valentina said.

"Gia puts a lot of trust in you," Norm said.

"She's knows talent when she sees it," Valentina said. "She's got a great eye for it."

They heard a howl, then another one, then another. Norm turned his scope to the police cruisers, could see the police looking around nervously. Then he saw some black Lupines from the shadows, running for the cars. They moved so quickly, like furry blurs, bearing down on the cruisers.

Some of the police officers saw them, but the Rupino werewolves were on them before they could do anything more than shout. The Lupines jumped on the hoods of their cars, crunching them and cracking their windshields with blows from their clawed arms.

The police officers began shouting and cursing, while the Rupinos went bolting off into the shadows, heading south. The cruisers turned on their sirens and lights and gave chase.

Valentina smiled at Norm with considerable satisfaction.

"There, you see? Easy."

Norm watched them go, then turned his gaze to the lake. He could see a boat approaching.

"Nice," Norm said. "Thanks."

"Happy to help," Valentina said. "Always. Good luck, Bro. Find my brother. Bring him back."

"Yeah," Norm said. "Nice chatting with you."

"Last chance to take me with you," she said.

"No way," Norm said. "No offense."

"It's alright," Valentina said. "I've got a hot date tonight."

"Yeah?"

Valentina nodded.

"A date with destiny," she said.

"Sounds portentous," Norm said, looking at her. She only shrugged, winking at him.

"I never kill and tell," Valentina said.

"Not my wife," Norm said, suddenly concerned.

"I wouldn't dream of it," Valentina said. "Okay, maybe I'd dream of it. But Gia told me she's yours, so there it is."

He left her in the shadows of the grove they'd shared and ran across the parking area toward the pickup point. He could hear the sirens of the police cars as well as the howls of the Rupinos serving as a distraction.

The boat pulled up, and Norm ran to it. There were three BEE agents aboard it, one on the front, manning an M60 machine gun. One was driving, and the other was aft, waving for Norm, who offered his confirmation code phrase.

"Long, grey day, eh?" Norm said.

"I prefer sunshine, myself," the agent said, throwing out a gangplank. Norm trotted over it and they removed the plank, speeding the boat from shore. The agents were alert and nervous.

"Nice to have you aboard, Driver," the agent said. He was a young man, short-haired and lean. He wore a BEE ballcap. "Any problems getting to us?"

Norm glanced back from where he'd come, could see Valentina there, wrapped in shadow, like a wraith, watching him go.

"Nothing I couldn't handle," Norm said, as they sped off into the darkness.

13

AFTER the encounter at Finnegan's Plate, the Daughters of Zooey had put out an all-call to their Chicago members. Sheridan had been enraged by the presumption of Valentina Rupino, the threat and the challenge she'd presented.

She'd fumed about it to the other heads of the Doozies. She was inconsolable as she paced in the building they had occupied for months. It had been the hangout of a gang of drug dealers, and the Doozies had murderously evicted them.

"We should just flee Chicago," Candace said. "Get away from here."

"No," Sheridan said. "That bitch is not chasing us out of town. Who does she think she is? Gia won't even take my calls."

Sheridan had thrown her phone across the room after trying three times to call Gia, getting only voicemail.

"We can't answer their challenge," Addison said.

Sheridan whirled on her sister, wild-eyed with fury.

"Of course we will answer it," Sheridan said. "But not in the way she suspects. We'll send hundreds after her. She thinks it's going to just be us showing up for her pathetic challenge. But we'll be an army. We'll kill those Rupinos and take their heads."

Addison was always the more cautious of the two of them, even before they'd become Infectives.

"Maybe they know you're going to do that," Addison said. "Maybe it's a trap."

"I don't care," Sheridan said. "We're going to run them down and kill them all."

Word had gone out through the Doozie network, that they were to meet at Trotter Field before ten o'clock.

"We'll be like a conquering army," Sheridan said. "Zooey would be so proud of us."

Nancy, Bobbie, and Candace were less certain, which only further enraged Sheridan. She turned on them.

"You should want this as much as we do," Sheridan said. "You saw that arrogant little thing, how she carried on. Threatening us. US."

"Yeah," Nancy said. "Still, Addison could be right. Maybe it's a trap. Maybe we should do something else. Like just not be there."

"And lose face? I accepted the challenge," Sheridan said. "I'm not going to lose face."

Addison tried to calm her twin.

"She's pushing your buttons, Sher," Addison said. "She knew you'd be infuriated by that. She did it on purpose to rile you up."

"Jesus, Addy," Sheridan said. "I don't care what her ulterior motive may have been. She's going to die. I'm going to kill her. Zooey would have hated her."

Nancy cleared her throat, looked vaguely uncomfortable.

"She's kind of like Zooey," Nancy said. "You know, like brazen."

That really burned Sheridan up. She got in Nancy's face, snarling at her.

"She's nothing like Zooey," Sheridan said. "That's an insult to Zooey's memory. Valentina's not a revolutionary—she's a reactionary. She's trying to put us down because we're threatening the established order. She's part of the Establishment. Trueborn aristocracy. That's exactly what this is. Aristocrats versus we Infective proles. That's precisely how this is playing out. I, for one, am not going to allow some blue-blooded Trueborns take down the Daughters of Zooey."

"Look, Nancy, Candace," Addison said. "You don't have to be there. The challenge was for Sheridan and me."

"And me," Bobbie said. "Personally, I'd like to take out those Furies."

"We're with you," Nancy said, glancing at Candace, who nodded. "Sisterhood and solidarity."

They held out their hands, and everyone put their hands together, until they were like a wheel. Sheridan let out a howl that they all joined in on, all of them transforming as they spun, turning into a multi-hued pack of werewolves in barely a minute.

Sheridan snarled and ran up the stairs toward the rooftop deck, followed closely by her sister and the others. Sheridan howled, and they joined her, the Daughters of Zooey sounding a terrifying chorus.

Sheridan was gratified to hear other howls going up across the city, and whether or not they were fellow Doozies, she imagined that they were. They ran for Trotter Field, tearing through the city at close to ten o'clock. Sheridan was pleased to see other Doozies joining them as they ran.

First there were five of them, then there were ten running, then forty, then seventy-five, then a hundred, then two hundred. Then three hundred. A pack of such ferocity and power that Sheridan felt like Zooey was with them again, brought back to life by the spectacle of their numbers.

The Daughters of Zooey retained the purity of Zooey's insurrectionary vision, more than any of the other Infectives. Sheridan and Addison had been thrilled to have kept that part of her alive.

All of them running, their voices joining in howls of war lust and rage, panting as they ran tirelessly toward Trotter Field.

In the dark, the Rupinos waited in their black-furred hybrid forms. Sheridan saw that with more than a little satisfaction. Valentina and the Furies were there, in the center of the field, waiting.

"Valentina's mine," Sheridan growled.

"She's ours," Addison snarled back.

The Daughters of Zooey fanned out into the soccer field, quickly surrounding the gathered Rupinos, who numbered only four.

What almost adolescent arrogance, Sheridan thought. *To think we wouldn't bring all of us that I could. We are stronger together than apart.*

"You showed up," Valentina said. "And you brought friends."

"You've bitten off more than you can possible chew," Sheridan said.

Sheridan wasn't about to banter with Valentina Rupino. Rather, she charged at her, mouth agape, while Valentina met her head-on, the Furies pouncing at Addison and Bobbie, while the other Doozies had formed a circle around the combatants.

Sheridan had left specific instructions that they were to wait. Should Addison and Sheridan fall, the Doozies were to set upon the surviving Rupinos and tear them to pieces.

But until that happened, the Grand Pack was to hang back and observe.

The Furies pounced on Bobbie, who clawed at them, but they outmaneuvered her, throwing her aside.

Addison went to help her sister against Valentina, her claws digging up clods of sod as she ran. The two of them were well-used to fighting together. It had given the Monroe Sisters an edge over the years, in fight after fight.

Valentina was limber, though, and was able to hold her own against both of the Monroes, snapping and clawing at them.

Blood was freely spilled on Trotter Field as they fought one another.

The Furies bounded for the Monroes, seeing Valentina fighting the Twins, while Bobbie was fighting to get to her feet and charge back in.

The audience of Doozies around them was a sea of red eyes and snarling faces, fangs bared.

Sheridan slashed at Valentina, catching her on her arm, only to have Valentina snap at her forearm, sinking her teeth into Sheridan, prompting Sheridan to cry out. Addison jumped to help her sister, but the Furies interceded, blocking access to Sheridan. Addison growled and stood her ground, her hackles up, while the Furies leered at her.

Bobbie charged into the Furies, tearing at them with her long claws. Two of the Furies went after Bobbie, while the third launched herself at Addison.

Valentina yanked her head this way and that, tearing at Sheridan's forearm, sending blood and flesh splashing onto the soccer field.

Grinning at her bloody-mouthed, Valentina circled Sheridan, who held her wounded arm in reserve.

"I never bite off more than I can chew," Valentina said. "See?"

Sheridan looked at her mangled arm and gnashed her teeth.

"For Zooey!" Sheridan roared, joined by the chorus of Doozies around her. The support of her sisters gave her power, and she slammed into Valentina, her shoulder catching Valentina in the ribs and sending her back.

Bobbie struggled against both of the Furies, who were splitting her focus between them, nipping and clawing at her in alternate turns. Bobbie committed to one of the Furies, trying to get at her throat, but the other Fury struck at her, yanking her head back with a clawed grasp of her furry head as the other Fury bit her throat, crushing her windpipe. And still the Furies attacked her amid the chorus that rang out in the darkness.

"For Zooey! For Zooey!"

But Bobbie dropped to the field, while the Furies flayed her with their claws, grievously—mortally—wounding her. It was not easy to kill a werewolf, but other werewolves could do it. And as they did so, Bobbie fell dead upon the field, while the Furies howled in triumph.

Addison saw Bobbie fall and let out an aggrieved howl-whimper and tried to get at the Furies who had killed her fellow Daughter of Zooey, only to have the Fury she was facing stop her with an outstretched claw and yank her back.

"Addison!" Sheridan said, seeing her sister in distress. She tore at Valentina with her claws, finding their mark on her furry frame, but

Valentina kept fighting even as Sheridan disengaged and tried to get to her sister.

The Furies had grabbed Addison—one held one arm, one held another, and the other held her flailing legs. The Furies were savage and relentless, slamming Addison onto the field with dreadful force that shook the ground and startled the onlooking Doozies into silence.

Within the ring, there was only growling and snarling and the rending of flesh, the splashing of blood. Addison's frame strained before the force of the Furies, who snarled and grunted as they pulled at her.

"Sheridan!" Addison shrieked, the Furies tearing off her arms in a horrid rending-popping sound. Addison screamed, flopping on the field while the third Fury smashed her onto the field again, her blood flowing from her torn body. The Furies raised Addison's arms aloft, watching them turn from their Lupine form to the arms of the young woman that she was.

The third Fury climbed atop Addison as Sheridan was clawing to reach her, only to clamp her Lupine jaws onto Addison's neck. The crunch was as loud as it was final.

The spectating Daughters of Zooey looked on in horror as Addison Monroe died on Trotter Field, her lifeless eyes on her sister Sheridan as she changed from her Lupine form into her pale and naked body. The Furies tossed her severed arms beside her body, turning to regard Sheridan.

"Addy," Sheridan wept, too late to rescue her fallen sister. She turned to face Valentina, who had gotten to her feet again, was sneering at her. "I'm sorry."

"She can't hear you," Valentina said.

"Hear this," Sheridan said. "Avenge us! For Addison! For Bobbie! For Zooey! For me!"

Her voice carried out over the field, and the assembled Daughters of Zooey raised their heads and howled as one, and they made to charge at Valentina and the Furies, but something was happening around the assembled Lupines.

Shots were being fired. Silenced, but unmistakable for the way the submachine guns and assault rifles coughed and spat silver bullets into the assembled pack from all sides. For while all eyes had been on the fight between the Monroes and Valentina and the Furies, the Rupinos had others who had gathered around the Doozies with weapons.

And they'd begun shooting just as Sheridan had tried to rally her pack.

The silver bullets could hardly miss at the range they were at, and the Rupinos went through clip after clip, firing into the panicking Doozies who sought to put distance between themselves and the firearms.

Valentina cocked her bloodied ear and smirked at Sheridan, who was panting and weeping by her dead twin.

"You hear that?" Valentina asked. "Modernity. Guess we're not so old-fashioned after all, *Spazzatura*."

Sheridan saw her sister packmates mowed down around her, saw Nancy and Candace flee into the silver-stinking throng and she vaulted toward Valentina, offering an intimate apology to Zooey, hoping to be able to kill the smug Trueborn before she died that night.

"I'M NOT A WOLF
IN SHEEP'S CLOTHING.
I'M A WOLF IN
WOLF'S CLOTHING."
—RICKY GERVAIS

GIA Rupino and several other members of the Black Hand held the trio of surviving Wargs they'd managed to catch in their chairs, having looped them—the length of silver piano wire, like a snare, put tight around their necks.

The trio were three young men who'd been intercepted tailing Gia's limousine. They'd become aware of them as Gia had made her way to the Rupino Urban Frontier Foundation for an art exhibit, and had arranged a trap for them, catching them and looping them before the Wargs could do anything about it.

Or almost—one of them had transformed as he was being looped and had cut off his own head. The point had been made, and the others had complied.

"What were you doing following me, *Infettivi?*" Gia asked. "You must know that I don't like to be followed."

"Go to hell," one of them said. One of the young men. "We don't want your kind here. Not anymore."

Gia glanced at her kindred, where they exchanged shrugs. The Wolves of God were particularly strident in their posturing relative to the Trueborn/Infective issue.

"Where? Chicago? America? The world?" Gia asked.

"How about all of the above?" the young man said. His blue eyes were full of malice, above and beyond what the lycanthropy had amply provided him. "This is our world, now. You old Wolf Mafia types had your day. It's *our* time."

"My boy," Gia said. "You have no sense of history. And, more importantly, your place within it. You saw the burning of your church, yes?"

"We saw," the young man said. "But we have plenty of churches. The Wolves of God can't be stopped by you or anyone else. We're ordained by God Almighty."

Gia strode in front of her captives. After the martyring of the Saint and the Deacon, the burning of the church and all of those Wolves of

God, the remaining Wargs had gone still more feral, trying to exact revenge where and when they could.

"To be what we are requires an understanding of one's place within it," Gia said. "You *Infettivi* always think you can upset that grand order of things. And it falls to us, the *Veronatti,* to make things right again."

"Speak English," one of the other young men said, with almost white-blond hair. Gia held out a gloved hand, and one of her men handed her a silver baseball bat.

"Respect," Gia said. "For your betters. For your history. For yourselves, even. This isn't going to go well for you, *Infettivi.*"

"What is that—a Silver Slugger Award?" one of the young men said.

Gia took a swing at the one who said it, cracking him across the face. The young man cried out, cursing. The bat left a welt.

"You tell me, *Infettivi,*" Gia said. "Did you feel that? Sterling silver works as well as pure silver. But you probably knew that already because you know so much."

"You bitch," the towheaded young man said. "The Bishop is going to kill all of you."

"No," Gia said. "I don't think he will. If the Saint couldn't, if the Deacon couldn't, the Bishop can't. Where's he at? The Créche?"

At the mention of the Créche, the bravado of the young man left him. Gia stepped closer to him, smiling.

"We will burn the Créche," Gia said. "Oh, how your Wolves of God will howl. Everyone's going to die there. The Bishop, all of them. Even the ones who try to run off into the forest. We will hunt them all down. You *Infettivi* do not understand us. We *Veronatti* are your betters. In mind, body, spirit. In everything. You're rabid dogs, and we put you down."

Gia cracked the towheaded young man across his thighs with the bat, and the young man howled in pain, began to transform, glaring at her, snapping his bonds, shedding his skin, sprouting white fur.

"That's it, *Infettiva,*" Gia said. "Turn for Gia. Show me how big and strong you are."

Where the loop of silver was, however, was cutting into the Warg's throat as he grew in size and stature before Gia, who watched with the bloody silver bat slung across her shoulder.

The loop of silver held, and the towheaded young man, the white wolf in front of them, strangled, blood pouring down his lovely white coat, his clawed arms reaching up to try to snap the strangling wire that was killing him.

But, as his transformation inexorably completed, the Warg beheaded himself, his great wolf's head tumbling to the ground, at Gia's booted feet, while his fellow Wargs wailed and cursed Gia with all that they could muster.

The great Warg body tumbled forward in a spray of blood, and the transformation reversed itself in moments, going from bone-white fur to pale man-flesh. The wolf's head boiled away, revealing itself to be only the lifeless, stunned face of the rude, towheaded young man.

"You see, *Infettivi?*" Gia said. "History. A knowledge of history is a powerful thing. You *Lupi Di Dio,* you think you can come along and upend thousands of years of history? All because of your dead preacher's mad sermons? My people—my clan—has been at this for a very long time. And there are older clans, who go even deeper into the maw of history. We respect it. You should respect it. You follow your preacher, but he is a fool, like all *Infettivi.*"

"We won't be Infectives forever," one of the young men said. He seemed to be the alpha of this little group. "We'll become Trueborn in another generation. Then you'll see. You Trueborn aren't all that different from the rest of us. You've just been at it a bit longer."

Gia could sniff something out, here. A hint of something hidden between them. A secret.

"Ah," Gia said, poking the speaker with the bat. "I already told you what we will do to your Créche. There will be no Trueborn Wolves of God."

She could see from their expressions that she had them by the throats with only her words and those loops of silver.

The other young man, the quiet one, finally spoke up.

"We are the Wolves of God," the quiet man said. "We herald the end of days. We are the righteous who cleanse the world of sin. We are the inheritors of the wicked world."

The mouthy young man joined in, and the two of them chanted this several more times, before Gia put an end to them with the sterling silver baseball bat, silencing their chanting with ringing swings of it. Gia swung hard for them, back and forth, her face a mask of Trueborn rage, her eyes glowing, her fangs bared.

She only gave herself enough Lupine to lend greater power to her swing of the bat, going back between them, catching them in their heads. The quiet man attempted to transform, an almost instinctive reaction to the assault, but the loop did its work as surely as Gia and her silver bat, and he garroted himself as he grew, while Gia still bludgeoned him with the bat. One of her swings helped finish the decapitation of the quiet man, sending his head tumbling across the room.

When they were dead, Gia then handed the bat back to one of her men.

She sniffed at the bodies of the Wargs, to be sure they were dead.

"Hang them somewhere they'll be seen," Gia said. "More martyrs for the Wolves of God."

Her phone rang. It was Valentina.

"What is it, Valentina?" Gia asked.

"He's headed to the place," Valentina said. One of Gia's men handed her a towel to mop off the blood she'd gotten on herself. "The place we discussed."

"Good," Gia said. "What about that other thing?"

"We're looking into it," Valentina said. "We're in a grey area, unfortunately."

Gia nodded. They always spoke very carefully, in code, because one never knew who might be listening. Bastion was stepping up things with his pack.

"Be careful," Gia said. "What about those other things? The sisters and the other one?"

"Handled," Valentina said. "Well in hand. We even called the BEE so they could put their Recovery people to work. They're cleaning up the mess as we speak. It was glorious."

"I'll bet," Gia said. "Find the Driver's wife. She'll lead you where you need to go regarding that other matter."

"I don't know," Valentina said. "After that raid, not so sure."

"Trust me, *Sorella*," Gia said. "Find her, follow her. You'll know when you know. And let me know when the Driver comes back ashore, and whether he brings company."

"I will," Valentina said.

Gia smiled, handing the bloodied towel to one of her men. She was very fond of Valentina, who, despite being one of the younger members of the clan, was at least as enterprising and ruthless as Gia was. She was confident she'd go far. If she understood Valentina clearly, the Daughters of Zooey were undone, which was one more thing she didn't have to worry about.

"Get some rest. You sound tired." Gia said, hanging up.

It had come up in years past, when they'd visited Ansel's gallery residence, looking for him. Valentina and Gia had been there, in his empty place, looking for some sign of him, where he'd gone. It was like he'd vanished from the face of the world. Valentina had been only 18 and had been excited to be included in the *La Grande Caccia*—the Great Hunt, as Gia had called it.

But someone had been there. Someone had broken in yet had not stolen anything. Someone lycanthropic. She and Valentina had taken the scent, stalked around the place. Whoever it was had been there, had combed through his place, but hadn't ransacked it. It was not a typical Infective incursion. Someone had been hunting for him. And not that long ago.

They searched his entire place, top to bottom, but there was no sign, only that hint of a scent. Gia and Valentina had gone to his deck and nursed a couple of Americanos in the dark, beneath the light of the moon, and hoped that the stranger might reappear, so they could deal with them.

Three nights, they remained, hoping to see a sign, but there was none.

"Who do you think it is?" Valentina asked.

"I don't know," Gia said. "Someone who cares about him. A woman, I think."

Ansel had so many girlfriends, had refused to settle down, to take his proper place in the Clan. Gia tolerated it because his work as an artist served the family's larger interests, but she still wanted him to find a mate. He'd always been so stubborn.

"A girlfriend?" Valentina asked, amused to the point of a sneer.

"Yes," Gia said, nursing her cocktail. "Your big brother keeps us at arm's length. He came to me in need, had said he had told me everything, but I don't think he did. I think Ansel kept something from me."

"*Fidanzata,*" Valentina said. "You think it was serious?"

Gia shrugged, leaning back in the lounge chair on Ansel's deck. "Could be. I would say the fact that he *didn't* tell me about her means it was somehow important to him. Or that she was."

"Ooh, we should find her," Valentina said.

"We took her scent," Gia said. "We never forget that. That, and her breaking into Ansel's home. She knew just where to go, how to get in. Have one of your brothers come and fix the lock."

Valentina's eyes brightened.

"I should just live here, Gia," she said. "I can lie in wait and when she comes, I can deal with her."

"No," Gia said. "This will keep. You have more important matters to attend to, *Sorella.*"

Valentina pouted into her drink. Drinking underage was the least of her youthful offenses. She'd already killed several *Infettivi,* under Gia's supervision, of course, before Ansel's disappearance had caused Gia to pull everyone back to find out what happened to him.

"It's just like your brother to disappear," Gia said. "For one so big, he can make himself very small. Like a little mouse."

Gia held up her finger in a pinching motion, and Valentina laughed.

"I'll find our brother, I swear," Valentina said. "No matter where he hides."

2

MINTON was not thrilled to see Norm. He'd called Norm into his office at midnight. Everyone had been happy to see Norm, since a visitor arriving at headquarters as a rare treat for the rank-and-file agents.

Norm was escorted to Minton's tidy, wood-paneled office, where big screens showed the news, featuring Norm's face, wanted in connection with the attempted kidnapping of Anne Stockwell and his involvement with the Polish terrorists.

"This is not the kind of news I want my Stingers to be making," Minton said. "In fact, I don't ever want them in the news. This is why I don't tend to pick married field agents, Norm."

Norm took his seat so Minton could give him his browbeating more effectively. He was always considerate in that regard.

"I hadn't planned on Anne to join up with Bastion, Sir," Norm said.

Minton looked exhausted. Still fit, still sharp. He'd taken to shaving his head bald and had started wearing glasses. But he looked about the same as he ever had. The managing of the Happening had taken a toll on him, but it hadn't aged him that badly.

"Still, this is heat we don't need," Minton said. "I had to call FBI, CIA, and everyone in between to let them know that you were on assignment, that nobody was to apprehend you. It'll take some time for that to percolate down to the lower echelons, but it'll sort itself out. I told you not to go after Bastion's men, didn't I?"

"Yes, Sir," Norm said.

"You promised me you wouldn't," Minton said. Minton glowered at him, actually took off his glasses to intensify the effect of his glare.

"But you did, anyway," Minton said. "Explain yourself."

"Target of opportunity I couldn't pass up, Sir," Norm said.

"Bullshit," Minton said.

"Shaw had my wife," Norm said. "Nobody was doing anything about it, so I did. I don't see the problem. Several dead Infectives. A successful operation. They were going to kill and eat some civilians, Sir. I had to do something."

Minton leaned forward in his leather seat.

"We have an arrangement with Bastion and Liminalix," Minton said. "I can't go about that with you bumping off his people. You promised me, Norm. You made me a promise."

Norm knew it wasn't his place to ask, but he asked, anyway.

"What is that arrangement, anyway, Sir?"

"Classified," Minton said. "You don't need to know."

"Ah," Norm said. "Still, I could probably do my job better if I did."

"Nope," Minton said. "No way."

Norm wondered what the big secret was, just as he knew that Minton would not spill. So, he just talked to see what kind of read he'd get off the man.

"Bastion's people are giving out Lupitol like candy," Norm said. "I'm guessing he worked some kind of trade with you—BEE lays off his people in return for him pushing Lupitol to help quash the Happening."

Minton mockingly applauded him.

"That's certainly part of it," Minton said. "Our mission is to stop this at all costs, by any means. Lupitol actually works to keep the Infectives docile, keeps them from going crazy and attacking and infecting more people. That's a win in my book. If Bastion is offering this, who am I not to take it?"

"Sir, doesn't it bother you to deal with them that way?" Norm asked. Minton shook his head.

"I inherited a godawful mess when I became Director," Minton said. "We're getting things under control, like really under control, for the first time in eight years, Stockwell. Worth it. Bastion came to us with a deal, won a contract, and he *delivered* on it. The man deserves a medal."

Maybe he was biased because of his history, but Norm didn't think anybody who had people like Todd Shaw on his executive team could be anything but bad news. And a Lupine who mass-marketed anti-lycanthropy medication? It was perverse.

"You know, he hunts people at that Free Rein country club," Norm said. "Upstate New York, I'm told."

"Nonsense," Minton said. "Urban legends. Who told you? Your *Synowie* friends?"

Norm wasn't going to say, but Minton said something, anyway.

"They're hardly beyond reproach," Minton said. "Fanatics."

"They've been good partners," Norm said. "And you put me in touch with them, for God's sake."

"To try to rein them in. They're wild cards," Minton said. "Immune to command and control. I reached out to them to try to wave them off the Trueborn. Their leader wore a damned ski mask when she talked to me. Did she meet up with you?"

Norm's phone pinged, but he didn't check it. The last thing he needed was Minton seeing that.

"Yeah," Norm said. "We talked."

"Did she wear a ski mask?" Minton asked.

"No," Norm said. Minton leaned forward, staring hard at him.

"What's she look like?" Minton asked.

"That's classified, Sir," Norm said.

"Nothing's classified from me, Stockwell," Minton said. "You're already in hot water with me for that stunt with Shaw. Hot water and thin fucking ice at the same time."

Norm made a judgment call on the spot.

"She's a brunette," Norm said. "Dark brown hair, blue eyes. Tall."

"What's her name?" Minton asked.

"Shari Bosko," Norm said.

"Shari Bosko," Minton said. "We'll look into that."

Norm just didn't want to give up Sonia that way. It didn't feel right. She had trusted him and been there for him, more than Minton had of late. That meant something to him.

"They know what they're doing," Norm said. "Whereas I'm trying to understand what the hell the Bureau's up to. I mean, Bastion, the Rupinos? What's next? Vampires?"

He'd said it to try to get a rise out of Minton, but Minton might as well have been poured from concrete.

"You know what's next?" Minton asked. "I got an anonymous call on my private line telling me the Daughters of Zooey are all dead in Chicago. That we'd best get Recovery to Trotter Field ASAP or else the news was going to have a field day with it."

"And?"

"I had Tiff fly over it and this is what she saw," Minton said, clicking one of his screens. There was a pile of bodies, alright. The image was particularly haunting on the night-vision camera flyover. It looked incredible to Norm, the carnage.

"Wow," Norm said. "What happened?"

"What happened was 245 Doozies were killed at Trotter Field around two hours ago," Minton said. "I had six Recovery teams there to clean it up. Thankfully, that area isn't heavily trafficked at night except for dog walkers and serial killers, but just look at that. And Addison and Sheridan Monroe were among the dead. Torn apart."

Norm thought about Valentina talking about her plans for the evening, what she'd said at Navy Pier. He assumed it had been them.

"This is what you wanted, right, Sir?" Norm asked. "The Doozies were a highly active faction."

"Not like this, Norm," Minton said. "A pile of dead women shot to death on a soccer field? If anybody asks, the cover story is that it was a mass suicide event by a Night Fever cult."

Norm pondered how that would play out.

"We cordoned the area off," Minton said. "Nobody could get close to it."

"Who did it?" Norm asked.

"This has Rupino written all over it," Minton said. "I called Gia and asked, and she claimed she didn't know anything about it. Said something about the Doozies being an erratic bunch, and that anything was possible with them. She denied it. Just like she didn't cop to the Tolkachev assassination. She's jerking me around."

Norm didn't understand why Minton was up in arms about this.

"It's what you wanted, Sir, right?" Norm asked.

"Not. Like. This," Minton said. "I don't want to be Sanderson 2.0, Man. I don't want mass graves and death squads on my hands."

Norm thought it was a matter of semantics with Minton but wasn't sure if he should push that in his current frame of mind. What did it matter if a few Stingers killed a few Lupines, versus a large-scaled takedown like this?

"Small ripples," Minton said. "In a big pond. I can handle that. Not big splashes like this. The Rupinos fucked me bad here, Norm. The media *cares* when women get killed. Especially white women. There were a bunch of white women dead at Trotter Field. Do you know social scientists have done studies that show that media coverage tends to be higher when white women disappear or get killed? I have 190 dead white women at Trotter Field. The Doozies were majority white women. Didn't matter that they were Lupines. So now, I'm participating in a massive cover-up for a mass murder."

"Uh, Sir, the BEE has been killing Lupines for years. No due process, nothing but rendition and assassinations," Norm said. "Since the Happening. Any of that truly gets out, we're all going to fry."

"The Lupercalian church fire, that was bad enough," Minton said. "But that one could be chalked up to arson. We clamped down on it. A tragic accident. But a mass killing on a soccer field? It looks just like what it is. We're just fortunate no news vans were around when it took place."

Minton looked unbelievably stressed.

"Right now, those dead Doozies have families and loved ones who are wondering what happened to them," Minton said. "All of them. They're just going to disappear. People are going to be talking about it. Night Fever is one thing. But a mass disappearance? How's that going to be explained away? Flying saucer abductions? Case-by-case, I can handle. But this many at one time? No way. There's no explaining it away. The cult story can maybe hold water. I don't know. But people are going to wonder. This is why Bastion's approach is better. Treatment, Norm. He's offering treatment for these people."

"I doubt any Doozies would have taken Lupitol, Sir," Norm said.

"Some are," Minton said. "Some have. We were making progress with them. Incremental inroads. The pills offer a path of treatment and recovery for the Infectives. A way out."

"The Doozies were a problem, Sir," Norm said. "Revolutionaries."

"Right," Minton said. "They really were a cult. The tri-state branches are losing it. They're on the social media, saying that the Rupinos murdered them. They're out for revenge. I've been sending Stingers in Wisconsin, Iowa, and Indiana to deal with that."

Norm could only imagine how they'd be "dealing" with that. He didn't want to be callous, but for Norm, it was only a volume issue.

Minton could tolerate one or two killings at a time, but when it got over, say, a dozen, then he got nervous. He supposed he couldn't blame him. Bigger kills meant bigger messes, which meant bigger problems for him to solve. More attention meant more trouble.

Although the timing couldn't have been worse, Norm decided to go there, anyway. He was already in a heap of trouble. Throwing a little more on top would have hardly mattered.

"I want to see Ansel Rupino, Sir," Norm said. That made Minton blink. Just one asynchronous blink, but Norm had seen it.

"Who says we have him?"

"I do," Norm said. "He's got to be here."

"Why?"

Norm didn't know how hard he wanted to push his boss, only that he needed to do it.

"As I see it, Sir, Bastion works a trade with you for the drug after the Rupinos offer their special skills to help you kill Infectives," Norm said. "But Gia Rupino doesn't give anything away for free. So, what're you offering her?"

"Amnesty," Minton said. "That's enough for them. They're free to take down the Infectives in their own way, free of interference. And we confirmed that Ansel wasn't on Wolf Island. But this Trotter Field Massacre has made me want to throw that amnesty right off the table."

"In their own way, Sir," Norm said, gesturing to the Trotter Field flyover footage.

The Director crossed his fingers over his big desk, tried to look as unruffled as possible. But one of the advantages of being a Stinger was the ability to sleuth out what somebody might be hiding.

"This was something else," Minton said. "And Gia flat-out lied to me about it, denying responsibility. She says that it could be anybody who did that. She accused me of anti-Lupine bias. Can you believe that?"

"Well, Sir, in fairness," Norm said. "We do have anti-Lupine bias."

"Come on, Norm," Minton said. "Give me a break. We're doing our jobs. We don't revel in it."

"Okay," Norm said, wanting to keep Minton on-task with his ask. "So, Ansel's not on Wolf Island, and nobody can seem to find him anywhere. His people have hunted all over the country—maybe the world—for him, and they don't find him. It's like he disappeared. He has to be here. We make people disappear every day."

Norm nodded at the Trotter Field footage. Minton paused a moment, holding Norm with his stare.

"Maybe he's dead," Minton said.

"I don't buy it," Norm said. "You'd be too happy if he was dead. You'd have to tell someone. You'd want to announce it. He's not dead."

"Maybe he *should* be dead," Minton said. "Maybe that would get Gia's attention."

"So, you have him?"

Minton's patience, never plentiful, was nearing its end.

"Why do you even care about him?" Minton asked.

"I want to talk to him, Sir," Norm said.

"Why?" Minton asked. "About what?"

"I'm sentimental," Norm said. "He's Big Black, Sir. The legendary lycanthrope we all wanted to bag. He was the one. Nobody ever got close. The *Synowie* were the only ones who ever did."

Minton had composed himself.

"Nobody ever will," Minton said. "He's gone."

"I don't believe it for a moment," Norm said. "Further, since I'm parked on the *Argent* for a bit, I'm going to comb every corner of this ship until I find him."

"Not if I have you confined to quarters," Minton said. "Under guard. Disciplinary action for gross insubordination. You have that coming."

The two men stared at each other for a few lingeringly silent moments, like they were playing a chess match on Minton's desk.

"I'll be here for days," Norm said. *Argent's* a big ship, but she's not that big."

Norm banked on Minton being fond enough of him to indulge one of his most successful Stingers.

"Fine, Norm," Minton said. "Yes, we have him. We've had him for years. But he offered himself into our custody on his own volition."

"What?"

"What I'm going to tell you is classified, Norm," Minton said. "You don't tell another soul. In fact, give me your phone."

He held out his hand, and Norm reluctantly gave him his phone, which he put on his desk. Minton got up and gestured to the Green Room.

"In there," Minton said. "You and me. Now."

Norm went into the soundproof secure room, while Minton shut the door. His office had been quiet, but the Green Room was particularly silent. Norm could hear his own heart beating. In the room was a rectangular table with six seats. Minton took the seat at the head of the table, and Norm sat at the other end of the table.

"In very late 2007, Ansel came to us," Minton said. "He identified himself and told us that he'd agree to being in our facility in return for him not being killed or extradited. His sequestration would allow us to conduct medical tests on him to attempt to find a cure for lycanthropy. That's part of the deal."

"So, he's your lab rat," Norm said.

"Yes," Minton said. "But only on condition of absolutely secrecy about his whereabouts. He doesn't want his family to know he's here."

Norm turned that over in his head a few times, trying to sort it out. Why would Ansel want to keep his whereabouts secret from his own family?

"Why not?"

"His official excuse is he felt guilty about his role in the Happening, and he wanted to make amends any way he could," Minton said. "Giving his body to science, as it were, well, that was part of it. We get our tests, and he stays with us."

"For eight years?" Norm asked. "As a prisoner?"

"As a special guest," Minton said.

"Weird."

"Yeah," Minton said. "Self-imposed jail sentence, I suppose."

"You said his official excuse," Norm said. "You suspect something else?"

"He's hiding from his family," Minton said. "He was very specific about us not revealing to anyone that we had him."

"But why?" Norm asked.

Minton shook his head, waved Norm off.

"You want to find out, you can ask him yourself," Minton said. "I'll give you clearance to drop by Dr. Holloway's labs. You can talk to him directly. But only on the condition that you don't tell a soul. After your lighting me up with that Shaw business, I'm hard-pressed to trust your word on anything."

"Sir, that was different," Norm said. "That was Anne."

Minton tapped the table with his index finger.

"Be that as it may, that's not the point," Minton said. "You tell any goddamned Rupino about us having Ansel here, and you're done. I'll revoke your Stinger status. I've got a lot on my plate right now, thanks to them."

Norm wondered how he'd square that particular circle with Valentina and the others.

"Sir, how long is Ansel's sequestration supposed to last?" Norm asked. "He can't just stay in custody indefinitely, can he? I mean, I would think Dr. Holloway has gotten as much medical information from him as she could, right? She's probably sequenced his genome years ago, for god's sake."

"Yeah," Minton said. "We've pretty much gotten everything we wanted from him."

"Okay," Norm said. "There you have it. How about you release him?"

"He doesn't want to be released," Minton said. "He's happy with us. We let him paint in peace. He answers psych questions."

It was crazy. Norm was more committed than ever to finding out what Ansel's deal was.

"Alright," Norm said. "I'd like that clearance, Sir. I want to talk to him."

"Don't kill him," Minton said. "Give me your word you won't. Your actual word, this time. Not just some shit you say to placate me."

"Jesus, Sir," Norm said. "I'm not a stone-cold killer."

"Right," Minton said. Even Norm didn't believe himself when he'd said it.

3

Pol had made short work of the Liminalix van. It had been a delicious diversion, a swift symphony of slaughter. They'd been intent on tailing Mina, hadn't expected company. Polly had transformed on the sidewalk, splitting her skin and taking on the monstrous mass of her other self, becoming the lithe and lethal creature she'd been so many times before, so many dark nights.

She threw herself at the van, her claws peeling the side of it like paper, seeing the startled Liminalix men in their grey jumpsuits, scrambling to control the vehicle while reacting to the unexpected attack.

Pol lived for this, biting the nearest man on the throat, snapping his neck with a shake of her head, while clawing the other man in the back with her claws, almost splitting him in two. The driver cursed and spun the wheel of the van while trying to grab his gun. The guy riding next to him was trying to get his seatbelt off to get a better angle on their attacker in the back.

"Nothing for you to do," Pol said, rending the passenger with her claws, almost hugging him around the seat, while she clamped down on his neck from behind.

The driver threw himself out of the van, gun in one hand, a radio in the other. Pol sprang through the open door, was on him even as he fired a shot at her with his sidearm. The bullet whizzed past her ear, missing its mark. She didn't give him another shot at another shot, ripping at him with her well-bloodied claws.

It felt so good to cut loose like this. Cathartic, Polly observed, deep inside the cell Pol had made for her, where she conjured up a poem while Pol did her bloody work…

LIMINALITY

Between two places
I wear both faces
She and me, we see

We're bound together
For eternity

The border between
What is her and me
The captious caprice
Nobody's fault line
Maybe just conceit

For we kill at will
And it's such a thrill.

The man was gone by the time her poem was done, Pol standing over his brutalized body. She sniffed the air, expecting the men to turn into Lupines, but they were normal men. The dead driver's radio crackled with chatter.

"What's your status, Hutch? Do you need assistance?"

Pol hopped away from the carnage, over the parked cars, onto the sidewalk. Nobody was out, so when she heard the slow-clapping, it startled her. There was a young woman down the street, wearing a black leather jacket and black leggings, wearing a black stocking cap. The young woman smelled like blood and death.

"Well-done," the young woman said. "Really, that was great."

Pol sniffed the air, ran toward the girl, who had no trace of fear. The girl sniffed the air, too, deep snuffs of it.

"Ah, there you are," she said. "I've been looking for you a long time. Ansel's pet."

At the mention of Ansel, Pol paused. She would have killed the young woman where she stood, but for that one word.

"Ansel?" Pol said, her voice a snarl.

"Yes," the woman said. "You're her. His *Infettiva* plaything. His chew toy."

The young woman's tone was mocking, her manner strangely threatening. No one could look at Pol and fail to be impressed, but this young woman most certainly wasn't.

"Where is he?" Pol asked.

"Not here," the woman said. "But I can take you to him."

Pol towered over this young woman who smelled unafraid, who smelled of the blood of others, who looked Rupino to her. Were they hunting her, too?

"Where?"

"Not here," the woman said. "I'm Valentina Rupino. I'm his baby sister."

"Sister," Pol said, her long claws scratching the sidewalk. "Cannot resist her."

"Rhyme time?" Valentina said, putting on a pair of black gloves. "Come with me, I'll bring you both together. *Un lieto fine!*"

Pol could smell danger. Valentina radiated danger, despite her small size. Pol loomed over her, and Valentina put one of her gloved hands on her hips, as if daring her to try something. The bravado in the face of the death that Pol represented was unlike anything she'd ever faced before.

"I'm not a dog," Pol said. "I don't go where I'm told."

And then she bounded off, racing away from the young woman, her claws skittering on the snow-dusted sidewalk, leaving puffs of displaced snowflakes in her wake. Pol had gone from hunter to prey in a heartbeat. She would not lead them to Sloane. She would run into the darkness, where they'd never find her.

She glanced over her shoulder as she ran, saw the young woman had slipped off her clothes and was running down the street after her. She could see fresh scars criss-crossing the young woman's body. It was true poetry, watching Valentina blur while she ran, both from motion and transformation, turning into a luminously beautiful black Lupine, strong and lean, chasing her, hunting her.

Pol ran hard for Lincoln Park, which wasn't much cover, but was better than none. Not since she and Ansel had killed Zooey had she encountered another Lupine like this. Valentina was closing the distance on her, which was stunning, given that Pol had gotten a head start.

"Run, Bitch, run," Valentina called after her, her she-wolf voice brimming with velveteen venom. Why she was hunting her was something Polly couldn't understand, although she remembered what Ansel had told her. Something about the pack. She wasn't welcome.

Pol charged across Clark Street and vaulted into the park, with Valentina half as far away as she'd been only a minute before. She was faster than Pol was. Pol would have to make her stand in the park. There would be no escaping this nasty little thing.

Once she'd gotten into the stands of trees, Pol turned, feeling the heat in her lungs as she panted in the shadows. Valentina was right behind her, stopping when she stopped, circling her. She'd effortlessly shifted from her four-legged form to her two-legged hybrid form, appearing to grin at her from a perfectly aligned cage of snowy whitefangs. Up close, Pol could better see the scars upon her furry flesh, the lines that spoke of bloody battle. Pol would give her more.

"I love Ansel," Pol said.

"Of course you do," Valentina said. "We all love him, *Infettiva.*"

"Why chase me?"

"Why chase him?" Valentina asked. "He's not for you."

"You don't get to say," Pol said.

"He's Rupino," Valentina said. "Whether he wants to be or not. Family first and foremost. We decide who gets to be in our family."

Pol flexed her claws, caught her breath, which came in gusty puffs in the cold air. Around them, their dark lycanthropic forms stood in contrast to the blue-white snow on the shadowy ground, far from the sullen glow of the sodium lights. The trees alone bore witness to them, silent, leafless sentinels.

"There's no place for you with him," Valentina said.

"I have a child by him," Pol said.

"Exactly," Valentina said.

"Is this a Trueborn thing?" Pol asked, which made Valentina wolf-laugh, yipping and dire in implication.

"You could say that," Valentina said. "Not that I have to explain myself to an *Infettiva* like you, but we don't let just anyone into our family. I've been hunting you for eight years. You did a good job hiding."

Polly didn't understand what lycanthropic protocol she'd somehow violated, what sacred Lupine line she'd unknowingly crossed.

"I've been a good mother," Pol said. And she had, in her own way.

"Where is the child?" Valentina asked.

"Safe," Pol said. "Safe from you."

"Dead?" Valentina said.

"No," Pol said.

"Then it's not safe," Valentina said.

"I don't understand," Pol said. "Why kill me? Why kill her?"

"Nice. A daughter," Valentina said. "Not her. You. She's safe with us. You, on the other hand…."

Polly's mind raced inside her prison, while Pol circled with Valentina. Why would they want her dead? What possible affront had she done to them? Besides birthing a Rupino bastard child with Ansel? What had Ansel said before? On that last night?

"I'm the right fit for him," Pol said. "He's right for me, you see."

Valentina laughed again, a strange sound from her Lupine visage, all teeth and baleful blue eyes as she kept circling.

"You don't get to decide that," Valentina said. "We decide. And if Ansel had thought you were the right fit for the family, he'd have married you and stayed by you. But he didn't, did he?"

"I could go away," Pol said. "I could leave."

"Oh, you'll be going away," Valentina said. "Are you ready to go away, now?"

Pol was animal instinct. That instinct told her to flee, not fight. But how could one flee someone who was faster than you? Maybe she was stronger than Valentina, though. Maybe she could fight her.

"Where is your daughter?" Valentina asked. And Polly knew if she told her, she'd be dead, anyway, and maybe Sloane, too. Valentina sniffed at her. "That's her scent on you. I smell it, even over all the man-blood you just shed."

"I don't deserve this," Pol said. "I've kept her safe. Without help."

She didn't count the money Ansel had funneled her way. Maybe that was part of it. Maybe it was the money he'd somehow secreted to her. Maybe that's what they didn't like.

"Ansel sent me money," Pol said. "Is that what it is? Is it about the money?"

Valentina's furred shoulders shook as she wolf-laughed yet again, almost like a hyena.

"We have all the money in the world," Valentina said. "It's not about the money. We didn't even know about that. It's about Ansel, and it's about your daughter. They're part of the Clan. You, however, aren't. And never will be, *Infettiva.*"

"I never wanted to be," Pol said. "I'm better than you."

"Are you?" Valentina said. "Want to find out?"

"Don't do this," Pol said.

"It's already done," Valentina said.

And then Valentina launched herself at Pol, moving like a black bolt in the night. The blood splashed across the snow like paint upon a canvas, and the howl that came when it was done shook the trees like well-honed poetry.

WHILE Minton had ultimately agreed to let Norm visit Ansel in his cell, it was only under strict parameters. It was with an escort of a trio of BEE agents Norm knew of. They were younger men, former military. He'd have said former Marines, but nobody was ever really a *former* Marine—once a Marine, always a Marine. They treated Norm with a great deal of respect since Stingers had particular (if covert) prestige within the BEE, and Norm more than most.

"We're honored you'd visit the Pens, Agent Stockwell," one of them said. His nametag said he was Piper. The other two were Squires and Haggerty by their nametags. All three were young and strong—Piper was black, Squires was Latin, and Haggerty was white. All three had short, buzzed haircuts and eager, earnest expressions. Norm qualified as a celebrity in BEE circles, especially with the news lately. What aggravated Minton charged up the rank-and-file BEE agents.

The Pens was the name for the cellblock within the *Argent* where the Lupines of particular interest were kept. These were apart from the other cells, where more ordinary Lupines—Lupines who would inevitably be bound for Wolf Island—were kept. That portion of the ship was called the Pound.

Right now, the *Argent* was at half capacity, which was a testament to the success of Minton's Archon-assisted program and his deals with the Rupinos and Bastion. The Lupine problem wasn't yet solved, but Minton had made incredible strides over the years.

In years past, Minton had sent BEE riverboats up the Mississippi as part of Operation Direwolf. They were a fleet of smaller prison ships, kind of test models for the *Argent* concept. These roving prisons had given BEE agents the opportunity to apprehend Lupines through ten states: Louisiana, Mississippi, Arkansas, Missouri, Tennessee, Kentucky, Iowa, Illinois, Wisconsin, and Minnesota. The BEE river patrol boats would then take their Lupine cargo—each river patrol boat could hold about fifty Lupines, and there were ten boats—and they'd trek back down to the Gulf.

Then the captive Lupines were loaded onto planes and flown to Wolf Island. The riverboats were then taken back up the Mississippi to hunt for more Lupines. Operation Direwolf had been such a success that it had gotten Minton recognition at the senior level and had led to the budgetary allocations that had paved the way for the deployment of the *Argent*. Minton's model was much the same with her, only instead of the Mississippi, she patrolled the Great Lakes, and eventually went out to sea, for the long trek to Wolf Island in the faraway Pacific.

The Pens were, like everything else aboard *Argent*, pristine and white-painted. The ship was immaculately kept, which contrasted with the shambolic nature of her cargo.

"Dr. Holloway won't like having you poking around the Pens, Sir," Haggerty said. "She's very protective of her patients."

"It's fine," Norm said. "I'm cleared for all of *Argent*."

"We know you are, Sir," Piper said. "We're glad you got away from those Loops that were after you."

"So am I," Norm said. "Definitely."

Norm was sure Dr. Vanessa Holloway would be less than thrilled to have a Stinger in her midst. She was a pure researcher on loan from the CDC's EIS branch—the Epidemic Intelligence Service. Ever since Mina had sent a message to her peer at the CDC, the EIS had been all up in BEE's business, actively studying the lycanthropic Happening.

Not that their expertise wasn't welcome—it was, of course, needed. But the CDC operated out of Atlanta, and it was a constant tug-of-war between BEE and CDC to hold onto their assets, and not have all of the Lupines summarily shipped to Atlanta for containment and study.

They reached the Pens, and, sure enough, Dr. Holloway frowned at him when he entered. She wore her white coat, her face caustic in its clinical assessment of him. Her ginger-hued hair was cut along the edges of her strong jawline, her brown eyes locked onto his.

"What brings you to the Pens, Agent Stockwell?" Holloway asked.

"I'm here to talk to Big Black," Norm said.

Holloway shook her head, smiling.

"About what, might I ask?" she asked.

"You know I can't divulge that," Norm said. The Research Division hated how secretive Operations was. The two halves of the Bureau were always stepping on each others' toes.

"Of course not," Vanessa said. "All the same, I'll not have you disturbing my patient."

"I won't disturb him," Norm said. "I promise."

"Okay," Vanessa said, confirming his clearances on computer. "Come along, Agent Stockwell."

Piper, Haggerty, and Squires followed on their heels, as they made their way through the Pens. Despite the name, they were clean to the point of being antiseptic, as Dr. Holloway had worked very hard to ensure that CDC containment protocols were upheld here. While lycanthropy was in its own classification, and its routes of transmission were clearly identified, Holloway maintained strict guidelines for any work carried out in the Pens.

"Aren't we going to be in hazmat suits, Dr. Holloway?" Norm asked.

"Not necessary, Agent Stockwell," Vanessa said. "All of the subjects are kept secure from the rest of us. And we all know how it's spread, now don't we?"

Norm nodded.

"You've still managed to not get bitten, Agent Stockwell?" Holloway asked. "Eight years in the field, and not so much as a scratch."

"That's right," Norm said. "So far, so good."

"Lucky you," Vanessa said, tartly. "Turn around and crouch for me, Agent Stockwell."

Norm did as instructed and felt Dr. Holloway check at the nape of his neck, shining a pen flashlight on it.

All of them had followed the Minton-directed protocol of getting tattooed with the BEE hexagon logo on either shoulder and with a bee at the base of the neck, using specific, proprietary inks that could not be falsified, and only showed up under black light.

Only BEE personnel could bear this tattoo, and anyone who didn't have it was at least under the suspicion of being a Lupine. Of course, to Norm, the logic of being able to do a black light check of a suspected Lupine was lost on him—if someone was a Lupine, you'd never be able to get that close to run that test.

But the BEE had its own bureaucratic traditions. Invisible tattoos were pretty much par for the course for the Bureau. The byzantine logic was that while visible tattoos were a clear sign of normalcy, they could also be faked. Whereas invisible tattoos were so insane that only Bureau agents in good standing would consent to having them.

"You know, they already checked me before boarding *Argent*," Norm said.

"I'm an empiricist. I wanted to be sure," Vanessa said. "Alright, you're cleared, Agent Stockwell."

They reached a security door, and Holloway took her yellow key card and opened it, ushering them through. Norm was noting the security for his own purposes, both in terms of the actual bulkheads and doors they had to clear, as well as the personnel.

It might have operated as a lab, but the Pens would have given a control unit prison a run for its money with regard to security. Breaking in here would be as challenging as breaking out. Minton had definitely learned from the lesson of the Kennel.

They walked down a corridor, coming to a particular unit, marked by a window of ballistic glass.

"Here we are," Vanessa said. "Big Black, himself, Ansel Rupino."

Norm gazed into the cell, surprised by what he saw.

Ansel Rupino was every bit as impressive as Norm had heard. He was painting in his cell, a portrait of Vanessa in red and white.

Older, now, he had some white at his temples, otherwise breaking the dark waves of his hair. He'd grown a beard, which had some white in it around his chin. His physicality remained as intense as ever, wearing a yellow BEE inmate jumpsuit with a serial number on it and the BEE hexagonal logo at his chest. On his back was GUEST printed in big, black letters.

"Mr. Rupino," Vanessa said. "You have a guest."

Ansel turned regarded Norm from the other side of the ballistic glass, paintbrushes still in hand.

"You let him paint in there?" Norm asked.

"It's therapeutic," Vanessa said. "It helps him."

"What do you think of my painting, Dr. Holloway?" Ansel asked.

The painting was lovely, her portrait seeming to live on the canvas, looking out at them all with intelligent, appraising eyes. The white of her lab coat stood in marked contrast to the sea of red Ansel had used as the background.

"Why all the red, Ansel?" Vanessa asked.

"You deal in blood draws, Dr. Holloway," Ansel said. "It's appropriate that I draw you in blood."

"Mr. Rupino, I'm Agent Stockwell," Norm said. "I'd like to have a chance to talk to you."

Ansel put his brushes in a jar, wiped his hands with a rag, and walked over to the glass. Even in his human disguise, he was formidably built. His blue eyes looked Norm over, coolly assessing him.

"About what?" Ansel asked.

"It's classified," Norm said. Norm glanced at Vanessa and the others, who excused themselves.

"I'll be in Room 113, should you need anything, Agent Stockwell," Vanessa said.

Norm watched them go.

"Do they tell you what's going on outside this place, Ansel?" Norm asked.

"What's your first name, Agent Stockwell? Or is your name 'Agent'?" Ansel asked.

"Norm," he said. "That's my name."

Ansel smirked at that.

"For real? Norm?" Ansel asked.

Norm nodded. "My parents loved 'Cheers' I guess."

He could tell that Ansel neither knew nor cared about the pop-cultural reference. He cleared his throat and continued.

"I have a twin sister," Norm said. "Fraternal. Norma. She lives in Seattle."

"Ah," Ansel said. "That's kind of weird, I guess. I'd kill my parents if they named me 'Norm.'"

"Would you?" Norm asked.

"Nah," Ansel said. "I love my family. Besides, both of my parents are dead."

Norm took a seat across from Ansel, who remained standing.

"Lycanthrope stuff?" Norm asked. Ansel eyed him warily—not caution, so much as reticence.

"Sure," Ansel said. "There's always attrition. Even for us Trueborn. Maybe especially us."

"Yeah, you're a real family man," Norm said. "You Rupinos are like that."

"Close-knit," Ansel said. "As families should be."

"Your sisters paid me a visit," Norm said. Ansel smirked at him.

"Which sisters?" Ansel asked.

"Gia," Norm said. "Valentina."

Ansel chuckled to himself, shaking his head.

"And you're still alive," Ansel said. "That means they have a use for you. My sisters can be bitches."

"Uh, well, we talked about things," Norm said. "I'm sure your cell's bugged, right? Cameras and the like?"

Ansel nodded.

"Dr. Holloway likes to keep tabs on her guests," Ansel said.

"I'll bet she does," Norm said. He pulled a signal jammer from his pocket and turned a few switches. "This is a signal jammer. Do you know what a Stinger is, Ansel?"

"They haven't told me," Ansel said. "Is that what that is?"

"No," Norm said. "I'm a Stinger. I'm a field agent for the Bureau."

"A 'Stinger' eh? Man, you BEE people really run with your motifs, don't you?" Ansel said.

Norm couldn't dispute it but wasn't about to defend how the Bureau went about its naming conventions to a Lupine.

"I didn't come up with the name," Norm said.

Ansel smiled to himself. His smile was menacingly handsome. It was as welcoming and warm as it was, in its way, threatening.

"Like the Wardens," Ansel said. "I remember them."

"Better," Norm said. "Anyway, your family needs you, apparently. Or they want you. Gia wants me to get you out of here. They think you're imprisoned here."

Ansel laughed, now, richly, his chest heaving.

"After years in here, my sister wants me free? Is this a joke? One of Dr. Holloway's tests?" Ansel asked. "I've been the Hive's pet lycanthrope for a long time, man. Ever since I turned myself in. You know, to atone for what I'd done."

"She wants you out," Norm said. "That's all I know. There's rumors about transferring these Lupines to the CDC facilities, off this ship. I think your sister doesn't want you disappearing in some bioweapon containment cell in Atlanta."

"Yeah," Ansel said. "I guess not. Fuck Atlanta. Still, it's rich. I've been hiding out here for years. I've been poked and prodded. They've done so many blood draws, I can't even remember how many. I screwed up. Across the board. Gia wanted me to fix it, but I didn't have that in me. Not that way. Not *her* way."

"Look, I don't know how much time we'll have to talk this out," Norm said. "Vanessa's going to be stomping back over here in a few once she realizes I'm jamming comms. Your sister wants you out of here and wants me to be the one to do it. And from what Minton told me, you're a guest here, not a prisoner. You can leave any time you want."

"This is bullshit," Ansel said. "It's some kind of trap. You're wanting to set me up so you guys can kill me or something."

"I think if anybody at the Bureau wanted to kill you, they'd have done it, already," Norm said. "Your family knows you're not on Wolf Island."

"Yeah, Wolf Island," Ansel said. "Everybody talks about that one. If it even exists. In my darker moments, I see it as a giant crematorium. Like they just burn all the Lupines that arrive."

"Wow, that's pretty dark," Norm said.

"I'm a werewolf," Ansel said. "My mind gravitates toward dark places."

Norm glanced down the corridor, either way. It was currently clear. That gave him hope that they could talk further without intrusion.

"It exists," Norm said. "I've been there."

"Look, Agent Norm Guy," Ansel said. "There's NFW your bosses would want you springing me from here. So, why in the hell would you even consider that? Does Gia have something on you?"

"That would make more sense, wouldn't it?" Norm asked. "She and I have come to an understanding."

"Ha," Ansel said. "I know what Gia's 'understandings' are about. Did she take some loved ones hostage or something?"

"No," Norm said. "Look, there's a lot going on out there. The Bureau's been really successful in dealing with the Happening outbreak with the help of your family. It's been largely contained—maybe not to pre-2007 levels, but better than it's been in years. Everywhere but Chicago, where there are still some serious packs in play. There's a real desire to get it sorted out before the next election, for fear that some other dipshit might take over and ruin everything."

"My sister has an army," Ansel said. "She doesn't need me for this."

"She wants you back," Norm said. "That's all I know."

"And you'll be the one to help me out," Ansel said. "Is that right?"

"Yes," Norm said.

Ansel couldn't believe him. The look on his face said everything. He'd been sequestered too long, his time here had etched away at him, eroded something of himself. Norm couldn't imagine hiding out on the *Argent* for years. It was insane. But then, Norm wasn't a lycanthrope, and couldn't say for sure that he knew how they thought about anything, what mattered to them, what didn't.

Which was a weird place to be, given how many of them he'd killed over the years. But killing someone wasn't the same as knowing them, he admitted. It was like looking at a photograph and trying to imagine the person in the picture.

"Then let me out now," Ansel said. "No time like the present. Why bother even telling me this?"

"I had to see you face to face," Norm said. "Had to let you know. And there's more."

"What more?" Ansel asked.

"You're a father," Norm said. "By way of Polly Drinkwater."

Ansel's face registered muted pain. There was a legitimate emotional connection there. For Norm, connections were tools he could use, provided him a degree of leverage.

"She was a friend," Ansel said.

"Oh, a little more than that, yes?" Norm said. "See, she had a child. A daughter. And damned if she doesn't look like you, Ansel. Cute kid."

Ansel grimaced, his mask of nonchalance slipping.

"A daughter?" Ansel asked. "And you think she's mine?"

"I'm willing to bet she's yours," Norm said. "She's a Rupino. You Rupinos look like each other. She's got your eyes, your nose, your dark hair. She's even got your scowl."

Ansel's eyes flashed and he paced in his cell.

"You can't tell Gia," Ansel said.

"No? I think she maybe already knows. Or suspects. She's pretty sharp."

Ansel shook his head, clearly agitated. "My family gets a little crazy about that stuff. They'll want to take her, bring her up in the family."

"Yeah, well, now you see why I had to talk to you," Norm said.

"Who's taking care of her now?" Ansel asked.

"Friends of mine," Norm said.

Ansel's eyes raked over Norm, trying to get a read on him. Norm had dealt with enough Lupines to know their body language and cues. He might not understand how they thought, but he knew how they reacted to things. They relied on their senses more than everyday folks. It likely bothered Ansel that he couldn't take his scent, to be sure whether or not Norm was telling the truth. Lupine noses were lie detectors.

"Why'd you tell me this?" Ansel asked.

"Because you needed to know," Norm said. He pulled out his phone and held it up against the glass, showing Sloane smiling. It was one of his surveillance shots, blown up.

"What's her name?" Ansel asked.

"Sloane," Norm said.

Ansel looked at the girl with shock and emotion that Norm couldn't entirely identify. Concern? Sorrow? Regret?

"Sloane," Ansel said, chuckling. "Such a Polly sort of name."

Norm put the phone away.

"I need your promise of good behavior," Norm said. "Don't sign any fucking consent forms or transfer documents, whatever Dr. Holloway puts your way. Will you come with me?"

Ansel shook off his shock and turned his eyes back onto Norm.

"Are you worried something might happen to you?" Ansel asked.

"Always," Norm said. "I wouldn't be good at what I did if I was too trusting."

Vanessa appeared around the corner and was clacking toward them, the security men on her heels. She didn't look at all sanguine about his jamming her comms.

"Time's up," Norm said, covertly reaching into his pocket and disabling the jammer. "Good luck with your painting, Mr. Rupino."

Vanessa reached them, looking at them both, trying to decipher what she was seeing. She was sharp-eyed and sharper-minded, and Norm felt altogether sheepish under her unrelenting stare.

"Hope you two had a nice little chat," Vanessa said. "Nice play with the scrambler, Norm."

"I thought you'd like that," Norm said. "Stinger prerogative, Dr. Holloway."

Ansel had shelved his shock, replacing it with the mildest of annoyance, laced with contempt. All Lupines were actors at heart. Acting normal, acting human, was something most of them tried to do every day. The bad actors didn't fool anyone, not even themselves. The best of them could almost masquerade as normal.

"What did you talk about?" Vanessa asked.

"It's classified, like I said before," Norm said. "Alright, boys, I'm ready to go."

"Stinger business or no: don't ever do that again," Vanessa said. "I try to maintain a secure environment for my patients. Running a signal jammer in the midst of my labs is just rude."

"Sorry, Doctor," Norm said.

She disabled the intercom with Ansel's cell, since he was eagerly watching and listening to them both. "Then again, you won't even be able to. I finally got the approval from CDC. We're shipping Mr. Rupino out to Atlanta at the end of the week if he consents to it. I'll finally get off this damned ship, to some proper lab facilities."

"You arranged a transfer," Norm said. Vanessa nodded.

"And a promotion," Vanessa said. "No more slumming it with you drones at the Hive."

"Good luck, Dr. Holloway," Norm said.

Vanessa smiled icily at him.

"Enjoy the rest of your life aboard the *Argent*, Agent Stockwell," Vanessa said. "I imagine you're not going anywhere, after all that you've done."

MINA had gotten Sloane into the safe house, mindful of everything around them. This place was a two-story home of brick, utterly unassuming in the manner of the *Synowie* safehouses.

Sloane had stirred a bit, waking up when Mina had set her down on the green sofa in the living room.

"Where's Momster?" Sloane asked.

"She's out," Mina said.

Sloane sniffed the air a moment, before sighing.

"She does that," Sloane said. "Goes out."

"What about you?"

"She doesn't let me," Sloane said. "Says it's not safe for me to go out at night. She's wrong, but she's my mom."

Mina felt sorry for the little Trueborn girl. What a strange place to occupy, to be a wonder in a world of wonder.

"She's right. It's not safe," Mina said.

Sloane looked down her nose at Mina from her spot on the sofa. She looked like the perfect fusion of her mother and father—Rupino and Drinkwater. She was adorable. What monstrous innocence.

"I'm not scared," Sloane said.

"You're very brave," Mina said.

"I've *never* been afraid," Sloane said.

How curious it was to be a female lycanthrope. For male Infectives, the bite was the primary mode of retroviral infection. But Infective females had two modes of transmission—the bite, but also giving birth.

Any child born of an Infective female would be a Trueborn lycanthrope. They grew up with their condition as a natural and inextricable part of their lives. They could transform at will. They healed so quickly, suffered from no disease, and only silver could truly hurt them. What a blessing for a little girl, knowing that she could tear apart anyone who ever crossed her.

"I'm always afraid," Mina said. "Afraid of losing control. Afraid of being caught. Afraid of being killed."

Sloane reached out a little hand and patted Mina's own hand.

"It's okay," Sloane said. "What's your name?"

"Mina," she said.

"Mina," Sloane said. "I'm Sloane Drinkwater."

"I know you are," Mina said.

"You're very angry inside," Sloane said. "I smell it on you."

"What?"

"You keep your real self all locked up tight," Sloane said. "She's *so angry*."

Mina wondered how the girl could tell all of that with just a sniff or two.

"I won't let her take control of me," Mina said.

"My mom would try that for awhile," Sloane said. "But she gave up on it. Fun fact: werewolves *always* win. You can't win with werewolves."

Mina smiled at that sentiment, even as she was frustrated by it. She felt like Animus was always gnawing at her, provoking her. The Lupitol took the edge off but didn't stop her from chewing away at her.

"No?"

Sloane shook her head.

"Why can't I win?"

"Just cuz," Sloane said. "It just waits in the wings for you to slip up, and then it pounces. The longer you keep it down, the bigger the pounce."

Lupitol would beg to differ, Mina thought.

"You should try to sleep some more," Mina said. "I'll keep watch."

"I'm not sleepy, Mina," Sloane said. "I should go find my Momster."

"No," Mina said. "She wanted us to be safe."

"It wouldn't be hard," Sloane said. "I'm a great tracker. I can find her anywhere."

"Yes?"

Sloane nodded. "I can track anything. I love smelling stuff. Smelling is like magical memory. Even yucky stuff is interesting."

Mina smiled at the sentiment. She knew her own sense of smell had improved when her infection had manifested, just as her vision and hearing had gotten better. Even with the Lupitol dampening Animus, she experienced those benefits.

Her phone chirped. It was Sonia. She got up and walked into the other room, so Sloane could hopefully sleep, whether she wanted to or not.

"What's going on, Sonia?" Mina asked.

"We've taken out the trash," Sonia said. "We're heading to your location. Are you okay?"

Mina wasn't sure how euphemistic she should be, felt an obligation to at least be somewhat cryptic.

"Umm, we had some people following us, but Mommy Dearest took care of it," Mina said. "I haven't seen her since, however."

"Okay," Sonia said. "Just stay put. We'll be there in an hour. How's the package?"

"Fine," Mina said. "Unharmed."

"The city's abuzz," Sonia said. "They're hunting. Greys, Blacks, Whites. Things are happening to the Happening. The Bees are buzzing in the park. Something big."

"Be careful," Mina said.

"We're always careful," Sonia said. "Just please stay put and draw as little attention to yourself as you can."

"Okay," Mina said. "But hurry."

They hung up, and Mina checked on Sloane, who had managed to get back to sleep, despite all odds. How nice it was to be so young and carefree. To be a Trueborn lycanthrope was the gift of knowing you were special from birth, that your other self was integrated in who you were, versus something you had to fight for control. For a Trueborn, it was like having an imaginary friend who was real, who would never hurt you, would always be there to protect you. It was like a guardian angel.

Stop fighting me, Animus growled from behind her Lupitol muzzle. *And there'd be no problem.*

Mina knew better than to engage with her other self. It was always the way one lost one's way, a little trick the virus played on its hosts. Getting into arguments with oneself led to a loss of a sense of self. Over time, the original self would be subsumed by the retroviral self, and when the lines blurred, one was lost to the infection, affliction, condition, curse. Whatever one wanted to call it. Maybe all four applied. Her younger self would have smacked her for that concession, but Mina accepted it for what it was.

Polly had left a book of poetry with Sloane when they'd fled her house. Mina looked it over, the little book with *Lupinia* as its title. It was a pretty little thing. Mina wondered if the woman's partial face on the cover was Polly's.

Lupinia: Selected Poems of Polly Drinkwater, 2007–2015

Mina paged through it a moment, seeking inspiration, salvation, whatever she could find. Then she went to the curtained living room window and peeked out, unsure what she might see. The street looked quiet and dark, with only the streetlamps offering anything by way of illumination.

A light snow was falling, and Mina could see someone walking down the street, a young woman limping. She thought it might be Polly for a moment, but decided the young woman was too petite to be Polly. The young woman was stumbling around, back and forth, like she was searching for something. She had a leather jacket and leggings and a black stocking cap. She moved like a shark, searching. Her movements were awkward, like she was in pain.

Mina backed away from the curtain, turned off the lights, and waited in the darkness for a few minutes before returning back to the window.

The young woman was still out there, still searching. She stopped at the car Mina had been driving, walked around it. She was sniffing the air.

Mina texted Sonia.

THERE MAY BE TROUBLE.

Then the young woman painfully crossed the street, heading toward the safe house. She walked back and forth on the sidewalk in front of the building, first heading next door, then walking back the other way.

She was pretty, with dark hair and big eyes, and Italianate features. Mina felt sure she was a Rupino. The young woman moved like a metronome until she settled in front of the safe house. Although lit only by the streetlamp, Mina could see she was smiling.

The young woman took out her phone and made a call. Mina couldn't hear what she was saying but felt fear clawing at her. Sonia texted her back.

WHAT IS IT?

A RUPINO, I THINK SHE TRACKED US.

THERE'S SOME TOOLS IN THE DINING ROOM SIDEBOARD.

Mina went over to the dining room and saw the dark wood sideboard, opened it. She saw a *Lupara* in there and a bandolier of shells. There were also some silver daggers. Mina grabbed the *Lupara* and checked to see if it was loaded. It was.

She'd never fired a shotgun before, but assumed it was pretty straightforward—point and pull the triggers. Two triggers, one per barrel. Okay. That made sense. She slung the bandolier over her shoulder and went back into the living room. She could smell the silver in the shells around her neck. They made her want to sneeze.

Going back to the window, she saw the young woman was wrapping up her phone call. Then she put away her phone and walked up the steps, using the railing to ease her way up. Mina could hear her trying the door, seeing if it was locked.

Rather than hiding, Mina threw open the door and pointed the shotgun in the startled young woman's face.

"Can I help you?" Mina asked.

"Whoa, whoa," the young woman said. She was bloody. Mina could smell it on her, could see it on her, despite the shadows. "You won't believe this, but I was attacked by a werewolf."

"Were you?" Mina asked, deciding she'd play along for the moment, since the young woman didn't know that she knew just who and what she was.

"I'm really shaken up," the young woman said. "And I'm hurt."

"Maybe we should call the police," Mina said. The young woman sniffed the air.

"No way," the young woman said. "I don't trust them. I think they're werewolves, too. I mean, I know it's crazy. Look, I'm really wounded. Can you help me?"

Mina kept the *Lupara* pointed right at her. At this range, even without being a practiced shot, Mina thought she'd be able to hit her.

"No, I can't," Mina said.

The young woman smiled at her. It was a becoming smile, and a wounded smile.

"Do you always pull guns on people who come to your door seeking help?" she asked. "Are you, like, a Bad Samaritan?"

"Only to those who deserve it," Mina said. "I saw you tracking us."

"Us?" the girl said. "You're not alone, then?"

"I'm sure you already knew that," Mina said. The young woman looked like she'd been in a helluva fight. She was bleeding on the front porch, drops that fell here and there, staining the snow.

The young woman stared at Mina, at the *Lupara*.

"I'm Valentina Rupino," she said. "I'm here to pick up what's ours."

"Oh, are you?" Mina said. Valentina sniffed the air again.

"You're an *Infettiva*," Valentina said. "So many of you, hard to keep count. Same stink, though—cowardice and confusion."

Mina wasn't a killer. Although she held the gun on the young woman, she doubted she'd be able to consciously pull the trigger, although she felt that she should.

"You're not *Synowie*," Valentina said. "Are you?"

"Yeah," Mina said. The young woman laughed.

"If you really were, you would have shot me down already," Valentina said. "The *Synowie* don't play. Let me tell you something. I already called my family. They'll be here soon. We're here for the girl. Give us the girl, and there'll be no problem."

Mina shook her head.

"No? Let me put it to you this way, *Synowie*," Valentina said. "Whether slugs or shot, you've only got two barrels. That'll do for me, but there are more of us coming."

"So, I should just shoot you now, is what I'm hearing you say," Mina said, feeling Animus on her lips.

"Whoa, take it easy," Valentina said. "I'm just saying don't start a fight you can't possibly win, *Infettiva*."

Mina sniffed at the young woman. *Two could play that game, the Lycanthropic Sniff Test,* Mina thought with satisfaction.

"That's not only your blood," Mina said. "It's also Polly's."

Valentina looked surprised.

"Nice nose," she said. "Yeah, we had words."

"You killed her?" Mina said.

"Sure," Valentina said, gauging Mina's reaction. "Had to be done."

"Did it?"

Valentina nodded.

"You killed the girl's mother," Mina said. "And you expect me to just hand her over to you?"

"I'm her aunt," Valentina said. "She's family. Polly wasn't."

"I don't think so," Mina said. "I don't care who you are."

Valentina cleared her throat, kept her eyes riveted on Mina and her *Lupara*.

"Look, you're not a killer," Valentina said. "I can tell you're not. So, why start now? That's a bell you can't unring. You give us the girl, and you never have to see us again. You look exhausted. What's your name?"

"Mina," she said. Mina didn't see a point in not giving her real name.

"Mina," Valentina said. "That's a nice name. Mina, you give us the girl, and you can go back to your so-called *Infettiva* life. What do you have to lose, besides, you know, your life?"

Mina knew the young woman was simply delaying her, trying to buy time before her family got there.

"Good point," Mina asked. She lowered the *Lupara* and fired it, striking Valentina in the legs. The shotgun roared and Valentina went tumbling down the stairs, her legs bleeding. Valentina cursed, crying out.

"Oh, fuck me," Valentina said, clutching at her badly wounded legs. "You shot me, you *Infettiva* bitch!"

Mina ran back inside, gathering up a startled Sloane, who'd jumped to her feet.

"What is it, Mina?" Sloane asked. "What was that noise?"

"Trouble," Mina said, grabbing Polly's poetry book while reaching for Sloane. "Come on, Kiddo."

She hoisted Sloane up and ran back out the front, closing the door behind her. Valentina was crawling on the sidewalk, cursing, leaving a smear of blood as she went. She glared at Mina, her eyes on Sloane.

"Baby," Valentina said, grimacing. "I'm your Aunt Valentina. I'm here to take you away from all of this. I'm just like you. She's not."

She threw off her leather jacket and started to transform, crying out as she did so, for the *Lupara's* silver shot hadn't been expelled the way ordinary bullets would, her wounds didn't heal the way they usually would. And Mina could see how badly wounded Valentina was. She was a mosaic of claw and bitemarks. Maybe she'd killed Polly, but it looked like Polly had fought very hard.

Valentina held out a clawed hand for Sloane, her nails long and bloody.

"Where's my Momster?" Sloane asked.

"She's not here, Baby," Valentina said. "She abandoned you. She ran off."

Mina wasn't about to be the one to break the news to Sloane about her mother, couldn't believe Valentina had said that.

She quickly put Sloane in the back seat, while Valentina pushed herself into her hybrid form, cursing and growling, propping herself against one of the neighborhood trees, in evident pain. She let out a riotous howl, shaking the fresh-fallen snow from nearby trees. People in the neighborhood who had turned on their lights after the shotgun blast were peering out their windows at the source of the howl.

Mina wanted to take another shot at her, but decided it was better to flee. She got in the car and drove away, leaving Valentina lycanthropically limping after them, receding in the rearview mirror, a bloody monster in their wake.

NORM had been frustrated by his effective exile on the *Argent*. A Stinger was most useful in the field, and least useful back in the Hive. He tried to occupy himself by studying the routines aboard the ship, to better figure out how he'd persuade Ansel to come with him.

The answer, obviously, was with Dr. Holloway's transfer. Norm would have to persuade Ansel to not sign that consent form and sign his life away. And if he did sign, Norm would have to take other measures.

However, that wouldn't be easy—the transfer team would be handpicked by Minton, and everybody would have clearance for it. Norm would not be welcome.

Norm decided to talk to Minton directly again, not in hopes of getting included on the transition team, but to hopefully get a sense of where Minton's head was at.

Minton was, as ever, busy, but made time for him, talking to him while reviewing the status board. It was a white board with a lot of scribbles on it. He'd already crossed out the *Volki*, the Babas, and the Doozies. He had a question mark by the Rupinos, and a circle around Bastion. The Brotherhood and *Lunares* had exclamation marks by them and dotted lines pointing to the Rupinos. The *Synowie* were in a circle by themselves, off to one side, with a line that led to "Mina" written in hard black lines.

"Did you know that Dr. Mina Milkowski was sheltering with the *Synowie?*" Minton asked. "That's where she's been all of these years. With them."

Norm debated whether to tell Minton, or whether to keep him in the dark. There seemed to be more advantage to the latter, so he chose that avenue.

"She's the one who shared all her research data with the CDC," Norm said. "She's not one of the bad guys, Troy."

Minton wasn't having any of it. He could be immovable once he got something in his head. It was easier to think that Mina was a problem to be solved.

"It was her data dump to the CDC that got them breathing down our necks to begin with," Minton said. "Before then, it was strictly Bureau business."

Norm didn't want to play devil's advocate but had to at least bring it up.

"I think the fact that Sanderson had massacred everybody at the Kennel had put her off playing nice with the Bureau, Sir."

Troy was working it out, putting a vintage BEE employee file picture of Milkowski on the white board, adding black dry erase question marks around her with a marker.

"She was bitten by Zooey Hummel," Minton said. "Like all the others at the Kennel. But Zooey is long dead, so that makes her a free agent, right? That's how it works?"

"More or less," Norm said.

"What's she doing working with the *Synowie?*"

"She needed help," Norm said.

"Goddammit, Norm," Minton said. "Haven't I been straight with you? You withhold that from me? How many times are you going to do this to me?"

"I only just found out, Sir. She's not a bad person," Norm said. "Infected, yeah, but she's been taking Lupitol. She's trying to do the right thing."

"The right thing would be turning herself in," Minton said. "Why were you in contact with her?"

"She has connections with *Synowie*," Norm said. "They'd reached out to me about Rupino, so I was using her to get insight into how the Poles were operating."

"Bullshit," Minton said. "I don't buy it, man. Why would those fanatics even work with Milkowski? Instead of, you know, putting two silver bullets in her head?"

"She's still a scientist," Norm said. "Maybe she worked a deal. Seems to be what people are doing these days."

"A deal, my ass," Minton said. "There's something that doesn't make sense to me, here. Something I'm missing."

"I don't think so, Sir," Norm said.

"Milwoski's been MIA since the Happening," Minton said. "You should have told me you'd contacted her."

It was a tricky thing. Norm didn't want Minton to know about the girl. He'd have one of the Bureau's Recovery Teams there in a heartbeat.

"We'd been in touch," Norm said. "Comparing notes, that kind of thing."

"That kind of thing," Minton said. "Show me your ink, Stockwell."

"You honestly think I'm infected, Sir?" Norm asked. He showed his arms, revealing his tattooed sleeves, as ever, and his official, secret BEE tats. Tattoos were one of the few vices BEE agents enjoyed with relish, because no Lupine retained their ink. It was a quick and dirty way to detect a Lupine. No ink or silver, maybe a Lupine.

Minton laughed bitterly as he studied them, running a black penlight over the BEE tats. "Yeah, I suppose not. You'd give a werewolf indigestion, man."

"Mina's one of ours," Norm said. "She needs our help."

"I'll have folks look into it," Minton said. "That's all you need to know. That's all you're gonna know, for that matter."

Norm resisted the urge to text Mina with an update. With Archon, Minton would be privy to exactly what he'd texted. He just hoped Mina would be alright.

Instead, he pivoted to something else.

"Has Rupino signed the consent form for the transfer?" Norm asked.

"Not yet," Minton said. "He's thinking about it."

"I want to be on the transport team for Rupino if he does," Norm said.

The transfer of Rupino would be a high security operation. They would likely try to tranquilize him, keeping him under while they moved him. It was simply too risky, otherwise. They'd gas him, then, when they were certain he was out, they'd transfer him to a PILL—Protective Incarceration Loading Lockbox—they were lozenges of titanium that were designed to keep a lycanthrope pinioned, unable to transform just because of the strength of the metal.

The PILLs were brute force solutions to the problem of a Lupine—a werewolf would literally bust a gut before they could breach a PILL. Each PILL had a little viewing window with air holes in it, so the Lupine could breathe and be observed. The ones that tried to transform when within a PILL would turn themselves into a lycanthropic stew that would take days to heal. It was a testament to their capacity to heal that they could even come back together after something like that. But it wasn't a pleasant recovery.

Once in the PILL, they'd wheel him to the loading bay, whereupon he'd either be put in a helicopter on the helipad, or else lowered to a waiting boat that would ship him ashore.

It was a coin toss whether Minton would transport by air or water. There were risks with either.

The helicopter was quicker but was potentially more vulnerable than the boat. He could have more security on the boat. Then again, the PILL would render Rupino helpless, as it was designed to do. The risk with transport was whether anybody else would go after the BEE team.

Once the transport reached the shore, they'd offload the PILL into an armored transport truck—or, they'd fly to the airport, and slip the PILL into a transport plane. After that, it was either a road trip to CDC (unlikely), or a flight there. Once at CDC, Rupino was effectively gone—they'd transition him from BEE to CDC, and he'd be lost.

From a planning perspective, everything hinged on the time they got Rupino into the PILL and off the *Argent*, to before the transport offload. That was his window. That would be when he'd have the most chance to make his move.

Ideally, he wouldn't have to.

"Ha," Minton said. "You know that's not going to happen. You're staying with me here on *Argent*, Norm. You were lucky I even let you talk to Rupino. If he consents, then he's going to CDC, and that's that. We're done here, Norm. I've got work to do."

Norm knew better than to argue with Minton. Once his mind was made up, that was that.

"Alright," Norm said, taking a risk by pressing the issue. "But I have another idea, something that's really next-level stuff, Sir. Something that'll keep the BEE front and center and not let the CDC override the mission."

That got to Minton, just a little bit. He was proud of the BEE, didn't want the CDC taking precedence in the R&D where the Lupines were concerned. It was as much agency rivalry and bureaucracy as politics.

"Tell me," Minton said. "You have three more minutes."

Norm's mind raced as he told Minton his plan. He knew he'd made some progress when Minton gave him three more minutes before he sent him on his way.

Norm walked down through the *Argent,* toward Research, wanting to see Vanessa, who he'd been meaning to see all night. One more all-nighter wouldn't kill anybody.

He card-keyed his way through to Research, where Vanessa had her menagerie, the Infectives she felt were worth studying, the row of women, the row of men. They were collector's items, now—two *Volki,* four Doozies, three Babas.

As he walked down the causeway, past the screaming, gibbering people, he saw that two-thirds of them had transformed, or were in the process of transforming—raging, pounding on that ballistic glass that so far seemed able to hold them.

Reds, browns, greys, blacks, tans, and golden—those were the dominant colors. To date, only Zooey Hummel and the Wolves of God had been white. Vanessa didn't have an explanation for that, at least not yet.

He saw Vanessa at the end of the cells, with Ansel, her prize. She never called them that, called them "patients," but that was just her being her.

She was sitting at a chair, taking notes, fully engaged in her work, not even seeing Norm approach.

"Vanessa," Norm said.

"Oh! Norm!" Vanessa said, startled.

Norm walked up, saw Ansel standing there, finishing his painting of Vanessa. It was a perfect rendering, sensuous and intense, gazing out from the canvas. The guy could paint. Dr. Holloway looked otherworldly on the canvas.

"Looks like you," Norm said.

"Ansel's a very skilled painter," Vanessa said, a trifle awkwardly.

Ansel looked at Norm through the glass without a trace of concern, without even evident emotion. He simply looked, appraised, surveyed. His artist's eyes saw through Norm, made him feel exposed, somehow.

"Did you sign the consent form, Ansel?" Norm asked.

Ansel glanced at him a moment.

"Not yet," Ansel said, eyeing Dr. Holloway.

"I wanted to wrap up my painting, first," Ansel said. "Then I'd decide."

"Yes, I see," Norm said.

"Looks just like her, doesn't it?" Ansel asked.

"Yeah," Norm said. "How is it you aren't suffocating in there? Those are oils, aren't they?"

"We've got his cell well-ventilated," Vanessa said. "You know I take precautions with our control unit cells, Norm. What are you doing down here again so soon, anyway?"

"I've just come back from Minton's office," Norm said, looking hard at Ansel through the glass. "The Lupines are getting stirred up in the city, by all accounts. Big things going on—the Rupinos apparently took apart the Doozies in the city. A massive massacre."

Holloway sucked her teeth a moment.

"*That's* why all those Recovery Teams went out," Holloway said. "I was wondering what had happened."

Ansel folded his arms. "I don't know anything about it, obviously. You can't pin it on me, I mean."

"Wasn't planning to," Norm said. "But I do have questions."

Vanessa studied Norm's face a bit, one of her searching looks, her scientist's eyes grazing over him.

Vanessa put her cool hand on Norm's forearm, wanting to offer him some comfort, since she could feel the vibe between him and Ansel, that sense of challenge between them.

"I suppose you think you're pretty clever," Norm said, gesturing to the painting. "What, are you trying to get into Vanessa's head with stuff like that?"

Ansel smiled. "She's beautiful. I couldn't resist. What can I say? Beauty moves me."

"You know, I'm sitting right here. You're making me blush, Ansel," Vanessa said. "I'm trying to persuade Ansel to sign the consent form."

"Signing your life away, Ansel?" Norm asked.

"Thinking about it," he said.

Ansel held onto his smile, took a seat in a wooden chair he had just past the barrier of the window. He was easily the largest lycanthrope they'd yet seen, back in the day.

"You're content to be shipped off to Atlanta?" Norm asked.

"Not really," Ansel said.

Ansel looked from Norm to Vanessa, who looked on, unfazed.

"He volunteered," Vanessa said, quickly. "I didn't coerce him."

"Right," Norm said.

"You see the problem, here?" Ansel said. "You have nothing to bargain with, relative to me. I have no reason to cooperate with you."

"Except what we'd discussed before," Norm said.

That gave Ansel pause, and he stewed a bit on it.

"Yeah, except that," Ansel said.

"Norm," Vanessa said. "Stop harassing my guest. Let me get back to work. We'll talk later."

"Where's Gia based?" Norm asked. "I need to talk to her again."

"Don't worry about finding Gia," Ansel said. "She'll find you."

Vanessa Holloway looked at both Ansel and Norm searchingly, trying to solve the puzzle of what she'd missed between them.

Ansel shrugged. "Dr. Holloway, this painting will need some dry time. I'd rather not have it drying in here with me. It needs to be put someplace where it can be left alone."

"We'll take care of it, Ansel," Vanessa said.

"You're not going to tell me," Norm said.

Ansel smirked at Norm.

"Why would I tell you?" Ansel asked. "Betray my own family for, what, you?"

"He doesn't know," Norm said. "He's full of it. Jerking you around, Vanessa."

"Norm, you need to go, now," Vanessa said, gesturing to the causeway.

"Yeah, Norm," Ansel said. "You need to go."

Norm smiled, shook his head, raised his hands in a mock surrender. "Alright. I don't want to interfere with your work, Dr. Holloway. Or whatever this exactly is."

Vanessa frowned at him, while Ansel smirked from behind the glass.

"Polly," Norm said. "She went looking for you."

Ansel's expression went from smug to concerned, and Norm noticed it.

"Yeah?" Ansel asked, trying to appear unmoved.

"Polly," Norm said.

"Polly," Ansel said. Ansel didn't react, but even with that mask up, he couldn't hide it. She mattered to him. Which meant that Sloane might matter to him, too.

The security in the Pens was very tight, but like anything, it could be breached. He glanced at his watch.

"Do you have somewhere to be, Norm?" Vanessa asked.

"I'd like to play another round of *Let's Ask Ansel,*" Norm said. "Minton gave me clearance to conduct my own interrogations."

"The way he indulges you," Vanessa said. "I can't fathom it. You're not the only Stinger, Norm."

"Sure, but I'm the best," Norm said.

Norm knew that would rankle Vanessa, who hated when Stingers got into her business. But, as Norm saw it, what was the point of being a Stinger if you couldn't make your presence felt.

"Go ahead, Norm," Vanessa said, irritated and waving him on. "Ask your questions."

"Thanks, Dr. Holloway," Norm said. "Ansel, I really want to know why you checked yourself into this place."

Ansel shrugged, his broad shoulders adding weight to the gesture.

"Penance, I suppose," Ansel said. "Atonement for what I'd done. I already said that, yeah?"

"Right," Norm said. "Like you said before. You negotiated your way into this situation."

Ansel looked at Norm through the ballistic glass, trying to sizing him up. Norm knew that if the two of them went at it and Ansel turned into Big Black, he'd be the death of him.

"I explained it already," Ansel said.

"You arranged this whole sequestration," Norm said. "Is that it?"

"I worked a deal, like you said. Protective custody," Ansel said. "They'd keep me under wraps, I'd offer information and insights into lycanthropy, and they wouldn't extradite and/or euthanize me. I offered key insights into Lupine behavior, stuff that helped your boss better navigate that world."

"Right," Norm said. He flipped off the microphone for a second. Vanessa looked at him curiously.

"What?"

"Are you treating him?" Norm asked. "Lupitol?"

Vanessa shook her head.

"Lupitol doesn't work on Trueborn," she said. "It rather has the opposite effect than on Infectives."

"How so?"

"It drives them berserk," she said. Norm wondered what Trueborns she'd tested it on, but with the volume of Lupines passing through the *Argent,* she may have gotten her hands on some. Or else she was privy to Liminalix research data. He wondered whether she was compromised, too.

"You didn't use it on him, did you?" Norm asked.

"No," Vanessa said. "I didn't want to risk him."

Norm was no pharmacologist, but that was a curious bit of information. It made him wonder about Liminalix and Bastion's whole enterprise. A drug that would moderate Infective symptoms but make Trueborn go berserk.

"Why does it have that effect?" Norm asked.

"We're still trying to figure it out," Vanessa said. "Likely it's a reaction on the part of the virus to being attacked. Lupitol works with an Infective's immune system, helping it against the retrovirus. But a Trueborn isn't the same biochemistry."

Norm flipped the mic back on.

"So, in return for leniency, you're offering information," Norm said.

"Least I could do," Ansel said. "After what I'd done."

"You feel guilty?" Norm asked.

"How could I not?" Ansel said. "One bad night, one relapse, and I set all of this in motion. I mean, I have to carry that with me every day."

"We all do things we have to carry with us," Norm said. "You're, what, content to live as a prisoner provided we give you stuff to paint with? You're going to hide here forever? Or at the CDC?"

Ansel sighed, looking almost shamefaced.

"I suppose," Ansel said.

"Come on, man," Norm said.

"What's the alternative?" Ansel asked. "Have my family put me to work killing hundreds of Infectives? At least here, I can't hurt anybody, and I get to paint in peace. I mean, yeah, it sucks, but it's not the worst thing."

Norm found Ansel's opacity and obtuseness frustrating.

"Nonsense," Norm said. "This is crap."

"What?" Ansel asked.

"You heard me," Norm said. "You're hiding out in here because you don't want to accept the responsibility for what you did. You're letting everybody else clean up *your* mess."

"Norm," Vanessa said, but Norm shook his head.

"You're evading responsibility for your part in it," Norm said. "Thousands of people are infected, thousands have been killed, on either side. All because you lost control one night."

Ansel looked pained at the thought, it slipping in on his otherwise impenetrable bearing. Norm knew how to get under people's skin, even if they were skinchangers.

"You took Lupitol that night you lost control, didn't you?" Norm asked.

Ansel stared at him through the glass.

"It wasn't Lupitol, yet," Ansel said. "It was underground stuff back then. I took a lot of tranquilizers back in the day. Somebody had gotten me some stuff. I didn't ask where. Nobody had anything like that, stuff that would work. A person had told me about something new they were working on. Keep in mind, this was before the Happening. Nobody had a clue."

"How'd they know you were what you are?" Norm asked.

"I'm a Rupino," Ansel said. "I don't hide that. Those in the know, they know, you know?"

"Who was it?" Norm asked. "A Liminalix contact?"

"A woman," Ansel said. "A pharma rep. I didn't trust her, but she told me there was something new coming to the market in a few years, offered me a free sample, made me sign an NDA."

Ansel paced in his cell, clearly agitated.

"I didn't think anything of it," Ansel said. "She'd told me she knew what I was, who I was. She told me about this program they had."

"Was it Anne Stockwell?" Norm asked.

"It was eight years ago," Ansel said. "Sure, I think so."

Norm produced a photo of Anne on his phone, held it up to the glass for Ansel to review.

"Yeah," Ansel said. "Her."

That pained Norm worse than anything.

Anne had been working the angles with Bastion even then, without so much as a word to him about it. She'd given Ansel some proto-Lupitol as a test case. Had Bastion planned for there to be an incident? For Ansel to lose control and go on a rampage, making it look like he'd just lost his way? Was the whole thing some sort of Trueborn power play? Ansel blows his stack, makes the Rupinos look bad, the Happening breaks out, suddenly Bastion has a way to get more funding for Lupitol and a fast-track to approval. Could it be as straightforward as that?

Anne had known all about the Lupines while pretending that she didn't. All that time. The depth of betrayal cut Norm even deeper. He was determined to talk to her again, to find out. But for now, he had to attend to Ansel.

"You've only served half your sentence," Norm said. "Our half. You owe the other half to your family, to your daughter."

"Daughter?" Vanessa asked. She looked shocked, like genuinely shocked. Norm tried to read her expression, and that's what he thought. It didn't look like she was faking her reaction. She didn't know.

"Yeah, he's got a kid," Norm said. "By an Infective mother."

Norm knew the possibility of accessing a Trueborn child was beyond tempting for someone like Dr. Holloway.

"So she's a Trueborn?" Vanessa asked. "Where is she?"

Norm nodded.

"She's safe," Norm said. "For now. But people are after her. They're thinking it's a way to get to Ansel. But we both know that's crap. People just assume that he'd care about that, but we both know that he doesn't."

Norm could see he was reaching Ansel on some level, could see some hint of anger in there.

"I'm going to deliver your daughter to Gia," Norm said. "She can grow up there, with Gia and your sisters taking care of her, teaching her how to be just like them. And you could be there, too, if you're man enough to shoulder the responsibility of fatherhood."

Ansel looked conflicted, paced in his cell faster.

"You're agitating him, Norm," Vanessa said.

"What'll that do to her, I wonder," Norm said. "Knowing that her own father didn't care enough about her to be there for her."

Ansel walked to the edge of his cell and glared at Norm. They were only inches apart, the ballistic glass between them.

"I didn't ask for Polly to get pregnant," Ansel said. "Didn't plan for that. It just happened."

"Yeah," Norm said. "Just like that night with Samantha Hain, you hopped up on a Lupitol prototype drug. It just happened."

"What do you want from me?" Ansel asked. "Just because I got Polly pregnant doesn't mean I'd be any good at being a father."

Norm tried another tack with Ansel.

"Let's put it another way," Norm said. "Let's say Gia and your sisters get their paws on your daughter. Then what? They raise her up in the family business. You know the business I'm talking about—the one you have tried your whole life to avoid. Is that what you want for your daughter? To be a killer in the Rupino lycanthropic crime family? I mean, it's why you took up painting, am I right?"

Ansel resumed pacing, faster now. He was seething.

"You became a painter because you didn't want to become a killer," Norm said. "You hid away here at the BEE for the same reason. You're *not* a killer, no matter what you really are. Except when you are—when you need to be."

"What's wrong with that?" Ansel asked. "Everybody wants something from me. Gia wants me to be part of the family business. She always has. I don't want that. I'll never want that."

"But you couldn't tell her that," Norm said.

"No," Ansel said. "You've talked to her. You know what she's like. We have a saying in the family: *Gia ottiene sempre la sua strada.* Gia always gets her way."

Norm smiled to himself, could see how that might pass for a Rupino family proverb. Gia was a formidable woman of vision and ambition. Ansel had grown up in her shadow, and who knew how that all played out.

"But she respects family," Norm said. "Yes?"

"Of course she does," Ansel said.

"And the way to protect your daughter from Gia is to claim her, by being her father," Norm said. "Otherwise, she's just an adopted soldier in your sister's empire. To fight and probably die for your family's honor—or whatever you want to call it."

Vanessa flipped off the mic and leaned into Norm, her eyes flashing.

"What are you doing?" Vanessa asked. "Ansel's going with me to Atlanta. That's where he's headed. You're ruining things, Norm."

Norm knew Dr. Holloway would be a difficult sell on this.

"You love having access to a Trueborn," Norm said. "But these are laboratory conditions. What about a chance to observe one in the field? To see how things play out in the real world?"

He could see her thinking it over. Norm flipped the mic back on.

"Think of all the research you'd gather from that," Norm said. "As I see it, we could continue surveillance, so Ansel, you wouldn't have to worry about anybody going after you. You'd be under our protection, so you wouldn't have to fear losing control—we'd be there to make sure you didn't. And Dr. Holloway, you'd be able to see the girl develop. No researcher, particularly no BEE researcher, has ever had that opportunity. Certainly nobody else at the CDC would have that opportunity."

"What are you talking about?" Ansel asked. "Me becoming, what, a fucking lycanthropic consultant?"

"Sure," Norm said. "Something like that."

Reality intruded on the idea in the form of a frown from Vanessa.

"Minton would never go for it," Vanessa said.

"Of course he would," Norm said, providing a folded memo to Vanessa, who snapped it up. "He already has."

She scanned it, dumbfounded.

"How?"

"If you extradite Ansel to Atlanta, Ansel falls under CDC authority," Norm said. "So, to keep him associated with the BEE, I pushed for the halfway house idea I pitched to you just now. This way, it stays a BEE matter, Ansel gets some semblance of a normal life—or what passes for normal for, you know, a werewolf. And you get an opportunity to continue your research."

Vanessa looked at Norm with more than a little curiosity.

"I never thought you had it in you, Norm," Vanessa said. "All this time, I just thought of you as a mindless, murderous triggerman."

"Wow, yeah, thanks," Norm said. "But it doesn't mean I don't think about things. I've killed way more than my share of Lupines. Nothing ever will change that. Those people didn't ask to be infected. I ended them. So, maybe this is part of my own way of atoning."

"What about the CDC?" Vanessa asked. "They're going to expect something."

"Give them some of the other Infectives, the particularly nasty ones who shouldn't be released. The Babas you have," Norm said. "Tell them there's been a change in plans."

Dr. Holloway stared hard at the Minton memo, looked back at Norm.

"What am I going to tell them?"

"You're smart. You'll think of something," Norm said. "Pack up, Ansel. I'm getting you out of here. You've got a family reunion to attend. Assuming you're willing, of course."

Ansel stared at him, shaking his head.

"Normcore," Ansel said. "That's what you are, man. Fine. I'll play your game."

MINA was driving through the city, without any idea of where she should go, while Sloane fussed in the back seat.

"Where's my mom?" Sloane asked. "Who was that crazy lady we saw? Was she really my aunt? She was all bloody."

Mina wasn't about to tell the girl that was her Aunt Valentina. That was the last thing she needed to do.

"She smelled like my mom," Sloane said. "I could smell her on her."

"I'm sorry, Sloane," Mina said. "Sorry you had to experience that."

"Why'd she say my mom abandoned me?" Sloane asked.

"She was just trying to be mean," Mina said. "Sometimes people just are mean. Especially werewolves. No offense."

She glanced at Sloane in the rearview mirror, could see the girl working through that. She was a smart little girl, and it pained Mina to know that her mother was dead. She wouldn't be the one to tell that to her, though. It was too painful.

"My mom left a poetry book back here," Sloane said, holding it up. "L-U-P-I-N-I-A. She has a lot of poetry books back home. Do you think she went back there?"

"The house isn't safe," Mina said, gripping the steering wheel. She dialed up Sonia, mindful of her little passenger in back, and that she didn't have a child seat. Then again, she could probably crash the car and Sloane would come out just fine. Sonia picked up on the first ring.

"What's going on, Mina?" Sonia said. "What the hell happened at the safe house?"

"A Rupino showed up to try to take…the package," Mina said. "I, oh, to hell with it…I shot her."

"We could see from the spillage," Sonia said, as obliquely as she could. "Where are you now?"

"I'm driving," Mina said. "I don't know where. I don't care. I don't know where I should go. Your safe spaces aren't so safe, Sonia."

"They are," Sonia said. "But you're a hot ticket, apparently. Makes things more difficult."

Mina was exhausted but didn't know where she should go. She was tired of living the refugee life, tired of feeling hunted all the time.

"What do I do, Sonia?"

"Let's meet up," Sonia said. "Someplace where they won't dare go."

Sonia texted her the business address:

FEDOROWICZ & SONS: SILVERSMITHS

Mina wanted to laugh, despite herself. It was downtown, not far away. She didn't relish heading into Bastion territory but didn't see herself as having much of a choice.

"Alright," Mina said. "I'll be there."

"Wait for my call," Sonia said.

——

She found a parking deck near the silversmith shop and waited, parking the car. Sloane was bouncing around in the back seat, half-talking, half-singing to herself.

"Aren't you sleepy, Sloane?" Mina asked.

"Nope," Sloane said. "I'm wiiiiiide awake."

Mina wanted nothing more than to get some sleep.

Her mind kept working through the thing with Polly, how she'd break that to the girl, or whether she should. Why had Valentina killed her? It had to be some sort of Trueborn pack dynamic thing. As an Infective, maybe Polly had no place within the family hierarchy. For the Trueborn, any Infective would be an omega, so that was at least a possibility.

Too often in her research, Mina had been studying lone Lupines. It wasn't her fault. It was what she had access to. Pack dynamics, on the other hand, were an area of exploratory interest that would be interesting to observe. She wondered how that was playing out on Wolf Island. After eight years, it was at least possible that some of the Lupines there had bred, producing their own Trueborn.

That was something she'd be curious to see, although she pitied any child born in that place. She wondered if Anya and Zach were still alive. She hoped they were, despite whatever horrors they would no doubt have had to endure there.

She wondered if Liminalix had made some arrangements with the BEE to administer the drug to the exiles on the island. Then again, she thought that nobody on that island would ever be allowed to leave. The story was simply too bad for the government—nobody would have wanted the story of an American penal colony. Lupitol or no, nobody was ever leaving Wolf Island.

Sonia pinged her.

WE'RE HERE. WHERE ARE YOU?

Mina replied quickly.

NEARBY. HEADING OVER.

"Okay, Sloane, ready to go?" Mina asked.

"Yes, Dr. Mina," Sloane said.

They got out, Mina wildly mindful of everything around them. She could hear police sirens and the periodic howl. Since the Happening, it was simply part of the city's evening atmosphere.

Mina listened for a moment, decided they weren't close enough to be a concern, and took Sloane's hand and went to the elevator. Sloane was humming.

"I love nighttime," Sloane said. "My Momster would always make me stay in bed, but I always wanted to go outside. You know, to run around. See stuff. Smell stuff. I love how stuff smells. I would go outside and smell the world."

"Would you?" Mina asked. Despite her exile from the Bureau, the paranormal researcher that she was remained.

"I'd sneak out when my Momster would go on one of her outings," Sloane said. "She'd sneak out when she thought I was asleep. She'd be gone for hours. Then I'd go out."

"Where would you go?" Mina asked. It only made sense for a Trueborn Lupine girl to not be afraid of the dark.

"Around," Sloane said. "Exploring. It was fun, although I wished Momster had been there with me. She was always going off on her own. We're better in packs."

The elevator took them to the ground floor and Mina led them out, her senses honed for anything out of the ordinary.

The lights at the silversmith storefront were on, and as they approached, Sloane sniffed the air.

"Oh, I don't like that, Dr. Mina," Sloane said. "Silver."

Mina didn't, either. The smell of it was almost overpowering. To a lycanthrope, silver smelled toxic, like ammonia. It was a strongly metallic scent that prompted an instinctive fear reaction.

"This is our hiding place," Mina said. "Where they won't come for us."

Mina went to the door and opened it, while Sloane moved with reluctance, pulling at her hand.

"We shouldn't be here," Sloane said, holding her nose. "I hate it."

Sonia and her brothers were there, taking off their *Synowie* ski masks.

"You made it," Sonia said.

All around the store were vintage silver pieces—tureens, plates, platters, goblets, cups, candlesticks, jewelry of all sorts. The place was radiant with silver. For Mina and Sloane, it was the olfactory equivalent of deafening noise. They struggled to approach it.

Sloane was really straining against Mina's hand.

"I don't want to be here," Sloane said, tearing up. "Dr. Mina, please."

Sonia watched them a moment before speaking.

"You're safe here," Sonia said. "Or safer, anyway."

Mina could barely breathe, there was so much silver around them. Even Animus, as doped-up as she was, thrashed inside her.

"Is there a place we can go?" Mina said. "In the back somewhere? Away from all of this?"

"Yes," Sonia said, leading them forward. Sloane was crying, and Mina's own eyes were watering. It was overpowering.

"We should have gone to the Landa Library," Mina said.

"This is good for now," Sonia said. The back room was a workshop, which still carried the scent of silver, but it was at least more muted than the showroom. "There's living quarters the next two floors up."

"I'm assuming Fedorowicz and his sons?" Mina asked.

"Janos is out of town," Sonia said. "So, it's perfect."

They went upstairs, using an elevator in the back. Having put still more distance between themselves and the silver, Mina and Sloane both felt better.

"That place is a nightmare," Mina said.

"You see why it's perfect," Sonia said. "No Lupine will voluntarily go in if they can possibly avoid it."

The Fedorowicz residence was nicely modern, contrasting the plethora of vintage silver pieces downstairs. The colors were autumnal, with low leather sofas and sectionals about, and a plasma screen television on one wall. Sonia's brothers turned on the television and got some beers from the stainless steel fridge.

"Looks like being a silversmith pays well," Mina said.

"Janos is kept very busy by the *Synowie*," Sonia said. "He has no complaints."

Sloane had let go of Mina's hand and gone running around the place, while Sonia took a seat across from Mina.

"So, bring me up to speed," Sonia said. And Mina did, relaying everything she'd encountered since their flight from the Drinkwater residence. Sonia simply listened, nodding. "You didn't see the girl's mother die?"

"No," Mina said, glancing to see if Sloane was in earshot. "I didn't. But Valentina claimed she killed her. I could smell her blood on her. Valentina looked wounded, as well."

"Odds are very good, then, that she's dead," Sonia said. "Trueborn versus Infective doesn't turn out well for the Infective in most cases. Does the girl know?"

Sloane was in some of the other rooms, humming happily.

"No," Mina said. "I haven't told her. Her mom apparently had a habit of running off, so the girl's used to that."

Sonia took that in, thinking.

"Norm called me," Sonia said. "He has found Ansel and has somehow worked an arrangement with the Bureau to secure his release. I'm frankly suspicious, but for the moment, that's how that's playing out."

"They're coming ashore?" Mina asked.

Sonia nodded. "Ansel's going to meet his daughter."

"That's good, at least," Mina said. As much as she enjoyed Sloane's company, she felt awkward carting the girl around. Not that Mina didn't love kids. It's just that the responsibility of minding one was too much for her over the long haul. "So, what do we do, now?"

"We get some much-needed rest," Sonia said. "It's been a long, long night. You and the girl can take this floor. I'll stay here, too. My brothers will take the floor above."

"Thank you for all you've done," Mina. "For me, for her, everything."

Sonia smiled at her.

"It's been a journey, to be sure," Sonia said. "You know, you'd be a good *Synowie*. I've put word to our leadership. We could use a researcher. Even a *Zakaźny* like yourself. No offense."

"None taken," Mina said. "I think."

The thought of joining the secret society was not something Mina had considered a possibility. She'd always felt like she was on borrowed time, that one day they would simply kill her.

"I can't imagine they'd want me," Mina said.

"There's a value you bring," Sonia said. "A unique perspective, even. And to be honest, we've suffered such attrition over all of this Happening business. Some new blood—even, my apologies, tainted blood—would be welcome. I'd love to get Norm, as well. Two former Bureau people would be great additions to the *Synowie*. The more I think about it, the more I feel that we need to update our approach. Modernize ourselves."

The thought of being part of a secret society of werewolf hunters amused Mina. The irony alone was enough to choke a horse.

Sonia watched her thinking about it.

"You've been on good behavior for eight years," Sonia said. "Sure, you had your bouts, but you have managed your condition in a way we've never seen before. While they like to paint us as fanatics and zealots, in truth, no *Synowie* who embraces that path lives for long. Death follows in our footsteps, and those who let their zeal and passion guide them find it sooner than later. But enough philosophizing. We need to get some rest."

Mina couldn't agree more.

Gia and the others arrived as Valentina was putting herself back together. Three black SUVs pulled up, and Valentina stood there, leaning against a tree, nursing her wounded legs, straightening her leather jacket. There were bloody lumps of silver shot on the ground where she'd dug them out with her claws.

Gia emerged and looked at her baby sister, at her bloodied legs, which had been badly wounded by the *Lupara* Mina had fired at her.

"We need to get you somewhere, *Sorellina*," Gia said.

"I'm fine," Valentina said.

"You don't look fine," Gia said, holding open the door to the SUV she'd come out of. "Please, join me. I can't stand to see you standing there like that."

Valentina painfully limped her way to the SUV, guided by her big sister, who helped her into the vehicle. Gia looked around at the spilled blood on the ground, shook her head.

"I told you that you should have waited for the Furies," Gia said. "You are so impatient, *Sorellina.* Who did this to you?"

"*Synowie,*" Valentina said. "Obviously."

"Not all of this blood is yours, I think," Gia said.

Valentina was clearly relieved to be off her feet, was doing her best to hide her pain. Gia got in and told them to drive on.

"If it were *Synowie,* I think you would be dead," Gia said. Valentina looked out the window, watching the city pass by as they drove, the streetlamps flitting by like will-o-the-wisps in the chilly night air. "You take too many risks, Valentina."

"It's not my fault," Valentina said. "Everything else went like clockwork, Gia."

"That other thing?" Gia asked. Valentina nodded.

"The problem is solved," Valentina said.

"Where?"

"In the park," Valentina said. "A few blocks away."

"Truly?"

Valentina nodded.

"We didn't see anything when we looked," Gia said.

"There are BEE Recovery Teams around for that other thing," Valentina said. "They probably picked her up as a dead Doozy."

"The girl didn't see, did she?" Gia asked.

"I'm not a monster, Gia," Valentina said. "Give me some credit."

"Tell me," Gia said.

The convoy drove through the city, toward a clinic the Rupinos had access to. She was not going to have Valentina suffer, despite her protestations.

"We fought in the park," Valentina said. "She fought well, for an *Infettiva*. She fought hard."

"You were impatient," Gia said. "You should have waited. Let me handle it. Especially after fighting with the Monroes. You are working too hard, Valentina."

Valentina turned took look at her oldest sister. Gia had led the Black Hand for as long as she could remember. She'd been the uncontested matriarch of the clan, which led to a curious state of affairs—the higher one got in the hierarchy of a clan, the less often one ever had the need to transform at all. It was like they rose above it, somehow. She hadn't seen Gia turn in years.

"I'm not afraid to get my hands dirty, Gia," Valentina said.

"This, I know," Gia said. "Look at you, *Sorellina*. You're a mess. Tell me who did this to you."

"I'll handle it," Valentina said. She knew Gia would happily send members of the clan after the Mina woman for daring to raise a weapon to her. That was the thing about Gia—she took care of her clan.

But Valentina would settle that particular account on her own terms, in her own sweet time. She'd taken the woman's scent, would be on the lookout for it.

"Not like that, you won't," Gia said. "Silver shot. I'm going to have someone look after you, let you heal. I cannot have Ansel seeing you like this."

Valentina was annoyed.

"I'm healing," she said. "I'll be right as can be in a week."

"He'll be here tonight," Gia said. "Mr. Stockwell called and informed me."

"He did it?" Valentina asked, eager for anything to distract her from the stinging pain in her legs. Some part of her was relieved that Mina hadn't shot her in the chest or used that other barrel on her. She would have been dead.

"Yes," Gia said. "He made an arrangement, if you can believe that."

"A deal? What sort of deal?" Valentina asked.

"He wouldn't tell me," Gia said. "But he only said that he'd recovered Ansel, that they were bound for shore."

"I *knew* Ansel was on that ship," Valentina said. "What are we going to do about him?"

"I'm going to talk to him," Gia said. "Set him right."

"Are you going to tell him about the Problem?" Valentina asked.

"I'll tell him about *Il Problema,*" Gia said. "He may not even know."

"Oh, he knew," Valentina said. "It's why he was hiding. Hoped we wouldn't find her."

Gia sighed. For too long, Ansel had denied his responsibilities to the clan. One of the biggest was starting a family. A pack that didn't sire children was not long for the world.

Ansel had been self-indulgent as a young man, had shirked his duties in that area, leaving that to his brothers to attend to. And while Giovanni, Marco, and Lorenzo had all done their part for the family, Ansel was the largest and strongest of them. His reluctance to do right by the clan was a source of endless frustration for Gia. It was lycanthropic logic—the biggest and strongest had to reproduce if a clan was to remain strong.

How much easier would it have been had she been a man, or if Ansel had been a girl. There would have been no problem. As it was, his reluctance to lead the Rupinos had been a boon for Gia, had allowed the matriarchal line to run the Black Hand since their father had died.

"Did you see the child?" Gia asked.

"Briefly," Valentina said. "She looked strong."

"Good," Gia said. "At least there's that. Strength I can work with."

If Ansel didn't take the girl, Gia would. She'd take her to one of their estates, where the girl would be able to grow up proper Trueborn, free and unencumbered by the everyday nonsense lycanthropes faced. She would grow up pure and wild.

"Why even bother with Ansel at all?" Valentina asked. "He's rejected us."

"No," Gia said. "He hasn't. Rather, he's just refusing his duty to us. He's just being a pup. I'll straighten him out."

Valentina frowned, playing with the zipper of her jacket, sliding it up and down absently. Anything to take her mind off the pain in her legs and elsewhere across her body. She had never been so badly wounded before.

"He's too old to be a *Cucciolo,*" Valentina said.

"That he is," Gia said. "I'll talk to him."

"You're always talking to him," Valentina said. "And he always plays you."

Gia smiled. One day, Valentina would succeed her as the head of the clan, assuming she survived that long.

The driver had reached the clinic, where people were waiting to get Valentina, who was chagrined at being tended to this way.

"I don't need this," Valentina said. "I need to be with you, Gia."

"You will be," Gia said, directing for them to take Valentina, who, if she'd been less injured, would already have transformed to try to get away from this. The fact that she didn't change was reflective of the extent of her injuries, all bravado aside. Valentina would die before showing weakness in front of her big sister.

"Give *Cucciolo* my regards," Valentina said, as they wheeled her off.

Gia watched her go, as Sia, Mia, and Bria came out of one of the other SUVs. The Furies watched Valentina leave, turning their eyes to Gia.

How beautiful they were, their dark hair slicked back, their strong Rupino features as implacable as statues. Few Trueborn were as feared as they were, but, for Gia, they were her baby sisters, younger even than Valentina, and she would do everything in her power to protect them.

"Come along, girls," Gia said. "We have to go pick up your big brother."

NORM'S mind was on a thousand things as they boated their way ashore. He couldn't believe that Minton had actually honored his request. He'd expected to have been locked up or kicked out of the Bureau, but he'd gone for it.

He glanced at Ansel, who was tasting true freedom for the first time in eight years. The man looked as unreadable as ever, smelling the air.

"I missed this," Ansel said. "The open air. Even cold Chicago November air can feel like bliss."

"Yeah," Norm said. "You've missed a lot."

"I'll miss Dr. Holloway," Ansel said. "Vanessa and I had a connection."

"I'll bet," Norm said. He knew Dr. Holloway was already making arrangements to go ashore and set up to be able to observe Ansel and Sloane.

Ansel had that whole strong, silent type thing down. Stoic guys always had that advantage, with women willing to try to breach the fortresses of their hearts, in hopes of finding treasure within.

He doubted there was much treasure to be found there in Ansel's heart. Then again, him being a painter was something else, would allow him to hide behind a canvas of his artistry as an excuse for his remoteness.

Ansel didn't even bother with a side eye.

"It wasn't like that," Ansel said. "She was a professional. Like you."

"Yeah," Norm said. "That's me. Professional as fuck."

Ansel glanced at him, before leaning into the wind a bit more.

"Why even bother with me?" Ansel asked. "Who am I to you?"

"Nothing," Norm said. "I mean, in your day, you were tops on my target list."

"I think I've heard that," Ansel said. "Look, man, I'm not that guy. I mean, I never was. I just wanted to paint."

"I've seen," Norm said. "You like painting women."

"Women are beautiful," Ansel said. "I paint them because they're beautiful."

He'd painted hundreds of portraits. Norm had seen them when they'd canvassed his gallery. Bureau agents had theorized that they were all his victims, but the more he'd looked into it, he was sure that they weren't. Ansel was an artist, through and through. It was neither posturing nor pretense.

It made Norm think of Anne, his own place of pain. Ansel noticed his pain, despite his efforts to conceal it.

"You have someone special," Ansel said.

"Had," Norm said.

"Me, too," Ansel said. "She's a poet."

"Polly," Norm said.

Ansel nodded.

"I mean, we have a thing," Ansel said. "Or we had one. Just a thing."

"Yeah," Norm said. "I hate to be the one to break this to you, but she's dead, you know."

That registered on Ansel's bearded face.

"How?"

"Your family," Norm said. It was easier to just rip the Band-Aid off, where that was concerned.

"I don't believe it," Ansel said, gripping the railing of the boat as it splashed, the Chicago shoreline looming larger. "I tried to hide her from them. Part of why I went into hiding. They get territorial about that stuff. Not like Polly and I were going to be mates. But you know that goes. I mean, you don't know, you can't know. My family keeps its secrets. They don't let just anybody into it. Poor Polly. How'd she die? Who killed her?"

"I don't know for sure," Norm said. "Signs point to Valentina."

"Valentina," Ansel said. When last he'd seen her, she was an 18-year-old pup, eager to prove herself to Gia and anyone else who'd pay her attention.

"One of your younger sisters," Norm said.

"Yeah," Ansel said. "She's fierce."

Ansel bowed his head a moment, his stonelike visage giving way to pain. Norm felt a bit of sympathy for him, trying to do the right thing, unsure what that even was.

"Sam had infected Polly," Ansel said. "I infected Sam, and she got Polly. Polly hated being a lycanthrope. I mean, she really hated it. She helped me take down Zooey, though. She was there for me when I needed it. She deserved better than to be killed by Valentina. I hate even thinking that happened."

"Sorry," Norm replied. He wasn't going to bring up all the times he'd seen her when surveilling Shaw's home. Those little moments he'd seen between her and their daughter.

"Does Sloane know?"

"I don't know," Norm said. "I'm just bringing you to them. I figured you can figure all of that stuff out."

"Fucking Valentina," Ansel said. "Proving a point."

"What point is that, anyway? Humor me with a glimpse into Trueborn family life," Norm said.

"It's a pack thing," Ansel said. "When you find somebody you want to get serious with, you have to talk to the alpha, to get their blessing. It's not like an arranged marriage or anything like that, but it's close. I skirted it by remaining a bachelor. Gia hated that. She wanted me doing my part for the family, serving up little baby Ansels and Anselinas for the clan. She always came down on me for that, for staying away from all the pack politics."

"But why does the alpha get to decide?"

"It's for the integrity of the pack," Ansel said. "For the clan. Back in the past, it was more a free-for-all. Maybe some packs out there are still like that, not sure. But for the Rupinos, there was real care in deciding who you'd let in. It's a big step for people, coming into a clan like that. And, for Trueborn, there's that, too. Infectives are looked down upon. They're just people who happened to be infected, not people born to lycanthropy. Gia's very proud of our Trueborn history, thinks Trueborn should be with Trueborn, to keep the line pure, and to root out the chaos you get with Infectives."

Norm thought about that as the city grew ever larger in their view.

"And since Polly was an Infective," Norm said.

"Bad blood," Ansel said. "From Gia's perspective."

Norm wondered how Sloane would take to all of that.

"Promise me you won't harm the girl," Norm said. "No matter what Gia tells you."

Ansel glanced at him, shaking his head.

"I don't hurt kids," Ansel said. "Least of all my own daughter."

"Not even for the integrity of the clan or something like that?"

Ansel looked at him a moment, then back out at the cityscape.

"I wouldn't do that," Ansel said. "I'll claim Sloane as my child. That'll put her under my protection. They'll have to respect that. By declaring her as one of mine, it'll keep her safe. Had I not sequestered myself, Polly would be alive. Had I known Polly was pregnant, I'd have never taken off the way I had. I wasn't in a good place back then."

"Clearly," Norm said. "So, you had no idea?"

Ansel shook his head.

"I'd have been able to protect her," Ansel said.

"Maybe," Norm said. "Or maybe she'd have been killed years ago."

"Unless I'd married her," Ansel said. "I'm not the marrying type, keep in mind. I would have done that if it meant protecting her. They'd have to have respected that. I was stupid. I should have just done that."

"Don't beat yourself up about it," Norm said. "You couldn't have known."

Ansel raised a finger, shaking it.

"But I did know," Ansel said. "I just didn't want to admit it to myself. Who I was, what I was, what my family was. Polly paid for that."

He suffered in silence, and Norm didn't push it, didn't know what to say to it, or to him. Ansel's family were a bunch of Trueborn killers, born and bred to it for generations. There was no changing that.

Norm's phone rang, identifying it as Anne.

His own problem with Anne was a trickier one, as he saw it. All the time she'd been with Shaw, he'd thought she was under his malign influence. He still thought she had been. However, what if she was complicit in it? What if she had found that she liked being a Lupine? Her association with Bastion and Liminalix had made her a fortune. That was as corrupting as the infection—there was no pharmacological treatment for greed.

He let it ring three times before answering, Ansel watching him.

"Yeah?" Norm said.

"We need to talk, Norm," Anne said.

"How'd you find me?" Norm asked. "This is a new phone."

"Chad talked to your Director," Anne said. "He had his people give him the number."

Minton had probably thought he was helping in some fashion. Or maybe he was trying to get into Bastion's good graces after what Norm had done. Maybe the whole thing was some sort of setup. Norm's eyes went to the shore, looking for anything that might seem out of place.

"What do we need to talk about?" Norm asked.

"About you, about me, about everything," Anne said. "I'd like to see you, so we could talk face-to-face."

Norm doubted that would go well.

"I don't think that's a good idea," Norm said. "Not with what you did."

"You put me in a cage," Anne said. "Like an animal, Babe. Like a prisoner."

"You are those things," Norm said.

He could hear her exasperation.

"They're going to kill you," Anne said. "Chad is. He's not going to let what you did stand. This whole thing is way bigger than you. It doesn't matter that you're bringing Ansel out of hiding."

Norm wondered how she knew that, too. How compromised was Minton? He muted the phone.

"Keep an eye out," Norm said. "I think something's up."

He texted Gia.

BE CAREFUL. I THINK M IS SETTING UP AN AMBUSH.

He went back to his call with Anne, who had been talking.

"Where'd you get the idea that I'm bringing Ansel out of hiding?" Norm asked.

"Babe, come on," Anne said. "Don't play dumb with me. You're not dumb. Naïve, maybe, but not dumb. You're being offered up as a sacrificial lamb by your own boss. Do you really think you could have persuaded Minton to give up Ansel just like that?"

With Anne, the penchant for mindfuckery was always sky-high. The key was sifting through the dross and figuring out what was real, versus what was bullshit.

Fact: Minton had given her his phone number.

Fact: Minton had told them about his release of Ansel.

"Why does Bastion want Ansel dead?" Norm asked. "They could have euthanized him any time they liked aboard the *Argent*."

"It's not Ansel he's after," Anne said. "It's Gia and the others. The Rupinos. Ansel's just the bait."

Norm muted the phone.

"It might be a setup," Norm said. "Bastion's set up some kind of ambush. You're the bait, apparently. Intended to draw Gia out, maybe the other Rupinos."

Ansel looked almost resigned to it, as Norm took the phone off mute.

"Why bother telling me all of this?" Norm asked.

"Because I don't want you to die, Babe," Anne said. "And I know you will. Chad doesn't care about you, but I do."

Norm wanted to believe that. He needed to.

Fact: If there was an ambush, Anne didn't have to tell Norm about it.

Fact: Anne maybe still cared about him.

"What do they have lined up?" Norm asked. "The ambush, I mean. Norms or Lupines?"

"I have to go, Norm," Anne said. "Just don't get killed. We need to talk properly. Meet me at the Art Institute tomorrow at five if you're still alive."

She hung up, and Norm cursed, wondered how far Minton had gone to screw him over. He looked at the three BEE agents who had accompanied them on the boat. They were younger, and, knowing Minton, he would have kept them in the dark about anything suspicious. Norm worked it over in his head.

Speculation: Minton was working with Bastion, trying to screw over the Rupinos, using Ansel as bait.

Speculation: Minton was actually trying to screw over both Bastion and the Rupinos, using Ansel and Norm as bait.

"What weapons do you have aboard?" Norm asked the skipper, who was driving the boat.

"Standard crew complement," the skipper said. He was a young black man with JONES on a patch on his chest. "Three M4A1s, three Glock 18s. What's the problem, Agent Stockwell?"

"I think we're in for something hairy ashore," Norm said. "Literally. Are the weapons silver-armed?"

"Yessir," Jones said. "Standard Bureau issue."

"You might want to have one of your men on the M60 at the bow," Norm said. Jones nodded, ordered Foster, one of his men, to the bow, told him to be ready.

"I need one of the M4s," Norm said. Jones ordered his other man to get him one of them. The BEE M4s had banana clips, which meant 30-round capacity. "Give me four clips."

They handed him the M4, which Norm loaded. He'd opt for three-round burst fire. Ansel watched him and cocked an eyebrow.

"Okay, so, like what the hell is going on?" Ansel asked.

"Trouble," Norm said, dialing Gia.

THE boat dropped them off, and Norm urged the BEE agents to leave the area as soon as possible. He didn't want them getting hurt or killed because of Minton's maneuvering. From where they were, near Navy Pier, everything looked urban-normal, otherwise open and unassuming.

Ansel walked with him, sniffing the air.

"Doesn't smell like an ambush," he said. Norm wanted to laugh but was too much on alert to do so.

"What do ambushes smell like?" Norm asked.

"You know, people in bushes," Ansel said. "That sort of thing."

"Ambushes aren't meant to look like ambushes," Norm said. He dialed up Gia, who picked up.

"I have you-know-who," Norm said. "But I also have on good authority that there's an ambush waiting for us. They're targeting you."

"Okay," Gia said. "Perhaps we should meet someplace else."

Norm was fairly confident the phone was likely cloned. If Minton was genuinely screwing him over, the phone would have been spoofed and they would be monitoring it directly.

"Yes," Norm said. "But we shouldn't discuss on this line. I need to get another phone. Let's delay the family reunion right now, and hopefully keep the trap from springing. How about we go to the…"

Norm thought of how he might euphemistically refer to Ansel's gallery condo in an oblique way that wouldn't tip off Bastion's people.

"…frame store?" Norm said. There had to be hundreds of frame stores in Chicago, which would otherwise occupy them if they tried to cover them. Likelier would be them watching to see where Norm and Ansel went, and tailing them.

"That would be nice," Gia said. "Can you put my brother on the phone, Agent Stockwell?"

Norm muted the phone, glanced at Ansel.

"Gia wants to have a word," Norm said. Ansel grimaced, took the phone only very reluctantly. While he was getting chewed out, Norm looked around them, trying to figure out where the Bastion people would be.

From there, the Lake Point Tower building was the dominant skyscraper. There were likely Bastion people there, watching them from above. On the ground, there might be people in the park area to the south, or on the other side of Navy Pier.

Norm made an effort to conceal the M4 but knew if a CPD cruiser rolled up there'd be all sorts of trouble. More so if it was one on Bastion's payroll.

Ansel handed back the phone to Norm. Ansel winced and shrugged in the same breath.

"Hello?" Norm said.

"Thank you, Agent Stockwell," Gia said. "We will see you in the frame store."

They hung up at the same time, after saying their goodbyes. Norm pocketed his phone, while Ansel sniffed the air again.

"Everything okay?" Norm asked.

"Between Gia and me?" Ansel said. "Hey, we're family. Family forgives."

"Right," Norm said. "Look, we're in a bit of a jam, here."

"So you say," Ansel said. "Although I don't see or smell anybody. Maybe your wife was just gaslighting you."

"While I can't rule that out, I don't think she was," Norm said. At the Pier, at night, the city lights only intensified the abundant shadows, and the ceaseless hum of traffic on Lake Shore Drive created a restless vibe to the area.

"What now, then?"

"We have to get out of there," Norm said. He called Agent Jones on the boat on his phone. "Jones, I changed my plan: meet us at the end of the Pier."

"Alright, Driver," Jones said.

Norm pivoted and started jogging toward the end of Navy Pier, Ansel following after him.

"We'll be trapped if we go here," Ansel said.

"That's fine," Norm said.

"I'm not letting anybody take me prisoner," Ansel said. "Against my will, I mean."

"Yeah," Norm said. "Might I suggest a wardrobe change?"

Ansel looked at him and laughed. He'd been wearing a black tee and blue jeans and sneakers.

"You serious?" Ansel asked.

"Yeah," Norm said. "Ideally before they come after us. Go, change. Do it."

"Alright," Ansel said, running off into the bushes near the Ferris Wheel. "But it's your funeral, man."

A CPD police truck came rolling toward them, a spotlight flashing at them.

"Drop your weapon, put your hands up," came a voice from a loudspeaker. "This is the police."

Norm wasn't going to waste silver bullets on the cops, made his jog turn into a run as he went down the length of the pier.

"Mr. Stockwell, throw down your weapon and surrender or we will shoot," came the voice, and Norm could hear the truck revving up as it followed. Who knew how many officers were present, and how much they knew? They'd seen both Ansel and him come ashore, for sure. At least some had to know he was part of the BEE. While law enforcement viewed the federal BEE with scorn, they usually viewed them with a degree of deference, too. Federal was federal.

Norm ducked into the side of one of the Navy Pier service buildings. Ansel had vanished. Norm dug out his phone and dialed up Tiff.

"Go ahead, Driver," Tiff said.

"Big Bad set me up," Norm said. "I'm at Navy Pier. There's an ambush of some sort here. Bastion's people. CPD."

"What are you even talking about, Driver?" Tiff asked.

"Send a drone or something," Norm said. "Do what you do. Like an attack drone."

Norm glanced back at the police truck, which was moving up toward his position, carefully. Because there was only one, Norm thought these were very likely some of Bastion's handpicked corrupt cops. Possibly Infectives.

"Mr. Stockwell," the voice said. "This is your last warning. Surrender now or we *will* fire upon you. There is no escape for you. Or your friend, Mr. Rupino."

Norm could hear the back of the police truck open, could hear three guys hop out.

"Mr. Stockwell," one of the unseen men said. "This can go one of two ways. Up to you."

He could hear the men grunting and yowling, knew what they were doing, and what he had to do. No hesitation.

Norm ran around the corner, bringing the M4 to his shoulder to fire on them. The metal doors of the truck were thrown open, obscuring his view. He could see one of the cops on all fours, mostly obscured by the door.

"What are you doing, Driver?" Tiff asked. "I don't have my drone deployed. I'm blind. I can't help you."

The cops were turning, and Norm could hear the rending sound at they changed. If he learned anything in his years of work at the BEE, it was that seconds mattered where werewolves were concerned. He went to fire on them when somebody swung hard on the metal door, striking Norm, sending him flying backward.

He saw a fully transformed Lupine standing there in hybrid form, brown-furred and huge, snarl-smiling at him, emerging from behind the door.

"You think we were just sitting in the back of that van waiting for you, Agent Stockwell? I was ready for you before we stepped out," the Lupine said. Norm thought of him as Speaker, because the other two were turning, but weren't doing more than howling and grunting as their flesh boiled away, replaced by fur and fangs.

Norm sought to get to his feet, the wind all but knocked out of him by the force of the Lupine's blow.

"That's it, get up," Speaker said, his voice a low and throaty growl. The Lupine jumped for Norm, grabbing him, knocking the M4 out of his hands with an effortless flick of his clawed hand. This police Lupine was large and menacing, even by lycanthropic standards. He had a darker brown muzzle and teeth that were bigger than bullets. Norm wondered where the hell Ansel was, hoped he hadn't ditched him.

The other two cops had completed their transformations, were also shades of brown. They looked over Speaker's big shoulders eagerly.

Fortunately for Norm, Speaker wanted to beat him a bit first, versus simply killing him, or whatever else it was they had in store for him. Speaker hoisted Norm off his feet, glaring hard at him, his yellowy eyes boring into Norm.

Norm drew his Glock 18 from his concealed carry holster and tried to shoot Speaker, but Speaker was too quick, had grabbed him by the wrist with his other hand.

"Um, no," Speaker said, giving Norm a bone-bending squeeze of his arm. "Drop it, Stockwell."

He talked to him like he was a dog, and Norm fought to bring his pistol to bear on Speaker, but to no avail. The pistol clattered to the ground.

"We should kill you," Speaker said. "But someone important wants a word with you first."

They were so intent on Norm, they didn't see Ansel rise up behind them: this massive, black-furred werewolf. He was amazing—a black-furred monstrosity who dwarfed the cop Lupines, one of whom turned in time to get Ansel's long claws across his face, while Ansel snapped the throat of the other one.

Speaker was in mid-speech, turning even as Ansel swung hard for him, his claws tearing through Speaker, cutting across his chest and shearing off his arm, the one he'd held Norm with.

Norm dropped to the ground as Speaker turned, choking, his blood splashing as he tried to face Ansel. Norm pried the grasping arm off him.

Ansel tore into Speaker, catching him by the throat and snapping off his head with a carnal crush of his great jaws. The Lupine Ansel had clawed was trying to get back up, his slashed face bleeding profusely. Norm grabbed for his Glock 18 and fired off three shots in close succession, catching the Lupine in the chest.

The police truck raced forward, the doors swinging, and Norm was grabbing the M4, trying to recover himself.

"Get that truck before they can call for reinforcements," Norm said. Ansel nodded and bounded after the truck, looking like a great black-furred boulder, his claws clacking on the walkway as he went thundering after the truck.

Norm walked to the dead and dying cops, who were in the process of becoming human again, and put two silver bullets in each of their heads, anyway, for good measure.

"Dealer," Norm said, dialing up Tiff again.

He regretted not talking to Tiff in person when he'd been on the *Argent*, but there'd been too much he had to get to. He trusted Tiff, hoped that wasn't a mistake on his part. In person, he'd be able to know for sure.

"What the hell is going on, Driver?" Tiff asked.

"Make sure there aren't cameras recording me," Norm said. "Or I'm in heaps of trouble."

"What'd you do?"

"Three dead cops," Norm said. "Infectives."

"Jesus, Driver," Tiff said.

"Bromide's people," Norm said.

He glanced down the way, saw that Ansel had caught up to the police truck, had torn the driver's door off and grabbed at the driver, yanking him from the vehicle.

Norm ran after him, hoping he'd get there before Ansel ripped him to pieces.

Ansel hurled the cop over the side of the pier, and the man landed with a splash, after bouncing off the surface of the water twice.

Norm ran to the truck, hopping behind the wheel, hitting the brakes. Ansel watched the cop swimming in the cold water, before turning his Lupine snout in Norm's direction.

"Took you long enough," Norm said.

"I haven't done that for awhile," Ansel said. "Not like that."

"What, did you forget how? Hop in the back, let's get the hell out of there."

Ansel went to get his clothes and then ran into the back of the truck, pulling the doors shut behind him, while Norm turned the truck around.

Although the truck was missing the driver's side door, it was comforting having the strong chassis of the truck in hand. Even the crackle of the radio was welcome.

Norm drove them out of there, past the three naked bodies of the dead cops.

"Cleanup at the Pier," Norm said. "Send a Recovery Team. Radio Jones from his boat. They're right here. They can do it. There's also a cop in the water. A witness."

Let Minton choke on that. It was his problem to solve. The bigger issue from Norm's perspective was that Minton had openly betrayed him.

"Driver, you need to lay low, not further raise your profile," Tiff said.

"Why don't you get your drone airborne?" Norm said.

"I'm not on duty tonight," Tiff said. "In fact, I was hoping to get some sleep when you called. Don't you ever sleep, Driver?"

"Not yet," Norm said. He was driving through the city, heading toward Ansel's place, keeping an eye out to see if they were being tailed. It didn't look like it, but that didn't mean they weren't.

"You need to please play it quieter," Tiff said.

"I'm trying," Norm said. "Big Bad has other plans, apparently."

"I'll try to find out what's going on," Tiff said. "Don't do anything more rash than what you've already done."

"I never do," Norm said.

Ansel's head popped up in the rear window of the police truck. He had returned to his human disguise.

"This is exactly what I was hoping to avoid," Ansel said. "I'm not a big fan of, you know, killing people."

"Right," Norm said.

"It's true," Ansel said. "You've never bitten somebody's head off or torn them up with claws. It's nasty."

The Reluctant Werewolf, Norm thought, bitterly. Ansel's memoirs.

"Dealer, I'll call you back," Norm said, hanging up on her before she could protest. There were cars following them, three of them. SUVs. "I think they've found us."

Ansel turned and went to the back of the truck, took a look out of the little windows.

"Who? Bastion people?"

"I don't know," Norm said. "Three SUVs."

He took a quick right turn and looked to see if they followed. They did. They weren't closing the distance. They were just maintaining it.

Norm dialed up Gia.

"We're on our way, but we've picked up three tails," Norm said. "Three SUVs, about a block behind us."

"Alright," Gia said. "Where are you right now?"

"Heading north on State Street," Norm said. "We're about ten minutes away, tops."

"Just keeping going on State," Gia said. "We'll find you. See you soon."

Gia hung up, and Norm put his phone away, kept an eye on the vehicles behind them, while Ansel reappeared at the rear window.

"So, what's the story?"

"Gia's going to meet up with us," Norm said. Ansel scoffed.

"Yeah," Ansel said. "That should be something."

Norm listened to the police radio crackling. It was normal police chit-chat, which confirmed his suspicion that whatever CPD guys Bastion was using, it wasn't the whole force that was after them. That was a point in their favor.

As he drove, Norm tried to keep it as informal as he could, while still maintaining situational awareness. He hoped that they didn't run into more CPD cruisers, because it would be damned hard for him to account for the missing door.

Minton rang him, and Norm debated whether or not to answer.

"You gonna get that?" Ansel asked.

"Fine," Norm said, answering. "Driver here."

"Driver," Minton said. "Dealer just told me you think I set you up."

"Yeah," Norm said, annoyed that she'd told him that. "There were people waiting for us when we got there. Lady told me you set something up with Bromide."

"And you believed her?" Minton said. "Driver, you're getting paranoid. Did it occur to you that she might be yanking your chain?"

Of course it had. Since everything had happened, Norm couldn't rule that out. But as to whether he trusted Anne more or less than Minton was up for debate.

"She's still got her hooks in you, Driver," Minton said. "Once you get the family reunion arranged, I want you back on the *Argent* for a proper debriefing. This stuff is getting to you."

"She said you gave her my phone number," Norm said. "She knew how to reach me. I picked that phone up on the ship. How'd she get that number, Big Bad?"

"I don't know," Minton said. "Maybe we have a leak. Something. Bromide's rich. He could have people here on his payroll."

"He could have you on his payroll," Norm said. "Lady has told me several times how rich she is from the drug money. Easy enough for them to feather your nest, too."

Silence on the line a moment made Norm wonder if he'd pushed too hard. Or else Minton was trying to figure out a line he'd swallow.

"You think I'm on Bromide's payroll?" Minton said.

"Not that hard to imagine, Big Bad," Norm said. "You've already come down on me for targeting Bromide, have waved everybody off him. Your partnership with him has paid off handsomely for you. Conflict of interest much, Sir?"

"You're way out of line, Driver," Minton said. "I want you back here immediately. Or I'm revoking your Stinger status, effective right now."

It was another hoop Minton had put out for him to jump through, basically. Another test. Norm wasn't about to set foot on that ship again.

"Driver?" Minton said. "Do you understand?"

"I wish I did," Norm said. Anne claimed she'd warned him because she cared about him, didn't want him getting hurt. If she'd said nothing, they might have been caught by those Bastion cops. Or maybe she'd warned him because she knew he'd kill them, which would get him in further trouble, would make things harder for him.

Minton had agreed to Norm's plan regarding Ansel, but why? Why had he agreed? If he'd wanted to kill Ansel, he could simply have done so on the ship. He'd kept him alive for a purpose. The question was, for what purpose? The rendezvous had to be the whole point of it.

"Drop off the package, and come back home," Minton said. "You're with us, Driver. We're your family, now. Don't let Lady get in your head, man."

"How close are you with Bastion?" Norm asked. He knew mentioning him by name on the line would really bother Minton.

"We can discuss when you get back, Driver," Minton said. "Where are you at?"

But Norm knew he knew where he was, because he was sure the phone had been cloned. Minton had been listening the whole time. He hung up and popped open the phone, taking out the SIM card. He peered through the open door, looked skyward for any sign of a drone. There had to be one up there somewhere, watching.

He tossed the phone onto the seat beside him.

"What's the deal?" Ansel asked.

"I think things are going to get festive," Norm said.

Then he saw three black shapes shoot out across the street behind him, smashing into the SUVs. The force of the attack was strong enough to cause the SUVs to swerve and crash. Norm put the brakes on and hopped out of the truck, taking his M4 with him, as well as the phone and SIM card.

Ansel popped out of the back.

Behind them, a block away, three black Lupines were attacking the SUVs and the men inside. The three of them were a chorus of snarls and slashing.

"The Furies," Norm said, tossing the phone and SIM card into a nearby trashcan.

"Oh, man," Ansel said. The Furies sprang from the ruined SUVs and bounded up the street toward them. Norm felt an instinctive fear at the sight of them, the three Rupino she-wolf enforcers racing for them. They had turned effortlessly from their hybrid forms to those of four-legged black wolves and were devouring the distance between them. For all of his experience with Infectives, seeing Trueborn do their thing was still bracing and more than a little frightening. There was none of the angst and uncertainty Infectives faced about their condition. There was an elemental purity to the Trueborn, something that had to be seen to be believed.

Norm again looked skyward, could see no trace of any BEE drones, but he knew that they weren't intended to be easy to spot, and if they were up there, they were up there.

The Furies reached them, sniffing at Ansel, who held his hands out and petted them.

"Mia, Sia, Bria," Ansel said. "You're all grown up."

They growled at him, bumped him, turned their blue eyes on Norm.

"We have to get the hell out of the open," Norm said, pointing skyward with a finger. "I think we're being tracked."

They quickly got off the street, headed toward the protection of one of the buildings, where there was an overhang.

"What makes you think we're being tracked?" Ansel asked.

"Years of working for the Bureau," Norm said. "Look, we know where we're going, where we're meeting up. So, let's all split right now and go our own way. That way, even if they've got drones up there, they can't follow all of us."

"Why would they do that?" Ansel asked.

"They're gunning for Gia," Norm said. "Bastion is. They're holding off until you're all together. That's what they're waiting for, I think."

"Why didn't he do it sooner?" Ansel asked.

"You were going to be transferred to Atlanta," Norm said. "Dr. Holloway had you all bamboozled, until I dissuaded you from doing that."

"'Bamboozled'?" Ansel said, chuckling. "Who even says that?"

"Shut up," Norm said.

Ansel glanced overhead, frowning. The Furies circled around Ansel, bumping him again. He was clearly happy to see them, as they were to see him.

"So, what do we do?" Ansel asked.

"You're the primary target," Norm said. "So, you should transform and just take off. All of you head off in different directions, like I said."

He saw that there were men emerging from the ruined SUVs. It wasn't like he'd been hoping they were dead, but he was kind of hoping that they were dead.

"I'll take the police truck and drive around with it, find a better place to ditch it," Norm said. "But we'll make them think that you're in it. Don't take off running until I drive away."

"Gonna bamboozle them, are you, Norm?" Ansel asked, nodding, smiling at him.

Norm gestured for him to follow him, while Ansel directed the Furies to remain where they were.

"Okay," Norm said. "You hop in the back of the truck again. I'll back the truck up to that overhang, where they can't see. Then you hop out, close it up, and I'll drive off. Wait a bit, wait until I'm out of sight, then turn and run off with your sisters. Make sure you're out of eyeshot of those clowns down the street."

"Got it," Ansel said. "Man, you're paranoid."

"Count on it," Norm said. He could hear police sirens in the distance. Whoever was still breathing in those SUVs must have called them in. "See you at the rendezvous."

Norm got back into the truck and backed it up when he heard Ansel get in there. He pulled it to the area with the overhang and Ansel hopped out.

Then Norm drove out of there, hoping what it looked like from above was them hightailing it out of there. He hoped he'd bought them enough time.

BASTION hung up from a call with Minton, while Dawn surveyed the city from the deck. He walked over to her and put his arms around her, nibbling on her neck. She smiled and leaned into it a bit.

"Gia stepped in it big time with Minton," Bastion said. "The massacre at Trotter Field really pissed him off. Your family would be pleased, right?"

"That field was named after me," Dawn said. "I donated the money to get it named."

"Ah," Bastion said, releasing her. "When?"

"Nearly a century ago," Dawn said. "Through intermediaries, of course."

Bastion laughed.

"Big soccer fan, are you?" Bastion asked.

"It was big in the 1920s," Dawn said. "Before getting upstaged by baser sports."

"Never figured you for a sports fan," Bastion said.

Dawn turned and stroked Bastion's cheek before gliding to another part of the deck. Bastion resisted the urge to follow her, then gave in to it. Dawn had fed on him earlier in the evening, and the euphoria it brought was unlike anything he'd ever felt.

"I'm a lot of things you never figured for," Dawn said. "Tell me about this call with the Director."

"Nothing fancy," Bastion said. "As I'd hoped, Gia Rupino'd the hell out of things, went a bit heavy-handed, and now four of the rival factions are effectively decapitated. Without Tolkachev and his senior guys, the *Volki* are in disarray. The Chicago Doozies are effectively extinct, the Wargs are annihilated in Chicago, and Black Sheep's freako Babas are largely dead. Gia went after them like a dog chasing a bone. As I knew she would."

Dawn looked back at him, her big eyes sliding over him.

"You knew, did you?"

"Yes," Bastion said. "I know how Gia rolls. She's old-school."

"What about the *Lunares* and the Brotherhood?" Dawn asked.

"Not worried about them," Bastion said. "They took my deal, the shares. Their leaders will be rolling in money soon enough. And, best of all, if they get greedy, or if their followers get envious of all of that money, then they'll bump off their alphas and presto, a pack dispute that'll shred them for us."

"And if they hold together?" Dawn asked. The city sounds were ever-present, the whir of traffic and the howl of the chill wind. Snowflakes danced around them, but neither Chad nor Dawn truly felt them.

"It'll all sort out," Bastion said. "I'll deal with them when the time comes."

"You're a very bright mortal," Dawn said. "I knew you were one to pay attention to. I can always tell."

Bastion joined her at the other part of the deck, gripping the cold railing. The winter scent of the city was its own thing, something he enjoyed. In Chicago, it was somehow pleasant. Out east, the cities had different scents. The age was upon them.

"Some might think it's unseemly, me being with you," Bastion said.

Dawn sighed.

"And when have you ever cared what they think?" Dawn asked.

"Well, I mean, I don't," Bastion said. "But amid the Lupine circles, you and me, that's, you know, not done."

"Who cares what they think?" Dawn asked. "What, you worry about what Gia Rupino might say?"

"Maybe," Bastion said. "She'd say I'm your dupe. Your pet, even."

"But you're not," Dawn replied. "I'm your partner. I am helping you."

"You're feeding on me," Bastion said. "There's that."

"I'm a parasite," Dawn said. "It's what I do."

She put a hand on his on the railing, gave it a squeeze.

"Don't call yourself that," Bastion said. "It's gross."

Dawn laughed, showing her teeth. Her laugh was guttural, devoid of humor. Her laugh always chilled Bastion.

"It's what I am," Dawn said. "I made my peace with it centuries ago."

"How long ago?" Bastion asked. It was one of those vampiric questions he hated asking, like calling a beautiful woman beautiful.

"Only five hundred years," Dawn said. Bastion did the math quickly in his head.

"1515," he said, whistling. "You're old."

"Not as old as some," Dawn said.

"Tell me something about 1515," Bastion said. Dawn sighed as if he'd put an undue burden upon her pale shoulders.

"Keep in mind, I was in Scotland at the time. It's where I was born," Dawn said. "But that summer, at the First Congress of Vienna, there was a double wedding between Louis, the son of King Vladislaus II of Hungary to Mary of Austria, who was the granddaughter of Maximilian I, the Holy Roman Emperor. Mary's brother, the Archduke Ferdinand, married Vladislaus' daughter, Anna."

"Wow, um, yeah, history," Bastion said.

"You asked," Dawn said. "It wasn't a particularly exciting year."

"Why were you made?" Bastion asked.

"I suppose my sire liked the look of me," Dawn said. "That's often how it happens."

Bastion put his other hand on hers, patting it.

"Do you like the look of me?" Bastion asked. Dawn smiled coolly at him.

"And the taste," she said. "You're delicious. I could feed on you forever. It's frowned upon, you know. I'd say 'my people' but we have no people. Not like your packs and clans. But it's considered impolitic to feed upon your kind. However, I got a taste for it."

Chad looked forward to their feedings more and more. His vitality sustained him, and she drained off some of it, which let him maintain his composure. It wasn't parasitical so much as it was symbiotic. That's how he chose to see it.

"My packmates would not approve," Bastion said. "I sent Blake and Wade back home to try to keep things settled. I'm sure they'll snitch me out to the rest."

"Who cares what they say?" Dawn said. "You're making them all rich. That was all you, Chad. Not them."

"Yeah, it was," Bastion said. "It was all me. All I did was monetize our affliction. I mean, brilliant, yeah, but you know. One of those simple ideas that just happens to be genius."

Dawn embraced Bastion, and he could feel his strength inside her, but he could feel her own strength, too. She possessed such power that she kept tightly restrained within her.

"How do you do it?" Bastion asked. "Persist, I mean? I don't know if I could stay sane over five centuries."

"You simply do," Dawn said. "You feed or you die. It's not all that different from what you do, except that in your case, you're alive. And me, I'm already dead. I died in 1515, and rose again three days hence, Christlike, I suppose."

"Hah," Bastion said.

"You could join me," Dawn said. "You should join me in eternity."

Bastion admitted to himself that it both appealed to him and frightened him. Dawn was beautiful but terrifying, too. Which was not something he was entirely willing to admit. He was the monster. What did a werewolf have to fear besides silver? Dawn was that thing.

"My siblings think the vampires sent you to keep tabs on me," Bastion said.

"We're not like that," Dawn said. "Not like your quaint Councils. We're more entrepreneurial in our outlook."

Bastion looked at her lovely face, forever young. He wondered about the Scottish woman she'd been in that other life. She was so lovely, and that would endure forever. And she was smart, and she was rich. She was perfect.

"Entrepreneurial?"

"We see opportunities and we take them," Dawn said.

"Am I that? An opportunity?"

Dawn smiled at him, showing her fangs.

"A delicious one," Dawn said. "I couldn't resist."

Bastion's phone rang, and he checked. It was Anne. He answered it.

"What's up, Anne?" Bastion asked.

"Norm and Ansel evaded your pursuers," Anne said. "The Furies attacked some of your men."

"Anybody killed?"

"No, just injured," Anne said.

"And Norm?"

"Driving north," Anne said. "I think it's a decoy. It looked like some of the Rupinos hung back and then they scattered."

"Stay after Ansel," Bastion said. "I'll call Minton and tell him."

He hung up, texted Minton that information.

"I thought you said you were going to call him?" Dawn asked.

"Texting is quicker," Bastion said. "Besides, I don't want anything else interrupting us tonight."

He pocketed his phone and took Dawn in his arms, and she let him.

"LOVE WILL FIND A WAY
THROUGH PATHS WHERE
WOLVES FEAR TO PREY."
-LORD BYRON

ANSEL and the Furies reached his home, where Gia was waiting with a handful of Ansel's cousins. Gia was wearing a camel-colored blazer with chocolate brown leather pants and caramel-colored boots.

"Ansel," Gia said, giving him a hug. "My wayward little brother. I should call you *Piccolo Fastidio* after all the trouble you've caused me."

"Sorry, Gia," Ansel said. "Where's Valentina?"

"She's been wounded," Gia said. "She's had a rough sort of night."

Ansel grabbed Gia and shoved her against a wall, which startled her and jarred the others. Gia, Sia, and Bria all turned and balled their fists, but Gia waved them off.

"Not the only wounded one, I think," Gia said.

"You killed Polly," Ansel said, hoisting Gia up, tears in his eyes.

"*You* killed Polly," Gia said. "The moment you had a child by her."

"I didn't know anything about that," Ansel said.

"Oh, *Cucciolo*," Gia said. "You always don't know what you do. It's always you, the innocent bystander to the disasters you bring. It's never your fault."

Ansel put Gia down, and she swatted his strong arms away with her gloved hands.

"Because I love you, I forgive you for laying hands on me like that," Gia said. "You never come to me except when you make a mess. You never told me about your *Infettiva* girlfriend."

Ansel fought to compose himself, while Gia smoothed out her blazer.

"I'm an adult," Ansel said. "I don't need to consult with you about these things."

"Oh, but you do," Gia said. "You are Rupino. You owe your life to the clan, Ansel. This is never just about you."

"You killed her," Ansel said.

"She was not suited for life in the family," Gia said. "Valentina told me. Not the sort of woman to give you plenty of children. Not a breeder. If I'm to believe what I'd heard, the daughter you have was an accident."

"Jesus, Gia," Ansel said. "It's really just down to that, isn't it? Having kids?"

Gia poked Ansel in the chest as she spoke to him.

"Yes. It. Is. It's the life of the clan," Gia said. "Children, Ansel. Strong children. You know what we deal with. The other clans. Always jockeying for position. You are the strongest of us, Ansel. I won't let that strength be squandered. I can't. I have let you play with your paints, I indulged you. Playtime is over, however. You need to settle down."

"You are too much," Ansel said.

Gia bared her teeth at him, staring hard up at him. Although she was smaller than he was, her power was undeniable.

"We have spent the last eight years cleaning up the mess you made," Gia said. "I've gotten into bed with the BEE, so they would not kill us."

"Yeah, about that," Ansel said. "I think they've decided to ally with Bastion over you. Especially after those big killings. Norm thinks that maybe they're using me as bait to get us all together so they can wipe us out."

Gia scoffed.

"They need us," Gia said. "We've helped them."

"I think they need Bastion more," Ansel said. "The Lupitol drug, all of that. It's safer for them than you are."

"We have a stake in it," Gia said. "Why would Bastion want to jeopardize our agreement?"

"Maybe you should ask him, instead of hounding me about starting a family," Ansel said. Gia waved a finger at him.

"You are not distracting me, Ansel," Gia said. "You are going to claim your daughter. That's the first order of business. The poor child is probably very confused."

"Murdering her mother was likely very confusing for her," Ansel said. "I want to see Valentina."

"No," Gia said. "You do not get to see her. Not yet. And even when you do, I do not want any bad blood between you."

"Too late," Ansel said. "You should have thought about that before you sent her after Polly."

"Valentina knows her duty to the clan," Gia said. "Do you?"

"I don't want to be part of the family business," Ansel said. "I don't think I could make that any clearer than I have."

Gia glared at him, stepping forward, jaw jutting at him, making Ansel step back as she did so.

"You are a spoiled brat, Ansel," Gia said. "And you always have been. You owe a debt to the clan. A debt that's only settled if you provide children to us."

"Stop," Ansel said. "Just stop. Even if I were to stupidly go along with that, do you really think I'd want children of mine to end up as killers and family enforcers?"

He glanced at the Furies, who pouted, sulked, and glared at him.

"We *are* killers," Gia said. Her phone rang, and she checked it, didn't recognize the number, turned off the ringer, pocketed her phone. "We have always been that. You are a killer, Ansel. Whether you want to be or not. It's what we are."

She pointed to the cage Ansel kept in his home.

"Your pathetic cage," Gia said. "Where you'd lock yourself up when you couldn't control yourself. This is no true life for you, *Cucciolo*. What about your cousins, Gianna? Alessia? Carlotta?"

"Stop," Ansel said. "Just stop it."

"They would be good matches for you," Gia said. "Strong girls. Broad-hipped and healthy."

Ansel was shamed to be having this discussion in front of his sisters and cousins, who all looked at him with wonder and shame. The rage boiled up inside him at being put into this situation. But this was how Gia worked.

"You came to me with your problems, Ansel," Gia said. "I'm solving them, *Cucciolo*. Don't whine because I'm solving more problems than you wanted me to."

Ansel composed himself.

"This isn't the time or place for this discussion," Ansel said. Gia shrugged almost operatically, so lyrical was her disdain.

"So you say," Gia said. "The Bureau triggerman, Norm, he says Bastion's using you to set up an ambush to get to me."

Ansel felt vulnerable in his own home, didn't want it to be a target of Bastion or anybody else. Seeing all of his things, he realized how much he missed it all.

"I don't know anything about that," Ansel said. "Only what I saw. They were chasing us. Norm thought his own boss maybe had something to do with it."

Gia was still irritated with Ansel, he could tell, but was willing to shelve that for the moment, as there were the larger concerns at hand.

"We should not keep Bastion waiting," Gia said. "If he wants to see me, we should arrange a meeting."

She dug out her phone, while Ansel looked around his place, and his relatives. The Furies watched him closely, a mix of love and contempt on their pretty faces. He was their idol, but perhaps he was a fallen idol to them, based on his own failures.

"Chad," Gia said, putting the phone on speaker. "This is Gia, yes."

"Gia," Bastion said, his voice all warmth. "How are you, Dear?"

"Fine," Gia said. "I was wondering if we might meet, you and me. I feel like we have things to discuss."

"Just us, or is this a Council sitdown?" Chad asked. "Am I on speaker, Gia?"

"Yes," Gia said. "Just us. And, yes, I put you on speaker. You know who is here with me? Ansel. My brother. You remember him, don't you?"

Bastion didn't waste a beat.

"How could I forget?" Bastion said. "Hi, Ansel. Finally got yourself out of protective custody, I see."

Gia sucked her teeth.

"Ah, so you knew where my brother was all along?" Gia asked. "All those times I asked Minton, you knew?"

Bastion chuckled.

"Of course I knew, Gia," he said. "Minton tells me everything. He didn't think it would be a good idea for you to know that your own brother had betrayed you and your family."

Gia's face went to a frown, and Ansel spoke up.

"I didn't betray my family," Ansel said.

"Ah, Ansel Rupino himself," Bastion said. "You know, you have this killer reputation, but I think it's just smoke, my boy. When Minton told me about the deal you'd made with him, I laughed. No Rupino would have tucked their tail between their legs so willingly, would have failed their own family so completely."

"You insult my brother," Gia said. "You insult all of us."

"I didn't want to kill all those Infectives," Ansel said.

Bastion laughed.

"Thanks to me, you don't have to," Bastion said. "My Lupitol is getting wider distribution than ever, more people are taking it to manage their condition. You should be thanking me. I did your work for you. Because of me and my company, Infective lycanthropy is going to be just another manageable condition people live with day to day. And I suppose I have you to thank for it, Ansel. We got you the early-stage stuff years ago, testing out how it worked on Trueborn."

"What are you talking about, Chad?" Gia asked.

"Any Trueborn who takes Lupitol loses control of themselves," Bastion said. "It works the other way on us. It compels a transformation, a loss of inhibitions. Funny, right? So, knowing who Ansel was, what he was about, I had some of my people arrange to get him some of the early stuff. We were still refining the formula, mind you. But we knew about him, his whole lycanthropic angst thing. Wanted to see how it played out. And it played out perfectly. He lost control, infected that girl—Samantha Hain—and then she infected Zooey Hummel, and, presto, we got the Happening. Perfectly played."

That Bastion was willing to say all of this on the phone spoke to how invulnerable he felt. Ansel was furious.

"You used me," Ansel said.

"God, yes, I did," Bastion said. "The perfect pawn. I mean, we'd done lab research, of course. But I wanted something in the field. And Trueborn aren't easy to come by. I wasn't going to risk myself or any of my people. But Ansel the Artist? The wayward Rupino? Perfect."

"So, can we meet up?" Gia said.

"Do you think I'm stupid, Gia?" Bastion said. "I know how you Rupinos work. Let's see, you and I meet, and you kill me, either yourself or with those she-bitches you use. I don't know what else you have in mind, but that's not going to happen. It's not happening, you might say."

Bastion laughed.

"This is my territory," Gia said.

"Not for much longer, Doll," Bastion said. "You know that, right? While you've been bumping off the other members of the Council, the outliers, I've been securing what I need to ensure that Chicago becomes mine. Part of that was getting you off the *Argent*, Ansel. That was important. Minton told me about that dumbass on his crew—Norm, the guy who murdered Todd and some of my men, working with those nutty Poles. How he wanted to get you off his ship, all of that crap. I told him he should just do it, and I'd take care of the rest."

"You're a dead man, Chad," Gia said. "I'll see you soon."

"I really don't think so, Gia," Chad said. "Bye, now."

He hung up, and Gia fumed, threw her phone across the room.

"We have to get out of here," Ansel said. "Like right now."

"We need to go after him," Gia said. "Nobody talks to me that way."

"It's what he expects," Ansel said. "He wants you to get angry and go after him. We can't do what he expects. But we do need to leave here immediately."

"Fine," Gia said, throwing up her arms. "Let's go. Somebody grab my phone. Call Valentina. Tell the others. We need to have a family meeting. Mia, Bria, Sia, scout our perimeter."

The Furies nodded, slipping off their clothes and transforming, going from the petite and lovely young women that they were to the lean, lithe, and lethal Furies. Their black-furred selves were a triptych of feral ferocity, and they pricked their ears and sniffed the air.

They went out the back door to Ansel's place, to his garage, and opened the door, slipping out into the night air, ears cocked.

Ansel went out with Gia, who was talking rapidly on her phone, while his cousins walked along, surrounding Gia.

"I want to take out Bastion," Ansel said. He could hear a buzzing in the air, something skyward. He looked up.

"No," Gia said. "He's mine."

The shot that came was silent. It struck Gia in the chest and came from above. Blood burst from her chest, and she gasped. At the same moment, shots came down on several of Ansel's cousins, and they exploded into plumes of blood, the scent of silver all around them.

Ansel dove back into the cover of the garage, while Gia fell dead to the ground as other shots came down from the sky, dropping other Rupinos where they stood. It was a downpour of silver bullets that rained down from the sky.

"Gia," Ansel said. "Ohmigod! Mia, Sia, Bria, get under cover!"

The Furies raced through the alley, while bullets sparked off the ground, tracking them. They dove back into the garage, only barely ahead of the phantom fusillade.

Ansel yanked off his clothes and turned, tears in his eyes as he saw Gia dead on the street, shot in the heart. He traded flesh for fur, let himself grow in mass, his claws lengthening, his teeth becoming fangs. His ears lengthened, and he could hear the drones.

"They're using drones," Ansel said, pointing skyward with a claw. "Let me flush them out, and you three try to take them out."

He could hear the whining hum of quadcopter blades and saw a gun-equipped drone drop into view, bearing the BEE logo. The thing looked like some kind of robotic wasp, with a single red eye and a camera, and the under-mounted gun, as well as its four rotating blades. It also had twin landing struts. Ansel grabbed a trash can lid and hurled it at the drone, knocking it aside. Then he dove for it, grabbing the thing and smashing it against the wall of the alley.

He could see a dozen other drones hovering overhead, training their guns on him. Ansel ran down the alley, while they pursued him.

Ansel zigzagged as he went, hoping that would at least make it more difficult for the drone pilots to gun him down.

Behind him, he heard the Furies vault into action, snarling and pouncing on some of the drones. As frightened as he was in the moment, he didn't want his baby sisters to be hurt, and he quickly jerked back around, narrowly avoiding a shot that smacked into the ground where he'd been only a moment before.

Ansel threw his rage and pain at the loss of Gia into attacking the drones nearest to him, grabbing one and throwing it into another, satisfied when they crashed. He stomped on them, not caring that the rotor blades cut him as he did so.

His sisters had already taken down four drones and were going for their fifth when Ansel had turned on the ones chasing him. The surviving drones flew up higher, and Ansel pursued them, scurrying up the side of the building in three quick strides. He threw himself at one of them, catching it on its landing struts, counting on his weight to pull the thing down. Not wanting to wait too long with this one and make himself a target, Ansel reached for the gun it carried and yanked it clear, satisfied by the crunch of metal and plastic as he pulled it free. Without its silver stinger, the drone was nothing but a nuisance.

He landed on the ground with the drone gun, hurling it at another drone, which dodged it.

"Come on," Ansel said to the Furies. "We have to get out of here."

The four of them sprinted out of the alley, while a half-dozen drones pursued them, buzzing angrily after them, far enough above them to be out of reach.

Ansel's mind worked as they fled. He didn't know how much power those drones had. But he assumed he and the Furies could outlast them. He also assumed that the BEE still wanted to keep things fairly quiet, which was why they used silenced guns to try to dispatch them, versus, say, a missile. The drones would offer a means to take them out without jeopardizing too many lives.

He led them to some of the neighborhood tree coverage, which would offer them some protection from the flying drones. He glanced over his shoulder, could see that three of the drones had slipped below the tree canopy, while the other three had gone high.

"Fan out, keep zigzagging," Ansel said.

He wanted more than anything to avenge the murder of Gia and the others, even as he wanted to keep the Furies safe. He would gladly take bullets meant for them if it meant no harm came to them. His rage continued to build, and he turned back on the drones chasing them, moving back and forth quickly, while they fired at him. They were effectively flown, but without the advantage of surprise, he felt that his lycanthropic reflexes were greater than the norms who were flying them.

Ansel leaped over the top of one of the many parked cars, satisfied by the crumple of metal beneath his paws as he jumped, catching one of the drones by landing on it, sending it to the ground, where he smashed the life out of it.

The other two whizzed to either side of him, pivoting to turn their guns on him when two of the Furies threw themselves at the drones, destroying them, tearing them apart with snarls and growls.

Three down, three to go, Ansel thought.

He shifted to a form he rarely used—his four-legged incarnation—and took off running, the Furies following suit, smoothly turning. In this form, they traded strength for speed and would make themselves harder targets for the drone pilots in pursuit somewhere overhead.

Several blocks west was Varro Park, where he thought he and the Furies might be able to make a stand against the remaining drones that were after them.

They ran hard for it, Ansel's mind working. He needed to get in touch with Norm, who could help give him insight into what was going on. The question was whether Ansel and his sisters would live that long.

NORM had ditched the police truck after taking what he assumed were his pursuers on a merry chase. When he got close enough to his home, he left the truck behind and took the assault rifle and snuck to his place.

Unaccustomed to not having a phone with him, he got to his condominium and tossed the rifle on his bed, fished out one of his backup burner phones.

He dialed up Tiff.

"Driver," Tiff said. "You survived."

"Yeah," Norm said. "So, did you deploy your drone or what?"

"A little busy right now, Driver," Tiff said. "Can I call you back later?"

Norm could hear an uncharacteristic edge to her voice, knew that it meant that she was piloting her drone after all, despite her protestations of fatigue. It meant Minton was up to something big.

"What's going on, Dealer?" Norm asked.

"Can't talk right now, Driver," Tiff said, hanging up.

That wasn't like Tiff at all. Norm dialed up Gia, but it went to her voicemail.

"Gia, I think something's up," Norm said. "Get somewhere safer than the frame store. I'll call when I can."

All at once, Norm realized that he wasn't alone in his place. It was an instinct borne of experience, and he whirled around, saw Anne standing there, wearing an ivory blouse and a jet-black leather skirt and black pointy-toed boots.

"Hello, Norm," Anne said.

"Anne," Norm said. "What happened to tomorrow at the Art Institute?"

"I didn't want to wait, Babe," Anne said. "And, honestly, I don't think you have much time left."

Norm reached for the Glock 18 he carried, but Anne just looked at him and sadly smiled. He thought he saw love in her eyes, but he had long since forgotten whether it was something he knew, or just something he imagined.

"I could say that about both of us," Norm said. "All along, you were in on Bastion's big scheme, yeah?"

Anne's face registered concern and care, and Norm couldn't read if it was genuine or not. Not when it came to Anne. He neither knew nor cared. Anne was always going to be Anne.

"You weren't the only one with secrets, Norm," Anne said. "Please, let's go to the living room and talk like civilized people."

Norm wasn't sure what her play was in this moment, so he humored her.

"Sure," Norm said. "Let's do that. It's just you, right?"

"It's just me," Anne said. She took a seat opposite him, while Norm sat leaning forward, feeling edgy.

"What do you want to talk about?" Norm asked. "Ladies first, right?"

"Yes," Anne said. "Absolutely. Babe, you don't need to fight any more. Chad's solved the whole Lupine problem. Lupitol is making everything better. He's solving it as we speak."

"But you won't take it," Norm said.

"Goodness, no," Anne said.

"I saw you take one," Norm said.

"Please," Anne said. "I was faking that."

"Why won't you take it?" Norm asked.

Anne sighed, leaning back in her seat. She looked as beautifully composed as ever. Anne never got ruffled, always maintained that coolly corporate composure. Norm loved that about her. It had been what had attracted him to her when they were younger. Anne always knew where she was going, and he respected that, whether or not he agreed about her destination.

"Babe," Anne said. "This is a gift. Lycanthropy's only been good to me. I have power, now. I'm rich. Why on earth would I give that up, would try to become ordinary again?"

"You've killed people," Norm said, and Anne actually laughed.

"Not as many as you, I bet," Anne said. "Or are those kill counts classified? Babe, we're *both* killers, you and me. We're just killing different people. How many did you kill in Afghanistan? How many with the Bureau? You're a killing machine. Don't try to lecture me about morality."

"You've eaten people," Norm said, realizing he should have led with that.

Anne shrugged.

"Small price to pay, given everything else," Anne said. "When Shaw and the others came for me, I was afraid. I knew what Liminalix was doing. I've been involved in their Lupitol project for ten years, Babe. Before the Happening happened. Chad laid it all out for us, his core team. He made us sign NDAs and everything. I couldn't tell you, I couldn't tell anyone. And I didn't want to. So many NDAs, so little time."

Norm listened to her talk, her honey-sweet voice, her blasé manner. She was perfectly at ease. Her comfort in his company was itself comforting, and Norm fought to resist the urge to go to her. She had that power over him.

"You jerked me around all those years," Norm said. "You knew who I worked for, what I did."

"Of course," Anne said. "That was a key part of it, honestly. Your work for the Bureau was invaluable. It gave us insight into how things were progressing. They're a very secretive organization, as you know better than anyone. I used the fact that you worked there to my advantage—nobody else on Chad's team had somebody with that kind of access."

"I don't understand why you'd even do it," Norm said. His heart was breaking to think she'd played him so badly, and he'd never guessed.

"Money, power, fame," Anne said. "Oh, sure, a corporate sort of fame, but fame, all the same. I'm *known*, Babe. Among people who matter. With Todd out of the way—thank you for that, by the way—Chad promoted me into his role. I'm VP of Sales at Liminalix, now. That was all you. Todd was never going to get out of my way on that one, but your murdering him was the perfect next step. I could kiss you for it. I would if you would only let me."

"No," Norm said, although he wanted her to. "Why bother telling me all of this?"

"Babe, I love you," Anne said. "I know this is a lot for you to digest, but I do. Do you think I don't know what toll this job has taken on you? Oh, I know, you're stoic and you just push all of that pain into some secret vault only you can access. But I know it wounds you. Every person you kill, it hurts you. They haunt you. I can take all of that away. Let me, you know, heal you, and you'll see: it'll all go away. You can be happy with me. We can be rich and free and do anything we like."

Norm couldn't believe she was even suggesting that.

"How long have you been one of them?" Norm asked. He could barely choke it out.

"Oh, you already know," Anne said. "When I wrote that note. Chad only offers the Gift to his most trusted people. He only extends his hand when he feels you've earned it."

"Wait, so *he* made you? Not Shaw?" Norm asked, his head wanting to explode.

"Yes," Anne said. "If I'm being honest, yes."

"If you're being honest," Norm said. "Fuck, Babe. Jesus Christ."

Norm's instinct was to shoot her right there. Everything he knew about himself, about her, about it all told him that was the right thing to do.

"All of that bullshit about Shaw was, what? A smokescreen?"

"Todd was in my way," Anne said. "He had no idea. You know how he was. He always wanted me. I gave him what he wanted. Purely a tactical move, incidentally. The man was such a prick. You were always right about that."

"You did all of that because you *wanted* me to kill him," Norm said. "You set me up."

"Bingo," Anne said, making a finger pistol at him, pulling the trigger. Norm raised his Glock 18 and pointed it at her. Anne's warm smile never wavered.

"What's to say I won't just kill you, too?" Norm asked. "Right here and now."

"Babe, I'm the one Lupine you'd never kill," Anne said. "Because you love me, and you always will. I know that, you know that, *we* know that."

Norm grimaced, holding the Glock level. Two shots would more than do it. At this range, all the lycanthropic reflexes in the world wouldn't be sufficient for her to evade it. She just watched him, no trace of fear in her. Only love in her eyes.

"And I love you," Anne said. "Now and forever."

The moment stretched out in eternity for him, sitting there, gun on her, and her, calmly, lovingly looking on.

"Fuck," Norm said, lowering the pistol. "It's not fair, Anne. What you do to me."

"Babe, I know," Anne said. "But that's love. Love isn't fair. If it was fair, it wouldn't be love."

Norm gritted his teeth, angry at himself, angry at her, furious at the world for even being in this mess of a place.

"You're a good man, Norm," Anne said. "I know that. You're a wounded man, but a good one. Don't you think I know that? I count on that. And I cherish that about you. You always do the right thing, no matter how much it hurts you. You did those tours in Afghanistan without complaint. I remember how that hurt you. Let me take that pain away. I can do that for you."

She held up her hands, her perfectly manicured nails. Her hands were steady. He knew she'd had to have that manicure done since her last transformation. That attention to detail was pure Anne.

"Not going to happen," Norm said. "I'm not becoming one of you."

"Chad thinks I'm crazy for holding on to you," Anne said. "He doesn't understand. He's Trueborn, Babe. They're entirely different from us. He's like two steps removed from humanity. He operates in another plane. He's a genius. Those Rupinos you're working with? They're nothing compared to Chad. He has them clocked. Sure, they have their whole criminal underground, whatever you want to call it. He doesn't even have to do that. He's the head of a major corporation—there are no shadows he needs to hide within. He's out in the open."

"Except for, you know, him being a fucking werewolf," Norm said.

"The norms can't handle that," Anne said. "They're sheep, Babe. A sea of sheep. The world is full of sheep, shepherds, and wolves. Which would you rather be?"

"And you're what? The shepherd's crook?" Norm asked. "I don't understand why Bastion would even cause the epidemic he wants to treat."

Anne laughed, throwing her head back and gustily laughing, her shoulders shaking as she did so. Her laugh was beautiful. Norm loved her laugh most of all. He treasured her laughter. Even with all she'd done, he wanted her to laugh. Her laughter was an expression of her joy, and her joy made him happy.

"You answered your own question, Babe," Anne said. "Chad knew it was an expedient way to make a fortune. Offer the treatment for the disease you've helped to spread. It balances the accounts."

"What about Free Rein? Does that 'balance the accounts' for him?" Norm asked.

Anne sighed, shaking her head. It was like he'd failed her somehow. And failing her, he felt wounded.

"Everyone needs a release from time to time," Anne said. "Babe, I know this is a lot for you to take, and you've had an exhausting several days."

She reached out and gently patted him on the knee. She reached into a pocket and produced a gold card case with her initials monogrammed on them. Opening it, she took out an ivory business card, put it on the table between them.

"Call me any time you need me," Anne said. "I mean that."

"Anne, please," Norm said. "You're sick. You're infected."

"Lycanthropy *healed* me, Norm," Anne said. "You'll never understand that. It made me whole for the first time in my life. It could make *you* whole, too. Chad has created the most exclusive and elite social club ever. You'd be amazed at how people in the know are coming to him, making offers to get infected. Can you believe it? *Paying* to get infected? They're powerful people, rich people, who see this as the next step in our evolution. And do you know what? They're right. Crazy Zooey Hummel had a good idea, but she didn't apply it properly—she wanted to infect everyone, to give them all the Gift and watch the chaos tear everything down. Chad sees something else—he sees the Gift as the means of opening a very particular set of doors to those who he sees fit to let through."

It was something Norm couldn't even imagine.

"A controlled infection?" Norm asked.

"You know how it is," Anne said. "There's no controlling the retrovirus once you are exposed to it. But in a controlled setting, well, that's another matter. He has people doing the work. Lab technicians, physicians, biochemists. A client gets infected and they go to a special clinic, where they can acclimate to their new condition without the pesky problems of infectivity. Managed infection. It's brilliant."

"Free Rein," Norm said. Anne nodded, smiling.

"That's part of it," she said. "A later stage. First, though, there's the initial infection within a controlled setting. You're observed and allowed to become acquainted with your new life. There are consultants and instructors there to guide the client stepwise through the process."

"Jesus," Norm said. Anne just laughed, her warm and buttery laugh that he missed so much.

"Once they're ready to be readmitted to society, they're free to go," Anne said. "Some get prescriptions to Lupitol, sure. Some can't handle it, and the Lupitol levels them. All of those idiot Infectives of Zooey's made the perfect test group. Those ones on Wolf Island. Thanks to Director Minton, they're only too eager to try it on them. We know how it works. Others, ones more in control of themselves, they can live their lives as they please. Chad just requires an NDA, has a team of lawyers handy to make sure they understand that it was a voluntary procedure. You wouldn't believe how many politicians want to receive the Gift. Anything for an edge."

Norm found his mind went into tactical places as she was telling him all of this. One thing he counted on with Anne was that she liked to talk, so he'd encourage her to do so.

"Does Bastion infect them all personally?" Norm asked. "He can't be biting all of those people, can he?"

He worried that if he did that, there'd be a veritable army of Infectives under his control, however indirect it may have been.

Anne shrugged as she recounted it.

"He has different packages based on the client's preferences," Anne said. "Some *want* to be bitten. Others are okay with an injection."

"What did you receive?"

"Oh, he bit me," Anne said. "The severity of the bite determines the speed of infection. I let him have at me. I didn't want to wait."

"Anne, what the hell?" Norm said. "How could you have done this to yourself?"

Anne laughed heartily again, like he'd said something funny. Norm couldn't even imagine how she'd ended up this way, what hole in her soul had existed to make her go that route. He felt like he'd failed her, somehow.

"Babe, I'm strong," Anne said. "I'm healthy like I've never been before. The vitality is a wonderful side effect of the Gift. I never get sick anymore."

"Because *you* are sick," Norm said. "You're part of the pestilence."

"Please," Anne said. "Don't judge, Babe."

She was right about him. He couldn't kill her. He wouldn't kill her. But not because she didn't deserve it.

"Chad is creating better people," Anne said. "The other Trueborn clans don't understand. They are mired in the past. Chad is doing something revolutionary—and evolutionary—far, far beyond anything they could have conceived. He was grateful the Rupinos threw themselves after all of those Infectives after the Happening broke out. It made him seem reasonable by comparison. Minton jumped at the chance to come up with a more humane solution. Lupitol was just that fix. The Rupinos are obsolete. They just don't know it, yet."

Norm's mind was awash with all of this.

"Why tell me all of this, Anne?"

"Because I love you, Norm," Anne said. "I don't want you to get yourself killed trying to stop something that's far, far beyond anything you've ever faced before. Chad is playing a bigger game than you can even imagine. However, because he's gracious, and he knows I care about you, he's allowing me to extend the Gift to you as an offer. You can join us and we can live the rest of our days in happiness, health, and wealth, Babe. Honestly, you're half a Lupine already— you've personally killed more people than most of the Lupines I know. The only difference is you'd be able to do it with even greater impunity than you already have, and without the guilt. All I'm asking you to do is think about it."

"About what?" Norm asked. "You can't possibly expect me to agree to let myself get infected and become one of those things."

"Just don't do anything crazy," Anne said. "Sleep on it, we'll talk again soon, after you've had time to process it."

She got up and walked to Norm, giving him a squeeze on his shoulder, leaning in and kissing the top of his head, then walked away, leaving Norm shaking and fighting back tears. Only when the door shut did he let himself go.

MINA woke up not entirely sure where she was, but when Sonia and Sloane turned up, she reoriented herself. It was morning, and she'd had her running dream. While Animus was so often Lupitol-locked inside her, she'd run wild in her dreams. In this one, Mina-Animus had been running through fields, feeling the exhilaration of unbounded motion. They'd been chasing something, but Mina could not remember what.

"Wake up, Mina," Sloane said. She looked a bit bleary, and Mina could feel it as well. Their close proximity to so much silver did nothing for the lycanthropic complexion. Sonia was making some coffee, while Sloane sulked.

"I'm up," Mina said.

"I miss my mom," Sloane said, watching Sonia make her coffee. "And I'm hungry."

Sonia pointed to some apricot kolacky that was in a white box on the counter. Sloane wrinkled her nose.

"Not sweets," Sloane said. "Meat. I'm *hungry.*"

Sonia shrugged, looked over at Mina, as if it were her problem to solve.

"We'll get some breakfast, Sloane," Mina said.

"No," Sonia said. "I'll have one of my brothers bring you something suitable. It's not a good idea for you to be out and about, Dr. Milkowski."

"Have you heard from Norm?" Mina asked.

"Not since last night," Sonia said. "I haven't heard from anyone. There was news this morning about something happening downtown, a three-car pileup. They're looking into it. They were Liminalix SUVs, so that could mean something. Sometimes, not-hearing is as much hearing as you get."

Mina smiled to herself, watching Sonia pour herself some coffee.

"Is that a Polish proverb or something?" Mina asked.

"*Nigdy nie odpowiadaj, gdy wilk puka do twoich drzwi,*" Sonia said.

"'Never answer when a wolf knocks on your door?' Now *that's* a Polish proverb," Mina said. "Where are you going?"

"To work," Sonia said. "I'm going to the library. I'm going to see what I can find out. You, however, had best stay put. Don't go out, don't get seen."

"What about school?" Sloane asked. "They're going to want to know where I am."

"I'll call you in sick," Sonia said. "Tell me the school."

Sloane did, looking a little sheepish at Sonia, who was no-nonsense.

Mina got up and got herself some of the coffee. She didn't look forward to being cooped up all day with a restless young lycanthrope.

She turned on the television, saw the news helicopters showing the three damaged Liminalix SUVs, which looked like they'd been smashed in from the side. Like they'd been attacked.

Sonia's phone rang, and she answered, even though it was a number she didn't recognize.

"Polski, this is Hum-Drum," Norm said, hoping she'd recognize his voice, hoping Minton wasn't mining Archon for any sign of him.

"Do I know you?" Sonia asked.

"We met the other day," Norm said.

"Ah," Sonia said.

"You still have the package, yes?" Norm asked.

"Yes," Sonia said.

"Do not deliver it to the intended recipients," Norm said. "There are others who are seeking to hijack it."

Sonia paced around, glancing at Mina, who was half-listening, while Sloane was running around, humming and pretending to be an airplane.

"We know that already," Sonia said.

"Others," Norm said. "Not just the ones you know. I need to sort out delivery instructions before the delivery."

"Okay," Sonia said. "We should probably meet. I'd feel better about that. Like maybe our lunch date we had planned?"

"Fine," Norm said. Tupelo's, she'd said the other day. "See you then."

Sonia hung up her phone, pocketing it.

"That was Norm," Sonia said. "Sounds like there was some trouble."

Their eyes went to the news coverage of the overturned SUVs for a moment before Sonia continued.

"Everything still stands as planned," she said. "You stay put, and I'm going to work. I'm going to meet Norm for lunch, and I'll find out what's going on. Once I know, I'll get back with you."

Mina nodded. The night's sleep had helped restore her, despite her running dreams. Sonia put her hand on Mina's shoulder.

"Just please stay put," Sonia said. "Nobody knows you're here except us. Let's keep it that way."

"Fine," Mina said.

"Also, be careful about the phone," Sonia said. "Just assume that somebody's listening."

"I know how the BEE works," Mina said, a trifle wounded. "Just because I was a lab geek doesn't mean I didn't know BEE procedure."

"Right," Sonia said, smiling. She grabbed a grey wool overcoat, put it on quickly. "I'll call you later, once I have more information."

"Okay," Mina said, watching her go. Sloane came back into the room, looking bemused.

"She's very serious," Sloane said. "She even smells serious."

"What does serious smell like?"

"A box of silver bullets," Sloane said. "And, like, steel wool."

SONIA met Norm at Tupelo's. It served Southern cuisine, was popular with both lunch and dinner crowds. Sonia wore a red turtleneck with a white scarf and grey wool slacks with black boots. She took off her grey peacoat and hung it on the hook that flanked their booth.

Norm looked worn out to her appraising eyes, as they went over their menus.

"Good morning, I hope, Norm," Sonia said.

"Rough night," Norm said. "Sorry if I look like hell."

"Ah," she said. "Seems like the Bureau should have given you something less, I don't know, arduous."

"I'm getting betrayed from so many different angles, I don't even know which way to turn," Norm said. "Promise me you're not going to do that, too."

"Never, Norm," Sonia said. "We're models of honor and propriety in our secret society."

"Hey, you rhymed," Norm said, managing a dry chuckle.

"Yes, I suppose it's going around," Sonia said. "Dr. Milkowski brought me a book of poetry from the apparently late Polly Drinkwater. I was paging through it last night. I'm thinking it'll end up in the Landa Library. I mean, for posterity's sake and all. A lycanthrope writing poems about her affliction? Probably a first for the cursed."

"You're doing it again," Norm said. Sonia smiled.

"You looked like you needed a laugh, Mr. Stockwell," Sonia said.

"Yeah, I'm not him, anymore, incidentally," Norm said. "I'm Grant Redding."

"Grant," Sonia said, trying it out, taste-testing his identity. "Alright, Mr. Redding."

She extended her hand, which he shook, smiling.

"So nice to meet you," Sonia said. "I'm still Sonia Gorski, the one and only."

The lunch crowd at Tupelo's was fairly standard, and Norm found some small comfort in being there, surrounded by what looked like everyday people. Being steeped in abnormality so often made those everyday moments feel more precious.

"You've changed your look," Sonia said. "I hardly recognized you."

"I did that last night," Norm said. He'd peroxided his hair and hadn't shaved, hoping that would offset all the shots of his face that had been trotted out by the media.

Their waiter came and took their orders—Norm got a catfish po'boy and Sonia ordered some gumbo.

"Let's catch up, Mr. Redding," Sonia said. "The Package is safe in our hands. But what about the recipients? You haven't heard, have you."

"No," Norm said. "I've tried to reach Gia, but it goes to her voicemail. That's concerning, because she always answers."

"My people reported some activity last night," Sonia said. "Something in Ukrainian Village. Something involving drones and Lupines. Black-furred Lupines."

"Hold on," Norm said, taking out a burner phone. He dialed up Tiff. She picked up.

"Who's this?" she asked. "Driver?"

"Yeah, it's me," Norm said. "What's this I hear about drones attacking Loops?"

"What is it that you're hearing?" Tiff asked.

"You tell me," Norm said. "You were flying last night."

"Nothing you need to worry about, Driver," Tiff said.

"Oh, I think I might," Norm said. "Were you chasing down Rupinos?"

"Can't say," Tiff said. "Sorry, Driver. We have our secrets, too."

Norm cursed, covering the phone with his hand before he did so. Sonia sipped at some sweet tea that was delivered to them.

"Big Bad is cleaning house," Norm said. "Isn't he?"

Minton came on the line.

"Driver, didn't I tell you to get back here?" Minton asked. "Didn't I tell you that?"

"Sir, what the hell is going on?"

"My mission, our mission, is to bring things back to normal," Minton said. "I'm doing that, do you understand? Everything I've done has been to get the country back to normal. You get back here, or you're through at the Bureau. I'm revoking your Stinger status, if you don't come back here this instant. You're messing things up, Driver."

"Won't be necessary, Sir," Norm said. "I quit. Effective immediately."

"You don't get to—" Minton said. Norm hung up on him and popped the SIM card out of the phone, snapping the phone in half and setting it on the table. Sonia watched this with an upraised eyebrow.

"Work troubles?" Sonia asked.

"Nope," Norm said, drinking some sweet tea of his own.

Sonia smirked at him.

"Want a new job?" Sonia asked.

"I might be in the market," Norm said.

She smiled at him.

"We offer excellent benefits," Sonia said. "Although there are a lot of occupational hazards associated with it."

"Hazards I can handle," Norm said. "It's the rest of it that gets problematic."

"I'll put a word in for you," Sonia said.

The server, a young man, came by, glanced at the broken phone without a comment. He looked nervous, which made Norm think perhaps that he thought they were Lupines or else that there may have been Lupines at Tupelo's. He quickly asked if Norm and Sonia needed anything else, but they politely demurred.

Sonia noticed the server's nervousness as well, and the two of them looked around to see if anybody stood out to them.

As werewolf hunters, there was an instinct that came into play when spotting lycanthropes. Norm's eyes raked over the patrons scattered about, but he didn't see anyone who looked suspicious.

"Do your people take in outsiders?" Norm asked.

"Sometimes," Sonia said. "If the expertise is there. To be honest, we'd give our eye teeth for a Bureau agent."

Norm nodded, only half-amused. He imagined Minton would give the other Stingers a bulletin informing them that Norm had quit. Not like he'd theatrically send them to kill him or anything, but he likely would notify them so that if Norm reached out to them for assistance, they could stop him. How they stopped him depended on how pissed Minton was. Or maybe he'd insinuate that Norm had died. He could play it any way he liked.

"Okay, I have to tell you some things," Norm said. "Incredible things."

Sonia smiled at the insinuation.

"Oooh, I love incredible things," she said. "Please do."

Norm did. He relayed everything Anne had told him while they had their lunch. Sonia simply listened attentively, taking it all in. Norm tried to compose himself, maintaining his mask of professional dispassion as he shared it all with her. When he was done, he took a breath and drank more sweet tea, which the server dutifully refilled.

"She's playing you," Sonia said.

"What?"

"Why would she tell you all of that if she didn't want you to do something about it?" Sonia asked.

"What, she wants me to set her free?" Norm asked, making a pistol gesture with his hand.

"Not like that," Sonia said. "Maybe she does still love you in some way, Norm. Maybe that's a vestige of her human self. Before she became an Infective. You're the last link to her humanity, the self she was before she took that Devil's bargain of Bastion's. You're the last loose end she needs to wrap up before she fully and freely commits to the path she's on."

"Hah," Norm said. "I don't believe that."

"Believe what you want," Sonia said. "You said it yourself—she didn't have to tell you any of that. She did so for a reason. Just like that whole elaborate 'kidnapping' kabuki she did with Todd Shaw. In that case, she wanted you to 'rescue' her, even though she had no desire to be rescued. She knows you, knows what you'd do. She presents you with this great big conspiracy, and she knows that'll bother you. You'll try to make it right."

Norm glanced around them, saw nothing out of the ordinary among the restaurant patrons, and was relieved.

"She offered the 'Gift' of infecting me," Norm said.

"She did that knowing it would offend you and that you'd refuse it," Sonia said.

Norm was used to thinking unconventionally. The job demanded it of him. But this idea was just beyond the pale.

"She's playing me," Norm said. Sonia nodded, shrugging.

"What are your options?" Sonia asked. "You can take her up on her offer, or you can reject her. Why didn't you shoot her?"

Norm hesitated before saying.

"I love her," Norm said. "I still do. Damned if I do."

Sonia nodded slowly, finishing up her gumbo. "I truly understand. What we do isn't easy. You know it better than anyone outside the company I keep. And when it's a loved one, that's the very worst."

"How do you handle it?" Norm asked.

"There's no uniform way. The *Synowie* take various approaches. We aren't centralized for a reason," she said. "We can't afford to be, with what we're fighting. We depend on individual initiative of our various cells. How they resolve it is their business."

Norm could see a white van pull up and park across the street.

"Yeah," Norm said. "That is the question."

"And what's your answer to that question?" she asked.

"I can't kill her," Norm said. "She's right about that. I can't, I won't."

"I can, if you need me to," Sonia said.

Her cool manner, her casual acceptance of it, was jarring. Maybe it was the work, but there was a ruthlessness to the *Synowie* that was always present.

"No," Norm said, perhaps more quickly than he intended. Sonia accepted that with a half-smile that was both jarring and strangely reassuring.

The server came back and recommended a dandy bread pudding for dessert, which they accepted, along with some coffee. The server still looked edgy, which made Norm edgy, too. He looked around without wanting to be too obvious about it.

"Something's up," Norm said. Sonia only smiled.

"Nothing's up," she said. "They think we're Lupines."

"C'mon," Norm said. "We don't look like them."

"It's true," she said.

Norm hated the idea of getting made. He was supposed to blend into the woodwork, not stand out. Part of him worked on ascertaining whether Sonia was right or whether it was all in his head.

"They're killers, we're killers," Sonia said. "When you're a killer, people can tell. There's just something about the way killers carry themselves. The hint of danger."

"Do people know you?" Norm asked.

"Lots of people know me," Sonia said.

"You know what I mean," Norm said. "Do they know who you are? *What* you are?"

She burned Norm with a caustic glance.

"What sort of secret society would the *Synowie* be if people knew about it, Grant?" Sonia said. "Nobody knows who I am."

Then Norm saw what was making the server nervous. Across the street were some Lupines. Pretenders. A small pack of them, members of the Lupercalians, wearing black suits and black ties with white shirts, preaching on the street corner. Three of them, young men, golden-haired and bright-eyed.

"There's the trouble," Norm said, nodding.

"Wargs," Sonia said. "Do you think they followed us?"

Norm scanned them a moment. They didn't seem to be paying attention to them, were instead preaching to the normies around them.

Part of him wanted to walk up and shoot them, but he knew it was better to keep under control.

"After what happened to them, it's surprising any are still in the city," Sonia said. "Must be lower-echelon. Dead enders."

Norm ignored the Wargs and focused back on the Anne Issue.

"Don't kill her, please," Norm said. "She's my problem. I have to deal with her."

"So deal with her," Sonia said, watching the server deliver the bread pudding and coffee. She addressed the young man. "Do they come by often, those people?"

"Every day," he said. "Same time of day. They come in here, too, sometimes. They're neo-nazis."

"Wow," Norm said. "The worst."

"Totally," the server said, moving away to one of his other tables.

"Can't you tell your people that Anne's off-limits?" Norm asked.

"Nobody's off-limits," Sonia said. "Where *they* are concerned. I can personally tell you that neither my brothers nor I will kill her. But the rest of the *Synowie?* I have to tell them what you told me. They have to know. Where they go with that is their business."

The chill in her voice was bracing, and Norm glanced at the Wargs, who had crossed the street to be outside Tupelo's preaching away. Were they closing in?

Sonia spooned some of the bread pudding seemingly without a care in the world.

At the rate things were going with the *Synowie,* Norm didn't think they had enough manpower to get close enough to Anne to credibly threaten her.

"We have plenty of *Synowie* associates among the janitorial staff throughout the city," Sonia said. "Not members, but they know to reach out to us if they need to. Bastion is a smart one—he doesn't use Poles among his janitors. We have no eyes on the inside. Smart. Then again, rules were made to be broken. A good *Cwaniak* could probably circumvent his defenses in his building downtown."

"I don't know what that is," Norm said.

"A hustler," Sonia said. "Are you a hustler, Grant? You seem more like a straight shooter to me. Steady hands, steady heart."

"I'll figure something out," Norm said, his eyes drifting to the Wargs, who were haranguing the pedestrians with their holy message.

"Prove to me that you're a *Cwaniak*," Sonia said. "Deal with those Wargs."

Angry by what Anne had put him through, Norm was all too willing. "Fine. Stay here."

She watched him get up, smiling while she ate more of the bread pudding.

"Are you kidding?" Sonia said. "I'm going with you."

"It'll be obvious if we both get up," Norm said.

"Ah," Sonia said. "Promising. You show *cwaniakować.*"

"Is that a good thing?"

"Very good," Sonia said. "What are you going to do?"

"I'm going to kill them," Norm said. "I'm a straight shooter, after all."

Sonia chuckled nervously, her eyes going to the other patrons.

"In broad daylight?"

"I don't see why not," Norm said.

"Then let's worth together," Sonia said. "I don't think they've made us. I think it's just you being paranoid."

"Either way," Norm said, getting up, leaving his half of the bill on the table.

"You be the bait," Sonia said. "I'll follow along."

"I was just going to shoot them," Norm said.

"No," Sonia said. "This takes some finesse. There's an alley a half-block from here, down the street. See if you can get the Wargs to follow you there. Provoke them and then head there."

"If it goes south, I'm just going to shoot them," Norm said.

"Finesse," Sonia said. "Trust me."

Norm didn't trust anyone anymore, but he knew that the *Synowie* were no friends to the Lupines. It was as clear as daylight.

Sonia settled the bill, swigging down the coffee and Norm strode out of Tupelo's belatedly wishing he'd tried some of the bread pudding. Streetside, he could hear the Wargs preaching. The alpha among them was a blue-eyed, lantern-jawed young man who looked fit and strong.

"The Church of the Apocalyptic Vision welcomes you all," the alpha said. "Join our flock, Lambs of God. Feast on the holy wisdom."

He was handing out fliers, and as Norm walked up, the Warg looked him over, decided he was suitably sheeplike to receive a flier. Norm glanced at it, seeing a church wreathed in light with a great cross hanging over it, surrounded by a pentagram that was throwing off radiant beams of light like the sun. PREY WITH US, it said in bold, black letters.

"You misspelled 'pray' on this," Norm said to the alpha.

"Did we?" the alpha said, smiling at Norm toothily. "We are the First Lupercalians. We bring light to the spiritually ravenous. Are you wolf or sheep?"

Norm brushed past them as they sniffed the air. They could smell the silver on him, he was sure.

"Lamb of God," the alpha said, following after Norm with the others close behind. "We smell the silver, Brother. Cast it aside and seek salivation with us."

"I think you mean 'salvation'," Norm said.

"I mean 'Salivation'," the alpha said. "Salivation IS Salvation with the Lupercalians."

Norm glanced over his shoulder and shook his head as he did so.

"I'm good," Norm said. He'd never been bait before. It was an unfamiliar feeling, and he started to pick up his step. The Wargs went after him, the alpha talking all the time.

"Run, lost lamb," the alpha said. "So far from your flock. Run, run, with salivation biting at your heels."

Norm broke into a run, gratified when they gave chase. Even in daylight, the instincts remained and he could see from the hunted looks on the faces of the other pedestrians that they knew what was happening and they were simply glad it wasn't they who were being hunted.

Norm's eyes went skyward and he didn't see any drones, felt that the Bureau was at least occupied elsewhere for the moment. Sonia's alley was just ahead, and he shot down it, hearing the clatter of the Wargs' hard-soled shoes close behind.

"Your hour of reckoning is upon you, Lamb," the alpha said.

For Infectives, Norm had to hand it to them that they remained as disciplined as they were to give chase as Pretenders and to not transform. The late Saint and Deacon had trained them well, whatever else they'd done to pollute their spirits.

The alley was the obligatory blend of telephone poles and well-battered dumpsters, blue plastic recycling bins, and litter crammed into corners. This particular one was old enough that the asphalt had given way to ankle-turning brick cobbles in places.

Despite his head start, the Wargs were gaining on him. Norm worked hard to stay fit, but they were paranormal and young, faster by far, so, when he got deep enough into the alley, out of sight of any streetside cameras he could see, he slowed down, pretending to be winded. He turned to face his pursuers, in hopes that they wouldn't surround him.

They stopped chasing him, surrounding him.

"You understand your place in God's great order," the alpha said. He tapped his well-tended hands against his chest and gestured to include his fellow pack-mates. "Predators."

Then he pointed to Norm.

"And prey," the alpha said.

Norm drew his silver dagger and the alpha's smile withered, because he could smell that silver more clearly, now. His eyes went to the dagger and Norm could see him weighing whether or not he'd be fast enough to jump Norm and snatch it away before Norm stabbed him.

That moment's hesitation was all that was really needed because Sonia felled him with a silenced shot to the back of the head. The alpha simply dropped in a spray of blood, while the other two turned and looked in shock at Sonia standing there in her black *Synowie* ski mask. It was almost achingly on-brand for her. He had images of humming *Synowie* grandmothers sewing those symbols with silver needles, using silver thread.

When one of them sprang for her, Sonia shot him in the heart, her pistol chuffing as the silencer did its job for the second shot. She was a steady hand with an unerring aim, her eyes calm to the point of uncanny serenity. It was like holy communion for her, made more ironic by the blizzard of Lupercalian pamphlets that flew about as the second Warg dropped. They littered the alley.

The lone remaining Warg turned back on his charge and dove at Norm, seeking to put distance between him and Sonia, wrongly viewing Norm as somehow less of a threat. He was blonde like his brothers had been, but his eyes were dark and wild, and he wasn't as handsome as the alpha had been. His eyes were close-set, his jawline a little too pronounced.

Norm threw a shoulder at him to drive him backward from his lunge and sank the dagger into his heart in one well-practiced stab, pulling it free a moment later, leaving a diamond-shaped hole in him that began to bleed as soon as he withdrew the blade.

The Warg cursed Norm, coughing blood, dropping to the ground, while Sonia was recovering her spent shell casings, fetching them with gloved hands and slipping them wordlessly into her handbag.

Norm stood a moment over the fallen Warg, watching him die. He so seldom knifed them. It was riskier to attempt if one was by oneself. Having a partner wasn't really something he'd factored in, but as Sonia walked up to him, he found he was grateful she was there.

She held out a handkerchief to Norm, who looked at her a moment, uncomprehending, as the Warg did, his head propped against the old brick of the alley wall.

"For your weapon," Sonia said. "Clean it."

Norm mopped the Lupine blood from the blade, then put his dagger back into its scabbard.

"Leave the handkerchief," Sonia said, taking it in her gloved hand, pinching an unbloodied corner of it with her fingertips. She set it down over the face of the dead Lupine, and Norm could see that the *Synowie* cross was embroidered on it.

"A baroque touch," Norm said.

"We are a baroque people," Sonia said. "Now, let's get out of here."

"I'm taking their van," Norm said, fishing out car keys from their pockets.

They slipped away from there, mindful of the various alley cameras they could see. They made their way as casually as they could. It made Norm wish he had a nice ski mask the way Sonia did.

"So, you *Synowie* have those great ski masks," Norm said. "Who makes them for you?"

"Trade secret," Sonia said. "If we initiate you as a member, you'll get one, rest assured. You'd look good in a ski mask, Norm."

They got to the other end of the alley, and Norm saw that Sonia had already stashed her pistol and whipped out her black beret, which she'd switched out with her ski mask, which was quickly tucked into her bag as she shook out her blonde hair.

Without missing a beat, she took to the street, striding down the sidewalk nonchalantly. Norm walked quickly to keep up.

"We should part ways," Sonia said. "As much as it pains me to do so. I trust you'll do the right thing where your wife is concerned."

"Yeah," Norm said. "Sure."

"Then good day, Mr. Stockwell," Sonia said. "We'll be in touch soon."

She pivoted away without a backward glance, leaving Norm looking on in bemused wonder. Nobody was the wiser, yet, but Sonia was wise to flee the scene. Norm got out of there, taking the Wargs' van.

VALENTINA was displeased to see Ansel, and he was even less happy to see her.

He and the Furies had managed to take out the drones that had followed them to Varro Park, and they had been on the run most of the night. They led him to the secret place where Valentina had been recovering. There were a dozen Rupino cousins there, keeping her safe.

Word had already gotten out about what had happened to Gia, and the Black Hand was in disarray. Ansel had shared what he'd witnessed, that the amnesty Gia had negotiated with the BEE was apparently ended.

"You got Gia killed," Valentina said, limping around. "Goddamn you, Ansel. You hide with your Bureau pals for years and the moment you get out, they kill Gia."

Ansel was in no mood to deal with Valentina.

"They weren't my pals," Ansel said. "I was practically a prisoner."

"You hid from your own family, *Vigliacco*," Valentina said, eyes flashing. "Gia loved you, always favored you. And you repaid her with, what? Disregard. Disrespect."

They glared at each other.

"I'm taking over," Valentina said. "I'm in charge of the family, now."

"My little sister," Ansel said. "I don't think so."

Valentina sneered at him.

"What, do you think you could lead this family?" Valentina asked. "No one would follow you, Ansel."

He was restraining himself because he wanted to kill Valentina.

"You killed Polly," Ansel said.

"Oh, that," Valentina said, rolling her eyes.

"Don't make light of it," Ansel said, stepping for her. But the other Rupinos got between Ansel and his sister. They glowered at each other for a long moment.

"She wasn't right for you," Valentina said. "Gia explained that to you, right? Before you got her killed? You led those drones right to her."

"No," Ansel said. "We didn't do that. We were careful."

"Not careful enough," Valentina said, tears in her eyes. It should have been something close to a happy homecoming, but it was anything but. Ansel ruined everything. "First things first. Anybody want to challenge me for the top spot of the family?"

Nobody in the room spoke up, except, of course, for Ansel.

"I don't accept it," Ansel said.

"Hah," Valentina said. "Of course you wouldn't. Do you think you could take me, *Cucciolo?*"

"Don't call me that," Ansel said.

He could see the rest of them watching him, wondering what he'd do. By Trueborn right, Valentina could be challenged for the alpha spot, and they'd fight for it. But he didn't want to fight his little sister, even after what she'd done to Polly. As wounded as she was, he felt like he couldn't do it in good conscience.

Valentina glared hard at him, holding herself steady despite her healing legs, her wounded limbs.

"Look, Bro, do you want to go or no?" Valentina said. "Lead, follow, or get out of the way. Don't pretend you even want to run this family, Ansel. If you gave a fuck about this family, you wouldn't have hidden with the BEE. You abandoned us. Got yourself that *Infettiva* girlfriend."

"I won't challenge you on one condition," Ansel said. "You let me claim Sloane as my daughter, and let me raise her on my own, away from all of your family bullshit."

"Ha," Valentina said. "No deal. Maybe you favor that daughter, but you owe us children, Ansel. All Gia wanted was for you to settle down and do your part. Gianna, Alessia, Carlotta? Those were three Gia had in mind for you. Pick one, pick all. I don't care. But deliver for us."

"No way," Ansel said. "I'm not doing that."

"Alright," Valentina said, raising a hand. "You claim your little daughter. But if you refuse to do your part by us, you're dead to us. On your own. You do that, I'll leave you the fuck alone, Ansel. We all will. Just what you've always wanted."

Mia, Sia, and Bria looked unhappy at that prospect.

"I don't want that, either," Ansel said. "I want to avenge Gia and our cousins. I want to kill Bastion and take out the BEE. The rest can wait."

Valentina pursed her lips and looked on scornfully at Ansel.

"You know, it's a good thing I killed Black Sheep," Valentina said. "Because you're the true Black Sheep of our family, Ansel. The never-ending disappointment, the *Pecora Nera.*"

"Somebody get me some paper," Ansel said. "I was on that fucking ship for eight years. You want to get revenge on the BEE? I can map the ship out for you. At least the parts I saw."

Valentina snapped her fingers and somebody provided a notepad. Ansel cursed, tossing it aside.

"I'll find something bigger," he said. "I'll draw something up for you. Would that help?"

"Sure," Valentina said, suspiciously.

Ansel rooted around the place and found some sheets of paper, drew out the map of the *Argent,* his painter's hands rendering the sketch skillfully, while the others looked on.

"You *can* draw," Valentina said. "I'll give you that. You always could. Drawing blood would be better."

"I'm going to kill Bastion," Ansel said. "That son of a bitch killed Gia."

"Whoa," Valentina said. "Whoa, whoa, whoa. That's for us to do. Not you."

"I'm doing it," Ansel said. "Fucker has it coming. You weren't there."

They watched him sketch it out in detail. Ansel indeed hadn't seen all of the ship, but he'd seen the Pens and the Pound, and they'd walked him around the ship under supervision often enough that he'd seen what he thought was nearly all of it.

"We should have two teams," Valentina said. "One for Bastion, one for Minton and his people on the *Argent.*"

"Not all of the people," Ansel said. "Just Minton. Maybe the drone pilots, too. You're better off trying to sink the *Argent,* versus trying to sneak aboard her."

Valentina shook her head.

"Blood for blood," she said. "They have to pay. All of them."

"Bastion might be an easier target," Ansel said.

"But the BEE sent the drones," Valentina said.

Ansel tossed aside the pencil, let the others study the map. Ansel told them what he knew, what was where, who was where.

"Okay, you want to play the Boss," Ansel said. "You decide which you go after."

"Minton," Valentina said. "We take him out first. Then we get that East Coast trash cut to pieces and sent back to his people in a pretty box. First we go after Minton and his drones on that goddamned ship.

Furies, you'll free the Lupines they're keeping there. And we'll turn that place into a ghost ship. Then we scuttle that fucker."

The vehemence of her tone was pronounced, and Ansel could see hints of Gia in her. The last time they'd seen each other, she'd only just turned eighteen.

"Are we agreed?" Valentina said. "Tomorrow night, Minton dies."

"Fine by me," Ansel said. "Assuming we know where he's at. Only I think the BEE's drones are the bigger problem. They shot silver bullets down on Gia and the others. If Minton deploys them around the *Argent,* we're going to have trouble."

Valentina wasn't troubled by this.

"Giuseppe, Alonzo," Valentina said to their cousins. They were young men, mid-20s, strong and fierce. "You two cause a distraction somewhere. I don't care where. Just make it distracting. Something that'll get the BEE people swarming. Something for their drones to fixate on."

"We will," Alonzo said, nodding. "I have some ideas."

"We don't even know if we can get to that ship," Ansel said. "It's heavily protected."

"Oh, I'm not worried about it," Valentina said. "I don't care about that. We're avenging Gia, and there's no price one can put on that. First the BEE, then Bastion. He lives downtown in his high-rise, in the penthouse of the Bastion Industrial Architecture Building, thinks he's unreachable. Gia told me all about it. Everybody get some rest. We're going to tear that place apart and hang those Bastion fuckers from lampposts. For Gia."

"For Gia," the Rupinos said, shouting. Ansel murmured it, and Valentina sat down and took oaths of allegiance from the other members of the pack once it was clear that none of them were challenging her. One by one, they paid their respects, with Ansel last. Valentina's eyes were on him the entire time.

"I'm disappointed, *Cucciolo,*" Valentina said. "You didn't challenge me. I was sure you would, to avenge your Polly. She died fighting. I mean, if that brings you any comfort. No groveling, which surprises me, because she seemed like the type who'd plead for her life. Then again, you know how it is with *Infettivi*—sometimes they find strength they never had in life. Her other half was her better half if you ask me."

"Are you trying to provoke me?" Ansel asked.

"She just wasn't right for you," Valentina said. "One child. Not a pack, like we need. One and done. She fought hard. She was fast for an *Infettiva.*"

"I know," Ansel said. "I'd fought beside her."

"Oh, right," Valentina said. She held her hand out for Ansel to kiss, like she was a queen. "How about it, Bro? Are we still family?"

"I thought you were casting me out," Ansel said.

"Just words," Valentina said. "Blood matters more than words. Besides, Mia, Sia, and Bria would never forgive me if I cast you out. They love you. I love you, too. I just wish you weren't so damned reluctant to be part of our family."

"Where are my brothers?" Ansel asked. "Seems like they should be here, too."

"They're trying to track this creepy Créche thing the Wolves of God made," Valentina said. "Someplace down in the Deep South."

Ansel was sad that Giovanni, Marco, and Lorenzo weren't here. He would have been more comfortable avenging Gia with the three of them with him. He missed them all. Being with his family brought things back for him.

Valentina's hand stayed out there for Ansel to kiss, for him to swear allegiance. He remembered doing that with Gia when he'd been the age of the Furies. It had felt a lifetime ago, and then he realized that it was.

"Come on, Ansel," Valentina said. "Don't mourn your lost *Infetti-va*. She, you know, died well. It's all we can ever ask for in this world."

"She deserved better than she got," Ansel said.

"We all do," Valentina said. "In this world, you only get what you take."

He wanted to avenge Polly, even as he knew that she never would have accepted any kind of life in his family. It was so clear to him.

"They hate me," Polly said, in his head. "I don't even know what I did to them."

Valentina's hand hovered in space, and Ansel could see the rest of them watching, waiting.

"For the safety of my daughter," Ansel said. "I do this for her, and her alone. Not for you, not for me."

He kissed the back of her hand, and Valentina smiled broadly at him.

"Call that an oath of allegiance, Bro?" Valentina said. "Repeat after me: may I be torn apart limb from limb if I raise my hand to Valentina. May I rot in everlasting Hell for breaking my oath to her."

Ansel said it, feeling disgust with himself for saying it. He could swear he saw Polly in the shadows beyond them, looking on. She looked sad, looking lovely as ever, her dark hair slicked back with her own blood. She was dressed in skintight red, until Ansel realized she was garbed only in blood, which pooled after her like a wedding train.

Ansel felt wounded, like he'd betrayed her beyond redemption. It was his fault she'd become an Infective, anyway.

"I'll avenge you," Ansel said.

"You'd better," Valentina said, not realizing who he was really talking to.

SONIA had shared with Mina everything Norm had told her, and the two of them, as well as Sonia's brothers and a very bored Sloane, processed it all.

"It's insidious," Mina said. "Almost pathological in its own right. Bastion's extending the lycanthropic franchise to paying clients. It's like the opposite of the Happening—a completely controlled spreading of the virus."

"We have to stop it," Sonia said. "Somehow."

Mina brooded on it a bit.

"I'm conflicted about it," Mina said. "Lupitol is a good thing. There's no two ways about that. But this whole secret werewolf social club? Terrible thing."

The Poles acknowledged that, sharing some red wine that Sloane wanted to try.

"I miss my Mom," Sloane said. "I miss her very much."

"I'm sorry, Sloane," Mina said. "We're going to take you to your dad."

Sloane looked suspicious.

"I don't know him," Sloane said. "My mom told me stories about him, but that's not the same as knowing him. I can find my mom, I swear. I can find her anywhere."

Mina patted Sloane on her head, which she seemed to welcome.

"It'll be okay," Mina said. "He cares about you very much."

"If he cared, he'd be here," Sloane said. "Where is he?"

"Soon," Mina said. "It's too dangerous right now. The bad people."

Sloane sulked. "I hate the bad people. I hate all the silver in this place. I hate this place."

She folded her arms and the sulk curdled into a full-blown pout. Sonia looked at her for a minute, then at Mina.

"In other news, Norm apparently quit the Hive," she said. "He's a free agent."

"Wow," Mina said. "What brought that on?"

Sonia told her about his experience at Navy Pier.

"What does that mean for us?" Mina asked.

Sonia drank her red wine and set the glass down.

"I think it means we should reach out to the Bureau," Sonia said. "They've already been making overtures. So, we take them up on their offer. I'm going to make some calls."

Mina felt herself grow cold at the thought. However much she wanted to be doing research again, the thought of the *Synowie* working with or for the Bureau made her feel unsafe.

"After what they did to Norm? I don't understand," Mina said.

"I'm going to get to the bottom of that," Sonia said. She took out her phone and walked to the other room, Mina following her. Seeing her approach, Sonia made a motion for her to be quiet.

"What are you up to?" Mina asked.

"Director Minton? This is Sonia," she said. "Yes, I was thinking about what we'd discussed. No, I haven't seen Norm recently. Not since our initial rendezvous. Really? Well, that's strange. Why? You can't say. I understand the need for discretion. Wolves of God? Yes, that may have been us. An embroidered handkerchief? Our people are funny that way. Listen, I was wondering if I could visit you on the *Argent*. Yes. I'd just like to see what all the fuss is about. I've talked with my people, and they are amenable to our common interests. Yes. Navy Pier? I can be there in an hour. Nice talking to you, too."

Sonia hung up.

"There," Sonia said. "I'm going to get a tour of the *Argent*. A chance for Minton to show off, and for me to do some reconnaissance."

"I should go with you," Mina said.

Sonia shook her head.

"No," Sonia said. "You should not. You need to stay with Sloane and wait for my call."

Mina felt afraid for Sonia.

"If you go out on the ship, you're at Minton's mercy," Mina said.

"Dr. Milkowski, I have nothing to fear from the BEE," Sonia said. "I'm only human, after all. You stay put here, try to stay out of trouble, and I'll call you when I need you. In the meantime, I have to make some other calls."

"Other calls?" Mina asked.

"Yes," Sonia said, nodding to her and going to the other room, closing the door. Sloane watched her go.

"Silvery secrets," Sloane said, a finger to her lips. She giggled. Mina smiled, unsure what to think.

The boat came promptly for Sonia, manned by BEE agents in their black and yellow jackets. This late in the year, the lake was getting choppier and the wind was blustery close to shore. Sonia had worn a black wool peacoat and a black fur hat. She didn't wear her ski mask this time.

"Ma'am, I'm Reginald Jones," the young black man said. "I'm skipper of this boat. My men there are Lou Green and Don Watson. We'll get you to the *Argent* safe and sound."

"Safe AND sound," Sonia said, smiling as she boarded the boat. "What more could I ask for?"

They let her into the warm cabin as the boat surged out onto the water.

"Gonna be a bit rough, but we're glad to have you," Jones said.

She texted Norm circumspectly on the new burner line he'd told her he was using.

GOING TO SEE TM.

Norm didn't hesitate.

WHAT? WHY?

DON'T WORRY WHY. JUST KNOW THAT I AM. YOU DO YOU. I'LL BE FINE. SG OUT.

Sonia didn't want to give anyone too much information if they were listening, so she muted her phone and deleted the messages, just in case.

The chop in the water was pronounced, but the BEE boat was able to navigate it readily and got them to the *Argent* in a half hour.

The big ship bobbed in the waves, and Sonia found herself relieved to be aboard the larger vessel, even getting screened by the BEE agents aboard to determine her humanity.

"Weapons, Ms. Gorski?" the female BEE agent asked. She was young and dusty blonde, with freckles across the bridge of her nose.

Sonia handed over her pistol and silencer, as well as her silver dagger. The agent took them and handed Sonia a yellow chit.

"You can reclaim them when you leave," the agent said.

"But I've only just arrived," Sonia said. "Where's the Director?"

Another BEE agent, a young black woman who introduced herself as Tiff Wilson, was there to greet her.

"I'll take you to him," Tiff said. "Nice to meet you, Ms. Gorski."

Sonia followed the petite Tiff Wilson, grateful to end up indoors, away from the chilly, turbulent air.

Minton's office was nicely appointed, wood-paneled and pleasant-smelling, like oranges and cloves. Director Minton got up and Sonia shook his hand.

"Ms. Gorski," Minton said. "So glad you reached out to us. Please, have a seat."

She could see the big screens in his office, monitoring Lupine activity. One screen showed a digital national map, the other was connected to a local news feed.

"Can I get you something? Coffee? Tea?"

"Coffee would be wonderful," Sonia said. "I can't fathom how you all live out here this way."

Minton nodded, smiling.

"It's not easy," Minton said. "But it's necessary."

"Do you leave the ship out here all winter?" Sonia asked.

"We move around sometimes," Minton said. "If the lake freezes over, we have to get farther out. We resupply annually, have a proper shore leave for the team for a month. That's a whole process."

After the coffee arrived, Minton got to business.

"Am I to believe the *Synowie* are considering our offer?" Minton asked.

"I don't speak for all of the *Synowie*," Sonia said. "But with the news of late branding us as terrorists, you can be certain we are angry about that."

Minton sipped his own cup of coffee, shrugged.

"I wouldn't worry about that," Minton said. "We can put the appropriate clearances and exemptions in place for that."

"It's a stain on our reputation," Sonia said. "To be outed that way. And undeservedly. We didn't kidnap Ms. Stockwell."

Minton listened to her, nodding.

"But you helped Norm," Minton said. "Accessories after the fact. Like I said, don't worry about that. Norm's really messed up. He's been in the field too long. I've seen it happen to field agents. It wears you down. Especially with Lupines."

"You look tired, Director Minton," Sonia said.

"Please, call me Troy," Minton said. "The work is demanding. But we're honestly nearing the end of it."

"I have it on good authority that your drones were hunting Lupines the other night," Sonia said. "Rupino Lupines."

"Yes," Minton said. "Things have changed. I'm not really at liberty to discuss that in detail, you understand."

"Completely," Sonia said. "Still, it's strange. Given how much you worked with them over the years."

"Can you get the rest of the *Synowie* on board with working with the Bureau?" Minton asked. "That would be a big plus from where I'm sitting."

Sonia shrugged and nursed her coffee.

"That remains to be seen," Sonia said. "We're a very independent bunch."

There came a knock on the door, and Sonia saw a tall, attractive woman in a white lab coat emblazoned with a BEE patch.

"Ah, Dr. Holloway," Minton said. "Vanessa, this is Sonia Gorski. Sonia, this is Dr. Vanessa Holloway."

Sonia stood and the two women shook hands. Vanessa looked to be roughly Sonia's age.

"Sonia's considering our offer of collaboration," Minton said. "She's *Synowie*."

"That's wonderful," Holloway said. "You're going to give her the tour, aren't you, Troy?"

"Of course," Minton said. "I think you'll be impressed by our facilities, Sonia."

They walked Sonia throughout the ship, touring the Pens, while Dr. Holloway spoke of the ongoing research they did. The Infectives in their cells watched them forlornly. They were a mix of people of every race and age and looked to be well cared for.

"What will happen to these people?" Sonia asked.

"Some will end up at the Wolf Island facility," Minton said. "Others will be sent to the CDC in Atlanta for further study."

"We don't just kill Lupines, the way you do," Holloway said. "We study them. Lycanthropy really is a fascinating area of study. I'm always learning something new. Such incredible creatures."

"Do you know Dr. Mina Milkowski?" Sonia asked. At mention of her, she saw Minton privately react.

"Yes," Minton said. "She was one of the unfortunates at the Kennel during the attack by Zooey Hummel in '07. Terrible business. She was one of our lead researchers before Vanessa arrived."

"What would you say if I could deliver her to you?" Sonia asked.

"You know where she is?" Minton asked. "She's been missing for eight years."

"We thought maybe she'd died," Holloway said. "Mina's research was pivotal for the Bureau and the CDC in those hectic early years."

"I may know people who can find her," Sonia said.

"We'd very much like to get her back," Minton said. "That would be greatly appreciated by the Bureau, Ms. Gorski."

"Still," Sonia said. "Given that you turned your backs on the Rupinos, I can only wonder if or when you'd do that to us."

Minton cleared his throat and Sonia saw him glance at Holloway.

"Big difference," Minton said. "You're human. First and foremost, the BEE allies with human beings. We forged an alliance of convenience with the Rupinos. We never lost sight of who—and what—they were."

"What about Chad Bastion?" Sonia asked. "He's a Lupine, too."

"Yes," Minton said. "Of course he is. But he's been far more helpful to us, to be honest, in putting an end to the Happening."

"The Lupitol," Sonia said. "The drug, yes?"

Minton nodded, and Holloway spoke up.

"It's been amazing," Holloway said. "The results have been impressive. So long as Infectives remain on Lupitol, they can keep unanticipated attacks at bay."

"Impressive," Sonia said.

They walked to the end of the Pens, where Sonia noted a high security door that was guarded by three BEE Operations men carrying assault rifles. The door said ABSOLUTELY NO ENTRY WITHOUT CLEARANCE.

"My, what is that?" Sonia asked. "Is that where Ansel Rupino is kept?"

"No," Minton said. "We actually released Ansel Rupino several days ago."

"Oh, that's a pity," Sonia said. "I would have loved to have seen him."

Holloway brightened at the mention of him.

"He was an interesting subject," Holloway said. "The only Trueborn we had on-site for years."

"So, what's behind that door?" Sonia asked.

"It's our high-security vault," Minton said. "For the most dangerous subjects."

"Like vampires?" Sonia asked.

Minton laughed.

"Yes," Minton said. "Like vampires."

"Can I see?" Sonia said.

"I'm afraid not," Minton said. "It's ultra-high security."

"And occupied?" Sonia said. "You have vampires in there?"

"I'm not at liberty to discuss that, unfortunately," Minton said. "Let's take you to our research library. I imagine you'd find that interesting."

"Absolutely," Sonia said. "But let me contact my people. I can bring you Dr. Milkowski."

"Yes, please do that," Minton said.

"Viktor, Sonia," Sonia said. "What we discussed, yes? Bring Dr. Milkowski. Get the boat ready. Put her on and get her to the ship I told you about. Be quick about it. Yes, I'm aboard. I'm talking to the Director right now. Yes, I will."

Sonia hung up, deleting the call log from her phone.

"Viktor gives you their regards," Sonia said.

"I can't say enough how appreciative I am of this," Minton said. "We'll send a skiff out to make the pickup."

"Not necessary," Sonia said. "We've got a boat we're sending."

"I'll have to notify my people," Minton said. "I don't want anybody on watch blowing her out of the water."

"No," Sonia said. "We can't have that."

"Dr. Holloway, can you take Sonia up to the main meeting room while I deal with this?" Minton asked.

"Of course, Director," Holloway said. "This way, Ms. Gorski."

The meeting room was very lovely, being a long wooden table with a bowed set of windows that offered a great view across the *Argent*. The lake was a sea of grey interspersed with whitecaps.

"She really is a lovely ship," Sonia said.

"We're very lucky to have her," Holloway said. "Although I must tell you I cannot wait to get back to Atlanta. It can be claustrophobic being on a ship as long as I have been."

"I imagine," Sonia said, pacing in front of the windows. The sun was obscured by clouds, which muted what illumination it provided, made the lake look particularly foreboding.

"I have to know: why did you ask about the vampires?" Holloway asked.

"Professional curiosity," Sonia said. "The Bureau doesn't only deal in werewolves, does it?"

"No," Holloway said. "Still, it was a curious thing to ask."

"I'm a curious woman," Sonia said. "Although not a researcher like yourself."

Holloway smiled coolly.

"You're a librarian, aren't you?" Holloway asked. "I heard a rumor that you were."

"Yes," Sonia said.

"That's kind of like a researcher," Holloway. "I suppose."

Sonia smiled at the snobbishness of Dr. Holloway. She was used to it.

"Do you know what my people call me?"

"What do they call you?" Holloway asked.

"They call me *'Zabójczy bibliotekarz'*," Sonia said.

Holloway smiled uncertainly.

"That sounds like a mouthful," Holloway said.

"It means 'Killer Librarian,'" Sonia said. "Funny, yes?"

Holloway laughed uncomfortably. Sonia could see that she was not used to making conversation like this. She was used to examining and interrogating her patients from their cells.

"It's a jarring image," Holloway said. "You don't seem like a killer."

"We never do," Sonia said. "That's why we're so good at what we do."

Holloway glanced at her phone.

"I don't know what's keeping Troy," she said. "I'm supposed to stay with you."

"Keep me out of trouble?" Sonia said. "That's the thing about trouble. Sometimes the trouble finds you."

7

NORM had driven the Warg van around town, stopping in a parking deck that was a stone's throw from the Bastion Industrial Architecture Building, which dominated the real estate for a city block.

He'd gotten Sonia's text, wondered what she was up to on the *Argent*. He wanted to ask but didn't want the Archon program to get her into trouble. He had tried dialing Gia again, had only gotten her voicemail. Something happened to her. She'd disappeared, which made Norm think that the BEE had somehow gotten her, although he had no way of knowing that for sure.

Instead, he called Anne.

"Babe," Anne said. "I'm glad you called. Have you thought about what we discussed?"

"Sure," Norm said. "I'd like to meet Chad."

"I'll bet you would," Anne said. "Chad's schedule is booked up solid. But you and I can meet. Where are you?"

"I'm near the Bastion Building," Norm said. He wondered if Anne was up there somewhere.

"What are you doing down there?" Anne asked.

"Spying," Norm said. "Obviously."

"Let's meet out front," Anne said. "Please don't do anything crazy, Norm."

"Why does everybody always say that to me?" Norm said. "Let's meet out front."

Norm was packing his Glock 18 and his silver dagger, as well as a .38 snub nose revolver in an ankle holster. He wasn't sure how Bastion's people would play it, but if he were able to get into the building and meet the man, he might be able to make something happen.

He saw Anne emerge from the Bastion Building, standing out in front of it, looking up and down the street.

He dialed her up.

"I see you," Norm said. "I want to see Bastion."

Anne was looking around, trying to spot him.

"He's a very busy and important man, Norm," Anne said.

"You have access," Norm said. "I'm sure he'd make time for his VP of Sales if she requested it. I'll wait while you do that."

Anne must have texted Chad, because she was quiet a few moments, and then spoke up again.

"Come down here, Norm," Anne said. "Let me see you, Babe. Don't be creepy."

"Alright," Norm said. "Be there in a sec."

He hung up and steeled himself, headed down to the street, careful not to get clipped by the traffic that rushed back and forth. Streetside, the Bastion Building looked as formidable and imposing as a mountain.

Anne saw him and held her arms out, flicking her fingers at him to draw him to her. Norm gave her a hug, the two of them embracing.

"Babe, I'm so proud of you," Anne said. "This is the right decision."

"Is it?" Norm said.

"Yes," Anne said. "It's a chance to be part of something larger. Bigger than both of us."

She walked them into the golden glow of the Bastion Building lobby, with all the modernist marble about, and the polished floors bearing a great big L in white with black rays emanating from it, like all points of the compass.

"You're armed, aren't you?" Anne asked quietly.

"Of course I am," Norm said.

"Babe, you need to give me those," Anne said. "I can't bring you in to talk to Chad if you're armed."

They went to the elevator banks and she called one of the elevators. She held out her big dusty lemon-colored handbag. Norm slipped his Glock 18 and dagger into the bag. Anne watched him do that, kept the bag open.

"And the holdout pistol," Anne said. "I know you, Babe."

The elevator opened, and Anne went in, urging Norm to follow. They went into the beautiful mirrored and wood-paneled elevator, and Anne used her executive keycard to access the penthouse.

"You know me so well," Norm said, fishing out the pistol and carefully setting it in her bag.

"Good boy," Anne said. "Babe, this is the best decision you could have possibly made. The whole world will open for you."

The elevator went up and up.

When the doors opened, there were three Liminalix security guys in suits, who patted Norm down. They were young men, strong and capable. Norm wondered if they were Infectives or norms like him. He really couldn't tell. Maybe they were on Lupitol.

The main foyer to the penthouse was a beautiful synthesis of cream-colored stone and well-polished dark wood that threw off a pleasant scent.

"This way, Ms. Stockwell," one of the men said. "Mr. Bastion is in the Vista Room."

"Perfect," Anne said. "Thank you, Dexter."

The Vista Room was a splendor—it was a lengthy room with lovely green sofas and coffee tables, gallery walls of art, and windows aplenty that offered a dazzling view of the city.

Seated in a deep green leather overstuffed chair was Chad Bastion, looking immaculate in a crimson sweater and grey slacks and black loafers. He was tanned and handsome, a man completely at ease in his surroundings. His sandy hair was cut short, and he radiated professional polish and corporate charisma.

"Norm Stockwell," Bastion said, shaking Norm's hand. "I'm glad we finally get to meet like this. Anne's told me absolutely everything about you."

"Gosh, I hope not," Norm said, sitting down across from Chad. Anne sat near Chad, in one of the other chairs.

"She told you about the Gift," Bastion said.

"She did," Norm said. Bastion smiled.

"Great," Bastion said. "I hope you appreciate her going out on a limb like this for you. I don't extend the Gift to just anyone, Norm. But you're important to Anne. And Anne's important to me."

"Thanks, Mr. Bastion," Norm said.

"Please, call me Chad," Bastion said. "You've amassed quite a track record. Including my own people."

Norm was going to say something, but Bastion stopped him.

"No need to explain," Bastion said. "I understand it. Were I in that situation, I'd probably do the same thing. I warned Todd about putting himself out there. I try to keep my top people in the Bastion Building with me. It's safe, here."

"Seems like it," Norm said.

"Todd was always a maverick type of guy," Bastion said. "You showed him the error of his ways. Ordinarily, I'd be pissed about that. But I'd made such headway with your boss—sorry, former boss—I let it slide. Again, you have Anne to thank for that. She talked me into not killing you. She really cares about you, Norm."

"Yeah, she does," Norm said. "I'm very lucky."

"This is a good time to get into the program, Norm," Bastion said. "We're diversifying, pulling in politicians, various heads of industry, military. I've got a program where we're going to be serving up lycanthropes in Iraq and Afghanistan. Can you imagine how they'll deal with that? All those crazy terrorist types out there, being hunted down by lycanthrope soldiers? It's all too good. Turns out, the government doesn't really care about Lupines, if they can put them to work for them. They're just another asset. I talked Minton around on it, let him see where the future was."

"Very thoughtful of you," Norm said.

Bastion laughed.

"You know, seeing you right here in front of me, you don't seem like a killer," Bastion said. "Everybody talks about what a killer you are, but I don't see it. You're just a dude."

"They never see it coming," Norm said. "I suppose I'm an ambush predator."

"Ha," Bastion said. "That's what I am, too, I think. I set traps for my traps. How meta is that? You want a drink, Norm? Anne?"

"Yes, please," Anne said.

"Sure," Norm said. Bastion got up and walked over to one of his wood-paneled walls and opened it, revealing a fully stocked bar.

"You seem like a scotch guy to me, Norm," Bastion said.

"Whiskey neat is fine," Norm said. "Whatever you have."

"I have everything," Bastion said. "Anne, you want a martini?"

"Yes, please," Anne said. She slid her handbag toward Norm, while Bastion's back was turned. Norm noticed, of course.

"Take it, Norm," Bastion said, not turning around. "You think I can't smell the silver? I could smell it when you came in. I'd like to see how much of a killer you really are."

He turned and gave Anne her martini and Norm his whiskey. Norm took it uneasily, unsure what to make of this.

"He's confused, Anne," Bastion said. "You confused him. Norm, do you think I'd let Anne come in with all of your toys if I was remotely concerned about them? You have no idea what you're dealing with."

Bastion took his seat across from Norm again. His confidence was terrifying, something Norm had never encountered before. He was used to fretful Infectives, not a cocksure Trueborn.

"Anne brought you up to speed, so I'm not going to go through all of that," Bastion said. "You already know. But my clan has wanted to oust the Rupinos out of the Midwest for decades. Killer clan, killer reputation. I'll give them that. The Rupinos play for keeps. But Gia and the rest, they're stuck in the past. They don't understand where the future is. Even a Lupine underground is just that. It's an underground. I want to get people used to their own monstrosity, to embrace it. We've got people lined up for the next presidential election, you won't believe how ready they are for it. The bloodthirstiness, all of it. Right there for the taking. I'm there for them."

Norm drank the whiskey, which was wonderful.

"Mobilize the norms," Bastion said. "They'll never be us, but they'll *want* to be us. And we'll show them how to be. We'll guide them. You're just a guy, Norm. A regular guy. And even with the Gift, that's only entry-level. That's not the end of the journey. It's the start."

"Is that right?" Norm asked.

"That's right," Bastion said. "What'd you think? Killing me would stop what's in motion? I have systems in place. You know why those *Synowie* pricks are so insane? They think they can stop us. They've been fighting us for centuries, and they still haven't eradicated us. Systems, Norm."

Norm set down the empty whiskey glass on the coffee table in front of them, wiped his hands on his pants.

"You going to do something, Norm?" Bastion said. "You going to stop me?"

Norm was angry at Bastion's blithe bravado. He was monstrosity incarnate. Bastion smiled, watching Norm work through it.

"I *love* norms, Norm," Bastion said. "You're so damned small. But your entire worldview requires thinking that you're not mundane. I respect your service in Afghanistan. I even respect your work in the Bureau. But it's just that. Small stuff. You are a little loose screw inside a massive machine. Whereas I'm the machine. Or I'm the guy who owns the machine."

"See, Norm?" Anne said. "Chad's a force of nature."

"No," Bastion said. "I'm *supernatural*, Anne. I'm above Nature."

THE commercial fishing boat pulled up to the *Argent,* while Minton, Sonia, and Dr. Holloway looked on from the meeting room. They had put on their cold weather gear, and were preparing to step outside

"I can't thank you enough for helping us in this Mina matter, Sonia," Minton said. "I'm a stickler for closure, and she was a loose end that just nagged at me."

"Glad I could help," Sonia said.

"Let's go, then," Minton said, ushering her forward. She and Dr. Holloway went forth through an outside portal, into the bracing November air.

The fishing boat, the *Aqua Vitae,* had slipped a few hundred feet alongside the *Argent,* the two ships bobbing forcefully in the surging water.

A covered skiff was lowered from the side and was motoring over to the *Argent* while Sonia and the others waited.

"When we get her aboard, I want you to get her to one of our debriefing rooms, Dr. Holloway," Minton said.

"I will, Director," Holloway said, eyeing Sonia.

The BEE agents had manned a hoist which they would use to get Dr. Milkowski over to the *Argent* safely. They readied it as the boat got within reach of the *Argent.*

The hoist was lowered, and Mina emerged from the covered skiff, wearing a parka and a hood and scarf. She fumbled for the hoist on the choppy surf. It took a few times for her to get it, to get her foot in the loops to allow them to pull her up.

As she went up, Sonia looked on, gripping the railing for steadiness. She hoped Mina would forgive her for this.

All at once, three black shapes burst from the covered skiff, clearing the distance in seconds. They were grandly monstrous, startling the BEE agents before they could react.

Fortunately, the turret defenses responded faster. The three shapes were airborne when the rotary barrel autocannons whirled and fired upon them, splattering the Lupines in the air, sending their bloodied bodies back the way they'd come.

The deck guns on the *Argent* turned to the skiff and fired, the autocannons blazing as they sent high-velocity silver bullets streaming into the skiff. Lupines aboard the skiff howled and cried out as they were cut down even as they fought to board the *Argent*.

Minton watched the slaughter grimly from the deck, while Sonia ran to one of the BEE duty officers, who was trying to bring his carbine to bear on the charging Lupines. She stomped on the man's instep, punched him in the face while he tried to compose himself.

Mina hung on the hoist line, looking on, stunned.

Sonia grabbed the carbine from the duty officer, caught him on the chin with the butt of the rifle.

The initial boarding of the Lupines had already been thwarted by the fire of the autocannons, which had already scuttled the skiff. The *Aqua Vitae* was trying to steam away, but Minton was barking orders on his radio over the roar of the deck guns.

"Fire up the engines, chase down that ship," Minton said.

Mina hopped off the hoist and landed on the deck, throwing off her hood and scarf, revealing herself. Minton cursed at the sight of her.

"Valentina Rupino?" Minton said.

"You double-dealing *Synowie* turncoat," Valentina said, glaring at Sonia. "I warned you."

She transformed in front of them in moments, shredding her cold weather coat and running for both Minton and Sonia, her face a vision of hateful rage as she gripped the deck with her lengthening claws.

"You're both dead," Valentina said. "I hope you're ready."

"I'm ready," Sonia said.

She shot Valentina in the head with the carbine, dropping her in a moment. Valentina fell to the deck, choking on her own blood.

"*Srebra*," Valentina managed to say, struggling to rise, looking up at Sonia with blood-red eyes.

Sonia raised the carbine for another shot, and took it without hesitation, catching Valentina in the forehead. Dr. Holloway gasped, her hands to her mouth.

Minton looked on, shocked, despite himself, as Valentina shuddered and died, turning back to her human form, while blood flowed on the deck from her ruined head, her gaping eyes staring sightlessly at the deck.

"Christ," Minton said.

"Belowdecks, Director," Sonia said, guiding him along with the carbine. "I just saved your life. You owe me this."

———

Sonia hadn't relished reaching out to Valentina, but she figured it was the best move she could make under the circumstances. The BEE wanted to hold the Rupinos accountable for the massacre at Trotter Field. Valentina had been one of the prime perpetrators of it, so Sonia had made arrangements with Minton to bring her to the *Argent* under the pretense of staging an ambush by the Rupinos to avenge Gia. She would deliver herself to the BEE that way. Valentina had been terribly amused by it.

"Wait, wait, wait," Valentina said. "So, you crazy *Synowie* have gotten yourselves a ticket to the *Argent* and you're wanting us to come along?"

"Minton will never suspect," Sonia said. "I'm human. Not one of you. He'll accept it. He already wants to deal with us."

Valentina laughed.

"Why would you stick it to Minton?" Valentina asked. "What's he done to you?"

"They've branded the *Synowie* terrorists," Sonia said. "That doesn't sit well with me."

"It's hilarious," Valentina said. "*Synowie* allying with us Rupinos to stick it to the BEE? Definitely can't say I saw that one coming."

Sonia had smiled as she talked to Valentina.

"In trade, send your Furies and Ansel to watch the Bastion Building," Sonia said. "Norm is going there. He'll need help against Bastion."

"You want the Furies to help out Stockwell?" Valentina asked. "My Furies?"

"Yes," Sonia said. "And Ansel."

"But I want Bastion," Valentina said. "Right after Minton."

"The best way to make sure that happens is to have your Furies there, to ensure that Norm doesn't kill Bastion," Sonia said. "Two attacks at once. They won't be ready for that."

Valentina considered it.

"Alright, yeah," Valentina said. "I see your loopy logic. The Furies and Ansel will keep Bastion on ice for me when I arrive. After taking out Minton. I see it."

"Perfect," Sonia said. "Do we have an understanding?"

"Yes," Valentina said. "You're fucking insane, but I love it. Hell, yes. I'm the head of the clan, now, and what I say goes. I say we go for it. But just know that if this is some kind of setup, you're dead, your family's dead, everybody you know and love is dead."

Sonia bit her lip.

"I understand that," Sonia said.

"Good, because that's what'll happen," Valentina said. "Everybody dead. There won't be a rock you could hide beneath."

"I know how thorough your people are," Sonia said. "And how long your memories are."

Valentina chuckled.

"Just wanted to make sure we had an understanding," Valentina said.

"I understand exactly who and what you are," Sonia said.

———

For her, it was a matter of survival for the *Synowie*. If that meant betraying the Rupinos to prove her value to the BEE and keep Bastion from taking them out, so be it. War made for bizarre bedfellows.

The general alarm sounded as the *Argent* chased down the *Aqua Vitae*, bringing her in range of her deck guns. The guns fired, buzzing like bees as they perforated the fishing boat and the remaining Lupines who were aboard her. The percussive sound of the shells striking the *Aqua Vitae* sounded like mad drums.

Minton stared down the carbine and shook his head at Sonia.

"Belowdecks? Not a chance," Minton said. "You don't have the clearance for that room."

Sonia cursed, but Minton had directed BEE agents to disarm Sonia, taking away the carbine. She was unwilling to shoot down the human agents. Even Sonia had her limits.

"Valentina would have killed you."

"Sure," Minton said. "You have my gratitude."

"For what that's worth," Sonia said, watching the *Aqua Vitae* begin to sink, having been shot full of holes by the *Argent*. Any remaining Lupines were shot as they tried to swim for it. In no time at all, the wavy water around the two ships was full of blood and bodies.

"It's worth more than you could possible know," Minton said.

"I have to make a call," Sonia said, dialing Norm up. She went to his voicemail. "Ghost, this is Parker. I'm on the silver ship. I need you to call me as soon as you get this."

Minton looked at her, rolling his eyes.

"Who's 'Ghost'?" Minton asked.

"Nobody you'd know," Sonia said. *"Synowie* stuff."

She pocketed her phone, watching the *Aqua Vitae* sink. Their ears still rang from the firing of the deck guns, and the fishing boat burned even as it sank.

"We're going to take the *Argent* out of there," Minton said. "We're going to Wolf Island before any this catches up to us. I figure it'll be easier to explain to my superiors when I'm in international waters. I'll start by getting us to the Canadian side of the Great Lakes and work our way out from there."

"I'm going to need every bit of help I can get," Sonia said. She doubted she'd ever live this down. The Black Hand would come for her for her role in that bloody night. She resolved that she would be ready for them when they did.

NORM'S phone buzzed almost the same time as Bastion's did. Norm didn't answer his, while Bastion picked his up.

Bastion listened, his face unreadable. Norm went for Anne's handbag, pulling out his Glock 18, while Bastion hung up.

"Well, Norm," Bastion said. "Looks like your were-friends were busy. Somebody attacked the *Argent*. The Rupinos, by the sound of it. It didn't go well for them, apparently."

"I don't know anything about it," Norm said, pointing the pistol at Bastion, who just smiled. His teeth were fanged, Norm noticed.

"Ah, you went for it," Bastion said. "I was hoping you would. Take your best shot."

Norm fired without hesitation. But, to his amazement, when his pistol fired, Bastion was no longer there. He'd simply zipped out of the way with a preternatural speed. He'd never seen a Lupine move so quickly.

"See? Too slow," Bastion said. Bastion's bodyguards ran in, but Bastion shooed them away. "I've got this. You have to shoot straighter, Norm."

Norm went to fire again, a burst this time, but Bastion appeared in front of him and knocked the pistol out of his hands. It went skittering across the floor. Norm's hand stung where he'd struck him.

"How?" Norm asked.

"Magic," Bastion said. "Next stage, like I told you. Lycanthropy is only the beginning."

He swung at Norm faster than he could see, and Norm went flying across the room, his head ringing. The strength Bastion possessed was incredible, especially in his human form.

"You don't see it, Norm?" Bastion said, zipping right in front of him, grabbing him. He tossed Norm again, Norm landing on a mammoth Persian rug that adorned the room and somewhat breaking his fall.

"I'm not just a werewolf," Bastion said. "Not anymore. I'm getting made."

"Made?" Norm asked. He glanced at Anne, who was watching the exchange with grave concern as Bastion struck Norm a couple of times with the back of his hand, knocking Norm to the ground.

"First things first," Bastion said. "A settling of accounts."

"Wait, Chad," Anne said. "I was just taking an opportunity that was presented to me."

"Sure, sure," Bastion said.

"I'm only doing what you would have done," Anne said. "What you do every day."

Bastion reached his arm out and stroked Anne's face.

"I know," Bastion said. "I want my people to be opportunistic. I also want them to be loyal. So, allow me to take the opportunity to show you how I deal with disloyalty."

Bastion grabbed Anne by the arms before she could protest. He hurled her, hard, toward the windows, and Norm saw her smash through them, flying out over the balcony and careening over the side, vanishing from sight with a scream.

Norm cried out and ran in that direction, while Bastion looked on, laughing.

He went out into he cold of the deck and peered over the side. He could hear a car alarm sounding far below. He could see Anne laying there on the ground, a world away, streetside. She'd landed on a car with a crunch, her body splayed on the ruined vehicle.

Bastion appeared beside him, looking over.

"Don't worry, Norm. She'll live," Bastion said, laughing. "But she'll wish she was dead. I mean, it's stupid. She actually thought, what—she'd fire you up and get you to kill me? And she'd take my place at the head of Liminalix?"

Bastion grabbed Norm and leaned him over the railing. Norm felt like a ragdoll in Baston's hands.

"You want to join Anne?" Bastion said. "That can be arranged. I always did like to play with my food. This'll tenderize you just right."

Norm fought to free himself from Bastion's grasp, but he was simply too strong.

"How?" Norm asked.

"Borrowed blood," Bastion said.

"What?"

The shot rang out from across the way, catching Bastion in the forehead. A silver bullet, knocking him to the balcony floor with a startled gasp.

Norm instinctively dropped, although he knew a *Synowie* onlooker had fired the shot. Then he saw the woman, the beautiful woman in black, with her long, thick black hair and big, dark eyes. She'd appeared in Bastion's living room, in a diaphanous dress of black.

And then she appeared beside Bastion, kneeling beside him, without having seemed to move at all.

Her ghost-pale face was plaintive.

"Bastion," she said. "What have they done to you? They've ruined you."

She took a fingernail that was more like a slender claw and dug out the bullet from his fractured skull, prying out the high velocity round and dropping it to the ground beside him. It landed with a metallic clink on the bloody snow beside Bastion's head.

"What the hell?" Norm said, stunned.

Ignoring him, she then bit her wrist with her white-fanged teeth and poured her deep red blood into his mouth, muttering something Norm thought might have been a prayer if he'd not known better. There was nothing holy in that moment, but he saw the wound on Bastion's forehead disappear, healing before his eyes, until it was gone, as if it had never been there.

He looked on in horror as the woman fed Bastion her healing blood.

"Leave us," she said in the quietest of voices, which spoke of a degree of control that Norm could not have possibly imagined. "Or join us. I don't care, Mortal. But do it at once."

Without hesitating, Norm ran out of there, grabbing his pistol and Anne's purse, and didn't look back, afraid of what he might see.

S**ONIA** called Mina, bringing her up to speed about what had happened, and where they could meet up with Ansel and the others. She'd picked a safe place, the lobby of the Landa Library.

Mina had seen on the news about the sinking of the *Aqua Vitae*, which reporters had said was a result of rough water on Lake Michigan. Authorities were investigating the cause of the disaster, and mangled bodies were washing ashore all night. Mina turned off the television and got Sloane ready. The *Argent* had left Lake Michigan, sailing off for parts unknown.

There was also reporting about an unidentified woman hurling herself from a skyscraper downtown, landing on a car, where she was thought to be dead at the scene. However, by the time paramedics had arrived, the woman was said to have fled. It would have been chalked up to Night Fever, but for the damage to the car, which couldn't be denied. That, and the photographs people had taken with their phones.

"Are we meeting my dad?" Sloane asked.

"Yes, Sloane," Mina said.

Mina had gone to the Landa Library with Sonia's brothers as an escort from the silversmith. Outside, the cold city air felt better, and anything was more desirable than being cooped up at that place with all of its silver.

The library felt safe. The scent of old stone and older paper and ink was soothing, and Mina was reminded why she enjoyed working there.

"Minton let me leave," Sonia said. "After saving his life. It's all he was willing to give me."

Norm kept quiet. He was stewing, had been brooding since that dark night in Bastion's tower. Bastion had been on the television that night, saying that some *Synowie* terrorists had attempted to attack him in his home. He looked as handsome and whole as ever.

"What kind of a country is this where a man—a successful man, mind you—can't even be safe in his own penthouse?" Bastion asked in the evening address to the reporters. His ethereally lovely girlfriend, identified as Dawn Trotter, stood close to his side, gazing at the reporters with her big, dark eyes. She wore a black coat and a black *ushanka* hat.

Mina's talk with Sonia brought him back to the moment at hand, and he welcomed the distraction from the memory of what he'd seen in that tower.

"He didn't let you see what was in that high-security area," Mina said.

"No," Sonia said. "He didn't. He wouldn't."

"Typical," Mina said.

Sonia put a hand out on Norm's forearm.

"Are you okay, Norm?" Sonia asked.

He looked at her, his eyes haunted. He hadn't said what had happened up in the penthouse, but Sonia had heard from her brother, Jan, who had fired the shot that dropped Bastion. The woman in black who had appeared. They were certain she was a vampire, and identified her as Dawn Trotter, but Norm wouldn't talk about it.

"I'm fine," Norm said.

Sonia didn't believe him. He didn't look fine.

"You're always welcome with us," Sonia said. "We never forget our friends."

"I'm done," Norm said. "For now."

Ansel approached them alone, his big frame and black wool overcoat making him look even bigger. Seeing him, Sloane smiled.

"You're my dad," Sloane said.

"I am," Ansel said.

"You're tall," Sloane said.

"That, too," Ansel said.

"Does that mean I'll be tall?" Sloane asked.

"If you're lucky," Ansel said.

Mina looked around them nervously. Old habits died hard. Even in the library.

"Where are the others?" Mina asked.

"Valentina's dead," Sonia said. "Shot while trying to attack the *Argent*. Minton had set up an ambush."

Ansel sniffed the air, looked at Sonia a moment. She looked back at him without expression. They all looked tired, and Norm looked more than a little sad.

"There's a future for all of you, if you'll have it," Sonia said. "In the *Synowie.*"

Norm grimaced at the thought.

"I think I've had it for awhile," Norm said.

They chuckled a moment, except for Norm, who was dead serious. Sonia understood, didn't push it.

The Society called it the *Wahanie*—the Hesitation. It was that moment when one's humanity came crashing up against the horrors that one had witnessed. Some never recovered from it. Others did and became *Synowie Srebra* again. She would wait for Norm to come out from under it and would be there for him when he did. He just needed time to heal, and if not to heal completely, to at least recover. There was always more work to be done.

"Who's heading the Rupinos, now?" Sonia asked. Ansel looked at her again, his face unreadable.

"My sisters," Ansel said.

"The Furies?" Sonia asked.

"Yes," Ansel said. "The Clan took a hit over this. They're heading back to Detroit. My brothers, all of that. We've got a bunch of funerals to go to. What happened on the lake wasn't pretty."

"I'm sorry," Mina said.

"Honestly, it goes with the territory, where we're concerned," Ansel said.

"Where were you, anyway?" Sonia asked. "You were supposed to help Norm up there."

Ansel shrugged.

"Sorry about that, Norm," Ansel said. "They didn't let us past the front desk. Bastion had apparently made it very clear that we weren't allowed into the building. My sisters wanted to kill the staff and work our way up, but I held them at bay. Didn't want there to be a scene."

"It's fine," Norm said. "No harm done."

Neither of them believed him when he'd said it.

"We'll find out for certain what happened with Bastion," Sonia said. "Don't you worry about that."

"And that's my cue to leave. Sloane and I are going to Polly's to stay awhile," Ansel said, having picked her up. She looked absurdly small in his arms. "You're all welcome to drop by."

Norm shook his head, while Sonia and Mina exchanged looks and shrugs.

"Bye, Aunt Mina," Sloane said. "Thanks for keeping me out of trouble."

"Any time," Mina said.

"Any time you want to babysit, that's fine by me," Ansel said, as he got into a cab with Sloane and drove out of there.

"Did he even thank us?" Norm asked.

"Nope," Sonia said.

"Such a werewolf move," Norm said, watching them go.

AFTER a grocery store run, Ansel drove Sloane to Polly's place, the scent of her still there, the remembrance of his time there years ago. Her scent was still fresh, and it shook him.

He saw the painting he'd made of her, the portrait, featured in her living room. He was proud of it.

"Mom loves that painting," Sloane said. "Let me show you *my* stuff."

"Lunch, first," Ansel said.

Ansel made her a roast beef sandwich with muenster cheese, lettuce, and tomato, which she eagerly ate.

"Where's the rest of the family?" Sloane asked. "All my aunts and cousins and everybody else?"

"We'll see them eventually," Ansel said. "Not yet."

"Boo," Sloane said, gobbling down her sandwich. She took his hand and guided him to her room, showed him her stuff. She had three scratch pads she drew on, showing pictures of things she loved—her mom, squirrels, the moon, the sun, trees, unicorns, dragons, acorns, steaks.

"You're good at drawing," Ansel said. "These are great, Sloane."

"Thanks," Sloane said. "I like to draw."

Seeing her there, he smiled. Fatherhood wasn't something he'd ever considered, but thought he'd give it a go with Sloane.

"I can teach you how to paint, if you'd like," Ansel said.

"Mom says you're a real painter," Sloane said.

"I am," Ansel said. "I live for it."

"I live for squirrels," Sloane said. "And running. Best things ever. Squirrels get so mad, Dad. The way they shake their tails and squawk. It's funny. Nothing so small should ever be so crabby."

"No?"

Sloane shook her head.

Ansel took her up to the widow's walk, after putting them in warm coats.

"Mom never lets me up here," Sloane said. "But it's cool. I like it. You can see everything from here."

"Yeah," Ansel said.

He'd taken up a canvas and some paints with him, set up an easel as the sunset crept along the horizon, screened by plentiful trees.

"You're really going to paint up here in the cold?" Sloane asked.

"Yeah," Ansel said. "I'll show you how to do it right."

She watched him work, humming as she did so. He found her humming somehow soothing. There was peace here, and peace was enough.

He started painting the sun setting in the tangled trees, thinking that he'd maybe be able to capture the light just right.

EPI
LOGUE

Here's how it happens: she wakes on the frozen grass in a sea of her own steaming blood. Not just hers, but most of it, yes, it's her.

She doesn't know where she is, at least for a moment.

The pain, the strain of it, the memory rushes back like a storm borne on hurricane winds.

A gasp, a grasp, a mournful lamentation of her fate.

She arises on all fours, like a dog, but she's a wolf.

First steps, a kind of crawl.

Make no mistake: she's wounded, and badly.

But there's something else, too: wounds heal.

Even crazy wounds caused by crazy things. Her wounds. The kind an ordinary person would not survive.

And she is far, far from ordinary, at last.

Through it all—the blood, the terror, the slashes, the anger, the everything—she is still herself, and more. She remains who and what she was, despite it all.

Breath comes, puffs of steam, and she scents the air. No sign of Nemesis.

Only herself, padding her way through the darkness. Traffic hums, the sounds in the distance. People sounds.

She hears the howls clearer, now. City howls. Not her people. She has no pack. She finds it in her to run. Incredibly, she runs. Memory fades. There is only motion, and one direction: forward.

Why am I not dead?
She asks herself this, another voice inside her head.
Telling her she should be dead.
The rhyme across the rime
Crunching of the snow beneath her paws
Sidewalk clatter of her claws
There remains only the knowing
Of the way she should be going

On and one she goes, through the pain. As painful as childbirth? Not by a long shot. That's what she tells herself as she goes along.

That was that, and this was this. A different pain, like another flavor. It is something to savor. That's how she gets along. A new experience, to be so wounded.

But not forever. The miracle that she has become won't let her die that way.

Nemesis left too soon, too impatient, too confident, too arrogant. Too much something or other. The words don't come clear to her. Not yet, not yet.

They will, however.

In and out she goes, in terms of memory, like snapshot flashes, a miserable Morse Code of dots and dashes. She sees, she forgets, she remembers. It's like a reunion that never ends, a party that begins and begins again, and the uninvited guests that are her memories never truly leave.

Each day, she gets better.

Each day that she is not dead is a better day than the day before.

This is progress, she tells herself.

Like a crawl that becomes a walk that becomes a jog that becomes a sprint.

She understands, and in that understanding, she heals. She feels. Days go by, and she can't remember everything. Only the things that matter.

She looks upon the wall and finds she is missing. She's not where she should have been. Someone has been there.

She bares her teeth, the violation, the intrusion, the severity of the temerity. Then she takes the scent, and as it always does, it jogs her memory. Her memory jogs, and she returns to what she had left behind.

The words roll back to her, her precious words. Playthings and partners in crime, they blanket her, warm her, soothe her.

"I'm not done with you, yet," she says to no one but herself.

It's enough, that missive.

She knows herself.

Both halves, an even split.

She and she, braided together, not broken or frayed.

Together, forever.

And in that knowing, she finds the strength to keep going.

That's why she cries in the night, a howl, her howl.

No time like the present.

To be present.
To *be* the present.
A late gift could be early, depending on your perspective.
I am the gift that darkens your door by the waning light of the gibbous moon.

She makes her way, the well-worn path, sure-footed.
Knowing where she's going.
The threshold awaits, and she, first-footing, passes through portentously at midnight.

They're there, they're waiting for her.
Somehow, they knew.
Sent by scent, those two.
Like breaths, they drew.
He's painting, and *she's* painting.
They're painting on bone-white canvas, brushes like stilettos, pushing intoxicating red oils across landscapes of their own imaginary worlds.

And he sees her, and *she* sees her.
Their eyes are alight at the sight.
And she cries as they cry out.
Not in horror, but delight.

"Took you long enough," he said, and he smiled.

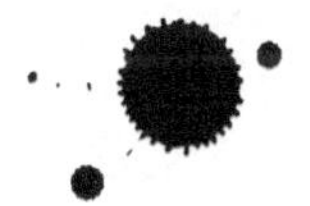

THE
END

ACKNOWLEDGMENTS

I would like to thank all of my readers, who offered their time, attention, and opinions to the writing and revision of this novella. I would also like to thank Christine Marie Scott of Clever Crow Design Studio in Pittsburgh for her wonderful cover art and her invaluable assistance with the layout of these pages.

ABOUT THE AUTHOR

D. T. Neal is a fiction writer and editor living in Chicago. He won second place in the Aeon Award in 2008 for his short story, "Aegis," and has been published in *Albedo 1*, Ireland's premier magazine of science fiction, horror, and fantasy. He is the author of *Saamaanthaa*, *The Happening*, and *Norm*, known collectively as the *Wolfshadow Trilogy*. He's also written the vampire novel, *Suckage*, as well as the Lovecraftian cosmic horror-thriller, *Chosen*. He has written three creature feature/eco-horror novellas, *Relict*, *Summerville*, and *The Day of the Nightfish*. He continues to work on several science fiction, fantasy, horror, and thriller stories.

NOSETOUCH PRESS

Nosetouch Press is an independent book publisher
tandemly-based in Chicago and Pittsburgh.
We are dedicated to bringing some of today's most
energizing fiction to readers around the world.

Our commitment to classic book design in a digital
environment brings an innovative and authentic
approach to the traditions of literary excellence.

*The Nose Knows™

NOSETOUCHPRESS.COM

Horror | Science Fiction | Fantasy | Mystery
Supernatural | Gothic | Weird

LUPINIA
The Selected Poems
of Polly Drinkwater,
2007–2015
A WOLFSHADOW BOOK